PAUL PICKERING
LUCY

S

SALT

CROMER

PUBLISHED BY SALT PUBLISHING 2024

2 4 6 8 10 9 7 5 3 1

First published in Great Britain in 2024 by
Salt Publishing Ltd
12 Norwich Road, Cromer, Norfolk NR27 0AX United Kingdom

www.saltpublishing.com

Salt Publishing Limited Reg. No. 5293401

A CIP catalogue record for this book is available from the British Library

ISBN 978 1 78463 324 0 (Paperback edition)
ISBN 978 1 78463 325 7 (Electronic edition)

Typeset in Neacademia by Salt Publishing

Printed and bound in Great Britain by Clays Ltd, Elcograf S.p.A *for Alice*

"No one has the right to obey."
HANNAH ARENDT

PART ONE

I

I AM FREE. The words rolled through him like thunder as naked and dark blue with dust he fled from his own all-consuming yellow fire.

He emerged from a ruined building a human flame and with one long scream ran up a mountain of rubble and destruction, the small arms fire chattering to a stop under clouds blackened with smoke and by the light of a strange and pale red sun.

There was an immense battle and he was not clear, his mind and memory gone, what he was doing there, or who the sides were. Or who he was. The hot dust stung his lungs.

The man tried to beat out the fire on his legs and chest and on the back of his left hand and stared up at the sky in a halo of his own flames and pain. His nakedness brought an intimacy to his inevitable death on a day when tens of thousands died. All reason then disappeared in another long scream.

Those watching missed a breath. Only a few women in brown uniforms by a red banner laughed at his infant nakedness. Men shook their heads. In his personal torment he was so completely vulnerable and magnificent as to be absurd in the faceless murder of the fighting. Too alive yet to die.

No one shot at him, or could tell which side he was on, although he came from the far end of the square, and there was a ragged cheer from among the huge blocks of stone and pillars that had exploded off the massive buildings. Several believers in their brown uniforms anxiously made the sign of the cross, interpreting his halo of fire as the devil's horns.

He raised his arms to the heavens.

Around him the grey rubble became horizons of smoky indistinction and indifference.

His arms outstretched, the man was trying to get the fresh spring air into his seared lungs, one last time, and onto his raw and charred skin.

His brain tried to work in the bubbles of consciousness between pain.

Through the smoke there was the glow of many fires. He knew at any second the spell of his sacrificial image might fail and a soldier would shoot him for no other reason than he presented a good, stationary target.

Yet in his ordeal he was so close to everything; at one with the soldiers who watched, and even with the broken statue as he reached the top of the hill of lesser stones. The statue had a three-cornered hat and a knowing smile on what now was only half a head. Yes, he was free, if only to fall down the other side of the small mountain, dead. And that was enough.

In his clenched left hand was something precious.

Then, without warning, the hill of stone he stood barefoot on, with the broken statue, was hurled into the air again and the colours and smells and tastes and pain vanished.

II

"HOLY SHIT! WHERE are you, man?"

A young American colonel sprinted into the blue-grey smoke that had been a hill of rubble and waited for the dust to clear. He had seen the burning man from afar and knew he had to save a heretic angel who had not given in to the surrounding madness. The colonel blinked away the grit in his eyes and found himself looking at an unconscious, naked man who had been terribly burned down the left-hand side of his head and body. The man had several wounds to his chest and there was a large hole in his skull; it was possible to see the pearlescent yellow-white folds of his brains. Yet he began to move. He was breathing. He opened his good eye.

He had an erection.

By the man was what looked like half the head of a statue of Frederick the Great. The colonel smiled. "Who wants to live forever?" he said, out loud, quoting the playfully ambiguous question to his troops by the King of Prussia. The colonel looked at his watch. It was exactly four in the afternoon on April 30, 1945, in the last days of the siege of Berlin, and what every sane person hoped was the end of World War II in Europe

The colonel had no idea where the last huge explosion had come from, which side had dropped a bomb or fired a shell, but then, a couple of yards away to his left, two Russian paratroopers shook their brown-clad bodies free from under the plaster and bricks. They must have heard him.

He levelled his pistol as one paratrooper, a man with sergeant's stripes, cocked his *papasha* submachine gun and pointed it at him while barking a command. The second paratrooper, a private, no more than a boy, turned his weapon at the man on the ground, smiling at the erection, but glazed over with the same fatal obedience as when ordered to kill one of his father's pigs.

"Please stop!" came a shout behind them. "*Pozhaluysta ostanovis'!*"

The private spun around. But the Russians did not fire. It may have been the use of the word "please" that startled them. The speaker nervously held a white handkerchief on a stick. Behind him was a small group of soldiers with American flag patches on their uniforms and for several more seconds the two sides aimed their machine guns at each other, breathless, terrified.

The colonel then dropped his pistol to his side, smiling and showing his white teeth, and took a packet of cigarettes out of his pocket. His long blond hair hung down below his helmet where someone had painted Hollywood in flowing script to one side of a silver eagle denoting his rank as colonel. The cigarettes were Lucky Strike. The red circle on the front of the packet shone like a ruby.

He threw them to the Russian private, who caught them easily with one hand. A tall, angular American soldier ran past the Russians to the man on the pile of rubble. The soldier had a Catholic chaplain's cross on his shoulder straps.

"This wretched man's still just alive. My God, he is. . . aroused." The priest picked up a cheap brown coat lying close by the man and grey with dust. He began to rub at the coat to expose a yellow badge. "There's the Star of David on this coat. If it's his, he may have been a prisoner in Gestapo headquarters, over there. He has the Jewish star. He's trying to say something in German. About love."

The young colonel's clear blue eyes had the innocence of the altar boy he had once been. He nodded. The priest was with them because he spoke good Russian and, Kells thought, to make the mission more idealistic than it was.

The man's infectious bid for freedom had even stopped the butchery for a moment or three. That had to be worth something.

"Tell the comrades we want this man. We are an observer unit trying to track down Americans who were being held and tortured in the Gestapo headquarters, near Mr. Hitler's bunker. We've clearance from Marshal Konev. Yeah, I see they know that name. We want to ask the burned-up man about our boys. This man is harmless and nearly dead. If they give him to us, we'll give them more cigarettes and chocolates. I'll get them Mae West's phone number from my cousin who's in pictures. How's about it? Is that a deal?" He talked fast and loud because he was shit scared and afraid he might dry up as a bullet zipped past.

The two Russian soldiers listened without emotion while his words were translated by the priest.

One turned to the other and shrugged. Americans were not officially meant to be in Berlin and the Russians, especially the private, looked as if they did not entirely believe in them, as they no longer completely believed in saints and angels.

Before the Russians could answer, there was another barrage of shellfire that landed in the park to the south and set fire to an asphalt path. The Zoo Flack Tower, a bulbous, dark, medieval-style keep that loomed on the horizon, raked the ground with fire from its anti-air-craft guns. The young colonel felt the heat on his face as most of his men hit the ground. The Russian private ran forward and grabbed the packets of cigarettes and chocolate from an orderly standing by the colonel and with his sergeant disappeared like rats into the labyrinth of desolation. Two more American soldiers appeared from the shelter of a nearby doorway carrying a stretcher.

"We got to get out of here before those Russians eat the chocolate and want Mae West," said the colonel, pleased.

Colonel Kells "Hollywood" Vardy was twenty-five years old and had been shot at now for nine months and twenty-four days and knew no one got past six months without a serious wound. That was not cool man, as the black guys in his unit said. But he had to save the burning man.

"If things fucking fall apart, at least bring something back," the infantry general had said. The colonel had expected to find the men he was looking for in the Swiss Embassy on Posierplatz, but there did not seem to be anything much of Posierplatz left. Maps are only any good when there are streets and buildings. There did not seem to be much of anywhere left and he had openly contradictory orders from military intelligence not to let the men in the embassy, in particular a Hyman Kaplan, fall into Russian hands as they had gone over to the other side, whichever that was, and to do whatever was necessary.

The colonel did not like this leaden "wink-wink-nudge-nudge" double talk. Killing resistance fighters was totally wrong, but if he objected, he might have bought all of them a boat ride to the Far East.

Still, the killing of the real Hyman Kaplan had most certainly been done for him.

The Russians were killing everyone. Sometimes, as with the last barrage, they killed each other. They even shot the animals in the Tiergarten Zoo. The colonel had seen two dead zebras and a strange kind of ostrich among the human bodies by the Ostrich

House, which was a fake Egyptian temple covered in hieroglyphics painted in yellow, blue and red. The primary colours howled out of the black and white newsreel of a day. It was like something from a studio film set he had been on with his writer cousin, after a surfing trip to Malibu Beach. The animals, not the men, made him feel sorry and angry and he said the "Ave Maria", though he had put his Catholic upbringing on the other side of a glass screen many years ago because it became too hurtful.

Kells lit a cigarette and stared at the awkward boned priest. He was a young man with an over-prominent Adam's apple and despairing eyes.

"This poor soul has been through a lot. My God. How's man expected to live such a life? He has something in his hand. . . It's almost too burned up. . . I'll be damned. . . It's the dried petals of a white flower."

The colonel smiled back, wistfully. "We fight on the side of romance! It may bring us luck . . ."

He fingered the Mickey Mouse Club badge he had in his lapel. His mother had given it him for luck when he went to high school.

He noted the disapproval of his new Italian sergeant, who was wearing a brown leather jacket and had a gold eye-tooth. You weren't meant to mention Luck. His sergeant did not think he took things seriously, that he did not pay war its proper respect. The colonel glanced around him as a bullet hissed past.

The intelligence operation they were part of that day was so fucking secret no one, not the army nor the intelligence people, had told him its name.

He had not felt part of this lunacy since parachuting into Normandy and had sleep-walked through his command. He felt no guilt, no need for absolution. Nothing.

The war was behind another wall of glass. Until today. Kells was fascinated with the burning man.

The wounded man was put on the stretcher and the colonel flicked his cigarette away. They dodged and ran through the Tiergarten and, now and again, amid the smell of burning and cordite and high explosive, there was the scent of blossom on the hot spring wind.

"Did you catch what the burning guy said?" Kells asked the priest, when they stopped behind a line of trees.

"It did not make sense."

"I doubt if it would. Try me."

"He said, *'Ich liebe Sie alle'*, I love you all."

"Christ," said Kells.

"Exactly, if I may say so," said the priest, with a smile.

III

TWO AND A half weeks later, the young colonel sat at the back of a light and airy green-painted room watching the man he had rescued slowly inhale and exhale in hypnotic, measured repetition. Kells' mouth kept falling open in childlike wonder. When he was young he might have called it a miracle. It was a miracle. From first sight the event had taken hold of him and he had not been able to get the transcendent image of the burning man out of his mind. Or the white flower gripped hard in a burnt hand. Or the words "I love you all." It spoke to everything Kells believed in before the war. At last there was something good. . . Kells had done good. . . A card in neat lettering was pinned at the end of the white tubular metal bed.

Kaplan, Hyman, type A blood, c. 35–50 years old? Condition: critical.

Propped on the cool linen pillows of an American military hospital outside Bonn was the man to whom Kells had given that name. The unconscious patient had a calm, beatific expression on the part of his face not in bandages. His head was covered in white lint and cotton wool and so were both his hands and arms and the left side of his body down to his left leg, secured to angry red-purple flesh with tape. There was a large cotton wool bandage over the left eye. His nose was broken and badly burned and had been covered in purple iodine. Kells fidgeted on his chair.

The man, even unconscious, had a weird magnetism and Kells was delighted for him and astonished at his survival, but personally there were complications.

The army were pleased with Kells, but he was going to be up to his neck in shit and trouble from the intelligence people for bringing Hyman back alive at all, and more so if they found 'Hyman' was someone else. Kells had disobeyed their orders, however ambiguous, euphemistic and army-speak, and had then wilfully deceived everyone that his rescued prisoner was Hyman Kaplan. From good intentions, Kells was in a steaming pit of deepest dog-excrement. In France, men had been shot for trivialities like getting lost. Kells had already come close. At least a firing squad was quick compared to a posting to a snake-infested death or glory island in the Pacific, where not even his Mickey Mouse Club badge might save him.

He sighed. He found it strange to be in a pressed new uniform and back in the "world". But whatever voodoo doo-doo he was in, he was righteously glad the burning man was alive.

It was now impossible for the man in the bed to disappear.

The newspapers and wire services had been kept from his bedside, but at a press conference the day before, Hyman Kaplan had been rightly declared a hero of the Jewish resistance and already given medals by France and Italy. It had been discovered Hyman Kaplan had been a distinguished professor at Berlin university, specialising in the Old Silk Road and the textile itself. He was an expert on the cultivation of silk, the silkworm and moth and held two doctorates on how its production had affected civilisation. Captured once, he escaped from the Sachsenhausen concentration camp north of Berlin and took part in a vital intelligence operation, the same operation that had been sent to kill him. The operation was simply described at the press conference as "vital to a new and peaceful world".

A reporter in the press conference started to ask a question about the operation, but was cut short when another wanted to know if it was true that the man had an erection, naked, on the battlefield. There was laughter. But a tall, dark-haired woman, who appeared to be a German interpreter with the French delegation, jumped to her feet, angry and lovely:

"How dare you! This man is a hero. I think you had better leave," she shouted in English.

Kells watched fascinated as a rangy newsman stood, smiled and dutifully left the room to applause. At the reception afterwards the woman had come over to Kells.

"Darling, I want to say you deserve your medal for saving that man," she said, and he had asked her to dinner, but she had looked disappointed and explained she was from Berlin, and he had smiled and said he was based there. They had stared at each other for what seemed an age.

Her skin was a pale ivory and had a luminous quality, a beauty that came with Berlin malnutrition. He then noticed that her black suit was mended and there was a small tear at the front of her blouse. Her high-heeled shoes were scuffed, but there was a visceral danger about her in that hand-grenade of a smile that made him blush. Her large brown eyes, one with green flecks, were wicked and playful and she had a dimple at the corner of her wide mouth. A gap between her two very white front teeth denoted passion. There were already lines of both sleep deprivation and laughter on her twenty-something face, making her look more sophisticated. Her eyebrows were arched and her lashes long and curled. She stood very straight and had the entitled but fun-loving air of a powerful mistress at a Prussian court.

She fingered his tie, her breath smelling of violet cachous, and said, "I have to go now, darling. I'll be back in Berlin in a few days. I'm in the Café Kranzler on the Ku'damm late Friday afternoons. My name is Gretchen. I sing in what's left of a club around the corner. You can buy me a hot chocolate. I have never had a hot chocolate with a real American hero." Her voice was lazy and deep. Then she was gone in a haze of no doubt second-hand, looted perfume, from the same ruined bedroom as the violet cachous and high heels.

Kells was left trying to frame a reply, but the muscles in his mouth would not obey him.

He had also tried to date a girl who was a nurse at the hospital. He had had no female company since Normandy. It was difficult as when he had leave he always had to look after his superior's wants or to organise something pointless for the men.

He had asked the delicate, freckle-faced nurse with red-gold blonde hair in a long shower of curls to come out with him on the first night he was here to see Hyman. Her eyes were a sea-green blue and he had assumed she was from a church-going Massachusetts town, of Scandinavian descent, or German. She had an aura of goodness. There had been a look of both panic and wonder in those eyes, like a child seeing the ocean for the first time.

Her sweet and innocent smile had lit up her scrubbed face and the room, and Kells. "Yes. That will be good," she said, in English.

They had gone to a PX restaurant, a cafe really, next to the hospital, and the food had just arrived when she rushed away, knocking a fork from the table in a clatter of big, white nurses' shoes. One of the waitresses told him in a whisper that the nurse had been in "the camps" and none of them could keep food down, even the ones they let work. And that she was Jewish. The waitress lingered on the word, as if as a warning. The nurse was called Rachel and was quite tall and painfully thin. There were dark circles under her eyes. Her cheekbones and hip bones were sharp as axe blades. There was a small, lozenge-shaped scar on her right cheekbone. She did not look Jewish.

Kells stood up as she now wobbled into the room on those white tea-pot nurses' shoes in a white uniform with the surgeon who had operated on the man in the bed. Her lipstick was very red. It shone in the green room like a magic lamp. She smiled at him, fluttered a delicate hand and then, to his dismay, left.

The surgeon, a gentle man in blue medical scrubs, stood by the bed.

"You wanted to ask me some questions, colonel? Well, Dr Kaplan, is certainly a lucky, lucky man. The wound to the head in itself should have killed him. It would have killed a moose. We call them elk. I have killed mooses many times with such a shot. My family is from Sweden. A section of skull and part of the right frontal lobe were removed. If the bullet had entered further back it would have hit the central brain and its blood vessels and most certainly have been fatal. We have repaired the missing skull bone with a lightweight metal plate, but he has lost brain mass on that side the size of a small orange. By that I mean a small American orange, approximately the size of a baseball."

The surgeon then paused, shifting his weight and making his sensible, leather shoes creak.

"No one knows what effect this will have until he wakes up, if he wakes up. I must stress that it is an 'if'. The shock alone of what Dr Kaplan has gone through would kill most healthy nineteen-year-olds. As well as the wound to his head, he took a bullet in his upper leg. There are also injuries to his chest, mainly from shrapnel, but these incredibly seem to have missed vital organs. Then there is the terrible burning. The burns along his left side and on his arms and hands are third degree and removed body fat, flesh and even the man's fingerprints. His hair and moustache were burned off and many teeth knocked out, which we will replace, but making him impossible to identify, even if we had dental records, and there are bruises that show he may have undergone a severe beating. Imagine, if you will, a roasting chicken that jumps alive from the oven."

The surgeon stopped speaking again, as if trying to understand what had happened.

"Dr Kaplan should not be here. He died several times on my operating table, but the angels do not want his soul yet. They must have a purpose for him."

Kells just shook his head.

The surgeon smiled. "Yes, it is a miracle. And you witnessed his priapism, his erection. Usually present in men who have been executed. This man must have a strong life force. Will he walk again? It may be so if he survives the initial shock. Will he regain his looks? Up to a point. We have a captured female German plastic surgeon, a fan of *Gone with the Wind*, who rebuilds most male faces as versions of the film actor Clark Gable. This man deserves the very best."

Kells nodded. "I thought you said Hyman here was going to die? For sure."

There was a playful smile in the surgeon's blue eyes. "It's quite hard to kill certain people. If a man is very committed, say. And we had fun with this one. We did. We took risks, and here he is. Though he is still critical. He can go at any moment."

Kells refused to want such a thing but who, exactly, had he saved?

"You think he'll remember anything when he wakes up? When do you think he will come round? He cannot hear us, can he?"

The surgeon shrugged. He seemed to sense the colonel's dilemma, though he had probably long since stopped trying to figure out such men and their wars.

"His heart may give out tonight. He may come around and start talking silkworms. It's hard to say. You have worried enough, colonel. You're going to come out of this very well. I heard they are flying you back to the States for your well-earned medal and promotion. You are a little famous, too. Don't be modest! I think so!"

Kells reached into his uniform jacket pocket and gave the surgeon a card.

"Please call me at this number, day or night, when he wakes up. I would like to know. My boys will like to know. They like lucky stories."

The surgeon was cautious, but moved, and raised his bushy eyebrows.

"That's very thoughtful of you, young man. I meet so many young men who have become cynical. I'll let you know the moment he wakes up. I am sure he'll be eager to thank you himself. One small formality. There has been talk among the Jewish refugees of an ideal community, a kibbutz, literally a gathering, in Germany. I do not think Dr Kaplan may ever be well enough, but I would like you to sign him over to us, so we can send him there, should the opportunity arise. He is technically your prisoner and, of course, as a German will automatically have to go to a POW camp. That is harsh after what he has been through, and most ironic. If you could sign this release form, please."

Kells hesitated and then signed with a pen his father had given him.

Kells stared at the man in the bed. There was something about this man that Kells was not at all sure of. He went to the side of the white-painted tubular steel military bed and drew close to the face. The breath came in and out with complete tranquillity. The terribly burned face, where it was not covered in bandages, seemed to glow.

Kells gripped the bed and sighed.

"There's no point in worrying," said the surgeon.

"Yes, I kinda figured that one," said Kells. "There is nothing you can do about the odds." Colonel Kells "Hollywood" William Bonney Vardy knew that for a fact.

The surgeon nodded. "You are young to be a colonel."

Kells took a deep breath. "I was on the staff and the men above me kept getting killed. Men who knew what they were doing. . ." He heard his voice frantic on the radio. "Hollywood calling New York. Kansas hit a homer." Kansas had been a major. New York was the colonel when Kells, Hollywood, had been a captain. Kansas had died from a stomach wound in a sewer by a river in Belgium. New York was luckier. An anti-tank round took off the top of his head when he stood up with cramp in his leg while giving a boring fly-fishing lesson with a drill stick he always carried. The blood had got into Kells' eyes and his hair. He had washed and washed his hair, which was longer than it should have been, and he combed it in a quiff, but bits had still stuck together with the liquid remains of New York. Every time someone was messily killed, Kells was promoted.

"Did you volunteer?" asked the surgeon.

"Yeah, fool that I am, I volunteered for the paratroops, the 101st

Airborne, because a sergeant had told me that jumping out of a plane was like surfing. I like surfing . . ."

In fact Kells had signed up first for an infantry unit and then changed to the 101st Airborne, the Screaming Eagles, to escape the endless latrine cleaning, petty power squabbles 'chickenshit' of the ordinary corporate military ant heap that makes you hate the army more than the enemy. But parachuting was not like surfing. It was freezing cold with the smell of vomit and urine, as grown men about to leap into the void were sick and peed their pants. The chute opened with a gallows jolt. You were meant to shout 'Geronimo', but everyone just said 'Fuck it'. It was all right in the end, though. Kells dug the floating around by himself in the white clouds and the quiet . . . He did his harness straps up super-tight for his tall, thin frame. It made him feel he was 'there'.

Even back home, Kells had only felt totally real when he was way out on his surf board and away from anyone else, looking for the big wave. He liked to be far out in the impossible surf he called 'candy thunder'. As a kid, his tall, slender frame was always bang-bursting to climb a tree or look to the next ridge, or flying around the basketball court. He liked the joyous certainty of being driven by a strong wave to the shore, to a more materialistic American dream he tried hard to understand and, on most days, avoid.

"Why did you want to fight?" said the surgeon. Kells saw the man was sincere, and he needed to tell the affable Swede. No one had asked him the question before, probably because they did not want the answer. He did not want to fight anyone.

"Maybe I was stupid. I could have worked in my father's armaments factory. I thought a tyrant like Hitler had to be stopped. By me, and that I would make the difference . . . All of a sudden everyone in my family and my girlfriend wanted me to go to war. They mostly thought of Hitler as the other team."

The surgeon laughed.

"In Normandy I landed on a roof in the wrong town in the wrong part of that region and rounded up other twenty-something-year-olds as lost and angry and confused as I was after a third of our force had been slaughtered by well-placed enemy machine-guns and searchlights that no one had thought to mention. In the end, I had a whole company of men, so shocked to the core they were totally useless, and I sheep-dogged them to a large and beautiful church, which the allied barrages had only half-destroyed. I did not realise I had broken a bone in my foot. It was not until later that it dawned on me that my rebel action might have been viewed as mutiny and gotten me shot against a ruined wall. A captain was shot, charged with looting for passing out bread to his men from a levelled bakery. But a general heard of my 'round-up' and immediately attached me to his staff. It all seemed like a dream."

Kells looked at the man in the bed. In the military it was hard to put a cigarette paper between triumph and disaster.

"So you have been with the general's staff since the landings?" said the surgeon, concerned.

"Yeah, all the way to Berlin, but you begin to feel like outside it all."

The burning man's words, whispered in the priest's ear, hissed like a snake in dry leaves.

"*Ich liebe Sie alle.*" I love you all.

Seeing awful stuff was not the worst thing, although he had walked through bloody fields of the newly dead and dying in squelching, oversize rubber boots, writing things on a clipboard in a shaky hand, making his reports. Wounded men cried out nonsense before they died. "I fucked whores in London town, then took my money back," Kells remembered one man sobbing.

It was not that war was unknowable, an unapproachable horror, but that it was inaccessible to the framework of civilised ideas.

Worse than seeing and noting the detached heads and legs of the slaughter itself was the absence of any coda, as if the solidity of goodness had been reduced to wet tissue paper, and a moral tumble weed was blowing down a long flat road, from nowhere to nowhere. Kells did not know if he had killed anyone, personally. The fights he had been in were such complete chaos and quick and nothing like training. He had only fired his pistol on a few occasions. There was not time to notice the effect. And his brain seemed wired to forget the incident as soon as possible. To be truthful, he had never liked guns.

"It must have been terrible," he heard the surgeon say.

"I am bad at talking about it."

"Everyone is, in my experience," said the doctor.

And all the time Kells felt he was not completely there. Not UP COUNTRY, not HOME, but NOWHERENOPLACE and not even that. He had thought actual occasional combat, such as his last mission in Berlin, might improve things, but it made him more removed. Floating among blurred and swirling pictures, like the distorted faces in a crowd he remembered from a French avant-garde film, even though at any moment he might be killed. He wanted to tell the nice Swedish surgeon that but couldn't.

"I bet you have something to go home to," said the doctor.

Kells nodded. "Oh, yeah. I hope to do a doctorate on Dante's *La Vita Nuova* . . . The New Life . . ."

The Swede shook his head. "I was meaning, is some girl waiting for you?"

Kells smiled and nodded, embarrassed. "Sure. She's called Betty. A former Miss Palo Verdes . . ."

He pictured Betty eating a strawberry sundae with marshmallows, a dab of ice cream on her lower lip as her breasts hung over the table imprisoned in a prim cotton dress. Her father was a senior manager in his father's factory, and Betty was the girl next door but two, who had left school at fourteen and was already planning where she and Kells were going to live. She was disturbingly clever and had always added up store bills in her head before the manager had got his pencil out.

Kells' mental energy was aimed at trying to grasp the whole show, the universe, the reason we are here and how to save mankind, while Betty liked sloppy romantic movies and a few pert kisses at the drive-in, but no gift of tongues or wandering hands. He had

known her since fourth grade and watched her grow into a volup-
tuous siren with long dark hair who caused traffic accidents in her
short, short, cheerleader ra-ra skirt and Bobby socks. Everyone said
Kells was a lucky man. But her strict father forbade Betty to go to
surfing beaches or parties. So Kells went on his own. He did not
feel he was cheating on Betty because she represented HOME to
him. The same HOME the army promised you for surviving the
war and them.

Betty had found him reading Dante's *La Vita Nuova* and he had
tried to convey to her how Courtly Love could be sublimated to the
divine and change the world and stop all war. How Courtly Love
was an experience between erotic desire and spiritual attainment, a
love at once illicit and morally elevating, passionate and disciplined,
humiliating and exalting, human and transcendent. He was about to
add, taking her small, hot hand, that he thought sexual love might
be elevated in the same way . . . Kells had never even gotten inside
her brassiere – to change the world and bring peace on earth.

Betty had looked up at him with startled blue eyes. "Courtly
Love? If folks get sent to court for what they get up to when out
courting, it must be completely disgusting. Please don't say such stuff
at our house. Is that what you'll be learning at your new university?"

He had not been sure if she was joking. At times she pretended
not to understand him to retain control. She still used the word
"courting" for going steady. She was adored by his mother and father.

"What news from Billy the Kid?" wrote his dad. Kells had toy
guns before he could walk and was brought up on cowboy movies.
Yet his mother had dressed him in her shorty nighties when he was
young. She had lost a little girl two years before he was born. His
mother had named him after the Irish national treasure, the Book
of Kells. Among the spiral of images in Kells' brain, the burning
man had begun to move him. To have weight and meaning. Like
Dante. He was real and not a dream.

"Am I still your dreamboat?" Betty used to ask after he had
been surfing.

"Goodbye, colonel and I hope you see Betty," said the Swedish surgeon, called away by a nurse.

Kells was miles away. "*Macht Nichts*" he said, mostly to himself. Literally it meant "that makes nothing". It was a thing all the guys said. It doesn't matter. None of it . . . The war . . . The whole fucking meaningless slaughterhouse . . . That's why Hyman here, the burning man, mattered a lot.

The surgeon looked at Kells curiously and left.

IV

THE MAN IN the bed, the burning man, the international hero, woke the next day with an intense pain in the middle of his brow. It hurt very much indeed when he tried to open his eyes. For a moment, he was afraid and grabbed at the sheets, but that only increased the thundering headache. He fell back, exhausted. One eye opened. He was in a green room that smelt of cleaning fluids. The sunlight was streaming in through a window and dancing on the walls in wavy patterns, possibly reflected off water outside.

He blinked his right eye. He could not see out of his left eye, which was now covered in bandages.

The window was slightly open and there were scents of spring, above the smell of bleach and polish. Through the window was a cherry tree covered in light pink blossom and beyond the blossom was blue sky. He attempted to turn his head but could not. There was a saline drip by the bed. On a hanger hooked on a white wardrobe at the other end of the room was a brown coat on which there was a yellow star. Was this garment his? This made no sense to him.

A piano was playing somewhere outside the window. He tried to remember what the music was but could not. He could not remember anything. He did not know who he was. The question seemed to stick in his dry throat in panic. He stared out at the cherry blossom and the intensity of his thought blurred and he passed back into image free unconsciousness. His head was not yet ready for dreams.

Three days later the man woke again in Isolation Room Six. Outside the window, probably under the cherry tree, a military band was playing modern American jazz.

The music stopped and an American voice shouted "Pennsylvania 65000!" and then the music started again.

It made the man now known as Hyman Kaplan want to smile and get up and dance, which was a joke. He was still not able to see out of his left eye and knew he was terribly wounded and at times felt he was on fire. Despite the drugs, he was in pain. There were bubbles of respite but then the pain came back and its absence was almost worse than the agony.

Yet he wanted to dance.

Had he liked to dance? The nurses, the older nurse and a younger girl, were looking out of the window and then began to dance themselves. Their big white shoes clattered on the wooden floor.

He must be careful, he knew.

He was in a hospital, but it may be the hospital of his enemy. They may be making him better only to torture and interrogate him again before killing him. He knew that was the way of things. The man did not understand all of the English, but they were talking of a dance called the Jive. It was an exciting dance where the partner was whirled around. The girl was laughing.

"That's it, Rachel. You got it, first time," said the older nurse.

Rachel was beautiful and so innocent. She stopped dancing and came over to the bed. He firmly shut his eye.

"The Swedish doctor said we should talk to him."

"Don't waste your breath, Rachel. He's deep-six, in a coma."

But he felt the girl's warmth as she came and leant over the bed and whispered in his ear, "*Der Chirurg sagt, Sie seien Dr. Hyman Kaplan und ein Experte für Seidenraupen.* The surgeon says you are Dr Hyman Kaplan and an expert on silkworms."

Her whisper was so close it tickled and sent a shiver through him. So he was German . . . Was he the enemy? He did not know the name Hyman Kaplan . . . Silkworms! They sounded like a contradiction or a pestilence. Surely he would remember? They meant nothing to him and he did not even know what a silkworm looked like. He did not care. Rachel smelt of roses and hope.

She was smiling now and "jiving" again with the older nurse at the end of the white tubular steel bed. He opened his good eye enough to see them. He knew one thing: if he did not die, he wanted Rachel. However impossible that was.

Whoever he was, he meant to have Rachel.

"Pennsylvania 65000!"

V

AN HOUR LATER, Rachel was one of two nurses who went into the room to change the saline drip of the resistance fighter the American colonel had rescued. "You change his drip this time, dear," said the older nurse. She was American and very experienced.

While she was attaching a new bag of saline solution, Rachel saw a flickering of his eyelid.

"He's awake! He's awake!"

The older nurse looked at the patient. There was a flicker of the right eye, and then nothing.

"Shall I go and get the surgeon?" Rachel said, excited and so happy. "Surely this is a good sign?"

The older nurse held onto Rachel's arm gently. "Don't get your hopes up too much, honey. Even when they start to pass in and out, cases like this. The next day or two will tell. All I am saying is do not get too fond of him. You must know that better than I can tell you, poor child."

Rachel, who was only twenty, was adamant the burning man was going to live. She had pinned back her red-gold hair under a white cap. She was so very happy she was able to help Dr Hyman Kaplan.

He was a hero. He was her hero. She pressed her lips together in determination.

The Russian soldiers had opened the doors of her prison camp weeks ago and let her free, with a group of other specifically political prisoners. Now Rachel found herself here, in this hospital, in charge of a man who had fought, really fought, and the Nazis could not kill. He was going to be so pleased when he realised he had woken to a new world. Dr Kaplan was going to live. No one knew how much she depended on that.

She finished securing the drip when the slightly fat and untidy middle-aged rabbi who was in charge of the group from the camps, came into the room. He had little round glasses and was so gentle. His grey hair curled at the sides and back of his bald head. He too had been in the resistance. Yet, he made every room he entered happy, a trick she knew might not tell his whole story. She had broken down and run out of the hospital the first time she tried to talk to him.

"Ah, Rachel, you are looking better, child, but you must eat more. Forty kilos is not enough at only twenty. Ah, to be that age again! I must give you some of my kilos from too much rum. You were going to tell me what happened after you left the camps last time, when you were called away.

Rachel took a deep breath, cleared her throat, smoothed down her dress and began. She was conscious that she made everything into more of a story than it was. ". . . When we left the camp we walked for several days. The Russian soldiers with us ran off with the food on the fourth day. Then in an abandoned suitcase I found no food, only a few lipsticks and feather boa scarves.

"Lipstick in the camp was only worn by those who became the doomed girls of the officers. I passed out the suitcase's contents. Then there was a miracle. Most of us were giggling, though others were crying, as we put the lipstick on, reds and pinks and one almost white. Even several of the boys joined in. I chose a pink lipstick. It tasted of Turkish Delight. I then put on a yellow feather boa.

Another girl put on one of deep blue and began to dance. We were women again.

"I felt like a film star. We had stopped, dazed, by a clump of trees, when three trucks came into view around a bend.

"'It's the Yanks,' said one of the boys, as they all saw the uniforms and the white stars on the lorries. It was getting dark and there was the smell of honeysuckle in the air.

"'My God, look at this,' said a woman doctor. Then they brought us here, to you. It was the start of the world again. The future."

Rachel was silent for a while, looking down at her white shoes. When the Americans told them to get in the trucks, she realised the girl she had been walking with lay dead by the side of the road, her muddy eyes wide open. The rabbi got up and got her a glass of water; she took a sip.

"I know this is hard, my dear. I remember seeing you the first time those doctors who found you brought you here. You said meeting a rabbi was like a distant memory . . . Can you tell me about your family? Were you arrested?

She put the glass by her chair. After telling the lipstick story it strangely became easier.

"We were not so religious . . . I was the daughter of a prominent doctor in Berlin who specialised in treating artists and actors. He was blond-haired and I looked more like one of the Nazi poster girls than Jewish. My father was denounced by a man who promised the world and then stole morphine from the surgery, which should not have been there and had been used to help my father's fashionable patients, who had connections with, or were lovers of, Nazi Party members. The very people who eventually arrested him . . ."

When she thought of her childhood, she always heard herself playing the cello, a sad, low sound that pulled at her soul with an exquisite melancholy she only now understood. A melancholy and a memory that was not straightforward, like many things she recalled and did not entirely trust.

Her uncle, who was a musician, an accomplished cellist, had taught her to play.

"My kind, funny father, kept thinking the Nazis would be swept out of power as they had swept in. Probably as a reaction to his optimism, I became involved in smuggling Jewish activists and communists out of the Reich in Red Cross ambulances. These were meant to meet wounded soldiers off the ancient, dirty clanking steam trains that smelt of damp wood coming from the Russian Front, that arrived at night into quiet stations outside big cities like Berlin, where they disgorged the blinded, and the maimed. I met a boy at the music conservatoire who hardly needed to convince me to help. I pretended to be a nurse, and it was like being in a school play. I did it several times and it all seemed so easy.

"One day we drove around a bend in a forest and there was a roadblock ahead. The driver tried to turn the ambulance round, stalled, and was shot in the head . . . There was blood . . . I got out of the door and tried to climb up the bank . . ."

She could still smell the rich forest earth as she had clutched at tree roots to get away.

"But a soldier grabbed me by the coat and then by the hair and another hit me in the face with his rifle butt. I was thrown into the ditch with the others and the soldier who had grabbed me shot one of the smuggled men in the face and laughed . . . I was screaming, screaming, screaming . . ."

Rachel was breathing heavily. "Take your time, my dear," said the rabbi.

She composed herself, the fear snapping at her like the soldiers' dogs.

"I was kept from the others in a little, freezing cell with a stone slab for a bed and a chair bolted to the floor. After three days a female warder came in with a tape measure.

"The warder said, 'Today, Rachel, you will go to the guillotine for what you have done and that you are Jewish. We have a travelling version in the van. It has been used successfully on those terrorist students in the Weiße Rose dissident organisation. Are you one of them? Come on now, stand up. We must get your measurements exactly right so the blade cuts cleanly through your pretty neck. It will soon be over. The less you fight and the more you obey the easier it will be. It is in the best interests of the Reich.'"

Rachel had wet herself.

She had heard her urine drip-dripping from the wooden chair and the warder had laughed.

"My hands and feet were put in shackles and I expected to be taken to die immediately. I was trembling and crying. But they took me in front of a panel who were silent for a long time. Two men and a woman. Very ordinary and in civilian dress. The woman had a pearl hat-pin and a fox-fur stole. They did not beat me, or shout, but I was quietly questioned and questioned for days by them and by night by guards, without sleep.

"You must tell us your contacts . . . Admit you are a communist . . . How long have you been a party member. . . ?

"I only knew those I had been arrested with. . .

"But they went on and on until I felt I was being separated from my soul. That there was nothing left. A husk.

"Then they stopped. . .

"I thought it was the end. That the guillotine was in the next room. From time to time I heard loud, mechanical sounds and then nothing.

"But I was taken back to my cell and the next day I was summoned by a different group of three men in army uniform. I told them I was a nurse and they were pleased, and even polite. They must have already decided I was of no resistance importance, and I kept myself hunched and most of my hair under a scarf.

"I was sent a long way in a van to a camp in a forest. There was an infirmary where a doctor and several nurses brought the torture victims back to a sort of a life, before they were tortured again. I made myself invaluable as a nurse, even working in the operating theatre, re-setting freshly broken bones. They liked me too because

24

I could speak German and French and English as well as some Russian and Italian. A pretty girl I was working with was taken to the officers' quarters. The girls were often sent to the officers' quarters and then, when the officers tired of them, to another camp where no one came back from, so I made myself plain."

She did not sleep for fear of nightmares.

One day she had heard the sound of a voice behind her. It was the surgeon commandant.

"What fine ankles you have, my dear."

She had shuddered and pulled her scarf closer to her head. She felt his breath on her neck.

His voice was soft and he was kind to her. Very kind. He gave her cake he made himself. He did not give her orders. It was confusing. He had been wounded in the legs in Russia. His name was Manfred. Rachel did not tell the rabbi about Manfred.

Here, in the American hospital she looked out as the blossoms fell from the cherry tree.

"Thank you," said the rabbi. "You are very brave." But she wasn't. If they only knew what she had done. The rabbi then put a hand on her shoulder.

"There is what we call a kibbutz, not too far from here, in the grounds of what was a leading Nazi's house. It is an ideal farming community. Everyone works the land and then has time to pursue their own specialities. No one is in charge. Everyone is in charge. Women are equal to men. Such communities existed in the early days of the Reich and were championed by certain Nazis as a way of getting we Jews to emigrate. It is a rehearsal for the kind of settlements that may be established if the Jews return to Palestine and would lay the foundations for a new Israel, though not in an old-fashioned imperialist sense. Or even as a state. We will take no one's land and everyone is free to join our communities."

The words filled Rachel with joy. She collected herself, sat up straight, and tried to smile. The people she had escaped with were all activists who hoped to establish a new way of living where there would be no more war. But she said, "I cannot leave my patient . . ."

The rabbi nodded and left and she looked over at the man in the bed. Again, she thought she saw an eyelid move.

VI

A WEEK LATER, the older nurse was teasing Rachel about the handsome American, Colonel Kells Vardy.

"He took you to dinner. He's interested in you . . ."

The colonel seemed a good man. He had insisted they go out for dinner. There was a PX store attached to the hospital and a restaurant there. The older nurse had encouraged her, but she should not have gone. It was all too soon. He had been very charming and polite, but she had rushed to the bathroom and thrown up. She then told another nurse to tell him she had forgotten to change a patient's bed sheets back on the ward, perhaps they could make it another time.

Rachel found it hard to imagine such a man, a boy, in a war at all. "That's the sort of young man who always gets rewarded. And he's after you. He wants to have fun. You could have a bit of fun too."

Rachel thought the American much better off without a person like her.

She must devote herself to the patient Hyman. She had to.

She heard the sound of American jazz coming from somewhere below in the building. They were having a party. The Americans always had parties.

Rachel had several books with her. She was learning Hebrew and she had found the works of the English poet T. S. Eliot, translated into German, which she read out loud. In the prison camp hospital when patients had been almost bludgeoned to death and were in a coma, reciting poetry to them, she believed, helped heal. She had recited Schiller and, when no one was listening, the forbidden Rilke. But it did not change the patients' eventual fate.

The eye of her patient opened and closed again.

Ten minutes later this happened once more.

On the next occasion, part of the way through a poem about a cat who was not there, the eye snapped open for over a minute. It was such a strong gaze in the direction of the cherry tree. She went immediately to get the older nurse, who went to get the surgeon. When they returned, the eye was firmly closed.

There were several false alarms like this over the coming days. The surgeon said that Rachel should sit by the patient full time. Rachel liked reading to Dr Kaplan. It made her feel safe.

Her father always said she had a calm and melodious voice and one morning started with a Chekhov short story, translated into German, called *A Boring Story*, which was anything but, about a silly university professor, anticipating his death, trying to right wrongs. The professor, it turned out, was not a stupid man after all; a little vain, perhaps. She bit her lip. Maybe she should not have read the patient that particular story as it involved death. She gave Hyman's hand a little squeeze and she thought she detected a murmur of pleasure as she wiped the saliva from his mouth. All the time Rachel listened to the breathing of Dr Kaplan, which she was convinced was growing stronger. When she paused, she saw Dr Kaplan's eyelid quiver.

There was a knock at the door and a man she had seen with the rabbi came in. He was carrying a book, in German, which he handed to her and left. It was about the silkworm, *Die seidenraupe*. On the front of the book was a picture of a smiling blonde-haired woman, not unlike herself, holding a little cocoon of silk. The book was entitled: *Der kostbare Faden*, The Precious Thread, and had been brought out in the early days of the Reich. She read:

"The process starts with the eggs hatching out on the mulberry leaves in a sericulture centre. The caterpillars eat their own homes they are so greedy and spin a cocoon of silk around themselves. They are in their finest outfits. All their greediness has clothed them in the best fashions. Then, before they can breed, and pass on any racial flaw, they are exterminated. This is done by steaming them over cauldrons of boiling water for hours and then they are right for spinning. Many thousands can be killed in a day in a modern centre, millions in a year. All to make the finest gowns or parachute silk for our airmen."

Rachel trembled and put the book down, in tears.

Outside the window the wind had become gusty, blowing around petals of the cherry blossom, and the band had started to play again.

Dr Kaplan's eye was wide open. The brown eye was looking out at the cherry tree as usual, but then swivelled towards her. What was left of the man's lips did not move, but she saw the smile in his eye. It seemed to have a golden quality. She ran.

The older nurse came in first. The rabbi, slightly out of breath, and the surgeon followed her.

They stood at the head of the bed and Rachel observed the patient's pupil darting from one to the other. He then tried to say something. At first it seemed too painful and she had to put her ear almost to his mouth.

The voice was a whisper. Rachel was sure of the words after the second repetition. She put her hand on the man's shoulder.

"What does he say?" asked the rabbi, worried.

Rachel smiled. "He says *Ich liebe Sie alle*, I love you all."

The older nurse crossed herself.

"Praise to God," said the surgeon, open-mouthed.

Rachel put her ear to the man's lips again. "He says he wants to live," continued Rachel. "I must live. I must live. '*Ich muss leben*'."

The rabbi was shaking his head in wonder.

"Don't you worry, my dear Dr Kaplan," he said, in German. "You are going to a better place."

The single eye looked at them worried, before closing.

A week later, the surgeon stopped Rachel in the corridor.

"It's time to get Dr Kaplan out of bed and into a wheelchair. I want him to go down to the garden tomorrow. It's important not to open the wounds again, but it is vital that the man's brain gets as much stimulation as possible. The neural channels are re-routing.

The bullet wounds are healing well and the burns will benefit from exposure to fresh air."

The Swedish surgeon paused. He seemed unable to think of the next words. Eventually he said, "You appear to be devoted to Dr Kaplan, in fact over devoted as I see from his chart, you even note his bodily functions. Perhaps, Rachel, it is time you moved on, away from the dying and wounded and into the light. You are so full of enthusiasm, as are all the young people who have come from the camps. And I hear from the rabbi of an ideal community you may all go to."

Rachel shook her head. "I cannot go from the hospital until Dr Kaplan is well."

The surgeon took her hands. "What I mean is that Colonel Vardy has agreed that if Dr Kaplan is well enough, he can go to the kibbutz too. Please do not tell him yet. This is still early days."

Rachel was so ecstatic she clapped her hands. She was smiling, smiling, smiling.

VII

"GRETCHEN, A MAN has been here . . . He says he will be back soon," whispered a waitress at the Café Kranzler.

Gretchen. That was what people called her, the name on her new papers. It was not her real name.

She sat at a small table, looking up the Kurfürstendamm at the ruined church, the Gedächtniskirche, the Kaiser-Wilhelm Memorial Church, 'the hollow tooth' as now its spire was missing. She had been inside a few days ago and burned a candle stub she had in her pocket, though it was a Protestant church, and asked forgiveness for her terrible sins – they were truly terrible, even to a God – and fled when a soldier shouted. The statue of Christ the Redeemer was pitted with shrapnel and with a scalded look in His eyes. He did not look as if He wanted to absolve her. Ever.

Well, fuck Him.

Gretchen smiled as she wondered what it would be like.

She slowly stirred her hot chocolate. Hot chocolate on a warm day. No excuse, but luxury. She thought of her father, dandy smart in a purple waistcoat with heavy silver buttons, and tears came to her carefully made-up eyes.

Outside, through the thick, cracked glass patched here and there with paper, there were many trucks but also processions of barrows and pushcarts and pony and traps as the ordinary people trickled back into the city, sent back by the Soviet troops who surrounded everything now. There were fresh leaves on the remaining plane trees. To get out properly she needed a passport and that was why she was waiting for a man, not a man she liked. To earn dollars.

The Frenchman who she had been translating for in Bonn had been annoyed with her after her outburst at the conference, which she staged on impulse to bring her closer to the American colonel, to get information for the man she was meeting. The Frenchman almost did not pay her when they went back to his hotel room, a fat, middle-aged Frenchman, who wore a tummy corset and had changed his mind when she showed him her vegetable knife, sharpened to a razor that she shaved her legs with. A nurse had told her the dreamboat American was very anxious about the expert on silkworms, Dr Kaplan.

Gretchen adored silk. She remembered a crimson and blue and gold silk shawl and her beautiful mother dancing around and around with that magical shawl to create the very vaults of heaven on earth. Gretchen's upbringing had been strict, so strict, and always on the road. Now she pursued a shadow life, as she once pursued the sacraments. By her right leg was her mother's old suitcase, two-tone cream and brown leather. When Gretchen had gone back to Berlin from the press conference in Bonn, to the room she shared with another girl, everything had been wrecked and there were drops of blood on the floor. Then she found somewhere else, much worse. That was why she was in the Café Kranzler on a Tuesday, when she only usually treated herself on Fridays before she sang around the corner. The trouble was no one realised what was happening in Berlin, underneath the surface. The killing.

She stirred her chocolate some more.

She had barely enough varnish to do her nails this morning and was wearing the last of her perfume. She had painted a stocking seam at the back of her long legs. She still kept herself supple, from an act other than singing, she thought with a wicked smile, but she did not need to stain her skin, she was brown enough, and the needle tracks she once had from the little Wehrmacht syrette syringes, like a toothpaste tube with a needle, were now gone. She must do something with her long, dark brown hair though, because of the brick dust and lice where she was living. She longed for the cigarette in her right jacket pocket, but did not smoke it because it was one of those disgusting half-cardboard Russian ones, and everyone hated the stupid Russians. She took another sip of chocolate. The man was late. She thought of the young American colonel with the angel face and floppy hair. You had to be careful of such faces, she knew. Such angels were capable of immense destruction, the *Blitzkrieg*, the other side of the patched window.

The door to the street opened and a man came over to her. It was not the man she was expecting. He wore a smart suit and carried a copy of the new *Berliner Zeitung* newspaper. He was scared. He put the paper on the chair by her. It was folded over an envelope.

"The money is there. They want to know more about this Hyman Kaplan. And the American. Now get out of here. People are after you. A team of three. I have been followed."

"What do they want with me?"

"They want you dead."

"Who?"

"Who do you think?"

Then he was gone.

Gretchen glanced outside the window and by the wreckage of a tobacco booth she thought she saw a bull-necked man she had seen before. She picked up her case, drank the hot chocolate and headed for the side door, shouting to a waitress she knew that she would pay on Friday. Perhaps she would see the young colonel before she sang. Perhaps he deserved someone like her, if only to make men like him understand what the world really was. Once outside, she looked quickly around her.

She waited for a group of Russian soldiers to pass and then crossed the Ku'damm, dodged down a side street, then onto a bomb site and, kicking off her high heels, she broke into a run up a hill of rubble. The stones hurt her feet. But her feet were hard from a barefoot childhood.

There was a shout behind her.

Gretchen heard a shot and dodged as a bullet hit a pile of bricks to her left.

The men behind were gaining on her. She half-fell, half-threw herself through the doorway of a ruined house, and headed up the broken staircase for what she hoped was the roof.

VIII

"YOU'RE SAYING HE'S who? Fucking tell me again," Kells demanded.

"I told you."

"Tell me again."

In Washington, before he saw the intelligence officer he was meant to be seeing, Kells was told he had to debrief a German prisoner in cells in the bowels of the State Department that smelled like a monkey house, even though they were in the brand-new Harry S. Truman building in Foggy Bottom. The boy, he was only eighteen, had told a story about a burning man. Kells sat by him on a prison bed. The boy was very frightened; he had been beaten recently and had an angry cut above his left eye. His father had worked on cruise ships and he spoke English.

"It was by the main bunker, sir. There were soldiers and bodies were brought up. My job was to watch the bodies burn in a shell hole and then to throw an old coat in. All around there was shooting and shelling. But I stood where I was told. There was a man with a head wound in a blanket and a woman and three other people. The man had been shot in the head at close range. I had seen many people shot in the Gestapo shower block after interrogation. The soldiers then threw benzine, you call it gasoline, and jellied benzine on five bodies, dropped in a match, and went back inside and I turned away because of the heat. Then there is this man running past me that has jumped out of the pit, still on fire. I try to put the fire out with the coat I am holding, but he is badly burned and then he runs off, grabbing the coat. I follow him because I was told to watch them all burn. He is naked."

Kells took a long drag of his cigarette. His hands were trembling. He did not fucking need this. "The coat? A simple brown coat? With a Jewish star?"

The boy seemed surprised. "How did you know that?"

Kells almost laughed. "Did the man say at any time who he was?"

The boy shook his head. "No sir, you do not make understanding."

"What don't I understand?"

"The men before you said I was mad. Who the man was. Like I telling you. Before they brought him out they must have given him one of those pep drugs that makes you always awake, like Pervitin, to interrogate him more. But they shot him instead. I thought he was only another prisoner. But he was not dead from the shot. And the drug was still in him. And even with all his wounds and his burns he ran off. Like a hare. Like the devil. And I saw clearly who he was. He ran into the rubble and fallen buildings and was set in flames again by a shell, and I ran the other way. Let me whisper his name to you once more, sir. It is a devil name. You will let me out now? I'm sure it was him. I am sure."

The boy turned and whispered the name in Kells' ear.

The name was unmistakable.

Kells punched the cell wall and the boy jumped.

"Are you crazy. Are you trying to get me in trouble? You're going to find yourself in all sorts of deep shit, believe me. You cannot be right. . . . Sorry, kid, but are you truly telling me the burning man is Adolf fucking Hitler?"

Several hours later, Kells was waved into a chair in an office at the State Department in Washington D.C.. Across from him was not a general, as he expected, but a man in civilian clothes, wearing a violently checked suit that did not go with the his deceptively soft voice. The man had kept Kells waiting in shabby rooms. His office was like a hotel suite and smelt of lavender.

"You've mostly done a good job, Colonel Vardy. You're sure that the man Kaplan, the real one, is dead?"

Kells nodded. "Nothing survived."

The man had a gentle smile. "You and your unit did?"

"We were not around for the initial Red Army artillery barrage."

The man across from him raised his eyebrows.

"You are quick, colonel. I like that. Quick. I like that a lot. Not usual in the military. But the man you have labelled as Dr Kaplan, thank you, by the way, for telling me the truth . . . That's so novel and refreshing. A badly burned nobody who survived that barrage . . . alive enough to have an erection . . ."

"Common in those who have been tortured or burned or under great emotional stress, the doctors say," said Kells.

"Ah, yes, the Prophet Mohammed had an erection on his deathbed and several popes censured priapism in Renaissance depictions of the Crucifixion. And I recall Saint Perpetua's orgasm as she died caused an earthquake?"

"I really don't know, sir."

"But you are sure your burning man is going to neatly die?"

Kells smiled and nodded. "He's at death's door."

"Where he's been lingering, teasing us, for some time?"

Kells looked the man in the eye. "Even if he wakes, the surgeon says he most likely will have no memory."

The man seemed pleased.

"No memory. I like that. What a luxury. Can you imagine what it must be like to have no memory of who you really are? To start again? Innocent as a newborn babe? A true wiping of the slate? I digress. What a thought, though! Of course, I have read your report and like and commend your suggestions. It is the sort of thinking we need. I noted in your file that you were educated at a good Catholic school, then California State University, Sacramento, and about to do a doctorate at Berkeley, on Dante's *La Vita Nuova*, because you don't want to join dad in the family hardware firm. My God. Perhaps you are too clever for intelligence? Don't worry, that is a joke. Your extravagantly failed Roman Catholicism more than makes up for any intellectual rebellion. As does volunteering for the war when your dad's airplane factory would have been a reserved occupation. I like contradiction. I suppose no one around this patient had an inkling of your selfish purpose for him?"

"Absolutely not." Why was it selfish to help another human being?

Hyman's phrase "I love you all,' jumped into Kells' thoughts.

The man stood up from behind the desk and his suit seemed almost to burst into song. It was grey and blue and he wore a yellow tie. On his feet were highly-polished Oxford brogues. Kells had no doubt at all that the man, his new boss, whose name he did not know and had not been given, was universally feared. No one wore yellow ties in the State Department.

He held out his hand to Kells.

"Names are best kept out of this. But the operation you were part of in Berlin that day was Operation Lucy . . . Lucy sounds a good operation . . . But there is some doubt now if it is ours . . . Good name, though. Didn't St Lucy gouge out her own eyes when she was about to be sent to a brothel as a punishment for helping Christians, and then was trampled by oxen before being burned? She has a pretty midwinter festival, where white-clad virgins don crowns of candles. This terrible burning, fanatic innocence is recorded with particular brilliance by the artist Juhn Baur on a Danish postage stamp of 1913. Lucy in a night sky of diamond stars . . . Then you'd know about St Lucy, being a Papist."

The man nodded sagely to himself.

"Lucy is patron saint of the blind, and her namesake operation may have completely confused and unsighted the German high command and may have turned the tide of war for the Russians in the Kursk Salient, the biggest tank battle in history on 1 July, 1943, that on the German side alone involved three-thousand tanks and forty-two German divisions. Thanks to Lucy, the Russians not only knew the date of the offensive but every intended German troop movement before the German tank commanders received their orders from Berlin. The battle was so decisive for the outcome of the war that it started certain of the more lunatic American generals talking of our next conflict, with Russia. The trouble is Lucy now confuses us, and probably the Russians too. We know many have been killed by her, people who were our agents. And then there are the double and treble agents we cannot trust and the dead ones we cannot ask, thanks to the blood baths after the plots on dear Adolf. We lost all our Lucy files in an air raid. One of our own, of course. You, for example, were operating as Lucy, but it is not clear where your orders came from in military intelligence. I want you to go back to Germany. Immediately. Tonight. You'll most probably be working for the Office of Strategic Services, Department S, and me, though there are plans afoot to temporally change the name to the Central Intelligence Agency until someone can come up with something prettier. If we refer to it at all, we will call it The Company. I predict a brave new building full of earnest clerks and typists. Yes, we lost most of our files relating to Lucy, with all the contacts, agent legends and code books, and need to find out more about the operation, operationally. Whatever it is, it's important, you can take my word. We think that the Russians, and even a few remaining Nazis or Lucy operatives, might take the bait and go after your patient, as the real Dr Kaplan. They all must be as uncertain as we are about what dear Lucy is now, and the good doctor must know many of her secrets . . . We'll see what your man brings out of the woodwork and interrogate them. Perhaps you should send a small team to the hospital. Unofficially, of course, for the present. Write nothing down. Hyman Kaplan may yet serve a higher purpose. You'll be on a flight this evening. There will be a humdinger of a storm. I hope that's not inconvenient?"

"I . . . There's a medal ceremony . . . I had assumed I was going . . ."

"Home? No, I do not think so. Your Silver Star will be posted to your family so you don't lose it as your life may become a little choppy in Berlin. It's lucky I am dealing with this or you might find yourself the subject of a court martial. We all must obey orders, mustn't we?"

Kells paused and swallowed, wanting a cigarette. His new boss anticipated him. He flashed a gold cigarette case at Kells, who did not take one. The man then lit a cigarette in an ivory holder for himself.

"Yes, your family and your girl in Los Angeles . . . I do think 'Hollywood' is a good name for you. Please feel free to use it in messages. Coded, always. You will receive a book. My code name will be Beatrice, by the way. Your spiritual guide through the many circles of hell. I bet your poor mother was expecting you and baking things. You have such a nice house and nice parents and that girl of yours is ideal for a solid American future. Give them a call before you go. And what did you think of the poor boy I asked you to debrief?"

Kells took a breath.

"I think he's shooting a line. I think it's too far-fetched and he was probably too far away from where we were. There's no connection with my burning man, or with Lucy. The boy is frightened and he thinks his lies will save him from jail. He just chose the biggest lie around," lied Kells.

The man in the loud suit then nodded and smiled and turned back to a book on his desk. It was a book about Italian Opera. He opened the book with one hand and waved Kells out with the other.

IX

"ARE WE EVEN sure who this Hyman man is?" said the older nurse.

Out in the hospital garden, sitting on a metal chair, Rachel's voice rose as she answered obliquely.

"Hyman's learning more. He can speak a few words."

The older nurse was shaking her head and extended a hand. "And you've done that so well, my dear. It's time to move on to this place the rabbi has been talking about. I know Hyman will be going too. Please don't spend all your precious time looking after him."

They sat in silence under the cherry tree that had now lost its blossom and was in full leaf. Rachel fiddled nervously with a leather bag she sometimes carried, spilling and gathering up the contents. The older nurse nodded her head and another nurse nearby smiled. Rachel then ran inside the hospital.

Rachel was breathing hard when she got to the small room she shared with no one else.

The instant she entered she took off the white nursing uniform she had to wear. She pulled off the nursing head-dress. She kicked away the awkward but well-made shoes. She then took off her brassiere and her government-issue blue panties and lay on the bed naked and hyperventilating. Her breath became faster and faster and each one shallower and shallower. She was not taking in much oxygen and the white, featureless room, with only a window strip high up on one wall, was hot. Then in her head she started playing her cello, as she did before everything changed. The low, steady notes in a minor key sawed at her heart and caught at the back of her throat. She was an innocent child again. It was Bach. Such music healed the division of people, whoever they were, from each other, and even from God. She fought thinking of the past and what had happened and why. For her the future started now. That's what she told herself. It was as simple as that and as she relaxed into those words, and the notes of her cello, her hyperventilation subsided. But she craved release.

She rubbed her hands against her flat belly. She touched herself between her legs. That helped more.

She liked to be naked in here on the bed. The Americans were always giving her things like Hershey Bars or soap, but she gave them away. All she wanted was to be responsible for her own body, her own mind. Her survival. Otherwise, the simple act of living, the minutes of the day, became unbearable. She could not now take on an ounce of another's load, albeit in sympathy. There was no one to trust but herself. She understood only too well about getting close to Hyman. Things fall apart. People die.

But Hyman was going to be different. She had to save him. It was the most important thing in the world for her. She needed him.

She put a finger inside herself. She felt a tickle again at the back of her throat.

She breathed out, pushing all the air out of her lungs. Some days she wanted to make plans. Then she did not want to make plans in case they were all smashed again. And the past was there again. Time was not simple. When she was working on the wards, the half-forgotten little girl in her expected her father to look around the door with a wink and a smile and say, "Come on. Let's go home for an ice cream." Rachel knew such fancies were the beginning of madness and suicide and that the past was dead; must be dead. She had suppressed her father's cheeky eyebrows totally in the camp, and his suits, and his hair and his cologne from Paris. Now, using two fingers inside herself, these ghosts were all breaking through once more and she saw clearly the salon with its floor-to-ceiling windows in her family house in Berlin and the pictures in silver frames on the piano.

There had been so much warning; there had been no warning. Her family had stayed as if hypnotised by a snake.

She ran her hand up and down her raft of pubic hair.

How can you expect something so completely dark happening

in a country like Germany? The country of Schiller and Goethe, Bach and Beethoven? That's what people said now. Seeking horror should not be in the nature of human beings. The honey-brown notes of the cello rasped in her mind. One ordinary day, storm-troopers had entered her house when she had been playing the cello. She was playing a piece by Bach, badly. When they burst into the salon, she took her bow off the strings and hugged the instrument to her. The cello had been a special, confessional friend growing up. She had brothers and sisters, but they were older, so she shared her hidden secrets with the cello her father probably could not afford, even though he was successful. It was worth a great deal and she told the young soldiers exactly how much and begged and begged them with tears on her cheeks to sell the precious instrument with its sensuous, sherry-coloured wood and preserve the cello's arrestingly beautiful voice. The boys, they were only boys, innocent looking, had stood there listening to her. She even told them the name she had for the cello. She called the cello Topsy, after a favourite aunt who had taught her to play the piano. The boys smashed Topsy with their boots and laughed right in her face, smelling of beer and sausage.

"We smash what we want. We smash all that is past."

Then they laughed more and tore off her white, starched blouse and held her face-down on a low stool and three of them had her, ~~raped her.~~ She could still see the intricate flower pattern on a fire screen. She recognised one of the young soldiers from her school, a boy who had been in the Hitler Youth. When she told her mother, her mother had said Rachel was always making stories up as a child. She had, it was true. There was nothing her father could do, even though he went to see a friend in the police. The local Hitler Youth commander had put the 'misunderstanding' down to high spirits and beer and what young men do. No one had used the word 'rape'. Her family had continued to act as if nothing was happening, as if they were not Jewish. The rape of a Jewish girl would make the crime one of *Rassenschande*, or racial shame. No respectable young German soldier could be guilty of such a crime.

Rachel still heard her father insisting at dinner that he could talk a particular Nazi round. Her clever, sophisticated father made the mistake of believing that he was dealing with one wolf, not a huge pack. And that pack had, by definition, no individuality. It acted as one pitiless animal. The pieces of the broken cello disappeared and her father managed through his contacts to get her another one from the Berlin Philharmonic, which he said he had exchanged for the old one. In the end she began to doubt if she had been raped at all and the cello smashed.

Her increasingly nervous mother, once a society beauty, said less and less, and chain-smoked gold-tipped Balkan Sobranie cocktail cigarettes, even at breakfast. She obsessively dusted vases and knick-knacks given to her by now missing friends, as if dusting ghosts.

Towards the time of her arrest, Rachel would hug her mother and her father, to be with them passionately. Their head-in-the-sand delusion, as much as the rape itself, was why she had joined the resistance, saving militants. Her memory of that was no fiction. It was real. Too real. The rabbi believed her.

Her capture had signed the death warrant for her family. They were walking dead anyway. But her action completed their murder.

She had been trying to help.

She moaned as she inserted her fingers again between her labia and increased the movement and pressure. In the camps she had even masturbated in the operating theatre by a new corpse. Especially in the operating theatre, among the blood and broken bones, when no one was there.

She smiled. Masturbating on the horror, playing herself like her smashed cello until she was empty, breathless, a husk again in front of her interrogators, was real. Real, like the living, electric air after a thunderstorm.

In the American hospital her head spun with the raw and painful kindness of complete strangers, who were like beings from another planet with their talk of home and apple pie. Her only way back to earth and reality was by pleasuring herself, becoming sexually aroused by the familiar horror of images from her past, by their dark music, by the swastikas and pain and stamping jackboots.

Rape and murder were the real world to her.

Nothing had changed. The past was still there.

The horror infected her present and her future.

She refused to hide from the horror like her dead parents. She pressed harder with her fingers.

Almost simultaneously she blinked back a tear, then shuddered with a spasm that made her cry out. There was a red smear on the pillow, like blood. It was her lipstick

She was becoming very fond of Hyman. If she was able to love him back into the world which had so abused him that would be something. Of course, nothing could ever, ever compensate for the things she, kindly Rachel, had done in the camp.

Rachel thought of Manfred, the surgeon commandant, and felt guilty. She thought of his wounds and twisted limbs and his tenderness and her survival. She thought of their love, it was love - he brought her little wild flowers - and making love. Of what she must do for Hyman.

But her sins were greater than being in Manfred's bed. They needed a darker catharsis.

Or how much of this was only in her frantic mind? What memories had she repressed, and what were pure fiction, the accusation of her dead mother?

Every dark atom of the past reverberated through her.

Her lips quivered.

It was a way of beating the past, the horror. With the horror.

Her hand was wet and she wiped her fingers across her face, sucking them, empty, breathless again. A curl of pubic hair went into her mouth.

What sort of creature was she? How could she be good or happy? Even in the future? Even if only half the things she recalled were true.

She orgasmed with a shout, arcing her long back. The swastikas again in her head.

X

ON HIS WAY back from Washington, Kells ran into a man he had met at Berkeley when he was offered a place to study Dante for a doctorate. The man was a fellow surfer and medieval poetry fan, who worked for the State Department and was helping organise the negotiations over the carve up of Germany under the victorious powers. They found themselves on the same plane from an airfield outside Bonn to Tegel in Berlin. As the man worked for the State Department, Kells asked about the individual code-named 'Beatrice' whom Kells had seen in Washington.

"You didn't ask his real name?"

"He said no names."

"No names. And you didn't ask?"

"I am new to this shit."

The State Department man smiled. "And he was wearing a loud suit? And a yellow tie? That's unusual there. Down in Foggy Bottom, Washington."

"He liked opera too."

"The motherfucker! I'll see what I can find out. Do you have a number? I'll try and call tomorrow."

Kells wrote his number down. "He said I must call him 'Beatrice' in all correspondence."

"Wow, man! He sounds a honey . . ."

The next morning Kells sat at the heavy and ordered German oak desk with cut-glass inkwells in the drawing room of the spacious detached villa assigned to him. He was not yet part of a unit and had no defined job, except to look into Lucy for a man whose name he did not know.

He gazed out into a garden of subtle greens and surprising flowers: stocks, tree peonies, Sweet William and late blossom, even though the house was close to the Kurfürstendamm, the main street.

It was one of the few properties in the centre of the city to come through without so much as a shrapnel mark. It had been previously occupied by a senior military historian attached to General Rommel, and the historian's wife was a keen gardener. Kells' mother would have loved the planted borders, stone walkways and high walls with trained quince trees, over which the piles of rubble were hardly visible. He missed her.

There was a random explosion somewhere towards the centre of Berlin that rattled the eternally smiling porcelain Dresden shepherdesses in a gilded glass cabinet. The house was full of old furniture, but not the heavy German sort. Kells guessed it had come from France, and the walls were covered in light papers, the floors in oriental carpets and the paintings were bright and mainly of Italian scenes; a rebellion by a trapped wife against Prussian uniformity.

There was not even a hint of the Nazi past.

A second larger explosion followed the first. Two planes flew over low and fast.

Before Kells left the State Department offices in Washington, the man in the yellow tie, who he was to refer to as 'Beatrice' in all communication, sent a brown paper parcel to the front desk. A man behind the desk had hailed Kells and said, "Do not open this parcel until you reach your destination, sir."

He opened the parcel now and inside was a book and a file, but no new ID card or official orders. The book had a cover that depicted a delighted Alice looking up at two gigantic Himalayan blue poppies.

It was a German translation of *Alice Through the Looking Glass*; *Alice hinter den Spiegeln*. It was published by Vita Nova, a small firm in Lucerne: 'A humanistic publishing house, anti-Hitler, anti-Stalin', stated the rear cover.

Kells' soul jumped. He had only planned to do a fucking dissertation on Dante's *La Vita Nuova*, – the Italian vernacular of the Latin Vita Nova.

But that was not all. In the Washington package there was a file marked Executive Order 8351, ABOVE TOP SECRET – SPECIAL ACCESS PROGRAMME, only TIER 5 clearance.

Kells did not like that. That was the very tops. What the bejesus, as his mother would say, had he got himself into?

In the file was probably all 'Beatrice' had on Lucy. On the first page was the information that the Lucerne publishing firm was run by a Rudolf Roessler, who was the head and founder of Operation Lucy. In a separate envelope, there was the picture of St Lucy that 'Beatrice' had referred to: an innocent young girl with masses of shining golden hair and lighted candles on her headdress, alone against a night sky of stars, ready to light the way out of winter.

The picture also had more than a hint of Alice in Wonderland, in its questing innocence.

'Beatrice' had obviously not made up his mind about Kells before the interview in Washington and preferred him to be surprised by the Lucy file and his own connection with *La Vita Nuova* when he reached Berlin.

In the book was a short note explaining it was to be used as a book code. The letters were numbered by page, paragraph, line and character. 'Beatrice' had exactly the same edition. Messages were usually, of course, mechanically encrypted now.

All of which might have been very helpful, except that when Kells immediately tried to send a short, coded message, signed 'Hollywood', asking how long he was meant to stay in Berlin, 'Beatrice' did not answer."

Kells sent several more messages only to receive an annoyingly open, uncoded one back on his wire machine.

PLEASE PROCEED WITH HASTE AND AWAIT CONTACT.

Kells' State Department friend was not going to call him back before the afternoon, he was sure, so he decided to go to intelligence headquarters. He took an approved taxi to McNair Barracks in the old super-modern Bauhaus Telefunken factory. A building even more soulless than the surrounding ruins.

He asked to see someone senior in military intelligence and was kept waiting for an hour. The old joke was that you waited for the rest of your life, because there was no shred of intelligence in the military.

"I just want to find out what I am meant to be doing. And about an operation called Lucy."

The man behind the desk looked at him strangely. "None of the US Army operations have girl's names, sir. Can you take a seat, please."

Eventually, a woman replaced the man and after several phone calls Kells was shown up to a diner decorated with Kandinsky prints and tubular steel furniture, where a two-star general had a cup of coffee and a bottle of rye whisky in front of him.

"Who the fuck are you?" asked the general.

"My name is Colonel Vardy, sir. I am most recently attached to intelligence. I wondered if you knew who my boss is here? I need proper orders . . . I have tried to contact Washington . . .

"He's dead. Washington."

"Yes, sir . . ."

"He had wooden teeth and smoked pot."

"I did not know that, sir."

"And he chopped down a perfectly good cherry tree."

The general poured more whisky into his coffee and took a drink. He then drew a large .45 automatic.

"I hate those fucking pictures," he said. "Do you think I should shoot them?"

Kells thought for a moment. "Only if they pose a threat to the free world, sir."

The general looked up at him with bloodshot eyes. "That's a good answer, son. You may go far. My advice to you is to enjoy yourself . . . Enjoy yourself while you can, my boy. All the physicality. Fallen women, strong drink and narcotics. That sort of thing . . . We deserve it for what we have done . . . Don't delay . . . Another fucking war's about to start. Already fucking started. Fuck it. Wanna drink?"

It was not the moment to ask about Lucy.

Kells got a ride back in a jeep and told the driver to drop him a few blocks south of where he lived. He wanted to walk. The city was coming alive again. Kids were tobogganing down mountains of rubble on bits of furniture.

He found the reason for the explosions he had heard earlier.

Ahead, sappers were blowing up the bombed buildings that stood like rows of decayed teeth.

There was a siren and he stopped before a loud bang and a building came crashing down, and people flooded out of the two next door. A wave of dust swept down the street. Men and women emerged blinking into the light, as if from a lost, subterranean species. Their skin was the dull white of a deadly fungus.

They were prepared to brave these explosions rather than hand themselves over to the authorities without papers, especially in areas where they were not sure who was in control. The allied bombing must have been far worse.

A pretty blonde girl in a satin nightie and one stocking halfway down her left leg, was being led away by brown-uniformed Russian soldiers.

Children with unsettling, adult eyes scuttled back into holes like feral cats.

A donkey cart with a large barrel with BIER painted on the side had stopped under a broken lamp-post. A man with a clown's smile painted on his face was selling the foaming beer in tiny glasses. Three men stood around the barrel. Kells had no Occupation Marks on him and paid with five American dollars. He motioned that everyone should have a drink on him.

'Danke," said the man with the painted smile, bowing low, and the others laughed.

Then on the bomb site in front of them a young man appeared

and ran though the rubble, changing direction, and there was a single shot. The man fell. The new German police, who were the old German police, or worse, did not bother to pick up the body that was still moving.

Kells started towards the man, but the beer seller took hold of his arm and stopped him.

"*Macht nichts,*" he said. "It does not matter."

The man with the painted smile then turned away.

Kells finished his drink and walked on.

He was glad to get back to the villa on Schiller Street, with its delphiniums and Dresden china shepherdesses. Almost as he stepped through the door he heard the phone ringing.

"Hey, Kells. This is your friend Sam, the only other surfer in the State Department. There is great drama! One of our senior players was killed in a traffic accident on the new bridge over the Potomac. Wipeout! As we surfers say . . ."

He paused. "Maybe he's your overdressed guy? You'd just better put your big surfboard Irish feet up and wait. There's going to be an incredible party on Saturday night in some old castle. A *Schloss*. Everyone will get Schlossed. I'll send you details and take prophylactics. And I will find out more about the dead guy. On that I will ring you tomorrow."

Kells read the details of the traffic accident on the Potomac bridge his friend had sent him on his wire machine.

He did not like the way 'Beatrice' might have died in a traffic accident. It probably was just a traffic accident in the alcohol-fuelled nights celebrating victory in Europe. The book 'Beatrice' had given him bothered him even more now given its publisher: Vita Nova, The New Life. He reflected on his proposed dissertation on La Vita Nuova, a book of poetry and prose; an autobiography of sorts by Dante Alighieri. In the book the poet showed the transition from Courtly Love to absolute love, on the same level as the divine. "Imagine if everyone's knowledge of personal love, all that ritualised teenage passion, was transformed into a sacred world-changing universal," a teacher at Kells' former university had said. It was a simple, subversive idea.

Was 'Beatrice' warning him in a subtle way with this copy of *Alice through the Looking Glass*, that Operation Lucy was, at least in the beginning, about a new vision for world peace? An upturned world order?

Exactly the kind of dangerous 'Commie' notion that got you killed on a busy bridge over the Potomac from the Pentagon war rooms. The sort of idealism that usually leads to war. Or was it only 'Beatrice's' idea of a joke? To make Kells interested and obedient.

Kells took a larger gulp of whisky. With Lucy there was not much to go on. He opened the sub-file on Rudolf Roessler, the man who owned the publishing firm, Vita Nova.

Uneasily, Kells started to read.

Rudolf Roessler had fled with his wife to Lucerne to escape Hitler in 1933, aged thirty-five. His Swiss identity card noted: hair, dark blonde; eyes, grey-blue; nose, straight; face, oval: distinguishing marks, wears glasses. The photograph on the card was of an ordinary man, possibly a clerk, but the signature had a princely flourish. A humble forester who had once wanted to be a priest, he was a veteran of the First World War, where he claimed to have met many significant men who went on to higher things.

Kells lit a cigarette.

In Lucerne, Roessler had set up Vita Nova and published much anti-fascist literature banned in Germany. He came to the attention of Brigadier Masson, head of Swiss Intelligence, who probably thought he could control Roessler by employing him. According to the file, Roessler claimed he was approached before the war by two German officers who both became generals: Fritz Thiele, now executed after the failed coup attempt on 20th of July 1944, and the aristocratic Rudolph von Gersdorff. Before the famous 'Wolf's Lair' 20th of July bomb, von Gersdorff had tried to kill Hitler on 21st of March 1943 with explosive charges hidden in his greatcoat pockets.

An intelligence staff officer, von Gersdorff was appalled at crimes against the Jews in the occupied territories. His plan had been to throw himself on the *Führer* in a death embrace as Hitler toured the Zeughaus, an old armoury on Unter de Linden in Berlin, converted to a museum on *Heldengedenktag* 'Day of Commemoration of Heroes', after which there was to be a *coup d' etat*.

"Fucking awesome," said Kells.

Von Gersdorff had set two timers to go off in ten minutes. Nothing could go wrong.

Until Adolf cut the visit short when he found one of his watercolours was missing, furious that his talent as a leading German artist was being questioned. Somehow, a frantic von Gersdorff managed to defuse the explosive charges in a toilet, sustaining terrible burns, and prudently went to the Eastern Front to recover in comparative safety. Dutifully schizophrenic in the Prussian manner, he later won the Knight's Cross in Normandy, fighting the allied invasion.

Thiele and von Gersdorff had initially told Roessler that they and their brother officers would supply high-level information. The sort of information that made allied 'code breaking' redundant. To Kells this was plausible and honourable. Yet the world 'BULLSHIT' had been written in capitals in the file margin at this point by someone in Washington.

A sheet of rain hit the French windows.

Kells stared at a photograph of Roessler in a raincoat too big for him. There was a fragility, and those eyes, large intelligent eyes, framed with oversized, square-shaped, thick-lensed glasses, had the endearing sadness of an orphaned bushbaby, or one of those strange lemur creatures from the twilight jungles of Madagascar. Kells doubted that the man in the picture, the man who was 'Roessler' in Lucerne, had ever been near a forest or wielded an axe. The file stated that he could not operate a radio, did not know Morse and even had difficulty with a typewriter. He was mild-mannered and unassuming, but despite his liberal and left-wing views, attended Mass in Lucerne's baroque Jesuit Church. And at first glance there was something about the sheer, dull normality of this cheaply-printed photograph that aroused Kells' suspicions and paradoxically suggested a high degree of planning and sophistication.

Kells wondered what the little man in the homburg hat, a meek, shabby refugee and amateur anti-fascist, desired for the future. Dante's *La Vita Nuova*, modestly written in the Tuscan vernacular, dealt with a new kind of love and life.

Kells tapped ash from his cigarette end into the ashtray. It all left him more confused and suspicious.

The rain was coming in sheets now and running down the panes.

Next, Kells turned to the coded documents the general previously in charge of the Office of Strategic Services in Berlin had sent to 'Beatrice', not the happier general who had told Kells to enjoy himself. The documents were like nothing he had ever seen, and did not correspond to any obvious book code from *Alice Through The Looking Glass*. On the first page the general had scrawled 'Goddam Commies' in angry pencil.

The page was headed:

DocSCS-StellaPolaris- Operation Lucy9609aTOPSECRET, then,

WHITE BLACK BLACK BLACK BLACK BLACK BLACK BLACK BLACK
BLACK BLACK BLACK BLACK RED RED BLACK BLACK BLACK BLACK
BLACK BLACK BLACK BLACK BLACK BLACK BLACK BLACK BLACK
BLACK BLACK BLACK BLACK WHITE BLACK BLACK BLACK BLACK
BLACK BLACK BLACK BLACK BLACK BLACK BLACK BLACK BLACK
BLACK WHITE BLACK BLACK BLACK BLACK BLACK BLACK BLACK
BLACK BLACK BLACK BLACK BLACK BLACK BLACK BLACK BLACK
BLACK BLACK BLACK BLACK BLACK BLACK BLACK BLACK BLACK
BLACK BLACK BLACK BLACK BLACK BLACK BLACK WHITE WHITE

The same pattern was produced on another sheet in splodges of poster paint.

Another sheet was even stranger:

"Shall we follow the ox-riding Highwayman over the Willow

Pattern Bridge?" said Myrtle, softly. She gently stroked the hairy legs of the strange creature with Bloody Horns. My uncle is not a tree. I should like You and Ezra Pound to Know that. I should like to get that straight from the Very start. Then we can go for a Soda at the Drug Store, like Amy. Or we might go shopping in Berkhamsted Castle with Chaucer."

The next day, after pathetically failing to break the codes, and being too late to go to the party in the Schloss, Kells had a headache and went out to sit in his ordered garden. It had stopped raining and the earth smelled wonderful. The delphiniums were starting to come out. The flowers were a glowing, impossibly Prussian Blue against the lead grey of the sky.

The rubble mountains were visible over his high garden walls.

Kells put his drink down and stubbed out his cigarette in a glass ashtray full of rainwater. There were two chairs and a table and he went back inside and grabbed a duster the cleaner had left on the fireplace and wiped one of the seats and sat at the table. He began to think of Rachel, the Jewish nurse who was looking after Hyman Kaplan. The doctor said Hyman was going to the kibbutz soon. Maybe Rachel too.

In Berlin everybody was being moved on, usually Stateside. Except him. The city was being divided into areas of influence.

He tried not to think of what the boy in the State Department cells in Washington had told him.

The elderly housekeeper, with a mole over her left eyebrow, who came with the house, walked slowly and purposefully to his table in the garden.

"There is also phone call, sir," she said, and shuffled off on bad feet.

He went inside. It was his State Department friend, Sam from Berkeley.

"Hey, Kells, the party at the castle was something . . . You should come to the next one. Anyway, surf's up on your man. I met someone at the *Schloss* who was working with your opera-loving boss with the yellow tie. Most sadly, Chief Yellow Tie is the one that had the accident on the Potomac bridge. My friend, she's a stenographer, also said that a young German prisoner had died the night before. Committed suicide. Hanged himself. With a rope and noose made from his trousers. *Die Toten Hosen!* What are our guards doing letting Nazis keep their trousers! Naturally, there's a shit storm and I don't know if the information is useful, or wise to pursue. Personally, I'd sit tight, work on your inner surfing, and forget there was a war. Enough of this death stuff. We must make pretty waves! Come over tonight if you like, there's a party again at the place on Müllerstraße. Bye. Hang loose, buddy . . ."

XI

HYMAN KAPLAN TOOK the piece of chocolate from Rachel's delicate fingers and let it melt in his mouth.

He had stopped feeding through a tube, though Rachel's attempts to give him broth and rice pudding were not successful.

She gave him another piece of chocolate, and she kissed the piece with her own lips to show him it was good, her mouth so near to his, and the bitter, fudge-like chocolate melted on his tongue in a rhapsody of complete sensual beauty. He thought he tasted a hint of lipstick.

Oh, how he would have liked her to pass the chocolate directly from her tender mouth to his ruined lips! How that excited him.

A stream of molten chocolate ran down his chin from a volcano of pent-up desire and she dabbed away his tyranny of wanting her with a soft cloth.

He laughed and that hurt so much inside his skull he thought he was going to die, but did not care.

Rachel was devoted to him. At times he pretended to lapse back into a coma and she filled the room with doctors.

She had her back towards him now, by the window, by the

cupboard. She reached out and touched the yellow star on the brown coat that she said was his and then pulled her hand away, as if she had touched something forbidden or a live electric wire. She had told him that all Jews were made to wear a yellow star and she had worn one too. In the camp. *Der gelbe Stern.* He had no memory of such an emblem. He saw from the tension in her shoulders that it was painful for her even to be in the same room as that star. There was a nerve that jumped at the side of her neck. Only once or twice. She had a long and delicate neck. Rachel also had the sort of female shoulders that made even her white nurse's uniform hang well, while the older American nurse did not. Rachel was still underweight and not eating, which Hyman liked. She turned back to him with those wide cheekbones and those large, sad blue-green eyes. She smiled as she saw him gazing at her.

She was teaching him English and, much worse, Hebrew. There was a shout in the corridor. Rachel was called away by another nurse and he was left looking at the coat with the yellow star. He was not sure what to think, or even how to think. His smashed head had retained an intellectual framework with which to make sense of the present. He remembered English words such as *mashed potato* and phrases like *thank you very much, Aunt Mabel*, but not anything clearly about the day they found him, except that he was running up a hill of rubble towards a broken statue.

He did not remember why, or who he was.

Why had they gone to such great lengths to kill him?

The doctor had told him he had a few petals of a dried white flower, possibly a gardenia, in his hand when they found him. A white flower?

He knew what memory was and attempted to remember. He tried to find the library of his mind. But his thoughts were like a labyrinth leading to the library where he imagined there was a door. Only he was not able to find the library door.

Now the pain was going he tried to remember. Oh, how he had tried. He had attempted to picture the face of his mother. His father.

His wife. The university. He tried to recall the last moments which had been described to him. But there was nothing.

"Most cases of memory loss are usually recovered in a few months, but parts of your brain, Hyman, have been irreparably damaged, or are missing," the Swedish surgeon had said. That meant Hyman's library had been smashed, its books burned, lost. It was with his brain tissue among the granite cobblestone rubble in the centre of Berlin.

"You are a hero, a Maccabee, one who fought impossible odds, who fought against the wicked in Germany . . ." said Rachel that morning and then became emotional and had to go out of the room. He did not pursue the conversation. What was the point? Perhaps Rachel knew his family had been killed in the war. He sensed something even darker, something they were not telling him as he lay there, still unable to raise his right hand sufficiently to brush a fly off his forehead. The insect crawled on what was left of his lips and its feet tickled. The fly was looking for Rachel's chocolate.

Two doctors entered and he closed his eye as they checked on him and whispered to each other. "They say he's getting stronger. The surgeon says he is getting stronger."

Later that morning Rachel came running in.

"They are letting you go outside today!"

She came over to the bed and Hyman thought she was going to kiss him. She patted his hand. He tried to hold onto hers and failed. He attempted to smile, which hurt. It came as a confirmation of sorts that he was going to live on and not die. If he was going to die from his wounds, he preferred it to be in the open air with the sun on his face and air in his lungs that did not smell of ether and disinfectant. The weather was perfect to go outside, sunny and not too hot, she said, and a hoist was wheeled into the room.

"Please do not worry," said Rachel.

But Hyman experienced great agitation as soon as he saw the hoist and the two big American soldiers. It was a contraption on wheels with a canvas seat. There was a brown mark of blood on the harness. He began to get a headache and wanted to open his mouth and scream and say no.

"This will only take a moment. It will soon be over." Rachel held his hand and smiled. The sun was coming through the window and caught the gold in her hair. He did not make a sound as they raised his head and back up from the bed, although it felt as if he was coming apart, and slipped the hoist under him. His sense of smell had not been damaged and he knew the bed stank today, despite Rachel's attentions.

He saw the disgust on one soldier's face.

The headache increased and there was a pain in his chest.

For several seconds he was swinging in the hoist, too vulnerable, like an animal on a butcher's hook. He was totally helpless. It was like being born and he wondered again who his mother was and if she was still alive.

An hour later, Hyman Kaplan sat in the hospital gardens in his wheelchair with his head back against a cool cotton pillow as he had been told to many times by the older nurse. If he did not do this correctly, he might be forced to wear a head brace, a metal contraption that had been shown to him and would make him look like the man in the iron mask, said the surgeon. Rachel had told him the novel, The Man in the Iron Mask by Alexandre Dumas, was an adventure story about the brother of the French king. The title hung in his mind, like an inn sign swinging in the wind. But the story was there also. He had begun to try to read himself now. With a book propped on a frame. He must have read a lot if he was a professor. A head brace would make reading painful, given his facial burns and loss of scalp and lip flesh, so he kept his head still, even though he was not the static kind; the surgeon said he made all sorts of movements all the time and probably had been very active before his injuries.

Why did he have those dried-flower petals in his hand when they

56

found him? They must have been precious to him. The surgeon, who told him about the flower petals, often asked him to try and remember the day when he was rescued by the American commando unit.

He concentrated now in the wheelchair, with the wind on his face, and thought about the centre of Berlin on the day he was found and tried to bring the scene alive, but without success.

All he could see were picture postcards.

He had been shown pictures in the newspapers of the devastation at the end of the Kurfürstendamm and near Potsdammer Platz, names which he knew. These pictures did not help, however. He tried to weave them into the only remembrance he did have, that of trying to climb the rubble hill to a broken statue. The young American colonel apparently confirmed this was what he was doing when first seen. What did come clearly to Hyman from the past was the smell of cordite and explosive and dust and soot and blood. Yet, he had been in a happy mood, exhilarated, joyous even, as he climbed his small mountain, on fire.

There had been dreadful pain.

Yet he did not remember the pain as important.

He heard the doctors saying that the colonel had insisted that he did not appear to be in pain, but in a kind of ecstasy, and the surgeon had nodded and said a strange, other-worldly perception was not uncommon in battlefield injury, and might, of course, be due to his initial head wound.

The nurses said he was tortured by the Gestapo secret police, and his mood, almost a rapture, may have been a mindless and impractical happiness in getting away from such horror and darkness; an attempt to assert a fictional control, to tell a different story. Yet he could remember not one thing about being tortured, what he might have said, what he might have known and, most important, if he betrayed his comrades. Of this the nurses had told him hardly anything, even Rachel. In fact, he thought it was forbidden for them to fill in his past. The surgeon and a female psychologist with a red birth mark covering half her face had told him they wanted his memory to knit together by itself. The psychologist, an American, spoke fluent German and said he should concentrate on the very last second of memory before he became unconscious and anything from his childhood.

He told her, "I do not have a childhood. I was never a child."

He did not recognise the name Hyman. The band outside his window had gone although there was a loudspeaker system that played popular American music most of the day. One could be in America in the hospital. English was the language used. The Americans appeared to be a fundamentally cheerful and practical people, no longer concerned with the war now it was won. There seemed no cult of the victor or the hero. The Americans regarded open-hearted, democratic friendliness as a fierce sacrament they were prepared to kill for, while their humour was therefore necessarily obvious and one-dimensional. They were uncomplicated, and mainly given to a dream of material plenty, with the exception of the young colonel who brought him here. The colonel had problems making sense of the war. Hyman thought he had overhead snatches of a conversation Colonel Vardy had with the Swedish surgeon. Kells had a darker sense of humour and Hyman imagined a heart as complex as anything in Europe, but what did he know? He was not even sure of his own name. The Americans were, said the older nurse, concerned with putting things back together, like mending a broken china vase that has been smashed into a thousand pieces by a madman.

When he asked about the madman, the older nurse did not help him.

The surgeon even told him he had had an erection that day, which only added to an air of absurdity.

On the lawn, to his right and left he did not see any nurses or guards or other patients in their wheelchairs.

In front of him was a line of tall lime trees past which there was a fence and a road. There was a single armoured jeep parked on the road. After helping him out of bed and into the wheelchair,

Rachel had reluctantly been called away to a meeting with the rabbi, who he liked a lot, and who had a sense of humour, about what she called a kibbutz, an ideal farming community. It was called Aviv and was here in Germany. Aviv meant spring in Hebrew. When she spoke of the kibbutz her face lit up and she became breathless with enthusiasm and a tear hung on the lashes in the corner of one eye. She was such a dear, sweet child. He had to prevent her leaving him.

There was no one else about.

The older American nurse who wheeled him out should have been with him and there was usually an orderly or a guard. The lime trees ahead of him were coming into blossom and the air was sweet with their pollen.

He breathed deeply even though it was painful. He wanted to get the good air down into his lungs. The sun was not that far from setting and there were pinkish shades and the temperature was dropping. He was totally alone for the first time since he had run burning up the rubble hill.

He tried to smile.

He had only been alone for minutes in his room. The hospital kept watch. Here, there was no one in sight. It was both liberating and a frightening. He wanted to get out of the stupid chair and dance towards the line of fragrant trees.

But he must not even move his fragile head.

"*Scheiße!*"

The flash and wave of heat on his face took him completely by surprise as part of the line of trees in front of him and the single guarding jeep were consumed in bright yellow flame, followed by the dislocating sound of an explosion. When the flames subsided into swirls of smoke, he saw two men in black, with black balaclavas running towards him, firing.

Bullets hissed past him.

He held his good hand up and then dropped it and gripped the wheel of the chair and leaned hard to the right, tipping himself onto the green grass. He felt no pain. The wet grass smelt of his absent childhood and green-stained knees.

At the top of the hospital building a nurse was screaming. Where was his Rachel? There was the sound of machine guns. Then single shots.

To his right a distinguished, dark-haired man in a black chalk-striped suit stepped from behind a tree with a long-barrelled pistol and a bright smile. Hyman saw two bodies on the grass. The dark-haired man picked up his ejected brass cartridge cases and put them in his jacket pocket. He swapped the pistol to his other hand for a few seconds and made the sign of the Cross. He wore black leather gloves. He did not go over to the bodies. They were no longer his business.

Hyman knew he was going to die. His enemies had come for him. It was a curious feeling, after not being able to die when tortured, shot and set on fire in Berlin.

The shooter walked slowly over to him and stood by the upturned wheelchair, his pistol pointing down at Hyman's face. He remembered saying certain last words when Kells found him. He was not at all sure what he had meant. He hoped they might work magic a second time.

"*Ich liebe Sie alle*," I love you all, said Hyman.

The shooter raised an eyebrow and his smile showed a gold eye-tooth. The man then laughed, shook his head, and pushed the gun's hot muzzle hard into Hyman's forehead . . .

PART TWO

I

"THIS IS IT, folks. This is your new home. The kibbutz!" shouted the driver in New York English.

"Will there be shooting here too?" asked a boy from the dark cavern of the US army truck.

"No, we will be safe here," said Rachel.

"Is Hyman dead?"

"No worries, people . . . You are safe now," echoed the driver.

"Do we know how Hyman is?" said a boy called Paul.

"Not yet," said Rachel, looking towards the back of the truck.

"Was he shot?" said Paul.

"They will come for us all . . . Like always . . ."

"He was shot."

"No . . . There is a problem with his heart . . ." said Rachel.

"You are keeping the truth from us . . ."

One girl, Anna, screamed, "They are taking us back to the camps to kill us." She jumped to her feet, but two of the girls got hold of her arms and sat her down and calmed her.

Rachel undid the flap at the back of the stifling, wooden-seated three-ton American army truck and jumped down. In front of the convoy was a small, but perfect, eighteenth-century country house across a ragged lawn with an old Italian-looking fountain. After the shooting at the hospital, the decision to bring the camp survivors from in and around Bonn here had been so quick the rabbi had not told her where exactly the kibbutz was, and the trucks had to travel in strict security with the flaps tied down. On the long, slow journey, Paul and another boy started to sing songs like they were going on holiday, songs mainly invented by their would-be exterminators, like "Der fröhliche Wanderer", The Happy Wanderer: "... *Mein Vater war ein Wandersmann, Und mir steckt's auch im Blut.*" My father was a wanderer, And it's in my blood too ... but they petered out.

Rachel had expected a stolid and forbidding castle. Instead, this house was from the age of Enlightenment, built in a French style, with long, delicate windows and painted a warm, daffodil yellow and white, and with grey cloche-style roofs in the centre and at both wings. It reminded her of the old Poppelsdorfer Schloss in Bonn, the palace in the botanical gardens, where her father had once taken her to a concert. A place of books and dancing and laughter and music. The other Germany. Her Germany.

The windows caught the sun and the house looked as if it was smiling. Across the patchy lawn, where thistles grew and bouncing flights of goldfinches foraged, sheep were grazing. A peacock screamed and she jumped. The boy, Paul, put his arm around her. She did not stop him. She flung her arms around him and kissed him fiercely on the lips.

"*Shalom!*", she said.

"*Shalom,*" he replied, laughing.

The house was surrounded by stands of chestnut, oak and cedar, whose roots reached back centuries.

The others started embracing and kissing each other as they got down from the trucks. Rachel had broken the spell of fear from the shooting.

All of those in the convoy, other than three orphaned children, were in their teens and twenties. There were more than a hundred in three army trucks, two jeeps full of American army guards and two ambulances, and several orderlies.

To the left of the house, Rachel glimpsed a lake and a herd of spotted deer.

"We are here!" shouted a girl.

"Where?" said a boy.

"Israel, stupid," said the girl and laughed. "This is Aviv. This is the kibbutz. Our homeland. This is springtime. That's what Aviv means. This is springtime. Always."

Paul shrugged. "I bet it belonged to Nazis."

Rachel stared at his wan face. Under the bravado she knew he was scared. "What does it matter?" she said. "Everything belonged to the Nazis. We belonged to the Nazis."

"I don't want their filthy things."

"They haven't given it to us. It's been taken from them. They are dead, or in jail."

"What about the shooting? We are not safe," said another boy.

It was then that Anna screamed again, "We have to go! We have to get out! Don't be fooled! This is a camp just like the others. If we go in, we will never come out."

The small, gentle rabbi had come with them from the hospital. He went over to Anna.

"There is nothing to fear, my dear. Not now. The shooting at the hospital may just have a been a robbery. Nothing more sinister . . . All of you, you must be hot from your journey. Go down to the lake and swim. We will bring you cakes and lemonade. This is a good place. It is quite safe, and I know you don't have your costumes, but no one is looking. Take Anna too. This is not a camp, Anna. It is the exact opposite. It is the end of camps. It is our hope for the future. And we were going to come here anyway. It was not just about the shooting and poor Hyman . . . First, we must all learn to have fun again."

Anna, still unconvinced, nodded her head and followed in the party that went down through the deer park to the lake. Everyone began singing again and there were whoops of joy.

Rachel stayed where she was. She was looking at the ambulance.

"You go for a swim, too," said the rabbi.

"I was waiting to get news of Hyman. They may send him . . ."

The rabbi shook his head. "There is nothing we can do. I am sure they will send him if he is well enough. I will telephone. Go and have a swim, my dear. Have fun. It is your duty. I mean that.

It is your duty now to be happy after evil people tried to make you unhappy. I am sure Dr Kaplan would want you to."

"Yes," she said, and followed the others, at first slowly then running to catch up. She loved to swim. She often swam in the Waldensee in Berlin, or one of the other lidos well into the winter, and once the whole year around, breaking the sharp ice at New Year, naked in the dawn with her then German school friends, shivering and laughing so hard when she climbed out. By the time she got to the lake's edge, most of the boys and girls had pulled off their clothes and were swimming among the water lilies. Many of the girls had left on their brassieres and knickers for the sake of modesty, but the boys bared all. They had been made to strip so many times in the camps. There was a jetty and she walked onto the wooden planks, picking her way through the clothes. Rachel stripped completely off, and dived into the cool, clear water and came up with a whoop. Everyone had a smile on their faces.

It was impossible, and was happening right before her eyes.

Rachel loved the cool of the water on her body as she swam into the middle under the dark trees. Her skin felt so soft in the lake that she laughed out loud. She trod water and looked at the others swimming out towards her. Everything was so clear and in perfect detail, as in a dream, but it was not a dream. She swam over to a white water lily and marvelled at the precise beauty of the flower, of the white petals around the glowing yellow heart and the stamens, as she had never done before. It was as if she was being given a second chance at life, and she was not going to miss an instant this time around.

She had not felt this way on the road after the camp or in the hospital.

Here it was different. She had entered into a magic future through a secret doorway, the gate to this great house, never to return to the old world. She tumbled over in a somersault in the water and stretched her body out with each stroke. One of the boys tried to catch her, but she did not let him.

Most of the bodies, especially of the boys, were thin to the point of starvation.

There was a colour to the skin that was beyond white. It was beyond even the white of the corpses she had seen so often in the hospital, after one torture session too many, when the man or the woman could no longer be revived for questioning or the pleasure of the interrogator. There was a white that went further. It was the white of the fungus deep in the heart of the forest; a strange glowing white that has an animus other than air and light. Before she had been arrested, she had always regarded white as a sacred colour, the colour of the virgin, of weddings, of doves, of light itself. She knew now that this was not the case. There was a dark white. The colour of nothing.

When she saw it in the face of a man or a woman she feared for them.

She was thin, but not sick.

The sound of the cello came rasping back to her.

She had better rations working as a nurse in the camp.

Rachel shook her head. She must not even think of that. The old world was gone.

She swam back to the water lily to reassure herself.

Even Anna now was smiling and prepared to believe as she dangled her feet in the clear water. They swam around and played and splashed like children and then some went to dry off on the little jetty or in the old rowboat moored nearby. One of the orderlies came down from the house with a pile of towels and left them on the warm planks and she got out and dried her hair.

"Shouldn't the girls cover up?" said one girl.

"No, men and women are equal in a kibbutz," said Paul.

Everything had changed.

A little later, as the sun was about to set, Rachel looked up at the house, which shone in the sun like a lily. She felt that everyone around her shared her feelings of joy, whatever they had been through: a girl near her was missing three fingers; a handsome boy an ear; no one talked of the past and everyone of the future. It was hard to shut a few of them up, not that she wanted to. She was glad of this moment, even though she did not know, or exactly trust, how it was going to end.

"I'm going to have dresses made in Paris. I am going to have twenty ball gowns."

"They'll come in useful when you are working on an orange farm in Palestine."

"All I want is to eat cake and dance."

"We must have a dance. That is the first thing we must do. We must organise a dance."

She saw reservations on a few of the girls' faces. At the camp Rachel had been in the officers liked to organise "dances" in their quarters.

"I bet there's a gramophone somewhere in this great house."

"They probably have an orchestra in the attic."

The sound of her smashed cello came again to Rachel's head.

A procession of servants from the house and two of the American guards then came down to the water in single file carrying baskets and several blankets, which they laid out on the ground. The old servants, the women in particular, traditional Germans, held up their hands to their faces so they would not see the nudity, and one older woman ran back to the house muttering in German to the laughter of Paul and the other boys. The blankets were then spread out and the baskets opened. They were small laundry baskets, which had become picnic baskets and were full of food. There was not just the cake and lemonade the rabbi had promised. It was a feast. There were roasted chickens and beef and sandwiches and iced cakes and even coloured jellies.

At first, there was hesitation. There was a serious look on one boy's face.

"It may be a trick."

"It may be poisoned," yelled a girl, and another began to weep.

Rachel stood up and walked over to one of the blankets and took a sandwich and ate it. It was of thinly sliced cucumber. She took another.

"See, I'm not dead. Don't be frightened," she laughed. "I am having so good a time I do not care if it is poisoned."

"I think it's all *Kosher*," said one of the American military guards, with a worried look. Rachel thought of them as guards.

There was laughter, and everyone came up and took food and ate slowly. There was no fighting and jostling. Rachel saw one boy unable to eat a piece of chocolate cake he had taken. He seemed transfixed with the glaze of the *Sachertorte*.

Three of the boys then ran down the jetty and dived into the water as the sun was starting to set. Still, no one officially seemed to mind they were naked. After what they had suffered, none of those old fusty values mattered. Those rules had not prevented what happened. Rachel looked up at the house again and the rabbi was standing on the balcony with a group of other men. Two of them, despite the heat of the evening, were in homburg hats and tan trench-coats, which hung around their painfully thin shoulders, like second-hand wings. She had seen such men before on the Nazi side. A shout distracted her and when she looked again the men were gone and she wondered if it had been her imagination. Ghosts she had brought to the feast.

"Come on, Rachel. Come in for another swim! The water is wonderful!" said Paul, the boy she had kissed, and wanted to kiss again. Then she felt guilty. Where was Hyman? She wished they had allowed her to see him before they all had to pack and leave.

II

KELLS HAD PUT the telephone down after calling McNair barracks in another fruitless attempt to find out who he was working for, when there was a knock at the door.

Joe, his sergeant, stepped elegantly into the room, smiling as usual. He was wearing his black, chalk-striped suit, which made him look even more like a crow than usual. Joe Crow was his nickname. His real name was Rimiggiu Macaluso Corbo. Rimmiggiu meant oarsman, which was apt. He was certainly a ferryman. Corbo meant crow.

"They came for the old burned-up Jew boy, like you said, boss. I got a lift back here on a plane. I like planes. Sure beats walkin . . ."

The man gave an unnerving throaty laugh.

Kells nodded. "He's dead? Hyman?"

"The Jew boy? No, they come for him, but they fucking miss him. He tip up his chair. It wasn't their fault. They was half-good men. But he tipped up his chair, the sneaky Jew boy. If you ask me he had the instinct. Knew they was coming to put him in a box. Knew someone was coming. I got the two triggermen. We grabbed a third, but he took a pill. He go straight to the hot place. Then we went to work on a fourth. He not a soldier. He had one of those blood group tattoos under his arm like the SS, but it was too new. They don't look like Russians either. Can I help myself to Scotch, boss?"

"Sure, so Hyman is okay?"

"Not exactly, boss. You never say what to do with him . . . I going to pop him, but I think he had a heart attack . . . He start talking and saying all that I love you all crap . . . and he goes still so I stick my gun in his face. Then his good eye go funny and he shiver like his heart is going pip-pip-pip . . . I seen it before . . . Then he still. I do not waste time. I go."

Kells poured the man a large glass of Scotch, which Joe rubbed between both hands and sipped. Kells then handed Joe a cigar from a cedar humidor on the desk, slicing off the end with the cutter, and took one himself. He lit Joe's cigar and his own. He was trying not to feel relieved at the possibility of Hyman's death.

"Thanks, boss."

"No one else was hurt? There wasn't a nurse with Dr Kaplan?"

Joe shook his head. "No. The Jew boy was on his own. Like a goat for a tiger."

Kells walked to the window and looked out at the garden. "Did the man you questioned say anything?"

"That one was not a soldier . . ."

Kells turned around and saw that his visitor was looking thoughtfully into his Scotch.

Kells had only met Joe, the Italian sergeant, on his last job. He was not a very tall man but stood very straight and had a sallow, handsome Italian face with anarchic black hair that flopped over his forehead and piercing but amused dark eyes. He was in his late forties. He had the old-fashioned manners from south of Rome. He looked like a modest store owner, though it took only a few moments in the field with a pistol in his hand to discover what was his real profession.

How had Kells come to know such a man? How could he explain Joe to Betty?

"So I am still working for you again, colonel?"

Kells went over and patted the man on the shoulder. "You are working for me."

"And they give you money?"

"Yeah. I got money. You want some, Joe?"

Kells went to a humidor and took out another two cigars and a wad of notes. "Take this. You're still in the transit-barracks, aren't you? You know about the new house on Friedrichstraße? Stay there."

Joe stared at the money and nodded. "I know about the house. From the officer who sent me here. Ain't that too much, boss? The money?"

Kells shook his head. "How did you know the fourth man wasn't a soldier?"

Joe put down the glass and slipped the money in his coat. Kells wondered if Washington ever decided to kill him they would use Joe.

"He had a soft body. He more of a boy. The guys I took beat him too hard, boss. But we had to do it quick. They use the pincers on his tits. Then one of the guys I take chokes him a bit and then too much. He go to the angels. Probably he so scared like a girl he prefer the box, The big hole. Big fucking coward. Maybe he was observer. Intelligence."

They were both silent as a grandfather clock ticked on. The cigar smoke drifted in the sunlight. Joe sighed with contentment.

"But did this boy say anything else? Anything at all?" asked Kells.

Joe shook his head and smiled wistfully. Kells sensed he was not being told everything.

Joe looked up at the ceiling.

"One thing. Again, it was strange and probably meant nothing. Before the choking he keep on saying, 'Nein, nicht der Mann. Der Mann. Der Mann!' Then he was laughing . . . Then he said Hitler. Not Heil Hitler. Just Hitler. And laughs again. My guy thinks he takes the piss and then chokes him hard and he die. Did maybe someone think the burning Jew boy is Hitler? Like because of where we found him? That's funny . . ."

"Yeah, Joe. A prisoner said that in the States. We don't know for sure."

"I can go back? No trouble. I don't mind killing a Jew boy Hitler. I shoulda looked at his dick. But I thinks he may be croaked anyway . . ."

Kells shook his head. "No . . . Please . . ."

There was the sound of the doorbell and the housekeeper came in followed by the priest that both of them knew.

"Colonel . . . Joe . . . This is such a wonderful surprise. I have been attached to your unit, again for my imperfect Russian. What are we going to be doing?"

Kells did not know exactly what to tell him.

"Not sure yet." Kells was wondering why an intelligence operative had been sent along in the attempt to kill Hyman Kaplan.

The priest was nodding. His name was Norton Wordsworth. He had formed a close friendship with Joe despite, or maybe because of, the man's profession.

The priest then sat down and said, "What is more, I have brought a cake. When did you last see fruit cake? I left it with the poor lady out there and she is getting us a pot of coffee. I spent most of my leave painting watercolours. You would be surprised how nuanced Southern Bavaria is at this time of year."

Four maddening days went by trying to break the nonsense code and the colour code and Kells eventually tried to call the hospital and speak to Rachel, but he soon found himself talking to the Swedish surgeon:

". . . I attempted to call you, colonel, but there was a communications black out. There was an attack on the hospital and the only person out on the lawns was poor Hyman. His wheelchair toppled over and saved him from a bullet, but we think he had a heart attack, and he is too weak to operate. He passes in and out of consciousness and we do not know if we will lose him. The rabbi has taken that pretty nurse, Rachel, and other camp survivors from around Bonn to their kibbutz experiment. This ideal farming community they are going to take to British Palestine to help create their Israel one day. They've all gone and I will miss them. Rachel was a very good nurse. I am so sorry about Hyman. He was due to go to the kibbutz with the others. He was talking more and more and now I am not sure he will survive. Before the shooting I knew he could drop dead any moment, but he persuaded me to let him go. He said he would rather have a few more days making a difference than sitting around in bed . . ."

"So this time he is going to die?" said Kells quietly.

"Best not get your hopes up, colonel. We did not think anyone would attack the hospital and still do not know why. I have the number of the kibbutz somewhere . . . I'll let you have it. Three of our people were killed and there might have been more but for a fire drill. A soldier in a jeep by the fence was blown up and one of my male nurses was shot in the face before they robbed the dispensary. Drugs were stolen. And, even more of a loss, is our plastic surgeon. Shot, too. So no more Clark Gable. Your man Hyman was her last."

Kells felt a shiver of cold up his back. Joe had not told him everything. No one told him anything anymore. He had not mentioned the dispensary nurse or the plastic surgeon or the drugs. Or who took them. It was probably part payment to the men Joe recruited.

"Did I tell you about the time I met William H. Bonney, alias Billy the Kid?"

Kells was on the phone to his dad and had heard the story, many times. In his childhood history, the tale was like a litany in the Mass.

On a fishing trip to the southern part of Texas famous for giant catfish, his father had run into a happy old man in a wood-shack bar who claimed to be Billy the Kid and to have killed eight men before Pat Garrett, his friend and fellow outlaw who became a marshal, said he shot him, but had let Billy go free. After travelling down to Nicaragua for a time as the bodyguard of a rich man who wanted to dig a canal, the old man said he, Billy, came back to the States and established a successful agricultural implement business and bought himself a bait shop in retirement by a peaceful lake as he always liked fishing. Kells' father had believed the story completely with the childish innocence of a sharp businessman on holiday, and he and the rest of the fishing party had all bought the old man drinks at the bar next door to the bait shop. The next day they drove out along the long, straight road to the dark blue lake, the only lake around, but they could not find the bait shop or the bar, yet his father clung to the quiet man's story like the Holy Grail and became obsessed with Billy the Kid.

Towards the end of the phone call, Kells did not know if his father realised that it was him, his son, on the line. Kells found it hard to resign himself to the fact his father's dementia had worsened since Kells last saw him. His dad kept saying, "'¿Quién es?' Who is it?"

The last words of Billy the Kid.

Kells put the phone down, gently. He was thinking about Hyman.

He stood up and walked around the desk and lit another cigarette.

The wire machine began to chatter. The message simply said: 'CLOSE DOWN OPERATION LUCY, MYERS, STATE DEPT.'

That evening, after eating alone, and finding there was no Myers at the State Department, Kells put on his coat and went out and strode around the city, over the bricks and the broken glass. He ranged from the sparse lights of the Café Kranzler on the Ku'damm with its spire-less church, to the bombed-out alleys and spaces where buildings had been, where stones moved and became strange, twisted people in the twilight, a scene lit by the occasional bonfire and candles and oil lamps that caused dancing shadows in the ruined buildings. In his pocket he had a small but heavy Walther PPK pistol that Joe had given him. He wondered, more than once, as he tramped the streets in the intermittent drizzle, if he had been selected by Washington as someone who would fail.

He was walking past the Café Kranzler on the Ku'damm a second time when he saw her, Gretchen, by the window, putting on her lipstick and looking at herself in the mirror of a powder compact. He went straight in and sat at her table. She did not seem surprised to see him.

"I've been looking for you," he said. "You told me you hung out here."

She nodded and stirred her hot chocolate very slowly. She then stared right at him and said, "You should get away from here. Get away from Berlin right now. Believe me, it is not safe. This café is not safe . . ."

"I work here. I am a soldier. I can look after myself."

"Don't look now, colonel. But the city has not exactly been protected by soldiers, has it?" She shook her head and laughed. Then her mood became lighter. "Come around the corner and hear me sing. Then we can go for a drink. I don't feel safe here."

The club was in a basement and packed and there was a negro band who played standards in a standard sort of way. Yet when Gretchen sang, from the first note, Kells was hooked. She began with the Gershwin song, 'It Ain't Necessarily So,' but in German to a jazz arrangement, and ended up with 'I Get a Kick Out of You' by Cole Porter. Yet Gretchen had received most applause when she sang old German songs like 'Lily Marlene', which silenced everyone. When she finished, the shouting and stamping was ecstatic, and as they left she kissed him and blew in his ear, which sent a tremor right to his toes. Then they were walking arm in arm to her place.

After a maze of dark and ruined streets and a dangerous staircase, she sat on her bed, smoking one of Kells' cigarettes and kicking off her high heels. Her small room in one of the ruined tenements was criss-crossed with twine on which she hung her clothes. A pair of silk stockings was drying. There was a fireplace and a blackened saucepan. She had sleepless lines under her eyes, but after the singing there was a stillness about her, a serene beauty that rose above the brick dust. She had tied her long, strong dark hair back, which emphasised her prominent cheekbones and large brown, green-flecked eyes. He sat on the bed beside her, looking around the room, wondering what to say, wondering what she did before her city was destroyed, her husband or boyfriend killed, when she laughed and blew smoke into his face. She grabbed his head and twisted it towards her.

"I thought you said I should leave?" he said.

"You're not part of this place. 'Bad' here is beyond anything you can imagine. Bad is this city's business. Its reason for being."

"Sounds like Hollywood," he said, laughing. "They used to call me that and I'm here until they get rid of me. Or because they want to get rid of me."

He was trying to sound cool and in control but failing.

Did she want him to put money down on the bed? He did not think of her like that. All of his body wanted hers. But he also wanted to tell her about his father and Billy the Kid. He wanted to tell her about the sea and what it was like sitting astride a board off the kelp beds and the delight when you catch the wave. Stupid stuff . . . She leant forward, taking him in, examining all of his face, as if making a decision. Not quite sure herself. Then she was kissing him hard, her tongue inside his mouth, pressing against his and then breaking away to take off her top, and he helped her unzip her skirt at the back and pull down her panties and unclip her garter

74

belt from her other pair of stockings. She kissed his neck and as he took off his shirt, she kissed all the way down his chest and belly and had his trouser buttons open and was sucking his cock and pulling the hard length in and out of her mouth. He then eased her back and moved down to lick her labia surrounded by dark black curls and she shuddered with pleasure as he probed with his tongue, her hot wetness against his face, as she pulled his hair. She forced him back on the bed and mounted him and they made frantic, passionate love. She climaxed with a scream and as he came he felt the empty edge of consciousness and all but blacked out.

She sat up, facing away, as if she had made a mistake and half-smoked another of his cigarettes in silence.

But then she turned and reached for his prick, kissing him again and again. They had sex a second time on her grey, Red Cross blanket marked *US Aid Not For Sale*. It was the start, and he knew he should not be there, as did she.

Somehow, he did not believe her real name was Gretchen.

III

RACHEL SLEPT SO completely, by the time she got up and drew the curtains in her room she knew it was at least half-past ten. She felt a moment of panic because she thought she had to get to her nursing shift that had started at six. She then remembered where she was, in a country house deep in the American Zone, in the kibbutz. At last she was safe, even though she did not feel it totally yet, and then she thought of poor Hyman, Dr Kaplan. She went and lay back on the bed, a small day bed next to the two-metre-high windows that led onto the garden. She was naked, having no other clothes than those she had acquired at the hospital which did not include a night dress. She looked down at a scar on her hip. A scar from a wound the day she had been arrested. Like the rifle-butt scar on her cheekbone.

She was going to think of a different way that the facial wound had happened. A fall at the seaside on a family holiday. She was going to steal her wounds back. A shaft of sunshine cut the high room in two, which was so large and so high for one person, so different from the single, white-painted cell she had in the hospital. She had been put in the big room because Dr Kaplan was to have been given the next room and, whatever else they set her to do, she had been going to be nursing him. And now . . . She caught her breath when she thought how easily the attack and killings had been. No one knew if it was a general attack on Jews from the camps in the hospital. She blamed herself regarding Hyman. He never should have been out in the grounds alone. If only she had not gone to see the rabbi. If the attackers were only trying to kill Dr Kaplan, it showed how important he had been to the resistance.

Her room was full of all sorts of massive furniture and pictures in a neoclassical vein showing gods and goddesses in an ideal landscape, not unlike the grounds of the estate. Were they safe here? In one corner there was a piano and she went over to it and lifted the lid. It was no ordinary piano but a grand, a precious Zimmermann, and she pulled out the little stool and sat there, naked, looking at the ivories. She put her bare feet on the cold pedals.

She played a little of Chopin's *Nocturne, Op. 48, No 1 in C minor*. The piano was not her instrument, but she was competent.

It was the first time she had heard the music since before the camp. It was so beautiful and sad, and the piano was meticulously in tune. When she stopped, she heard the music of her cello. She reverentially closed the lid of the piano and got up, fearful.

Rachel had let the past in through a familiar door, the door of beauty. She had told the rabbi a little about the camps, but she could not tell him about the surgeon commandant. Manfred. Or about what happened on the last day. She shivered.

She had no way of contacting those in the resistance she worked for. They always contacted her.

She was going to put on her nurse's uniform, which was the only clothes she had, as they had left in a hurry, but there was a knock on the door. It was a gentle knock. She grabbed a sheet from the bed. "*Bitte*," she said.

Outside was one of the younger maids carrying a pile of clothes, jeans and work shirts, but also dresses.

"They were giving these out. There are no sizes." The girl giggled.

Rachel smiled. "Yes, please."

"Would you like to see the house?" said the girl, who put the clothes on the bed. "They will all be having lunch soon, but I can show you around before that, if you like. It is a labyrinth. Everything has been kept up because it was used in the end by Julius Streicher, who was one of the original Nazis, when it ceased to be a kibbutz, of course. He is in prison now and they're going to try him and execute him. Even the older German servants did not like him. They liked their old master, the man who came before him whose family originally owned the house. He was killed in a tank battle somewhere in the East early in the war. I am not sure . . . I'll let you get dressed and come back in ten minutes if you like?"

Rachel wandered around the house with the girl. The thick blue jeans and the baseball boots fitted well and the plaid work shirt hung loose around her. They were all brand new. When she had changed, she had also found a box of toiletries with lipsticks, even perfume, and more surprisingly, military washable male condoms in a plain yellow carton. The girl hurried along beside her. "Three of the women working here are French. We were caught here by the war and it was safer to stay. The only thing that has happened here in hundreds of years is that Frederich the Great visited the Graf of the time with Voltaire. That and the creation of the kibbutz by 'moderate' Nazis who wanted the Jews to be anywhere but Germany and thought they would all go to Israel. But, of course . . ." The girl did not finish the sentence.

After room upon room of unexpected, mainly Italian, art works, including what looked like a Botticelli, and a library full of books from every corner of the world and viewpoint, they came to a double-height dining room with a large fireplace. The walls were hung with tapestries and hunting prints. It was the only specifically Germanic room in the house, with its long dining table and heads of deer and boar on the walls. By the fireplace was a photo of a kind looking soldier standing next to Hermann Goering, who grinned like a happy, small-time gangster invited to the country, invited here: the same *Reichsmarschall* Goering who created the Gestapo and ordered the Final Solution. A man now on trial for his life. On a side wall was a group photograph of obviously Jewish faces, dated May 1937. Had they felt safe here?

"Do you want to see the maze?" said the girl. "There is a real labyrinth. There were wild parties here. Even in winter. They found a couple in the centre dead from the cold . . ."

Rachel had been in a little maze when she was eight in one of the water parks in Berlin where her uncle had been playing a concert. The hedges came up to her hips and it was a safe and pleasant puzzle. You could easily see your way out. She remembered that concert well. It was the first time she had seen people in brown shirts with swastika armbands. One had lifted her up and given her a small *kinder cone* full of sweets.

The maze at the back of the house was different. It was built from yew, which Rachel's father had always told her was poisonous. Suddenly, an older woman called to the maid who smiled and said. "I must go. Don't go in very far. You can get lost. *Allez* . . ."

Rachel went to the entrance of the maze, which was a hole cut into a bush three metres high. Inside it was dark and cold and there was a feeling of dread that was not in any of the rest of the house.

She had stepped into a wicked fairy tale. Where a bad person always had control.

An aunt from Hamburg had insisted on bringing Rachel strange books of German fairy tales when she was a child, where the outcome was always far from happy. The maze was like the forest in 'Hansel and Gretel', with its cannibal witch, and the air of unavoidable punishment, the same as in *Der Struwwelpeter*. One day Rachel had taken all those books and left them on a tram, and then regretted what she had done because the creatures in them might run riot in the tram and scare other children.

The yew walls of the maze were impenetrable and rose for two metres, even four metres in places. There was a strange haunting smell of damp and rot. Every now and again there was a circular space with a bench. Inside, it became darker and darker. The green of the yew turned to grey. White stones glowed around the little stone benches like skulls.

The low remembered note of her smashed cello sounded among Rachel's thoughts. She turned quickly, and walked back to the house, hoping to get news of Hyman.

IV

"HERE HE IS ... Dr Hyman Kaplan! He is back with us and alive. He is a hero and has survived." He heard the shout, as two American military orderlies took him from the back of a civilian ambulance. Another soldier folded out his wheelchair and he was put into the seat as he stared at the welcoming committee in front of a large country house.

"Hyman! Hyman! Hyman!" The chant went up from the young people.

Hyman, he was still not accustomed to or totally content with the name, even less so with Dr Kaplan. Then he saw Rachel, who ran up and gave him a little kiss on his good cheek and he experienced a warm wave of pleasure. His mouth curled into a painful smile and all thought of his name and the hurt in his body vanished.

Rachel was about to say something when there was another shout. "He looks like Clark Gable!"

His facial bandages were gone now and the driver of the military ambulance he came in said he was the double of Clark Gable in *Gone With The Wind*. Hyman approved of the work. He was the image of the American film star he was shown in magazines, which was probably an improvement. He had wanted to thank the plastic surgeon, but understood she had sadly died in the crossfire at the hospital.

Rachel took hold of his hand. "Isn't this a wonderful place! I have been swimming in the lake. As you see! There are water lilies and swans! You must come, I think most of the others are still down there. They'll want to see that you are all right after that unforgivable shooting. You were heroic in saving yourself from those madmen. You could have been killed by the fall. Your body is so full of shrapnel."

He nodded. But he put up his hand at what she was saying. Tipping over his own wheelchair to avoid a bullet was hardly a heroic act.

"I would like to go to the lake," he said, slowly and in the whispering voice that he now had. Outside the light was fading.

Rachel was such a romantic dear, he could forgive her anything. She was so beautiful standing there, still wet, with her red-gold blonde hair and pale white skin. Even in baggy American jeans and a T-shirt. She was like a famous painting in oils he had seen but could not remember.

"It's such a lovely house, isn't it, doctor?"

He wanted to say she was beautiful, but he only nodded his head.

She insisted on calling him doctor, or Herr Doktor, even though he had tried to make her call him Hyman, which was better than Kaplan, or Dr Kaplan, which sounded too ordered for his circumstances and pain. He felt like weeping that she and the other young people cared at all about him. They all felt so guilty about him being left alone the day of the shooting. They were all slightly in awe, because they thought the shooting was to assassinate him, personally, by the remaining Nazis, because of his fight for the Jewish resistance, about which he had his doubts. However strong an ideology, it does not survive total military defeat.

The attackers probably had come to rob the hospital for drugs, for penicillin or morphine. They shot at the first human being in their way, even though he had been swathed in bandages and in a wheelchair. Or, they may have thought he was someone else, someone important they had been sent to kill. He remembered well the jowled face of the dark-suited guardian angel who probably saved him, who in his estimation was not a good man, although he may have once yearned to be. Even if Dr Hyman Kaplan was high up in the Jewish resistance, why would they bother to kill him now that the war was over and he was more than half-dead? Perhaps they thought he knew something that he had now forgotten completely, which was equally absurd. It made his head go around and around. Rachel, mercifully, let the brake off his wheelchair and pushed him out into the cool of the evening and down past a herd of grazing spotted deer to a lake overhung with trees. Here all the young people were sitting around, some naked, like another painting that he could not remember the name of, or the artist, and when they turned and saw him there was a cheer. He raised his good hand stiffly to salute them and they cheered again. He had a peculiar feeling that such young people had cheered him in the past. He hardly deserved them after all they had been through.

"Doktor Hyman!"

Six of the boys ran over and they were now propelling him along the little jetty and, for a moment, he thought they were going to tip him into the lake.

That would put an end to his doubts!

"Careful with him!" shouted Rachel, running behind.

Hyman did not care if they did tip him in to feel the cool water on his itchy wounds and he completely trusted them to fish him out again. There was not an ounce of badness in any of them. Why did countries sacrifice their young people in wars? Now he had the gift of speech, however slight, he must ask Rachel more about what had happened and to explain what she said he had done in the wartime. There were so many things to understand and he still did not even understand what was really meant by the term 'Jew', although he knew he was meant to be one and it had a lot to do with the Yellow Star that was on the half-burned coat when he was found.

Hyman looked out on the darkening water and the flies playing over the surface. A fish jumped clean out and splashed back, causing ripples to fan out into the pond around the swimmers. What must that fish feel like, suddenly in another dimension, another world?

That was how he felt.

Rachel was rubbing his hand and gave him another small kiss on his cheek, the side that could feel, delicate, like one of those small strawberries one finds in the forest. One thing he did know was that he was among friends, and so very happy.

"*Ich liebe Sie alle!*" I love you all!

Later, exhausted, he was taken to his room, next to Rachel's, that was bright and airy and immense, with ceiling mouldings, French windows, gilt-framed mirrors, two-metre doors and a chandelier. It had ancestor paintings and a canopied bed and oriental silks on the walls and was next door to its own conservatory.

"There is another house near the fields where you can experiment with your silkworms and mulberry plants," said the rabbi. "The mulberries are important as they might trigger memory."

"I saw a tree on my way into the grounds," said Hyman. He had been reading all he could about silkworm production to try to prompt his memory. Everyone had been very gentle with him, especially the small rabbi, whose eyes were often full of an inexplicable joy.

"You will have a willing staff to help you, if you want. They all love you," said Rachel.

Hyman nodded. He liked the rabbi and asked, "Do the young people ever talk about the camps the nurses told me of?"

There was a silence, Rachel looked away and then the rabbi said, "They talk occasionally of the camps in low voices, embarrassed almost, and there is fear in their eyes. No one talks of the camps directly. They do not speak of revenge . . . They mention details: a rose by a fence, a cockerel that was eaten by a guard, swallows and swifts in the sky . . ."

Rachel sighed and said, "One boy, Paul, who was by the lake and will show you around tomorrow, had a horrific time but managed to escape from a train while being transferred to a death camp, by dropping through the truck floor when the train slowed down and chancing a roll between the wheels as it crept into a station . . ."

Hymen realised he had asked too much.

He then saw that the orderlies had put a cardboard box containing his few books on silkworms and the coat with the yellow star on the table. The soldiers were so kind and cheerful and had fed him their chocolate ration and given him more Hershey Bars for later. He must have always had a weakness for chocolate.

"Let's have some American chocolate," he said, taking control.

The next day Hyman was in his wheelchair in the conservatory that was next to his room and Rachel had gone out to the fields with her young friends, as she should. There had been more army lorries arriving, and more young people, former students mostly, young and strong. Hyman had no memory, still. They had told him who he was, the good doctor, but nothing they said touched him. He made no sense of his past because, perhaps blissfully, it was not there. Dr Kaplan had no family or friends that might inform him on personal matters. They had all perished in the camps, he had been told. His only immediate family had been his deceased mother and father.

There was absolutely nothing. And nobody.

Nor did anything else trigger recollection. The half-burned coat with the yellow star was in his luggage, but he did not remember who gave the garment to him.

There was a knock at the door. The door opened.

"My name is Paul. We are going to take you for a ride on a horse and cart, Papa . . ."

Hyman was not sure he wanted to be called Papa. But the sun was shining and the house looked very pretty with wisteria and other climbing vines. One of three other boys pushed him in his wheelchair out onto the gravel. Paul had fair hair and a scar on his cheek, like an old German duelling scar Hyman had read about. They were all so passionate and so fragile.

A butterfly landed on Hyman's leg when, with the help of the other boys, Paul pushed Hyman up a ramp of planks and onto the cart. The horse was enormous with a great bridle and the cart quite low and small. The horse was the only one that had not been taken off to the war. A piebald, it was so beloved by the general who originally owned the house, he ordered the servants to take it into the forest, or the maze, if the army were to come to requisition it for meat or transport.

"The general said the horse was too intelligent and kind for the army," said Paul. "His name is Bismark."

Hyman knew that was a name he should know.

"You are not the only one here to have trouble with memory," Paul said, without explanation, taking the reins and setting the cart off. "Bismark is the name of a very famous German chancellor, an ill-fated Nazi battleship and a type of herring."

The gentle Bismark took them for a slow and very stately tour around the grounds and three farms of the estate that had become the kibbutz. They stopped to pick up Rachel and several others. It was obvious Paul was very fond of Rachel. "This is wonderful," Hyman said to her.

Near the house, the hilly fields had been landscaped and the herds of deer, both spotted and red, were extensive.

At the bottom of the hill was a simple, two-storey house.

"It was the former home of a manager of the estate," said Rachel. "It has a walled garden and a small gatehouse. It will be the home of your silkworms. It has mulberry trees."

As they got nearer, Hyman blinked and sat up and craned his head at the old trees in the garden with those large, dark green and unmistakable leaves. Two names in Latin popped into his mind as the right-hand wheels of the cart went over a rock. *Morus alba* was

84

the white mulberry where *alba* can also mean dawn, or new dawn. *Bombyx mori* was the silkworm, which gorged on *Morus alba* and had brought such prosperity and then destruction to China. For a second, he could not breathe, every detail of the leaves and the silkworms and the surreally beautiful moths was so clear! Was this a memory? But a little dismayed, he realised he must have read it in a book, and this was not a sudden window to the past.

Rachel took his hand. "Isn't it lucky to have such fine mulberry trees here? The rabbi is so enthusiastic about your silkworms that he is getting the Americans to fly them in from places in England and Italy. We can set up a silk farm. Everyone needs silk." She then kissed him again on the cheek and that again left him breathless.

They entered the walled garden of the house by a large gate and the horse was brought to a stop. The rabbi came out of the house and joined them as they got Hyman down from the cart and he was pushed about the overgrown paths to the mulberry trees. They had such a mysterious darkness. There was a pungent scent to the leaves. Rachel's hand was on his shoulder all of the time. "We can harvest the leaves and use the house to raise the silkworms," she said. "We must obtain more books. But I am sure it will come back to you."

The rabbi smiled and said, "Yes, it will, and we would also be honoured if you could take your place on the committee. If you will be secretary of the committee, please."

"I might try," said Hyman.

"We are having a meeting in several days and I am sure you will be elected."

Rachel nodded and kissed him on the cheek. He gripped her hand hard with his good hand.

Already there was pinkish fruit on one of the mulberry trees and a boy, a close friend of Paul, began to speak of the poet Ovid and the Babylonian myth of Pyramus and Thisbe. "Thisbe killed herself under a mulberry tree with Pyramus' sword after he had been killed by a lion who he thought had killed Thisbe. The gods then turned the white mulberry fruit to blood red to mark their deaths. The blood cries from the trees for the innocents."

Hyman felt the mood change. He raised his good eye and glimpsed the fruit through the leaves. He shook his head and attempted a smile.

"That fairy tale is a stupid one. I do not respect gods that murder lovers. Especially with such young lions around me." The young people all laughed and then cheered him again.

V

"KEEP STILL, KELLS. I do not want to cut you. They will probably shoot me. We can be shot for having kitchen knives now."

The proclamation about knives was a recent one. Gretchen was shaving the back of his neck with her very sharp little vegetable knife.

"You should be careful with that blade. It could splice a hair."

She laughed. "Oh, I am. But if you are a colonel working for the peace, you cannot look like a tramp. You needed a haircut . . ."

"Perhaps they will tell me what I am doing now. The guys at McNair barracks."

She scraped away at his neck a little more. He was opening up to her. She was in her dressing gown.

"And how is the old guy? The one who got burned and then they shot in the hospital? Is he dead?"

"I don't know . . . They have not told me. I am still not sure who he is . . ."

She flashed a compact mirror in front of him.

"Is that to sir's liking?"

His expression was serious.

"You must have learned all sort of things . . ." he said.

His words caught her by surprise. "What do you mean?" she said, wiping the knife carefully on a cloth.

"In the war . . ."

"Oh, we did . . ." She stroked his face.

86

"I meant in the bombing . . ."

She laughed and kissed the top of his head. She was relieved. He trusted her.

"Ah, the bombing. We used to run up to the top of a high building and wave to your brave boys. They often used to wave back."

"It must have been Hell."

"You probably get used to Hell. Now are you going to give me a kiss for my fancy haircut?"

He stood up and kissed her. He then passed her a cigarette and lit one for himself.

It was his fifth visit. Gretchen stared for a long time at the glowing end of the cigarette she was smoking.

"Watch this, Kells."

She kicked off a shoe and put the cigarette between her toes as she sat down on the floor boards. She then raised the cigarette to her mouth, before taking it back in her hand and jumping up again.

"We learned to keep fit in the war, I am very bendy. I have folded myself into a dustbin to hide from a Russian patrol."

He looked astonished.

"I . . . I have to go now. Thanks for the haircut, Gretchen. Next time I will bring you a treat. I promise." She kissed him again as he went through the door and she heard him skipping down the stairs.

She liked Kells, oh, how she liked him, the softness of his flesh and the fact that he was so clean and polite. She liked his Mickey Mouse badge. A clean and innocent killer. She must not forget that, and what he wanted from her like all the rest. She must not forget that she was a woman alone in this ruined madhouse of a city, made and unmade by men. A piece of plaster fell from the ceiling onto the bed.

She laughed.

Kells had no idea about her war.

Gretchen remembered with a shudder the days of the air raids when she was starving and homeless and could not even trust the ground to stay still and straight. When she had slept on a thick rope in the cavernous ammunition store of the Zoo Flack Tower fort with hundreds of others. It had been an emergency air-raid shelter, a *Luftshutzraum* or LSR, and a wit had scrawled *Lernt schnell Russisch* by the initials, Learn Russian Quickly. There were seven thick ropes stretched across a large area under the guns, used to store live shells and where heavy brass shell cases, glowing hot, which were not ejected properly above, came crashing down, injuring and killing. You rested your shoulders against the rope and tried to sleep, twenty or thirty men and women a rope, as the guns thundered above and the Russian shells and bombs exploded and the place stank of bad tobacco, cordite, urine and snatched sex. Gretchen said the "Ave Maria" and prayed to the Virgin. She was constantly being woken with propositions and then one night, forced entry. A gunner had come and led her away with the promise of coffee. Coffee! It happened to all the younger women and the older ones and a few of the younger men.

The choice was a man inside you, or you outside.

Life (and rape and coffee) or death.

"Pray for us sinners, now and at the hour of our death . . ."

She remembered the total, screaming panic of waiting for the bomb to drop when she was caught outside, of falling over in the blackness on sharp tiles and bricks and glass and, on more than one night, the revolting touch of pieces of flesh still warm, while the shrapnel from the flack tower guns flew down like swallows and thudded and scythed into the ground. The old and the ugly and the wounded and those who did not obey were put outside. When the big bombs went off you could feel the detonation in your teeth, inside your skull. She had been blown off her feet like a leaf in the wind once and the sheer air-bending power of the explosions had caused her nose and her navel to bleed and her period to come. She cried out to her mother in Alanya in Turkey, "Mother, my nose and my navel are bleeding!"

Before that her periods had sometimes stopped, probably with the terror and panic of thinking she was never going to eat again, and it was her fault and the fruit of her sins. The war. The bombs. Her ravenous animal hunger. That her mother had left her father.

A tear ran down her cheek, and she brushed it away. The tear was not for herself, but for the enormity of that remembered darkness. She took a long drag of the American cigarette, a Lucky Strike, shifting her position on the moist mattress where love had now gone clammy and cold. Gretchen laughed.

She blew a smoke ring.

"Look on the bright side, girl," her father used to say.

Gretchen smiled her biggest stage smile. Her trapeze-artist smile. She had performed in the circus since the age of four. She would never have been able to afford such a good address as this, or have such educated company as Colonel Vardy before the war. And what food he brought her. She loved Kells, but knew she had to despise him.

There was the sound of shooting in the distance.

Yes, the hunger was the worst.

VI

"GET FUCKING DOWN!"
Two days after seeing Gretchen, Kells had walked out across a junction being directed by British Royal Military Police. The sun flashed briefly on the visors of their red military hats. Their brasses shone on their white webbing belts. In contrast to the drab brown of the Russians, they looked like toy soldiers. At first, Kells thought they were waving at someone else.

"Get fucking down!" one of the policemen shouted again, in English. "Get down, sir!"

Kells only just had time to avoid a car that then swerved to a halt in front of him. It was an old blue Russian Gaz saloon. There were many in the city. A man inside had a pistol pointed at him. The barrel was a long one. There was a smile on the man's face. He had not shaved.

"Stop . . . Halt!" another policeman shouted and drew his revolver. The saloon accelerated down the Ku'damm and turned off.

Kells showed his American Army ID when the policeman came over to him.

"Are you all right, sir?" he asked. "Begging your pardon, sir, but it looks like someone's got it in for you. Big time. Better go careful, like."

Kells walked quickly for two blocks to hide his trembling. Everyone, he thought, was looking at him. He steadied himself against a crumbling wall of old sandstone and was nearly sick.

He stopped at a wide road and looked carefully around him, even though there were no cars in sight. He had not thought to reach in his pocket for the gun Joe had given him. At his feet was a beggar on a board that had the little metal wheels of the kind you put underneath furniture. Kells noticed the board had once been an intricately carved wall plaque. There were two words, *Alter Kämpfer*, old fighter, one of the Nazi party originals, and honorary term for often the most extreme. There were now forbidden swastikas at both ends of the board. The man, who had lost his legs, extended his hand for a coin towards Kells. The look in the man's pale blue eyes was one of complete hatred. As Kells started to reach for a dollar bill, the old veteran rolled his prized board away along the broken paving stones of the sidewalk.

Perhaps the man in the car was a German who wanted to scare Kells because he was an American invader, nothing more.

Kells crossed the road and hurried along the cracked pavements in front of missing or broken houses. He looked over his shoulder frequently, his hand on the cold pistol in his overcoat pocket.

When Kells got home he went to his study and had a drink of whisky. He heard laughter from the garden. He looked outside to see Joe and the priest playing chess.

"My Lord! How did you do that again, Joe? I do not seem to be able to win."

Kells poured two more neat Scotches, put them on a tray and went out into the garden. Joe turned around and immediately knew something was wrong. He stood up. The priest looked worried.

Kells sat down on one of the metal garden chairs as two planes flew over, very low, making the window panes rattle. Joe put a hand on Kells' shoulder, but only for a moment.

"You okay, boss. You gone all white."

Kells tried a laugh. "Burning the candle at both ends, Joe . . . I need a drink." He didn't want to tell them what had happened. Then he said, "Why don't you two guys move in here? There's plenty of room. It's more comfortable than the other place."

That was all he needed to say. The next day they took up residence.

Kells tried to see Gretchen a week later, even though, and partly because of knowing his movements, she might have been part of the attempt on his life. Was she a plant and he a choice target for her? Or maybe someone had got to her.

But he didn't want to think that and most of him didn't care.

He went back over to where she lived, checking all the time if anyone was following him, but it was so hard to know in those ruins of streets. She had certainly got to him. He wanted her arms around him again. There was such a warmth about her, however faked.

The trouble was he could not find Gretchen's building. The map had changed again. Two whole streets had been reduced to rubble by the sappers. She had disappeared and, around every mound of bricks and plaster, memory and history had been erased. A dog barked and barked and barked on top of a thick wall, turning through every degree of the compass. Kells imagined the unshaven face of the man in the car with the gun, and that smile before the saloon drove away quickly down the Ku'damm.

He had also called Rachel from a number the surgeon had given him. There had been no answer at the kibbutz.

A girl he had not even kissed.

VII

"SHALOM," SAID THE rabbi on the main steps of the house as Rachel and the rest of the kibbutz assembled on the grass in front.

A message had been sent around that the rabbi was going to give a talk and then they were going to have another picnic. Paul pushed Dr Kaplan's wheelchair to a suitable point near the front of the crowd. A small table was put in front of the rabbi by the old butler. The rabbi coughed and said again, "*Shalom!*"

He then continued in German. "That is a greeting on meeting or parting. It means 'peace' in modern Hebrew, as in peace be with you. I speak in German because that is our common language, although some of you may speak Yiddish. I have spent my last years here in Berlin. Peace! That is what I want, that is what we all want after the dreadful times we have lived through. We all know what we have suffered so I will not go over any of that. That is past. What I see is sunshine on so many young faces now you have all settled in. What I feel from being with you is happiness. That is the recipe for driving away the darkness. The monster is dead. The monster is dead and the shadows that were so long cannot touch us anymore!"

Everyone got up and clapped and cheered and the small fat rabbi held up his arms in a suit that was too small for him.

"My name is Isser Leib and I am from a small village in Poland, but that does not matter. You can call me Izzi or whatever you want. I do not care. You do not need my blessings. You are my blessing. It does not matter much that I am a rabbi. Not that much. I have never been a very good rabbi. I drink too much rum. It does not matter even that I am a Jew. I am not a very good Jew, either, always doing what I shouldn't on the Sabbath, drinking rum."

There was laughter.

"We hope to take this kibbutz to what we may again one day call Israel, in British Palestine. I do not need to tell you that despite the British Balfour Declaration for a Jewish homeland to be formed in 1917, the path has been thorny. The League of Nations at the San Remo conference in 1920 granted the British a mandate in Palestine and it has been a British protectorate ever since. A sleepy colony, growing big oranges for the London market. The British only understand the world in colonial terms and their era has passed. The British have done nothing about Jewish plans to live in Palestine after the Holocaust and now they are fighting the Unified Resistance Movement, made up of the *Haganah*, the *Lehi* and the *Irgun*. Our kibbutz is peaceful, but I do not need to tell you the importance for defence against those who try to destroy us."

The rabbi was silent.

"There are non-Jewish people here, and that does not matter. What matters to me is that we are all free. We are free to organise this kibbutz, this seed of a community, whose prime aim is not defence, or even return to Israel. My Israel is a spiritual place that gives me strength. We have a greater task than mere return, my little oysters. Our task is quite simply *tikkun olam*, to repair the world. We have to establish a community that will not only give succour to our people, but that will mend the world. We must mend the world. We must tie it together again."

There was cheering.

"Whatever you have presumed, I'm not a Zionist and this is not a religious community, though you can follow your own religion if you like. I believe that when God destroyed the temple, he meant Jews not to have land until the temple is restored, and no one should rebel against God . . . That there should be no physical state of Israel although the kibbutz is possible . . . That is only what I think, though . . . This kibbutz is always open to non-Jews who want to break their backs in our fields." There was laughter again. "To mend the world we will start in very small ways. While there will be people in charge of groups, who are responsible for everyone in those groups, they are not there to give orders. In this new spiritual Jerusalem, for it is that, men and women will be equal. A woman will refer to her husband or her partner as *ishi*, my man, if we are speaking Hebrew, not *ba'ali*, my master. We have had enough of all those little men who call themselves masters and wanted to invent a master race. You are the future, my children. You are the seeds from which a million flowers will bloom. If you go to the physical Israel you will make the desert bloom with the smiles that are on your faces now. You are the future and that is our task. We must create Jerusalem in our hearts. We must create a welcoming, peaceful Israel. For the whole world, not just for us. Not just for the Jews."

The crowd then rushed up to the rabbi who for a moment looked scared. One of the older German maids went inside and slammed the door. The boys grabbed hold of the rabbi and carried him round and round the lawn, eventually putting him down. Smiling and blushing, he made his way back to the steps. It was obvious to Rachel that the rabbi was not as old as she had thought. He made a great mess of trying to tuck his blue shirt into his trousers.

"Let me now read you the lists of working groups . . . Hyman will be our kibbutz secretary . . ." He then read the list of those in charge of them . . . Rachel Weinberg . . . She dropped her notepad when the rabbi read out that she was in charge of Group Three: twenty workers and had responsibility for the silkworm production and three of the large fields beyond where sugar beet, a strategic crop, was to be grown. Rachel looked across at Hyman, who was smiling at her and raised his right hand slightly. She had expected Dr Kaplan to be in charge of the silkworms. She sighed. Perhaps this way he would be able to devote his entire energies, other than being the kibbutz secretary, the formal head of the kibbutz, to breeding the moth caterpillars. The rabbi then opened the door of the house and the butler and the man servant looked out as if they had expected a riot. Everyone laughed.

Next picnic baskets were brought up from the kitchen. "The future must eat," said the rabbi, raising his arms and inviting people to help themselves to the food. He walked off towards Hyman and Rachel. Paul and Anna sat nearby.

"I loved your beautiful speech," said Anna.

The rabbi smiled. "Thank you. But please excuse me. I want to take Dr Kaplan to the summer house near the lake. We have things to talk about. Serious things. It is better if we are alone." With that the rabbi pushed the wheelchair down to the lake. Everyone watched as they headed off into the distance.

"Do you believe what the rabbi was saying? Do you believe people like us are capable of those things? That we can mend the world?" asked Anna.

Paul said, "I cannot even mend my window in the house. It will not close. There are owls outside, and I fear that one might get in."

"What do owls do?" said Anna, worried.

"They are very clever and can see the tricks of someone like Paul, here," said Rachel and the people around them laughed. "He wants us to do it for him."

"Listen to the big . . ." and then Paul stopped himself. He flushed and dropped the piece of bread and cheese he was about to eat. He went quickly down to the lake. Anna was going to go after him.

"Was it something I said?"

"No," said Rachel. "Leave him. He'll come back. Leave him."

It was not a Saturday, if they were going to observe religious matters, but there was no work for the rest of the day. They all sat there, a little stunned at what the rabbi, a man they all liked, had said. It seemed too ridiculously simple, Rachel thought. The day was hot and a group of girls started dancing.

Hyman had not come back by the time Rachel had eaten, but neither had Paul.

"I have lost seven people. I have lost my whole family," said a girl called Itka, out of the blue.

"We are your family now," said another. A boy danced on his own in the middle of a circle of dancers. The dance was made up from nowhere. Hands were clapping.

"This is insane!" shouted one of the girls, her face so happy.

Laughter swept through the picnic and Rachel found herself in the circle, whirling round and round and round.

Laughing now and dizzy, she left the dance as more joined and walked towards the lake. She felt there was no past. No sad note of her cello . . .

She found Paul sitting on the wooden jetty. He had taken his new baseball boots off and was cooling his feet in the water. In the sunlight they were glowing white beneath the surface.

"What was it? I'm sorry if I offended you. But it was not my words about the window. What was it?"

He shrugged. He was more handsome angry. He softened.

"It was the shadow. The shadow of the dark angel."

"There are no dark angels. There is only me and you by this beautiful lake."

He breathed in the air slowly and looked out at the water, shaking his head.

"There were many shadows in the camps. Many dark angels. There was the cold and the dark and the pain and the anticipation of the next blow. What is going to happen? The hunger. What is going to happen to me? More hunger. How are they going to kill me? Everyone is happy here, but that dark angel is still there. Getting in my broken window. I have many broken windows."

"We have left that behind."

"Have we?"

"I believe what the rabbi said."

He stared into the distance.

"We have survived. We have survived, but not because we are good. We have survived because we are the strongest. I did things that I regret."

"We all did. I did too." She thought of the last days. The last days before she fled from the camp. She thought of the resistance operation of which she had been a part. Had she made that up as well, like a lot more? Rachel did not want to think of what she had done anymore.

Paul kicked at the water. Out in the lake a big fish jumped.

"I nearly called you a *kapo*."

"I know."

The ugly term for a Jewish collaborator overseer in the camps intruded on the bright day.

They were silent after that, watching the dragonflies skim over the water. Rachel put her hand on Paul's shoulder, and eventually he spoke.

"I did not regard myself as a Jew. In fact, at university I had nothing to do with Jews. It wasn't a political thing. It just didn't happen. I didn't realise I had a Jewish ancestry. My grandmother was Jewish and we were denounced. The next but last camp I was in was Buchenwald. Even there I did not think of myself as a Jew. Even when they sent me to another camp to be killed. Can you imagine that? Can you imagine the self-delusion? The scapegoat that denies he's a goat. In my head I was still doing philosophy at the University of Heidelberg and wondering about a thesis I was doing on *Die Metaphysik der Sitten*, *The Metaphysics of Morals* by Emmanuel Kant, can you imagine? I was put in . . ."

Rachel placed a finger on his lips and then kissed them. His light hair contrasted with his dark eyebrows and eyelashes. He looked as German as she did.

"We are in a new place. We are in Aviv. This is springtime."

He kissed her back.

She pulled him to his feet.

"Come on, *ishi*. Let's go find the future."

He smiled and they skirted the bulrushes of the lake and went into a thick wood of oak and beech trees where they made love.

VIII

A STORY THAT Kells knew well was being told again. The story of the burning man, by a drunken Russian interpreter.

"And you know what?" said the interpreter in English. "He had an enormous hard on."

A Russian colonel with an aristocratic demeanour and carefully pressed uniform, who sat across from Kells, stopped laughing and struck the table in front of him with a bottle and became sombre. He stood and spoke passionately in English. "That man must have a destiny. A holy purpose!"

Kells nodded in agreement. He was on the edge of being drunk too.

The Russian sat down again and started to tell the story in Russian to the person next to him, a British major, who was cackling uproariously at everything anyone said, in any language, but had a great sadness in his blue eyes. The Russian became irritated.

Kells was at a formal dinner with flown-in champagne and lobster, and Russian folk-dancing that was being held in the Schloss Tegel, a chilly nineteenth-century building constructed around four square-sided towers that looked like an up-market Massachusetts mental institution, in the sector of the city by the airport controlled by the French. The dinner was meant to be an informal prelude to more *Kommandantura* administration talks as part of Operation Talisman, about Berlin being split into formal zones. The Russians so trusted the intention of the meeting they had come with their side arms. Kells did not care. He was thinking of the delicate Rachel. His calls had not been returned. For all he knew she was on her way to Palestine, to her Israel. He had not been officially invited to the dinner at the massive walnut tables, but it had been fixed for him by his friend in the State Department. There were tapestries on the walls and a Frenchman was speaking on the need for peace and co-operation and understanding between the allies in a very broad Breton-accent, so the Frenchman to Kells' left had informed him, which even his colleagues probably did not understand.

Kells had gone to the dinner for the sole purpose of meeting the affable general he had met at McNair barracks who hated Kandinsky and who Kells had since learned was the head of American military intelligence. He wanted to ask again what he was meant to be doing and if there were any files the general knew of on an Operation Lucy. Since he had seen the man with the gun in the Russian car, he felt he had to know.

A young man from the general's office shook a minatory finger at Kells, guessing what he was about.

Kells was fascinated with the general, who at the top table was either asleep, comatose drunk or, dead. Occasionally, the elderly man slobbered and his jowls quivered, and when the Frenchman giving the speech paused for effect, the general snored, quietly.

The waiter brought Kells another large balloon glass of French cognac and a cigar and he sat back and blew the grey-blue smoke at the intricate wooden ceiling. Kells did not catch what the Frenchman said next, as it was in halting Russian, but the Russian colonel, who had liked the story of the burning man, leapt onto the table and ran along it to the top table with surprising agility, and kicked the Frenchman in the face.

The formal dinner then quickly degenerated into a Wild West bar fight.

Kells decided it was time to leave, none the wiser about his mission. He got to the cloakroom to find his trench coat had disappeared and, despite his protests, the hat-check girl selected a cashmere overcoat with an astrakhan collar. He tipped her and she giggled, pleased with the five dollar note. He was still clutching his brandy and puffing on his cigar. He placed the cigar in an ashtray and the brandy on a table while he put on the heavy coat, which two men could hide in, over his uniform.

PEACE IS OUR PROFESSION, read a sign in the hall.

Eight men, all in uniform ran past him, fighting, and there were bloody footsteps on the marble floor.

Kells heard a man behind him speaking English. He turned and asked, "What was it that offended the Russian?"

The man was short, with a winning smile. His brilliantined, light, slightly curly brown hair was neatly parted and his accent almost ridiculously British upper class.

"I don't quite know what the froggie meant to say. He seemed to be having great difficulty speaking his own language. Or someone has been having a game with him. What it came over as was. '*Vse rossiyane nasil'niki i pridurki.*'"

"And that means?" asked Kells.

The man's eyebrows went up. "I thought all you college boys in Berlin spoke Russian? It means, all Russians are rapists and cunts or assholes, which you saw did not go down very well, as it is the truth. The very worst thing you can do with Ivan is tell him the truth. It makes him go completely berserk. The consequence of living on a windswept steppe, eating dog shit and believing it is the best of possible worlds, while also under the delusion this is an idealistic war and not just another Roman exercise in colonialism for land and gold and slaves. I do hope he has not killed the poor frog. The food tonight was most agreeable. By the way, the French have set up a telephone room along this corridor if you want to make a call for a car or a girl or something. Might be safer than walking. Bye now. Remember, be very careful with the truth."

The man then vanished into the heaving, fighting crowd.

In a storeroom off the telephone room, Kells heard the sounds of love-making.

The mention of rape had penetrated Kells' fug of cognac. He doubted the Russians were worse than any other lousy army. In Belgium he had come upon a scene where a grandfather was pleading with four American paratroopers to pause while raping his daughter, so she could feed her baby and stop the child crying. She had eventually used the politely formal words "*Excusez moi s'il vous plait*" as she detached herself from her rapist and took the child in her arms, blood on her thighs. The paratroopers had then turned and seen Kells and saluted, as one man pulled up his trousers. Kells had not bothered his general or ordered a court martial, but had sent the four of them, young, white, well-educated boys, up the line, and they thought they had got off lightly. He had heard a whoop outside his temporary office in a village café. A new innocence shone from their neatly parted hair. Innocent as the picture of St Lucy 'Beatrice' has sent him. They started to play scissors-stone-paper for who would go and get their milk ration. They were all killed the next day, blown to pieces in a mortar strike.

The unthinking wheels of the great mechanism he was part of had turned. There was no place for the individual in the modern corporate structure.

Kells stubbed out his cigar in a helmet inexplicably left by the phones and lit a cigarette. First, he dialled the international operator and put in a call to his home that he should have made earlier. He got through to his mother. He could smell her floral perfume.

"Whenever you call, I always think you're going to be dead."

"The war is over here, mother."

"Then why aren't you home and at my kitchen table?"

His mother paused.

"They've taken your father away. He had ripped off all his clothes and was shouting nasty words at the coloured women who clean. Two women who know me from St Mary's. He was shouting 'I can make you famous', like Billy the Kid. He then ran after them. He thinks he is Billy the Kid. Our lawyer rang me saying that he tried to change his Will. He wanted to leave all his money to Pat Garret, who I think killed Billy the Kid, and the water company. I can almost understand the Pat Garret bit, because he's had enough of life and me, but not the water company. Why would anyone want to leave their money to the water company? He is in a home now near Laurel Canyon and they've given him a cowboy hat, only he keeps pestering them for a gun. I am sorry to sound upset, but it is because I am. I am. I really am. I wanted a quiet time after worrying about you in the war and being so proud of you. What have I got to look forward to now? Are you bathing? Do you have provision for baths over there? Is there running water? Are you washing . . . down there? I have seen the newsreels and Berlin looks completely destroyed, which is what they deserve. I will give you the number of the home your father is in, it's a private asylum really. It's the strain of running that damned airplane factory. God's children are not meant to work in those termite heaps . . . He was so looking forward to you coming home for good. Your fiancée Betty came round today and we talked curtains and soft décor for your future house. She wants to talk to you about them. She has your Silver Star in case your father ran off with it pretending to be a sheriff. She is so proud. I'll give you the number of the home. He won't recognise you. Your voice . . . I don't know what you are doing over there in that rubble pile. You cannot expect to do good to those cruel, ungrateful Nazis. I refuse to pray for them. It would be better to drop a heavy paving stone on them all. Come home. Your father's mind has gone. He'll only talk to you if you say you are a member of the Hole in the Wall Gang."

Kells told his mother he loved her and put the phone down. A flush-faced American officer and a Russian woman soldier came giggling out of the storeroom and laughed more when they saw Kells.

Back in the entrance hall of the castle there was more pushing and shoving. Another punch was thrown. The Kandinsky-hating general, who had passed out, was being carried by on a stretcher.

Kells walked into the summer night, more than a little drunk. With all his mother had said he had forgotten to call Joe, who had newly acquired a former German staff car, down the backseat of which was a blue and gold *Mutterehrenkreuz*, the Nazi order for patriotic motherhood. Kells didn't want to go home, probably the result of talking to his mother. He asked a cab to take him to the Ku'damm, near the Café Kranzler.

"If you try and rob me, I will shoot you in the eyes," Kells tried to say in German, and the driver drove quickly and did not look round.

"I am a member of the Hole in the Wall gang . . ."

When he had paid off the cab, Kells spent half an hour walking from the boarded-up department store and the Café Kranzler, away from the broken-spired church and the divided circle sign of the Mercedes building, for about a mile to a check-point and back again. He knew he should not do what he was going to do next. If anything, it was his mother's worried, relentless voice that drove him to it.

He plunged into the comparative darkness of one of the side streets, blinked, blundered on, and saw everything once more in welcome degrees of black.

It was crazy to do this drunk and in uniform at night if a Russian patrol caught him. The Russians were still in charge, although the other allies, like himself, were seeping in, the diplomats, bankers and spies.

Kells lost his way several times and climbed to the top of one of the ash piles. On one side he saw a small square he recognised. On his way down he slipped and slid the rest of the way on a chest of drawers. At his feet was a headless teddy bear. He stood up and brushed the dust from his new cashmere coat. He hurried on. He was going to where he thought Gretchen lived. To try and find her again. But they had re-arranged the buildings even more.

He found the square. The buildings were now only intact on one side, and a lone tree leaned almost to the point of falling into a bonfire. He remembered the tree. A tall man was pulling a cart along with a piece of string. A yellow balloon was tied on the back. The firelight flickered on the cart's load of worthless objects scavenged from the bombed houses. There were empty bird cages, parasols, and a pile of pot steins. At the back was a large bottle that was full of glass eyes, next to a broken doll and part of a carousel horse. The man pulling the cart had sallow skin and yellow eyes, and when he smiled his teeth were broken or missing. "Ja, ja, ja," he said, as if he had found gold. A man across the road struck a match and lit an oil lantern. Kells thought he recognised the doorway he wanted. He walked quickly past a group of men who shouted after him and he felt for the pistol in his uniform jacket pocket.

"No Yank! Your girl is not in there! They have all moved to

the house at the end! The rats have better manners!" shouted one of the men in English.

Once inside the correct building, he ran up the stairs and after knocking on several doors, all to rooms occupied by young women, mostly with the doors open to keep each other safe and shout alarm. "*Gretchen, dein Yankee!*" one of the girls called up to her and she was in the doorway as he pushed past her and sat on the only stool. A three-legged stool, like one used for milking. Her second pair of silk stockings was drying in the fireplace. There was a two-tone suitcase by the window. She looked surprised.

"Did you not expect me to come and see you again?" He spoke in English. He said the words quickly. Breathless.

She did not answer at first. She was wearing a thin silk dressing gown that was torn. Then she said, "They have been blowing up streets. Everything changes. I was worried. How did you find me? And at night. That was foolish."

He shrugged.

"Sheer good Irish luck."

He must have betrayed his suspicion of her in the way he said "luck". You should never talk about luck. She blew out smoke from her cigarette.

"You think I am bad luck? What is it that I have done?"

He lit a cigarette. "The last time I came here a man in a car pointed a gun at me on my way home."

Instantly, Gretchen was on a knife-edge of anger.

"You think I'd do that to you? You think I am something to do with a stupid man in a stupid car? You are from a foreign army in a cut-off city. Only a fool would think he had no enemies. And if you suspect me, why do you come back to me again? Why do you come here in the night? To hurt me? I thought you trusted me, at least?"

She stared at him, sad-eyed now, and lay down on the bed. She put the cigarette out on a saucer.

They stayed like that, looking at each other, for five whole minutes. He could see the dial on his wristwatch as he sat awkwardly on the stool in his overcoat with the astrakhan collar. She was more than lovely in the light of the smoky fire, which was heating a pan of water. There were sounds of laughter in the house and a wind-up gramophone playing opera. There was a scream from the street and in the distance a two-note German police siren.

Then he got onto the bed with her, and she was taking off his clothes. Faster and faster. He made love to her again and again, until the grey light and chill of morning, and they did not exchange a word. All she said was *scheiße*, as she burned her hands taking the blackened pan off the fire.

There were no curtains on the window and, as the pink light grew, she kissed him once on the forehead and swung her legs off the bed. He looked at her full breasts and her tangle of pubic hair and reached for her.

"*Bock*," she said, but smiled, and they began again. She then quickly dressed. She put on heavy shoes to negotiate the rubble.

"I will go and find coffee. I will go and get real coffee, you see." She spoke in English.

"You won't get the bad guys?"

She laughed at him. "So who bombed and blew up all these fucking houses and the babies and children in them? The good guys?"

She went to the door and opened it and half went through. She then popped her head back. Her hair was up in a ponytail again. In the dawn she looked younger, as she might have before the war, and the gap showed between her front teeth. Her expression as she left was playful, that of a long-time girlfriend. He heard the sound of her shoes on the bare wooden stairs and there was the smell of cabbage cooking from far below. The nineteenth-century house must have been elegant once.

Kells felt strangely calm with the sunlight streaming in through the window. He pulled the overcoat with the fur collar up around him. He took his Mickey Mouse Club badge from his uniform and pinned it on the overcoat.

Outside in the street he heard the sound of a vehicle. A loudspeaker crackled into life. A man's voice said in German, "Please leave these buildings. They are due to be demolished. It is unsafe to stay here."

Windows went up and there were jeers. "Do you expect me to go to my suite in the Kempinski Hotel? Go and fuck yourself with thistles."

There was laughter, even though the watchers knew that the soldiers followed the vans and one could be shot for disobeying an order of the new *Kommandatura*. There were rumours that the entire city was to be raised to the ground as a punishment, like ancient Carthage.

Kells lit a cigarette.

Gretchen came back with two small cups of coffee and smiled and sat on the bed and they sipped the strong, sweet liquid.

"There is a man in the basement who will not come out. All he has is several sacks of coffee beans and some sugar, a filter pot and an old grinder. He makes coffee for everyone in the house. He does not ask any money. I do not think he eats. I fear for him when the coffee runs out. He thinks things are all right when he is making coffee."

Kells nodded and more sunshine came in through the window.

He dipped into the inside pocket of the coat and brought out a small hip flask filled with brandy the owner of the coat had left there. She shook her head and he put it on the bedside table. He offered her one of his cigarettes and she took it and lit it from his.

"I do not drink in the morning."

Kells smiled.

"That is most commendable. I have faith in the new Germany."

She raised an eyebrow.

"I am not good at drinking."

"Nor am I. Nor is anyone. You should have seen the dinner I went to last night."

She nodded.

"Where do you live in America?"

America? His America? He thought of sitting on his surfboard with the brown heads of the kelp dancing up through the ocean around him, his legs in the water, ready to catch the wave, his whole body and entire existence directed to that thrilling and totally meaningless task, save that it made him and others happy. He would like to take Gretchen to that beach and teach her to surf, take her to restaurants and parties, and do the normal things people do when they date.

"I live in California."

'With the film stars?"

He smiled. "Of course. They all live next door. Errol Flynn lives at the bottom of my father's garden."

Her eyes widened and then she reached out and tickled him under the ribs.

"Oh, you are joking with me."

He shook his head and kissed her and took another drag on his cigarette.

"I have a cousin in the movie business. He was a writer and now he is something else and wants to be a director. He started out as an actor. He met lots of the stars. He has Mae West's phone number. He met Ingrid Bergman for a whole minute."

Gretchen seemed delighted with the news.

"I am sure she was completely in love with him for all sixty seconds. You like my coffee?"

"I love your coffee."

"Thank you."

"You speak very good English. It is almost without an accent."

She nodded.

"I wanted to go to the university."

"To do English?"

"Perhaps. There are many books in English that I like. I like *Wuthering Heights* by Emily Brontë. I am not sure though what Wuthering means. Is Heathcliff a negro?"

Kells nearly dropped his coffee. He laughed and they both laughed although there was no reason it should be funny. She continued: "I very much like the Shakespeare too. And Herman Melville. The story of the Great White Whale. How Captain Ahab makes a devil's bargain. He sacrifices his soul, his ship, and his men to kill the whale. Germany knows the type . . . And, of course, Sherlock Holmes, which is very good for English sentences no one talks. I like Dr Watson. I do not believe anyone in the world is like Dr Watson. He is so comforting. He is like sweet tea with milk. Even if he is not real, I like him. Perhaps you are a Dr Watson?"

She was telling him the whole earnest truth. At least about Dr Watson.

"What did you do? What was your work?"

She sighed.

"I worked as a typist and then a secretary. Tap-tap-tap-Ping! I used my English. I worked as a secretary in the Foreign Ministry." She looked away. She had said too much.

IX

"THAT IS VERY good, Hyman," said the rabbi, coming up from behind. "Very good indeed, you have talent . . ."

Hyman was painting a watercolour, sitting at an easel on the stone path under the largest of the mulberry trees in the walled garden of the house he was converting into a silkworm farm.

"I am not so good," said Hyman, who was becoming more used to the name that he still did not believe in. For a detail he held a small, watercolour paintbrush between his teeth, guided by his good hand, and had been painting the rolling fields over the wall up to the thick oak and pine forest on the hills. The boy Paul, who seemed to be increasingly fond of Rachel, had found a watercolour set in the attic of the main house and sheets of paper and brushes. Paul had also brought him the paints so Hyman did not take up so much of Rachel's time.

"You seem very professional to me, but what do I know? I don't think anything in our researches indicates Dr Kaplan is an artist."

Hyman nodded. He took the brush from his mouth.

"It speaks to memory. What surprises me is that I have this knowledge of painting with watercolours. I instinctively wet the paper thoroughly and filled in the light blue of the sky first before drawing in the darker colours and going for effects with a little squee-gee sponge. The problem is the mobility in my right hand, which is fine for broad movements, but cannot be relied on for subtlety. So I had to put the brush in my mouth and look like an idiot."

After practice, this technique allowed him to get the precision needed for the little figures in the fields beyond the gate. He kept looking for Rachel, but could not spot her. It was so wonderful that she had a position of real leadership. A group of young people passed the gate to the garden on the way to the fields.

"Hello, Papa! Hello rabbi! *Shalom!*"

"I love to hear them sing on their way to work," said Hyman. "They are going to help me set up the mesh cages for the silkworms when they arrive."

"Ah, yes," said the rabbi. "The Americans are kindly getting the silkworms and the equipment you need from the south of France. They will fly it into an airstrip nearby. Everyone is very happy having you as secretary, Hyman. You give them someone to look up to. A decorated hero of their people. Especially the way you went out on the cart with a few of them and disarmed the local who was threatening those in the fields with a shotgun."

Hyman laughed but it hurt.

"Oh, that was nothing. They exaggerate . . . They talk all the time about Palestine. They may meet men with guns there who think these young men and women have no right to the land."

"Ah yes, the new Israel . . ."

"It is fantastic about the silkworms. I shall have to read up on them even more."

"I think you will find that second nature."

The rabbi peered at the front of the easel again. Hyman coloured in a blue figure in the distance, using only his hand.

"I try to remember if I was ever connected with any sort of

Zionist movement, but my memory does not answer. A huge door to my library is closed. I imagined it as one of those metal-studded temple doors under a great arch. To me Zionism is still as alien as silkworms. It is amazing how much of our identity is memory."

That was why it fascinated him that he painted watercolours.

"There is so much to fill in," said the rabbi. "So much I wish we could forget . . . There was the Great War, as it is called, from 1914 to 1918 when we had a Kaiser. The German economy never recovered from the defeat and the ordinary people never were able to recover their pride as human beings. Instead, they became bewitched by a devil of a man, a man who could charm the birds from the trees, a man who preached a thunderous message of hope based on hatred of minorities, in particular the Jews . . ."

Hyman listened as he painted a tree. The rabbi continued.

"At first, we Jews were excluded. Made to wear the yellow star. Like the one on your jacket. Then there were the camps. Then extermination with insecticide on an industrial scale as if we were cockroaches. A genocide. The attempted removal of our entire race and culture."

Hyman stopped painting. "I am a Jew . . . You are a Jew. You were in a camp and escaped . . ." He reached out and touched the rabbi's hand. The rabbi had become very upset and tears ran down his plump cheeks. "All the young people here at Aviv have this horror in common. As do you, Hyman. As I do."

X

THE TELEPHONE ON Kells' desk rang and made him jump. "Surf's up, Colonel Vardy!" said his friend who worked for the State Department. "Be ready tonight at nine. I'll come round. We are going to another *Schloss*. No fighting this time. I missed a treat. There's a different kind of party."

His friend Sam's voice was full of such adolescent, fraternity-boy earnestness Kells could not say no. The *Schloss* was in the Grunwald and according to his friend, who was not always reliable, was near a lake called the Krumme Lanke.

Kells felt a little guilty. He had visited Gretchen every day for a week. He tried to tell himself she had useful information, but knew that was phoney. He begged her to let him get her other accommodation in a better part of town, a nice room, a nice flat, but when he did she changed the subject or just laughed. He took her tinned food from a store cupboard he found at the house. He took her champagne and even a tin of caviar among the rations of corned beef. The cashmere overcoat had large inside pockets that seemed tailor-made for the lothario or black marketeer. Every time he visited her now he also left her dollars and hoped she was beginning to trust him.

When Kells got out of his friend's car he stared and stared at the *Schloss*. A very modern Bauhaus-inspired, brilliant white, two-story house with balconies, had been tacked onto a grey stone blockhouse of a castle, that was more frightening than romantic. Sam broke the silence.

"Yes, it's a funny sort of house, really. Built by an industrialist in the last century to a style which is replicated in White City, Tel Aviv, believe it or not. Part of it is got up to look like a castle. Inside it really is quite civilised. But we didn't come for the architecture."

They went in and a small band of black musicians was playing. The band spoke German and American English to each other, and Kells wondered where they had spent the war. They all looked uneasy, and viewed all white people with suspicion. A waitress handed around glasses of champagne on a silver platter, and on a small dance floor couples were already skin close, as if they were going to be sent to the front the next day. A group of Russians were hog-whimpering, roaring drunk and passing around a tray of glasses with a flask of vodka, knocking back a shot before throwing the glasses into a fireplace and roaring for more. A sweeping staircase with portraits of expressionless, straight-backed men on horseback led to upper rooms.

"Have a drink down here and one of the girls will take you upstairs."

"What?"

"They will take you upstairs. No charge . . . and don't ask why."

"No shit? Are you kidding me?"

"No shit."

"Whose place is it?"

Kells' friend shrugged. "I'm told it belongs to a French countess, who is a friend of Marlene Dietrich. Everyone is here. All I can say is that both sides like to meet here, off limits, so to speak. If I say more someone will probably kill me. Grab a good time while you can because they will be closing things down soon. The new CIA head, Allen Welsh Dulles, is interfering with the conduct of all and sundry. Apparently, Dulles thought Hitler was not as bad as he was painted. Dulles is a presbyterian minister's son and he hates Catholics more than Nazis. The only thing we have in common is Dulles is a sex maniac and has slept with hundreds of women. Did you get any proper orders?"

Kells shook his head. His friend continued, "Well, Dulles is probably busy with the next hundred girls. I tried to find you on the intelligence lists and failed. I saw a memo today on his new departments. Having been involved in intelligence combat operations, you may come under SAD/SOG. Neat, huh? Take that as gospel from a State Department man from Foggy Bottom. I suppose as you started out under State Department orders you are Sad Soggy Foggy. And you a surfer from out among the kelp beds. I mustn't joke. You are probably in the Special Operations Group of the Special Activities Division of the all-new Central Intelligence Agency, who make a point of not even telling their own people what they are doing. You should feel special. If you are part of SAD/SOG, your team motto is *Tertio Optio*, which stands for third option. I am pretty sure that is not meant to have a sexual connotation, even for the priapic Dulles."

"No, I should not imagine so. So I am not listed? I get orders coming on the wire."

His friend smiled. "Oh, that is usual. Things get mixed up."

"But I cannot go home to mother?"

The State Department man sighed. "No. They would shoot you."

"Even if my father's gone mad and thinks he is Billy the Kid?"

His friend shook his head.

"Unfortunately not. That may be a common excuse in the wild west. I'm sure all will become clear. Well, enjoy yourself. It won't last. I got to slide off. There's a girl over there I want to talk to and more. Let's not wait for each other. There's no shortage of safe taxis when you call it a night or a morning. Or as safe as they can be in Berlin."

Kells finished his glass of champagne and then asked a waiter at the bar to give him a whisky and soda. He turned round and a small, dark-haired girl with a black lace blouse and dreamy eyes took the drink out of his hand, drank the whole glass, and led him to the dance floor. She was French, imported like the champagne, and they danced and danced. Kells had forgotten how much he liked to dance.

"My name is Céline . . . We will go upstairs now?" whispered the girl in Kells' ear, as the band played a slow number. He followed her.

He thought about Gretchen and then decided that this was like going to the beach surf parties when he was with Betty. He did not feel much of anything, and certainly not guilt. Tonight was off limits, out of time.

Down a carpeted formal corridor, hung with more paintings and tapestries and decorated with pikes and swords and, at the end, a very small suit of armour, a naked girl stepped out of a room, giggled, and ran into another. A man in a shirt, clutching a champagne bottle, came out and looked around and then went back into the room he had left. The girl then came out of the room she had gone into with two more champagne bottles and went back into her original room. There was a low whoop of pleasure.

"There is a room at the end I like," said Céline, leading him into the room at the end of the corridor.

It was hours later when he got out of the bed. The light was already coming up across the lake. The sky was pink, and it reflected in the water. It was a particular type of light strawberry pink that reminded him of California. The forest at either side grew down to the water's edge. He looked back at the bed and saw Céline smiling to herself in her sleep. He felt exhausted and happy. He dressed quickly.

He opened the door quietly and put his shoes on outside.

At the other end of the corridor another door was open. He glanced inside as he passed and stopped.

He saw Gretchen.

She was standing there, fully dressed. There was something about her being fully dressed that scared him. She was not even dressed for a party. She looked like she was going to work in an office in the neat suit he had first seen her in at the press conference.

He took half a step towards her, but Gretchen shook her head.

The door slammed shut.

The next day before lunch he went out without his jacket, walking up towards the Ku'damm. He was going to get himself a cup of coffee, just to step out of the house, buy a newspaper, smoke a cigarette. He had been sitting pouring over his few original files, thinking of Gretchen.

He was rounding the corner when a boy ran towards him and had his hand in Kells' trouser pocket and was then away.

"Little motherfucker ..." he said. Two pedestrians looked at him and shook their heads. Everyone was stealing in Berlin.

There had been nothing in that pocket. Kells kept his keys and a small pocket-knife in the other and his wallet was in his jacket and his pistol in the top drawer of his desk. But when he put his hand back in the always-empty pocket he felt something. There was an envelope. He turned around quickly and went back to the house.

He had been intending to phone his mother to ask how his father was, but he went straight to his study and opened the letter. Inside were two typed pieces of paper, typed on a small machine, that had a fault on the letter 'e'. Such were the explosions in the centre of the city in the last days that most typewriters, if they survived at all, had some identifying fault.

The two pages contained a list of names and then a series of numbers.

Kells read through the names. There was no heading. A first list comprised seven persons, all very high-ranking military officers or civilians in the Nazi administration. It began with Major General Hans Oster, chief of staff to Admiral Wilhelm Canaris, the head of *Abwehr* (German military intelligence) and ended with Carl Goerdeler, ex-mayor of Leipzig, and head of the conservative opposition.

"Shit," said Kells, out loud. This list could have been an alternative government.

Two people stood out. The names of von Gersdorff and the executed Thiele had been in Roessler's file that 'Beatrice' had sent him.

The radio was playing jazz in another part of the house. He read a second list, sub-headed, *Lucerne*. Again he recognised two names: Rudolf Roessler, code-named 'Lucy', and a Rachel Weinberg. That was Rachel's name, the nurse, it must be a coincidence.

"Who the fuck has sent this . . . ?"

After the list there were a series of numbers and letters. It must be book code.

Kells span around in the chair. He then reached for *Alice Through the Looking Glass, Alice hinter den Spiegeln*. After only a few numbers the code was obviously "his" book code sent by "Beatrice". It reminded him of doing Latin at his expensive mountain school at Los Alamos. Who the fuck had sent this?

The coded passage read: "There are many others on these lists, working for Lucy, both witting and unwitting. Lucy itself is a cut-off, acting independently as a go between. A cut-off is a mutually trusted or distrusted intermediary. There were individual agents who acted for Lucy, some of whom your side killed, but many were killed by Lucy to protect Lucy."

Kells swallowed. Rachel was the last person he would have

thought was involved. Could it really be her. Was she in danger? He must warn her. He read on.

"At the end of the war Lucy had four hundred agents in the field supplied with information by four top sources code named Werther, Olga, Teddy and Anna, with access to the *Oberkommando der Wehrmacht*, the High Command of the German armed forces, and other top departments, if not Hitler himself. Their identity is not known. Someone you already know very well may give you the rest of the information. If that is what you want. My advice is it is better not to know. Do not open Pandora's box."

Kells stared at the beautiful picture of St Lucy that 'Beatrice' had sent him, on top of a file.

The sender, a secret friend, must be wrong about Rachel. He must warn her.

XI

T HE FIRST, PUNGENT smell of silkworms is not easily forgotten.

Rachel and the others caught the scent before the crates were offloaded from the trucks. Initially it seemed to be almost a pleasant mixture of musk and spices, but then the smell of rot, that of human decay and excrement that she and the others knew too well, hit the back of their throats. She thought of the rotting bodies piled by the wire on the last day in the camp. It was also a smell from the camp latrines, the bubbling soup cauldrons and overused mattress straw. A smell of life and death. One of the girls hid her face and ran up the lane back to the big house. Rachel let her go.

"Best thing is to put a scarf around your face and cover it with wintergreen or some such. Tiger Balm is good. My brothers are in the Pacific and sent a load home. We used to use it down on the farm when we found fallen stock," said the American in charge of unloading the trucks. He was a lieutenant, a rangy man with a southern accent. "Who'd have thought a pair of silk stockings would smell like this? C'mon boys, let's get these things off and get back to the depot."

Rachel was always surprised how fiercely hard Americans worked. As if they were building the Promised Land. The racks and rattan mats for the mulberry leaves were soon off the truck and into the small house with the walled garden. There were lots of them, already covered in leaves and fat caterpillars. Then came larger equipment and bottles of butane gas, followed by the spinning machines.

"We picked these up in Alsace. The factory got bombed. This was left so I don't swear to things working. The factory got pancaked, but these little wormies went on wriggling. They say each one can make a mile of silk. That true? Damn useful."

"That's what they say," Rachel answered, pushing the hair out of her eyes as the American in charge moved close. She knew the Nazis traded in "useful" teeth and bones and hair and skin. The American was going to say something more, but the smell from the lorries was blown their way. She laughed and so did he, embarrassed by the mortal perfume and how it whispered of the war.

There was something, too, about the American that reminded her of the colonel who had saved Dr Kaplan.

With a gunning of engines, the trucks were turned around and the young American officer came over and gave her a box of chocolates and cigarettes before jumping on his truck. "See you again, honey," he said. "I don't doubt we'll be back with more."

It was nine and she had been in the fields since six and did not feel like a honey.

The officer's men sang in the back of the trucks:

"Who ya makin' the bacon for, honey?
If ya not makin' the bacon for me?"

Rachel was sure they did not mean any harm. The wind changed and a cloud blew across the sun and the song was carried away and the sound of the trucks and the smell of the silkworms vanished.

The walls of the small house glowed ochre as the sun appeared again.

Paul had wanted to come with her from the fields and help the Americans unload, but she had not let him. An old groundsman swore it was going to rain the day after tomorrow and the hay had to be got into the barns for winter feed. Rachel knew nothing of such things and took the old man very seriously. He had no teeth and smoked a clay pipe with chapped lips. Paul was furious. He scowled at her and drove the enormous, gentle horse and the cutting machine as fast as he could through the long grass.

"If that's the way you want it?"

"That's the way I want it."

There was a silence between them when she returned. A raven, wheeling over the fields, searching for prey, let out a low, guttural cawing, and Rachel stepped past Paul. She could feel his anger, his confusion and his love.

"We will all stop for a break at ten," she shouted to the others, who were smiling and laughing as if they were on a school picnic. "Paul and David, could you please go up to the silkworm house? They need strong men."

She wiped her forehead with her sleeve. Since they had made love, Paul acted as if he owned her. He had wanted to take over. He had wanted to be in charge of the silkworm house, he had wanted to be in charge of Dr Kaplan, even though Hyman was Kibbutz Secretary, and she had said no. It was not going to work. It was not going to happen. But neither did she want him wrecking all the work in the fields.

She lit a cigarette one of the GIs from the trucks had given her. They had no problem with her being in charge. Perhaps things were changing after a war that had drawn in everyone. She walked back to the silkworm house and leant against the garden wall that was warming in the sunshine. Quince plants had been trained on trellising against the wall, but there were gaps of honey-coloured stone from which the wall and the house were built. The silkworm house had four rooms on the ground floor and four bedrooms and two bathrooms on the upper floor. She guessed it may have been built before the great house and had a steep, old-fashioned slate roof, where all the slates were rounded and looked like tears. She remembered seeing houses like these as a child when she was taken by her father to concerts. They had often stayed in a manor house of a music lover outside town and she remembered icy runs to the toilet along creaking wooden corridors, scared she might wake the dogs downstairs, or a ghost. She had carried her teddy bear with her to keep her safe, a Steiff bear, from when her father used to go a lot to Munich and bought by her mother. She could smell her mother's perfume, Chanel.

She took a long drag of her cigarette.

The American soldiers flirted with the other girls, asked them on dates, although there was nowhere to take them and their orders forbade them to do so. They never asked Rachel. Perhaps they sensed something. Only Colonel Vardy asked her out frequently in telephone messages. He was certainly different from other soldiers. The poor man was trying to understand himself and the war. She wondered whether he was really attracted to her. Did he want to protect her, as most men did? Americans, she had observed, said they loved freedom, but they craved order; always frightened of the savage wilderness inside them. They liked to finish the quest, solve the problem. Get the girl.

Rachel blew out smoke and coughed. She wondered what Colonel Vardy would do if she told him her secrets. All she remembered, true or not.

She glanced up at the house. All of the rooms were being emptied to make way for the munching silkworms and pieces of furniture and bookshelves and books were being carried out into the garden. She hoped to put them on a cart and store them in the great house.

She went inside.

Already in the house, in what had been the sitting room, everything had been stripped away. Shelving now lined the walls with the rattan mats of fresh leaves. Everything had been cleaned and there was a smell of disinfectant over that of the moth caterpillars.

Rachel stood there alone watching the fat green creatures, about as long as her little finger, munching away at the mulberry leaves which had been brought in from the tree outside. She did not need to put her ear close to hear the sound of their jaws. Munch, munch, munch.

They appeared to be getting fatter by the minute, like businessmen in a *Weimar* cartoon by George Grosz. They were greed personified. She remembered restaurants she had been to with her father where many of the men measured more around the middle than they were tall. She thought of the Nazi propaganda of the greedy Jew and then the emaciation of the camps. She tried to remember a resonant note on her cello to drown all that out.

Rachel stamped her cigarette out on the wooden floor, stripped of carpets and rugs.

She picked up one of the worms. Its body was soft and warm. It did not let go of the leaf it was eating.

Rachel turned to see Hyman behind her in his wheelchair. He was beaming.

"They are happy with their new home! They brought me books as well, the Americans. I must once have known all this, but I will have to learn it all again. It is said that silk was discovered more than four and a half thousand years ago by the Empress Xi-Ling-shi, when a cocoon fell from a tree into her cup of tea. She picked at it, and found the thread stretched across the garden. Imagine that! In China they call her the silkworm mother. I want to be the silkworm mother here." He laughed.

"You mustn't work too hard," Rachel said.

He looked offended.

"I must disagree. I must. Everyone else is doing their bit and more. I never expected to have a present, let alone contribute to the future."

She went with him into another room. He was expert with his wheelchair and there was only a thin bandage under the homburg hat he wore, which one of his helpers had found in a wardrobe.

The other large room on the ground floor was full of silkworm racks and she heard the sound of furniture being carried downstairs.

"Must everything go? You need some furniture."

Hyman held up his good arm.

"I have what I need. Thank you for leaving me in charge of my silkworms."

"You should not overtire yourself."

He turned his chair and looked up at her. His good eye was determined. The doctors said he was never going to see out of the other. He reminded Rachel of Manfred the surgeon commandant who never complained about his wounds. Hyman smiled:

"Anna said we are all citizens of a new spiritual Israel. That the word Israelite means a person who wrestles with God. If I am to wrestle with God, I cannot be tired."

Rachel laughed and gave him a kiss on the forehead as she used to do at the American hospital, and then she went upstairs.

There was a small bookcase left in the first room she went into. A boy had a book open.

"It's Rilke," he said, and read out loud. "'Perhaps all the dragons in our lives are princesses who are only waiting to see us act, just once, with beauty and courage. Perhaps everything that frightens us is, in its deepest essence, something helpless that wants our love.'"

"That is so beautiful," she said.

She looked at the leather-bound volume. Rainer Maria Rilke, *Letters to a Young Poet*. It was well used and had been important to someone.

"Who do you think lived here?" she asked.

The boy sighed:

"A poet, or someone very interested in poetry. It is different from the big house. The library there has all the usual books. These are the books of a writer. They should be taken up there. But Paul says they are all to be taken out and piled in the garden."

"What?"

"Paul said . . ."

Rachel shook her head.

"Hyman is in charge in this house."

"Paul said that Hyman was in charge of the silkworms and he was going to deal with the rest. He said it was all Nazi shit. But there is everything here. Schiller, Tolstoy and even Mayakovsky. There are banned books. Jewish books. They should not be got rid of. Can I keep these?"

Rachel smiled. Something dropped on the floor.

"Oh, and that. That's a wooden foot." He picked it up. "It is really small. I think it belonged to a lady. The lady that had this house. She was probably the poet and had all these books. Most of the furniture is French. There were photographs."

Rachel looked at the boy, who had adopted the name of Jacob. He could not bear the name he had before. He could not bear to think of his family. There were many at kibbutz who had taken other names. Their old ones were detonators to the past.

It was then she smelled burning over the stink of the silkworms.

She ran downstairs and out into the garden.

Paul was standing by the old farm labourer and two of the others. He had set fire to the pile of furniture and was throwing on books that had been brought out of the house.

"Put it out!" she shouted. "Get water!"

"It is too late," said Paul, folding his arms.

"I said it was all to be taken to the big house."

"You did not say anything to me."

She turned to him.

"You are not in charge. Everyone, get water. Get water now!"

Her voice had changed. They all obeyed immediately.

Ten minutes later, the main bonfire was out. The furniture and books that had not already been put on the flames were saved. She picked through them. She saw a copy of *Peter Pan* in German. Hyman had come into the doorway of the house to watch them. She had the books and the best bits of furniture put into a small lodge by the gate in the walled garden, which had not been emptied.

Paul, who had not shown any urgency in fighting the fire, laughed.

"There was nothing important. It does not matter. It was a stupid German's old books."

Rachel walked up to him. "What language are we speaking? Chinese? Where did you grow up? The moon?"

There was a smirk on Paul's face.

"We are going to Israel. To what will be a new state. And have you forgotten what they did to us?"

She stared at him.

"You seem to have forgotten how they burned books at Nuremberg? I will not have you on my work detail anymore. Go back to the house and I will discuss later with the rabbi what to do with you. Beaten dogs bite. You are still obeying the soldiers in the camp, Paul. If you do, you are no better than them. Now get out of my sight. I am sorry that I ever knew you. We must be better than this."

She thought he was going to hit her. Hyman shouted "stop!" and Jacob ran toward them still carrying the wooden foot of the nameless woman who liked poetry. The farm labourer laughed and showed his bad teeth. He liked to see the arrogant young man told off by the slip of a girl. Paul turned and strode back up to the house.

XII

"YOU HAVE TO be realistic," said Paul. "You can't be serious about all this working with the local Arabs stuff? No one is going to give us the land in Palestine. No one is going to help us hang on to it unless we create a state." Paul had come to speak at the Sabbath meeting of the Kibbutz Committee.

Rachel shook her head. "For me the kibbutz is an ideal, an example to strive for by all peoples, not the first settlement of an old-fashioned nation state. It can be a model for everyone. Not just Jews . . ."

She had been busy discussing progress, or sometimes the lack of it, with the harvest and repairs and renovations in the meeting at the great house and even the cutting back of the Gothic maze. The discussions had gone on late into the night. Paul was the only one to object to Rachel's methods of organising the farming, but tried to make light of it when she pointed out he had not noticed that Bismark the cart horse had lost a shoe, and began to shout when she suggested he would be better employed up at the great house. After that, he spoke increasingly passionately about assessing if they were ready to go and establish a kibbutz in occupied Palestine, to be a spark for the new state of Israel.

Rachel was still furious with Paul for burning the books, especially the books, and the furniture. She should have never let him inside her.

Then Anna was whispering in Rachel's ear.

"Hyman has been sleeping on an old settee these past nights covered with a thin blanket only. He won't stop working . . ."

"You left him there? On the sofa? Hyman? The secretary of our kibbutz?"

Anna nodded. She was trembling. She did not like the argument that had come to the ballroom in the big house like a thunderstorm.

"Hyman should not sleep in that stench. He is a real hero. And he should sleep on something flat or the metal in his body may kill him," Rachel said, striding out of the meeting, even though the rabbi tried to catch her. He, as ever, had been attempting to calm things down. She was glad to get out into the cooler air of the summer night. There was a nearly full moon, which was reflected in the small lake. She stopped for a moment, watching the fish rise and snap at insects and send ripples across the surface of the reflected moon. The frogs and toads croaked and by degrees she relaxed. It was unbelievable to her how they could all have gone through so much to have the same old arguments.

She skirted around the pond and ahead of her a small deer or wild boar broke cover and made her jump. She looked up at the moon and the stars and was thankful that she had survived. Thankful and so guilty and more guilty, she knew, than some of her friends. Rachel's guilt was not merely survivors' guilt. What she had done on that last day was probably unforgivable. In that context, who was she to judge a person like Paul who talked tough because he was still so scared?

The sound of the cello was back in her head. Bartok's *Rhapsody No 1*. Search as she might, she had not found a cello in the house like the one the SS smashed. If it was really smashed. She did not know anymore.

An owl began to hoot; she must not think like this. There was only the future now.

She let herself into the silkworm house and turned on a battery torch the Americans had given her. She found Hyman on the remaining couch in one of the downstairs rooms, covered in an old blanket. The smell had become worse. It was not sanitary. His wheelchair was by the couch. She had to shine the strong torch on him, though mindful of the shock it might cause being woken in the middle of the night.

"Hyman. You must not sleep here. Let us go to the gatehouse. There is furniture there."

He did not protest as she folded him into the wheelchair. He had lost weight since she had known him in the hospital. He held onto her hand as she wheeled him through the front door into the moonlight, shining silver around the bird-winged leaves of the black mulberry trees. She pushed him into the gatehouse and lit an oil lamp with the paraffin lighter she had in her pocket.

"You are too good to me. All of you."

"Nothing is too good for you. You work until you drop."

In the other room was a bed which was slightly damp, and she made it up with bedding that had been put in the room from the main house by Jacob. Tomorrow she would light the range and dry the place if she could not persuade Hyman to go back to the big house. When she had finished making the bed, she wheeled Hyman into the room and lifted him onto the sheet. Then she undressed him, and he did not protest. She was his nurse again. It was like undressing a child. She looked at him in the kindly, creamy light of the oil lamp and his wounds were still pitiful. More pitiful than the surgeon commandant Manfred's at the camp. In places the skin on Hyman's face was purple and black.

The lamp was on the bedside table on the opposite side to him. It was an old-fashioned bed with a brass bedstead. She went round the bed, turned down the lamp and took off her clothes. She took off all her clothes and got under the blanket and blew out the lamp. She stayed there like that for many minutes listening to the silence and then she reached across and touched him, and pushed back the sheet in the silver and black moonlight. The scars and the burns on his body filled her head, excited her. They made her feel real. Each of his scars and burns was like a precious jewel she wanted for herself. She worshipped his destruction. But her indulgent phantoms dissolved back into the present, and she was there with a man she had come to love. Yes, love. He made a small sound and she felt his erection. At first this dwindled to nothing and then revived as she caressed him gently, not wanting to hurt him. She took him in her mouth.

He sighed.

His damaged skin smelt of new bread and soap and she moved on top of him and they were together.

He held her hand very tight as he cried out, and she did too. She kissed him tenderly. With great thanks.

When she woke in the night the sheets were lit by the powerful harvest moon, and he was awake, propped on his side looking at her, in a position that must have been painful. One side of his mouth had that wistful, slight smile of his.

What he said surprised her.

She knew, too well, it was not true.

"You're a good person, Rachel," he half-whispered. "Please God, you are the future. You've made me so happy. I am the happiest man in the world. *Ich liebe Sie alle.* I love you all."

XIII

THE MOMENT HAD almost come in the silkworm house.

"Please go up to the house and fetch the members of the committee," Hyman said to Jacob, one of the boys helping him, who looked worried. "It is urgent. There is not a second to lose."

Hyman had thrown himself into his work the day after that first night with Rachel with a renewed passion and joy.

He had won her, as he intended.

Hyman ordered more shelves, and oversaw the harvesting of the mulberry leaves from the trees in the garden and others he had found on the estate. He re-read the books he had been given and watched as the worms became fatter and fatter and began to turn into chrysalises. A few already had and he could not wait. He stoked the fire on the downstairs range to make the old house impossibly warm. Now was a crucial moment he wanted to share with her.

Rachel was in another evaluation planning meeting, choosing those who might be considered for the first wave of settlement at a new kibbutz in Palestine, if they were able to get in, or persuade the British to let them.

When he thought of her, he was walking on air. He wondered if he had died all over again and gone to a heaven of his spiritual and physical dreams. He had been so attracted to her since he first saw her and loved the touch of her delicate fingers against his cheek, or when she had washed his body in the hospital. Her long-fingered hands made him moan with pleasure and she had told him how she used to play the cello. He knew that she was devoted to him and he delighted to hear her voice, especially when she read him poetry and, suddenly, the emotion came through and her voice sounded more childlike. He loved the tiny kisses on his undamaged cheek, and even on his wounded side, kisses that had lingered of late.

Hyman had not expected any more than that. Anything more than her dazzling smile when something surprised and pleased her, or when the protective shield she had constructed around herself was let down and she was all sunshine and thistledown.

He never dreamt of intimacy beyond the subtleties of touch and subtexts of speech that had occurred, that might be more his hopeful imagination than reality and he did not ever expect her to share his bed. He thought of himself as revolting, beyond all relationships, a monster from the sort of particularly cruel German fairy tale Rachel had been talking of the other day, but she did not see that. The bandages were off his face and body now and, if anything, the normal side of his face made the other, reconstructed section, even more terrible. It was as if a painter had put his hands on a portrait before the oils were dry and smudged and ridged his work.

That there was more than a hint of the actor Clark Gable, made what he saw in the mirror even more disturbing and revolting now, especially as he did not know how he looked before. He was at first satisfied with his new face. He sighed. He knew that these adolescent thoughts and doubts started after he and Rachel had made love.

The rest of his body was in an even worse state and there were still bits of metal and shrapnel beneath his skin and deeper, around the vital organs, that one day were going to kill him. At times he felt them moving, as if they were living entities, wriggling inside his flesh like the silkworms. He might well die when making love to her. To die while making love to her seemed so appealing because she could not spend her life with a wreck like him. But then he thought how much it would upset her and how much it grieved him even to think of parting from her. To go into the ground, when she walked in splendour above. She made him want to go on living. He saw her inspiration in every leaf of the mulberry tree, every living vein on those dark, pungent leaves. He was in love with Rachel. One day she would go physically to her new country, Israel, in Palestine, and he doubted very much if he was going to be allowed to follow her. What use could a new state have for a ruin like him? He stopped still and put another small log in the stove and wheeled his chair over to the sink and filled a large saucepan. He put it on the top of the range and waited for it to boil. The young people were going to scold him when they came in for doing things by himself. They told him he could have an accident at which he always smiled and said he was an accident. These young people were going to preside over a better world than the one he had lived through. He was no hero, as they said he was.

A true hero takes responsibility for the sins of others, and changes those others.

He went to an old, handmade kitchen cabinet and took out a metal colander. He then wheeled his chair back into the silk-worm-raising room and fetched the three cocoons that were ready. Inside, the caterpillars had pupated and were ready to turn into silk moths, if he had his timings right. It was a critical window. Too soon and too late and there was going to be no silk. The water was boiling now and he placed the colander on top as he heard voices in the garden and the front door open. He was happy and excited.

XIV

"FIRST WE MUST kill Goliath," a young man was saying, as Rachel saw a boy come into the meeting and speak to Anna, who looked over at her.

The boy, Jacob, had been working with Hyman. She had not directly mentioned moving into the lodge with Hyman. She assumed that everyone knew, and no one had mentioned anything. It was none of their business, but she had said she was anxious that Hyman might have a fall from doing too much. He was so happy in his work. Perhaps that was why the boy had come. Two women the rabbi had recommended had been invited to the meeting, one who had come from British Palestine and one who had fled to France, but before doing so had been part of the early kibbutz movement in Germany, which she said was supported by several rich Nazis who wanted no "Jew-lice" in the Fatherland.

The problem, for Rachel, had been the three representatives from the *Haganah*, who had come with the other woman from Bonn, and said the new state should have a strict selection process and what they required were soldiers, not farmers. They were thin, scowling men who had spent the war years shouting at each other in Egypt. They had no interest in understanding what the people at the house had gone through, and they said this often. They saw the future as a battle with the British and any ideal society, agrarian or otherwise, would have to come later. They wanted to build a defendable nation state, not communes.

"First we must kill Goliath. The British are as bad as the Nazis," the young man repeated.

Rachel did not like any of the three, especially the one with pebble glasses who had just spoken. Only one of them had been to Palestine, and none of them to the liberated Nazi death camps, or been in one. She had observed before that those who had not fought in a war mythologised it most. Their leaden skulls were a fantasy of guns and monsters. The same was now true of the camps. The horror of what happened was being lost in crude politics.

Yet another part of her sympathised with them and their raw anger. Who knew what their terrible histories were? And she was more guilty than most of editing her past. But she opposed them.

"We all go or none of us go," Rachel said, as Anna came over to her. "We take land that is given to us or we reclaim from the desert. We are at the end of angry men telling us what to do." Rachel fully intended that Hyman and anyone else who wanted to go to a kibbutz in Palestine, to a new and peaceful spiritual home, should be allowed to, or nothing made moral sense.

The *Haganah* man curled his thin lips in a false smile. "I can understand why you have such an attitude living in a country house like a countess, being fattened up for propaganda by the Americans. You should be ashamed."

"Kindly do not be so rude," said the rabbi, in a voice as cold as winter that none had heard before, and the young man stamped out of the room and slammed the door.

There was a mirror behind the remaining two *Haganah* members and when she examined the back of their heads and scrawny necks, they all looked like boys. Rachel had seen what "boys" can do.

"I have a message from Hyman," said Anna, taking advantage of a pause. "Please go to the silkworm house immediately. He wants members of the committee. It is important."

"Oh, silk is more important than survival," sneered the man with the thick glasses, who had come back into the room.

Rachel ignored him, and immediately left the meeting.

She ran past the lake and down the slope to the silkworm house with the boy and Anna. The grass was still wet with dew.

"Is he all right?"

"I think so," said the boy. "But he was very insistent that you come."

They burst into the kitchen and saw him red-faced by the stove. He had the large colander in his hand.

"The cocoons are ready. Now I shall kill them with the steam. Please watch."

Hyman was smiling.

"No!"

Anna rushed back out into the garden and Rachel followed her.

"I cannot watch that . . ." she began.

Rachel put her arms around Anna and held her close. They stood like that for minutes, trembling into each other, overcome by what Hyman intended to do.

When they went back in, he had dried the cocoons on the kitchen table.

He was picking at them with the nails of his index finger and thumb.

"It has not worked with three of the cocoons. I think I was too soon. But look at this one. There is a thread. Take the thread, Jacob. Anna, why are you crying? What have I said? Take the thread and go out of the door. Carefully, now. We have to see how it unwinds.

Look, it is silk! We have produced silk! Why did you rush out like that? Keep going, Jacob. Keep going."

In the end the thread stretched all the way from the stove to the gate lodge. Anna rushed out of the house again. She could not stop crying.

"Look at that thread, Rachel. With that we shall bind the world together again. We will make everything new and whole! Look how strong it is! A single thread. There must be twenty-five metres. There must be. I will measure it. I will."

The next day one of the soldiers gave Rachel a lift into the nearby village of Katharinenburg, where the Americans had set up a small transport depot. They were bringing in new equipment for Hyman, including a gas-bottle oven, which was said to be better than steaming the cocoons. But another batch of silkworms would be ready before then and Rachel was in search of a bigger pan and a bigger colander from the cafe there. The Americans always had too much of everything. She had not discussed the matter with Anna. They both could not find the words.

She arrived in a jeep.

"The canteen is over there, ma'am."

It pleased her when they called her ma'am. That it was accepted that she was in charge, a woman was in charge. Perhaps that was going to be one of the positive things to come out of the war.

She went through a door and into the kind of American diner she had seen on films. There was an Italian espresso machine and at a table three soldiers were eating hamburgers. At another sat Colonel Kells Vardy with a piece of apple pie and two coffees in front of him.

She stopped. It made her angry, she had been set up.

"Why are you here? I do not have time to return your calls."

He pushed away his piece of pie.

"Well, for one thing, I hoped I might see you. Please sit down."

He stood up and pulled out a chair for her and offered her a cigarette which she took.

"And the other?"

He lit her cigarette with a gold lighter and sat down again.

"I was wondering how Hyman Kaplan was getting on? Most of all, I wanted to see you. I cannot get you out of my mind. I really can't." He blew a smoke ring. "Whenever I think I know who you are, you go and change. I hear you are more or less running the kibbutz now. When I first saw you, I thought you were too pretty and delicate to be a nurse."

She laughed.

"A pretty little girl who you thought you could get into bed and fuck?"

The conversation stopped abruptly on the next table.

"Did you set this up? My lift to a nowhere village?"

He sighed. He looked very handsome in his uniform. She wondered what it might be like to go to bed with him. She wondered what he really wanted.

"I knew you were coming here. But I was coming already," he said.

"I am not sleeping with you. Ever. I am sure you have lots of women in Berlin, grateful to be liberated."

Again the conversation on the other table faltered. Kells half-turned and the men all started to get up and go.

"May I take you somewhere else? For a drink? Perhaps something to eat? "Dinner?"

"The answer about fucking will still be the same."

He paused.

"I think you can help me. All I want to do is talk."

XV

TO KELLS IT was the same old story.
The more she pushed him away, the more he wanted her. That had been so true with Betty.

"Shall we go?" he said.

The three drivers still were in the diner and they were waiting for her to say no.

"Where to?"

"There is an inn nearby."

She laughed.

"There always is, colonel. There always is. But I am expected back at Aviv this evening."

"I know," he said. He left a tip on the table and then held the door open for her. They walked over to a staff car and he dismissed the driver. The car was a Mercedes.

"I'll drive," he said. "Come and sit up front."

They then drove to the inn, a half-hour away, like two young people going on a first date. The countryside of small fields and horse-chestnut trees gave way to a thick pine forest. She smoked and blew the smoke out of the window on the warm wind. They passed workers coming in from the fields and a line of army trucks and the forest became deeper and darker. He pressed the accelerator.

"If you skid and hit a tree, you will burn down the forest," she said, and giggled.

"Why is that funny?"

"You come over here and say you are going to build. Instead, you smash everything. You want to take a girl for a romantic drink and end up burning down a forest."

"Absurd, perhaps. I am not sure that's funny, though."

"I am. But we Germans have a darker sense of humour."

"I thought you were Jewish?"

"And I thought you were here to liberate us from race science?"

She then touched him on the hand as he changed gear.

"I'm sorry. You are just trying to be a nice American boy. Where is this Inn? Or are we lost? Are you lost, colonel? Lost in a dark German forest with a woman you do not know?"

He found the inn, which was several miles from where he thought it was. A bar was full of fighter escort pilots from a nearby base and several German girls. A man was playing the piano and another two men sang quite tunefully. They all stopped and looked at Kells and one of the officers said "'ten-shun" but then they all went back to what they were doing and Kells made his way through them to the bar.

"Hi, honey. I'd watch out for the colonel. He's a known child-snatcher," said one of the pilots.

Kells asked if they could get something to eat and if there was somewhere quiet. The barmaid directed them to a room at the back, inquiring if they also wanted a room for the night. Kells shook his head and Rachel smiled. They were then brought wine and a basket of dried sausages, followed by venison stew with potatoes. The inn defied rationing, thanks to the forest and the Americans. She had sips of the sweetish white wine, but hardly ate a thing.

"Don't you like it? I forgot you don't eat much."

The look on her face was playful.

"There was a time when I never thought I would eat again. Especially meat. It is something to do with the smell of meat. The smell of meat burning in an incinerator. I think you know what I am saying."

He nodded. He had finished his stew.

"Yeah, I do. All the time I came though France. You are right. We destroyed villages and towns, burned them down, and I did not feel shit when I should have . . . Villages and towns with no strategic or tactical importance. Civilians who were waiting for us to liberate them are dead and bulldozed into mass graves. Corpses burned with gasoline. That Sunday-afternoon barbecue smell. I kept joking around and did not feel enough. I wasn't even properly frightened. It was like being in a movie. I wake up in the morning and feel a hollowness and an emptiness, which is the opposite of feeling, as if somewhere I lost myself. It isn't postponed fear or shell shock. I don't know what the hell it is."

She took another sip of her wine. "Well, if you didn't feel anything you can go home to your girlfriend and go bowling or whatever

Americans do after a day at the office. You can forget about us. We won't mind."

He was silent and then she did something surprising. She leant across the table and gave him a kiss on the cheek.

"I am sorry. I am being a bore. Thank you very much for this. It is the first time I have been taken out somewhere unexpected by anyone since before the camps, let alone a handsome and dashing colonel. Let's enjoy ourselves. After all, the war is over."

XVI

RACHEL WATCHED KELLS go to the washroom after the plates had been taken away and the waitress brought more wine. She was a local girl who looked like she had escaped the worst of the war. She gave Rachel a knowing wink.

"He is from the American base? Your man?"

"He's from Berlin," Rachel answered.

The girl had been including her in the wave of prosperity she could hear in the laughter of the girls in the other room, as if Rachel was one of them. She had taken one look at Rachel's blonde hair and blue eyes and fair skin and made her assumptions. They were in the same boat. It was only the mention of the word "Berlin" that had turned the edges of the girl's mouth down. Perhaps it was the ghost of the previous regime, or a relative, formerly of the SS, hiding in a log cabin deep in the forest. The man who shot the deer they had just eaten.

The waitress smiled again.

"Berlin. Poor Berlin . . . You can go outside, you know. There is a garden through that door. There are seats and a path into the wood. It is a fine evening."

Rachel nodded. "Yes, we may do that. The dinner was delicious, thank you."

"You are not from round here are you?" said the girl.

"Not far away these days," Rachel said.

"It's your accent."

"Yes," Rachel lit a cigarette. She offered one to the girl who took it and put it behind her ear.

"You speak English too. I wish I could speak English."

Rachel smiled up at the girl.

"You will."

There was a silence.

"I grew up in Berlin," Rachel said. She stared at the girl who became nervous and then left the room. She took a long drag on the cigarette, one of the colonel's cigarettes, and looked around at the rustic decor. There were carved wood mushrooms on the bar, but also a few fibres of red on a nail above, possibly from a flag. On the other wall by the window was an amateur oil painting of alpine mountains, but next to it was a lighter rectangle where another picture had been, perhaps a photograph. Around the rectangle was a black band made by grease and dust. It was usual to have a photograph of the *Führer* in every room in a bar. It did not necessarily indicate a party member, but anyone who put up a photograph was not likely to help those who opposed the government.

She was reaching for another of the American's cigarettes when he came back. She stopped herself.

"We can go outside. There is a garden. We can take the wine. I didn't order coffee."

He smiled.

"Let's go."

When she got outside, she gulped down the air. She had been suffocating inside from what she saw and surmised. She steadied herself against a wooden table.

"I ate too much of the food, even if I didn't eat much. I'm not used to it. As I said, I'm not used to going out on dates with men."

He caught her and for a second, she thought he was going to kiss her, but he didn't. It was so important for Americans to think of themselves as good. There was a smell of honey in the air and she saw there were rope beehives by an old wooden shed. By the shed vegetables had been planted out in rows, but the owner of the garden had refused to dig up the rest of the garden, in particular the roses, a couple of which were coming into flower. And there were the usual flowers of the old-fashioned German garden: red hot pokers, big daisies, and spikes of acanthus.

"Do you like gardens, Kells?"

"Doesn't everyone?"

She laughed. He had made one of those literal, generalised comments that European writers thought defined the innocence of Americans. Even when that innocence was violent and destroyed cities and governments. Americans feared the wilderness and gardens were self-evidently preferable. Only a short step away from that was gardens MUST be preferable, and Uncle Sam would go to war to protect them.

The collective noun for Americans could be an Innocence of Americans.

"I would have thought being a soldier is to be the enemy of gardens," she said playfully.

He nodded and smiled. "My mother loves to garden and my father loves to look at her gardening while he reads the sports pages."

"What does he do?"

"Oh, he has been running a munitions factory. He had his own hardware business, built up from one shop. I guess his pots and pans now fly. He checked every nut, bolt and washer personally. He had made it and didn't need to do the war stuff. He hated all the impersonal corporate nonsense and memos and forms the most . . . Now he's had to stop. It's driven him over the edge. My mother's very worried about him. We were from St Louis, before moving to the coast. His father was a gambler and lost the family farms, so it made him as he is. Checking every nut and bolt of every bomber."

Kells sat down at the round wooden table, wondering why he had told Rachel more about his father than he had Gretchen.

Rachel pulled up one of the wooden chairs next to him. Her smart red coat was inside, but she did not need it. The evening was warm and the sun was still shining through the trees. She could see the colonel was upset about his father. He pushed his blond hair back on his forehead. She saw that he loved his father very much.

She patted his hand. "I am sure he is very proud of you."

"He is very proud of what he thinks I am."

There was a silence and in one of the apple trees a blackbird began to sing.

He was silent for a long time.

She got up.

"Let's go and walk in the wood."

He laughed.

"If you don't want to find wolves, don't go into the forest."

She held out her hand.

"*The Idiot*, by Dostoyevsky?"

"Yes"

He stood up and took her hand. His was warm.

The trees closed above them and in twenty yards they had left the plantings of a human garden for another place entirely. It was cool and dark among the trees as the sun was dropping. In the bushes to her left something big like a wild boar moved, breaking twigs, and then a blackbird flew up making its alarm call. It was the colonel who was startled.

"This is where all our fairy tales start. German fairy tales. They often do not have very good endings."

"It would be easy to become lost in these woods."

"It is. Are you lost, Kells?"

He did not reply.

"What was the last thing your father said to you? Has he had a breakdown? Can they make him better?"

Kells paused. "I really don't know. I was studying English Literature and a bit of Dante, but he was never interested in that. The last conversation we had was about Billy the Kid. He thinks that Billy the Kid wasn't shot by Pat Garret. My father met a man called Billy in a bait shop when he went on a fishing expedition in the South, long before I was born. He is sure he met William H. Bonney, alias Billy the Kid."

She looked at him puzzled.

"Who is Billy the Kid?"

There was a helpless look on the colonel's face.

"You must know. Billy the Kid? He was a gunfighter. An outlaw. It's a cowboy story from the old west. They say he killed eight men."

Rachel drew closer to him and she smiled as she said softly, "Eight men? Not even a dozen? Wow! As you say. That's not a lot now, is it? Not with so many dying. Your command in France probably killed far more than that in an hour. Yet we remember this gunfighter, this boy, as dangerous. These stories became popular because they were used to mask the truth about the land grabs by the railroads and the mining companies."

Kells shrugged.

"He thinks I am Billy the Kid sometimes."

She took hold of his arm in sudden, complete affection. She leant her head against his. Cheeks touching.

"Perhaps he will return from his dream when he is ready. And this romantic outlaw, Billy the Kid, lives forever for him in you."

He stared at her.

"It doesn't make a lot of sense."

She didn't reply. Then she said, "You work for intelligence now, I know. The rabbi said. The rabbi knows everything. He says even the Christian God tells him secrets."

She made a half-mocking sign of the cross.

"Do you believe in God?" Kells asked, surprised.

"I believe in the rabbi."

She inhaled the smell of the forest. The smell of the pine needles and below that the smell of fungus and rot; a sweet smell on the wind. She wondered what had happened in these woods.

"I'm getting chilly. Let's go back for our wine," she said. She could see that he was again going to try and kiss her but didn't.

"Did you go to university?" he asked.

She shook her head. "I thought about it, but my father was a doctor who loved theatre and music and my brother was a singer and two of my sisters played instruments well. I played the cello and went to the conservatoire for a whole lovely year. I was beginning to play in concerts. I thought it could last forever. My father thought he had contacts, you know. Our house was also full of books and we always had people around arguing about this and that. They argued so much about modern art they forgot to look out of the window."

A warm breeze hit them as they came out of the forest.

"What happened to your father? Is he all right?"

She looked at him puzzled.

"None of them are all right. They are all dead. My father, my mother, my three sisters, my little brother. All dead in the camps. The American Hospital people checked. We Germans keep excellent records. Then there are all the aunts and uncles and cousins. As far as I know, I am the only one who has survived."

She took a sip of wine.

"I am so sorry," he said.

"Yes."

She sat down and so did he.

He looked really anguished.

"I am sorry."

She smiled at him.

"Are you?"

"I have something I must tell you . . . It's something you can help me with, maybe . . ."

"And what is that?"

He took a gulp of his wine. "Your name is on a list. A list of names of the Lucerne resistance group in Switzerland. We call it Lucy. They got information from high-placed Germans and passed it on."

She shrugged. "That must be someone else. I joined the resistance as a student because no one was doing anything. I was arrested and was to be executed, then I was sent to a camp where I was not in a position to get information from high-placed Germans, but I am sure being caught and sent there led to the death of my entire family."

He swallowed.

"I am so sorry I asked."

"No, you are not. You are a sensible and clever human being trying to make sense of meaningless shit. Only you have come across things that are nonsense to the point of being beyond absurdity. Like the death camps. You have stepped through the Looking Glass, colonel."

"Why do you say Looking Glass?" He looked alarmed.

"Isn't that what people say when the world is back to front?"

He took her hand across the table. His hand was warm. She wanted so much to trust him. Then he said:

"You survived."

The words had an instant effect on her, as if a door to a deep cave had been opened and the universe was filled with a great noise.

She overturned the table and sent the glasses and the bottle flying.

"What . . . ? What have I said . . . ? I'm sorry."

"Please drive me back to Aviv. Drive me back now."

She went back into the small room at the rear of the bar and looked around for her red coat. It was not there. The waitress who had served her came for her money.

"Where is my coat? My red coat?" Rachel demanded in German.

The waitress pretended not to know what she was talking about. Rachel moved close to the girl.

"Whoever has my coat, get it back now. That's my coat and I want it. Otherwise, things will go very badly. You will discover who I am."

The girl looked scared and rushed off into the bar. There was a small argument and then she returned with the coat and could not meet Rachel's eyes as the colonel paid. The waitress held the coat while Rachel slid her arms into the sleeves and then buttoned it up.

She was thinking of the dark outline where the picture had been. She then walked out of the inn.

In the car they drove in silence for mile after mile, even when he nearly ran over a deer. She saw the fear in the animal's eyes. It was a doe. It must have brushed the front of the car as it leapt across the road. It made Kells jump. Rachel did not move, or comment. The lights on the car were not good, being toned down for the black-out, she supposed. She sat next to him, seething with anger one minute, and in despair the next. When he glanced across at her he must have seen a tear on her cheek. How could he be so stupid and so clumsy? Perhaps he was only trying to tell her that she could be in danger from being on that list. She did not speak and she did not even smoke a single cigarette.

She pulled her red coat closer around her.

He drove past the gatehouse and up to the big house and stopped on the gravel drive in front of the old building. Lights were on and she saw the young people inside. A guard came over and, seeing Kells' uniform and Rachel, went away again.

Kells turned to her and then she was kissing him, franticly. She could taste his lips, his skin. She held onto him like a mad person and then drew back.

"I'll see you, won't I? Why not next week?" he began.

She nodded. She then kissed him again and ran away into the night, down towards the lake, away from the house where the light from the high windows did not reach her. This was not the dark love she felt for Hyman, rooted in the vicious past. In making amends. This was love in the present tense. She wanted the darkness to shield her from the terror of such love. That was for good people.

XVII

"I KNOW YOU want to ask me a question," Gretchen said. "It has been in your head all night."

She pulled down her white lace panties with one hand and exposed her black pubic hair before jumping onto the bed and kissing him on both eyes. They made love twice and then she poured his brandy into two small glasses as the ruined tenement shuddered to a nearby explosion. It was a whole week after he had returned from the kibbutz to find the priest and Joe discussing repentance in a very serious way. Kells could not bring himself to repent of Gretchen, and had no trouble in finding her this time.

"You want to ask me a question?" she said again.

He did not say anything. He sipped the cognac he had brought her. The glass was the size of a large thimble. The alcohol burned the back of his throat and warmed him.

"You want to ask me what I was doing at that party?"

Again he thought it better to let the question lie with her. Her breasts were full, but he could make out every one of her ribs. He put his finger out and touched one of her nipples.

She gave a little yelp, giggled, drank her cognac down in one gulp, coughed and laughed. "Did your intelligence people, your nice State Department friend, tell you I worked for a famous general for a time, Rudolph von Gersdorff?"

"No one tells me anything."

Only part of him thought he was being clever in not telling her all he knew. He leant over and kissed her nipples, each in turn. She was so beautiful, lying there, drinking good cognac in a building that could fall down on them any moment. He hated to think he had been guided towards her, that he was in a trap, that she had been put in his way for a purpose. But, he told himself, she could still help him, and he could help her.

"The general, a good and kind man. He had an aide and I was the aide's lover," she said. "I think he was killed in the bombings on the last days, for sure. He was called Walter and he told me what was going on and I had to pass messages for the people against the Nazis. That is what I am still doing. Passing messages . . . That is what I was doing when you saw me the other night."

Kells looked around him at the bare plaster of the room and a pair of stockings hung over a string washing line.

"I live here because I have to. There are people who want me. From both sides," she said.

"And why is that?"

He put down his glass and moved on top of her.

"People want me to work for them. People think I work for the other side. Others want to question and kill me."

"And who do you work for?"

She smiled at him and there was a dimple to the left of her wide mouth. She put on the heavily accented voice of a street girl.

"I work for you. American soldier! My liberator! *Mein Helden!* I work for the Yankee dollar!"

She giggled again. Then she stopped. "I should not tease. The Russians took me to their headquarters nine days ago and asked me the same question. Who do you work for? I thought they were going to kill me. They have my lover from just before the war. Not Walter the general's aide, another man. A normal man. A doctor. If I do not work for them, they will harm him. I took a message to a man at that party where you saw me."

He kissed her lips.

"Do they know about me?"

"They want me to get information from you. I do not think they tried to scare you with the gun in the car. But I could be wrong. They are interested in the man you rescued. But most of all they are interested in an old operation called Lucy and who else knows about that. They are very interested in Lucy."

There was an argument in a room somewhere below.

"What were they doing? The Lucy crowd? In the war?"

She looked at him surprised. "You don't know?"

Kells shook his head. She was sure he must. She reached out and held his hand.

"They passed on information to the Soviets, from the British, from their code breakers and spies, about German operations, but mostly from Lucy's own people, in particular about the military plans in Kursk. The big tank battle which lost Germany the war. The battle Germany should have run away from. But at the back of this there were other things going on. Walter said there was an Operations Sunrise which involved the surrender of the German troops in Northern Italy and was organised by a General Wolff of the *Waffen SS*. There were lots of these operations . . . la-la-la . . . This one was negotiated with a man with a stupid name. Dulles. But it was all more than that. Wolff was part of Lucy. So was my general and Walter. Another girl working for the general took details of these things to a man called Roessler in Lucerne, and a roll of camera film in a cassette box in an intimate place. She did not believe what she saw."

He kissed her left thigh.

"Americans?"

"No, stupid. They are all mad. Lucy. She said there was a Mad Hatter's Tea Party and they were all dressed up as animals or characters in *Alice in Wonderland*. Walter and I were going to run away together. He told me all I know about Lucy. But he was killed in a big air raid on the south of the city. Poor Walter."

Kells was thinking of the Alice code book.

He kissed her on the lips.

"So whose side is this Roessler on? The Reds?"

She smiled. "I don't believe Lucy takes sides in the national sense and thinks that old-fashioned. Even more so now, as Lucy is a bigger lady. She is a side in herself. A player in the game. Walter said there was something in the message the girl who went to Lucerne brought back that was, *schlechte Nachrichten* or 'bad news'."

Kells felt he was actually being told the truth. It made him fear for her.

"And what was that?"

"My poor Walter said that behind Operation Sunrise there was another American and British operation approved by Churchill called Operation Crossword, a plan to invade the Soviet Union . . . This scared Walter and everyone . . . Even the general. It scares people even more now . . . There are such crazy things going on. Killings. I want to be out of here, please Kells. Can you get me an American passport? I can get papers that may be of use to you. But please leave Lucy alone, she is dangerous . . ."

They made love again and when they had finished she tried to warm coffee on the fire. They shared the steaming coffee in a glass and he had to put it down on the old, varnished boards it was so hot. They shared a cigarette and he watched her full lips purse as she inhaled. There was lipstick on the cigarette as she passed it to him. Ash fell onto her bush of pubic hair and she laughed. Music then came out of nowhere, funnelling up through the holes in the building. Not opera today. Loud American music. It was Glen Miller with a female singer on "Doin' the Jive."

Gretchen got lazily off the bed with a wolfish smile on her face and pulled him after her.

Her body and her heavy breasts were moving to the music.

The volume was turned up. A girl was singing: "*You clap your hands / And you swing out wide / Do the Suzie Q / Mix in a step or two / Put 'em all together / And you're doin' the jive*".

Gretchen ducked expertly under his arm. She giggled. She threw herself back and then they were together again.

She rubbed her belly against his and there was a rasp of pubic hair.

Then she pulled apart in another sort of jive.

Kells threw his head back and laughed.

Holy shit! He felt there! For an actual, emerald moment he felt he was 'there'. Despite all the war shit. He felt! In that instant.

In the eternity of that instant.

Kells was about to tell her when there was a cracking sound and the boards and beams underneath them gave way as she was coming back towards him and the floor collapsed in a cloud of dust.

He hit something soft very hard and she was on top of him.

He had banged his head and there was a strange feeling in his nose and bees and stars exploded from the dirty plaster.

They found themselves on a bed in the room downstairs, looking up at Gretchen's possessions hanging from hooks or fluttering down towards them. Gretchen's bed was wedged at a strange angle above, threatening at any moment to fall on them.

But the music did not stop.

The same record played again as they coughed out the dust.

"*Do the Suzi Q . . .*"

They could not stop laughing. Every time they tried the laughter started again at the corners of their mouths.

"The house is at war with itself," she said.

He kissed her.

"I have fallen for you," he said.

"I have fallen for you, too."

They laughed again.

"Better come and stay at my place", he said. "I'll hire you as a secretary. The United States of America formally hires you as a secretary and Lucy consultant."

She shrugged. "I have previous experience of that role."

Gretchen was excited and slowly and carefully they retrieved what they could of her possessions, which were few: a good dress, some jewellery and papers hidden in the mattress. She hugged him and kissed him most affectionately now she had no home. She was, he thought, being completely open. First they went to the Café Kranzler and he bought her milky coffee and a chocolate cake. He had to tip to get a table as they were still covered in plaster dust.

She ate her chocolate cake slowly and then paused and said, "The Russians are very interested in your Hyman Kaplan. He worked for Lucy and knows much . . . They suspect everyone. They suspect many ordinary people, like my doctor friend, of being secret Nazis. They thought he was Walter. He is nothing like Walter. They tried to take your burning man from the hospital. There is even a rumour that Hitler escaped. I don't think they found Hitler, as they said, and sent his prick to Stalin in a bottle. The Russians lie about everything. That is typical of their stupidity. To think your old burned up Jew, Hyman Kaplan, is Hitler. That's what one of the simpletons asked me. Do you trust me, Kells? Talk to me. You have gone very quiet."

XVIII

A T THE KIBBUTZ, Aviv, the third crop of silkworms was almost ready and Hyman Kaplan was so excited he did not know what to do with himself. He was on his own as it was five in the morning and he could not sleep and had left dear Rachel in bed. She had been up with plans and plans and plans all night, so he had got into his wheelchair himself and pushed the wheels to the silkworm house, over the stone cobbled tracks of the garden underneath the mulberry trees. He could see Venus, low over the southern horizon, and clearly make out a tiny moon. He liked the expression, Transit of Venus, when the planet travelled like a beauty spot across the face of the sun. It was not very scientific, but when he thought of Venus he thought of love and when he thought of love, he thought of Rachel.

When he got to the silkworm room, the kitchen, he saw that nearly all of the crop were in the cocoon stage and one had turned into a silk moth and was flying around. There was a dreamy quality to its looping flight that somehow made him even happier. He ran his wheelchair around the big table, knocked off a bowl and then stopped. He did not want to disturb Anna, who was sleeping upstairs; she was going to help him get all the cocoons picked off the rattan mats ready for the boiling water. She did not want to see the creatures killed. She was a lovely, sensitive child and he was glad that she would soon be going to a kibbutz in Palestine, to her spiritual Israel. The new communities needed women like her. They needed people with heart, as well as courage and intelligence. She had nightmares too, but not like his.

Hyman's nights had been very long and dark, before Rachel. He liked the light.

Through a gap in the curtains sunlight illuminated the table where he was looking at the silkworm cocoons. It was such a beautiful moment that not realising what he was doing he put his feet on the floor, pushed himself up from the wheelchair and without a second thought, stood in wonder. He supported himself with the table. He was standing, holding onto the table bathed in sunlight, and then he let go.

He was standing by himself, like a man!

He tried to take a step and fell head-first onto the red-brick floor and laughed. He laughed and laughed as the silk moth that had escaped the hot water banked and dived in its swooping glides over him. He must get back into his wheelchair. He must prepare to place the cocoons in the boiling water. He never could have been so happy as he was now. And visitors were coming to see the progress at the kibbutz that very day. He was going to give them a surprise.

XIX

"PLEASE LOOK, COLONEL," said Hyman in English.

Kells' mother had always said she was able to read his face like a book. So when he arrived at the kibbutz after what Gretchen had told him about the Russians also suspecting Hyman was Adolf Hitler, he tried to maintain a neutral expression, but he knew he still showed things too much in his eyes. It was sunny and so today he wore sunglasses, even in the dark house with the walled garden where the silkworms and Hyman Kaplan were. He found the Swedish surgeon there as well. Rachel, who Kells had really come all this way to see, was elsewhere in the fields.

"Please look," said Hyman, in English. "Look, Colonel Vardy."

Kells looked around the table. He thought it must be something to do with the silkworms.

Hyman then stood slowly from his wheelchair.

The Swede was excited and took Kells' arm. "Look, colonel. This is the man you saved! He can stand. As a doctor I do not believe in miracles, but I have never found a will like exists in this man."

Kells was glad of the sunglasses. A young man had brought in coffee and handed him a cup and saucer. The room was packed with many from the kibbutz.

"Thank you," said Hyman, and then sat down again in the wheelchair.

The man before Kells looked so different. A mop of straight dark brown hair had now grown back over the slightly off-centre face modelled on that of Clark Gable. But it was his sheer charisma that made Kells take seriously what Gretchen had heard from the Russians, and what the conveniently dead young German had told him in Washington. For Chrissakes, what was he thinking?

"Good to see you have made such a great recovery, sir. And are hard at work again," said Kells.

There was a moment of silence.

"I owe everything I have now to the colonel," said Hyman, without emotion.

"Yes," said the Swedish surgeon. "He is your saviour."

They were both looking at Kells.

"You'll soon be walking around," Kells said, as Hyman was putting the silkworm cocoons into a large sieve while a pan of water began to boil on a gas cooker. There was the pungent smell of bottled gas from a faulty valve.

"And now I have to get back to work," said Hyman. It was time to extinguish life in the cocoons, a prospect he seemed to relish. There was a smile on only one side of his face, like a mask of comedy and tragedy.

"And Hyman may soon be leaving us," said the surgeon.

"Yes, I may be in the first party from here," said Hyman "But I think one of the other younger ones should take my place. They would be of much more use than a crippled old man. A dream needs women and men at the start of their adult lives."

Even before he had finished speaking, the young people about him had started to shout him down, in a very affectionate way. They obviously loved him.

"He's coming to Palestine with us, to the new Israel, aren't you, Hyman?" said one of the young people. "After everything he has been through, he is our lucky charm. With him we are invincible."

Kells dropped his coffee cup.

It smashed on the tiled floor. It was delicate china and smashed into hundreds of tiny pieces.

"Israel?"

The question was lost in the general hubbub and Kells left the silkworm house and went into the garden with the Swedish surgeon. They walked around looking at the flowers as Kells wondered what it might be like to explain to Betty how he had gotten a medal for sending Adolf Hitler, disguised as Clark Gable, to British Palestine to help create the infant state of Israel.

There was no sign of Rachel.

"I have never seen a recovery like this, colonel," said the surgeon at last. "I may offer a paper to the *Svensk Kirurgisk Förening*, the Swedish Surgical Society. I have seen young, fit nineteen-year-old paratroopers die of shock after multiple injuries and burns. He must have great faith in something."

Kells nodded, glaring down at a row of tobacco plants. "He's not got his memory back?"

The surgeon shook his head.

"I have a feeling that he may never get it back. We know so little about which parts of the brain govern memory. Hyman has been able to retrieve the intellectual framework he had before and is cultured and well-educated, extremely adaptable and calm, given what has happened to him. He happily accepts that the war is over. That's something very few people I deal with seem capable of. Have you noticed that, colonel?"

Kells paused and stared down at the light shining on his immaculate shoes.

"Yeah," he said at last. "I know what you are saying, I think. Lots

are still fighting in their heads. But the whole war thing is crazy . . .
On that last day . . . When we found Hyman. That was the only
day the war seemed real to me . . . Seeing the burning man. Hyman
. . . Am I making any sense?"

The Swedish doctor lit his pipe.

"I think all soldiers feel a sense of unreality. Many of my badly
wounded crave meaning."

Kells kicked at a stone.

"Seeing him again brings back that day."

The Swedish doctor blew out smoke. "Hyman has been having
dreams. Do you have nightmares?"

Kells shook his head.

"No, if anything the opposite. Most times I don't feel enough.
About anything. Like I am in one of Hyman's cocoons."

The Swede laughed.

"Not a good position to be in."

"No."

They were both silent for a while.

"He has been having dreams?" asked Kells.

"Oh, yes."

"About the war?"

"Yes . . . They only started recently. I think it's because he feels
completely relaxed and safe here."

Kells tried to frame his next question carefully.

"You have no more indications . . . ? About verifying his identity?
I'm sure there is no doubt, but it's just my superiors in Washington
always like to dot the i's."

The surgeon nodded. "And cross the 't's. Yes, I am familiar with
the expression. A good one. I suppose you could ask me how many
testicles he has, or if he is circumcised. I should not joke. There
are lots of people who suspect that all sorts of high-ranking Nazis
have got away. But I do not think this man is one. He has such a
sweet nature. I think he is who you told me he is. Hyman Kaplan,
a survivor of brutal policies of the Third Reich. I do not think a

man who has settled in at Aviv as he has and is as loved as he is, could be a fake, a pretender."

Kells smiled.

"Sorry, I have to ask these questions."

"I know, my boy."

Kells waited for a moment. He hated to lie to the surgeon. He still was not working for anyone.

"So what are these dreams?" he asked.

"I should not tell you."

They walked around a few of the flower beds and stopped under the mulberry trees.

"I don't want to be boring, doctor. But I am interested from an intelligence point of view. I mean, you have your job. I have mine," Kells said.

He had no job. He didn't mean what he said to the surgeon to sound like a threat.

The surgeon's brow furrowed, then he blew a cloud of smoke from his pipe and said, "Every day I am still trying to cope with the results of your former job."

Kells did not reply. He was watching a hawk high above the fields.

The doctor took another drag on his pipe.

The hawk fell on its prey.

Kells sighed. "It's so damn beautiful here."

He let the words hang on the warm breeze.

The surgeon stared at him hard, still trying to work him out. Eventually he said, "Okay, what I say is confidential. I have told Hyman they are survivor's dreams. Dreams to expiate a Holocaust survivor's guilt. He, like you, like all the young men in this war, is trying to make sense of what has happened to him. He has been dreaming that he is Adolf Hitler. Adolf Hitler giving speeches at rallies and riding in a car before cheering crowds. There, I have told you."

Kells nodded, but the breath had gone out of him. He turned

on the path towards the gate and the road that led up to the house. The Swede came hurrying after him.

"If you are going to see Rachel, I'd be diplomatic about what you discuss. They are together now. Together. Rachel and Hyman. That also has made him very happy."

On his way back up to the big house, leaving the surgeon to check on Hyman, Kells stopped several times and finally was violently sick on his newly polished shoes. He was hardly able to suck air into his lungs and his hands and lips were trembling. He wanted to scream "Fuck it", but no sound would come from his dry mouth. His mind was going too fast even to frame the words that might explain what the good-natured surgeon had told him. It was one thing for Rachel to prefer the mutilated leavings of a man from guilt. Yet after such a passionate kiss in his car, Kells had not expected this. And Rachel had no idea who Hyman was.

He wiped the vomit off his shoes with a large dock leaf.

The sun came from behind a cloud again and he looked up at the sky.

Kells wasn't usually religious, but today God had surpassed himself.

"Mother-fucking bastard!"

XX

RACHEL CLAPPED HER hands. She was excited, but not because Kells was downstairs, pacing the gravel outside the front door. She had kept him waiting after coming back from the fields.

On the old general's desk, in his study by his bedroom, on the first floor of the house overlooking the lake, Rachel had the photographs and files of the twenty or so young survivors of the camps who would be going to British Palestine in the first party. There were several strong and intelligent boys who were committed to the kibbutz ideal and to a spiritual state of Israel, but were not fanatics. Otherwise, it was merely another form of colonialism. The list included Ben, who was training to be a doctor and, of course, Paul and a few of the other boys who took a harder line, but who she hoped might be softened by the necessities and hard work of 'making the desert bloom' and the need to let the personal go, while never forgetting. She wanted to include sensitive Anna among the girls to preserve the caring, feeling side of life at Aviv. And many happy others. She wanted laughter in the desert. And then there was the question of Hyman, and if Hyman went, she must go with him. He was so passionate about his silkworms and selfless and brave when the talk came around to Israel and taking a rusting old boat from Piraeus or Marseilles to run the British blockade; she was not sure yet which it was going to be. He had started training Jacob and several of the girls in all that was needed for silkworm production and had the Americans consult libraries in London and Paris about silk cultivation in Syria in the Middle Ages. His energy was incredible.

A peacock screamed and she jumped. Throughout the war, no one had killed the peacocks for food, which surprised her.

She stood up from behind the desk and walked to the windows.

She heard and saw Kells scrunching his military shoes on the drive. She had expected him for days.

Rachel went out onto the balcony and smiled.

Kells had not seen her because the small butler was heading towards him with a glass of champagne on a silver tray. The American tried to move around the German butler but the small man would not let him. "*Bitte. Mein Freund.* I bring you champagne. You are the victor and must drink the wine. The victor must drink the wine."

Whichever way Kells stepped, the butler was always ahead of him. It was like a dance and Rachel laughed. Near to losing his temper, Kells took the glass and drank the wine and replaced it on the silver tray. He then looked up and saw Rachel on the balcony.

The butler turned, laughing. "I always serve the victor!" he was shouting. "*Ich diene immer der Sieger.* I always serve the victor!"

The day was now one of bright yellow sunshine from a child's colouring book, and Rachel went down to meet Kells in the main hall with its hunting trophies and swords and pikes and muskets. She had taken off her cardigan and was wearing a long, flowered summer dress. She had found the dress with Anna in an armoire upstairs. In another cupboard she had finally found a cello. It was a very precious instrument. But she closed the cupboard door and turned the key. The cello music, the sad sound that clawed at her, had disappeared lately. She had locked the room.

On the stone flags of the hall, Kells looked annoyed and confused. He had a way of biting his lip nervously, which he must have done as a child. He had taken off his hat. He ran his fingers through his floppy blond hair. She gave him her brightest of smiles.

"It's so lovely today. Let's walk by the lake," she said.

"I have questions."

She shrugged and smiled. "There are always questions. But they can wait on a day like this, can't they? Did you smell the roses out there? Do you like roses, Kells?"

He was about to say 'yes', but she held her finger up to his lips. His blue eyes had a sudden flash of panic. He swallowed and she watched the motion of his Adam's apple. She left her finger in place for a second. It was such an instant of frivolous intimacy and power.

She pointed upwards.

"Careful, you may wake the tiger."

A stuffed tiger head looked down.

The American was doubly neat today in his uniform and she felt that ever since he tied his tie in the mirror, he had wanted a row with her.

The tie was tied in a Windsor knot, like her father used to tie his. "Never trust a man who ties his tie with a Windsor knot," he used to say. She had never asked him why that was. She supposed that men who took such trouble with their appearance were often narcissists, and that narcissists were capable of being psychopaths. She hooked her arm into his, and he did not move away. Kells was not a psychopath. He was an innocent, left dazed and wide-eyed at a crime scene, like all the pretty soldiers. In a way she felt as responsible for him as she did for her friends at the kibbutz, but his questions were a threat.

Over by the bushes at the end of the gravel, another peacock shrieked.

She moved closer to Kells, her hip touching his, and as he moved away, she slid after him. As they walked her hip was now touching his in a synchronised movement. She had always been a good dancer before she was sent to the camps. There the girls often danced with each other after lights out, humming hit songs like Cab Calloway's 'Minnie the Moocher', or other banned music, daring to be free for a few rebel minutes, even though they knew that girls who were taken to 'dance' with junior officers in their quarters rarely came back. Yet Rachel had danced with the precise, mannered Surgeon Commandant, Manfred, in his hut, even though it must have been painful on his shattered legs. He held her to him. He had a collection of jazz records. He closed his eyes when he danced, thinking of his wife. He told Rachel so. Before he made love to her the first time. Music and dancing made him both sad and gentle. That was the way of things.

She pulled Kells even closer, and then stopped and took off her high heels. They were unsuitable for the grass around the lake. They were good shoes that the maid had found in another of the *armoires* upstairs.

Rachel hooked her arm in Kells' again and they walked past a group on army blankets, which included Anna and Paul. She caught a suppressed look of disapproval on Paul's face, but the others shouted a happy 'hello'. They were having a picnic, and talking of Palestine.

"It is not all desert."

"I never said it was."

"Where we are going is green. It has grape vines and olive groves."

"We are not colonialists. We are staying."

"So do colonialists like the British. Doesn't the devil say in Faust that we are all colonialists now? Who did the land belong to? Specifically, not the biblical shit."

"It has been purchased."

"Who says?" asked Paul.

"The rabbi." No one questioned the rabbi's word. "He says even purchasing is wrong and cursed . . ." Then someone whispered something, possibly about her and Kells, and there was sudden laughter. Rachel could not care less. All the old rules in her life, all the old embarrassments, the fetters which prevented freedom, were gone. Now she did what she wanted.

Rachel and Kells walked on to the furthest end of the lake, where there were many trees and the grass was long. She was barefoot and seemed to feel every leaf of the wet grass. The trees towered around them and dragonflies darted across the pond.

At one point they passed a motionless grey heron, beak held a few inches above the water, waiting for a fish to come close. The sunlight danced on the bird's grey feathers.

"I hope we don't get bitten to death by mosquitos," said Kells.

She laughed.

"Only the idle man has time to swallow flies," she said, and danced in front of him.

He looked at her admiringly.

"Is that a Jewish proverb? One of the rabbi's?"

She shook her red-blonde hair. They could not see the others now, or hear their voices.

"No, it's Nietzsche."

Kells seemed both impressed and confused.

"I haven't read . . ."

She raised her eyebrows, and shook her head.

"It's not. I just made it up."

Rachel led him further around the lake.

She chose her spot carefully.

There were high reeds, sedge and yellow flag irises. The greenery was so close together and powerful, she thought.

She lay down on the damp grass, rolled over and looked up at him, a half-smile on her face.

"So why did you come all this way to see me, colonel?" she asked, in a serious voice.

"I wanted to ask you . . . ? To tell you . . ." he began, but never finished the sentence.

She was up on her feet and kissing him, again and again, not allowing him time to breathe, let alone get another word out. He was trying to say something, but then he was kissing her and holding her tight, so tight, as if he was frightened she was going to fall off the world and break, like the fine china cup Hyman said Kells had dropped in the silk-cocoon-killing room.

Afterwards, Rachel lay in the dappled sunshine under the endless green of the trees listening to the laughter from the other side of the lake, sucking on a sweet stem of wild oats. She was completely naked. The inside of her thighs was wet and she was in that pleasant, still, haze of satisfaction. Her nipples were hard and her cheeks hot. Her legs were shaky. A peacock shrieked up near the house. She had pulled Kells to the ground and slipped out of her dress and bra and panties. Her hair shone and curled on the thick grass.

He still was wearing his ridiculously neat uniform.

She had felt in his hardness the power of all the earth as they were together in the howl of orgasm and touched the stars, which then exploded inside her.

It was strange to be made love to by a man so properly dressed and wearing his medal ribbons.

Perhaps that was it, the human mistake. The world was scared of standing naked.

She wanted to reach for him again but stopped herself. She wanted him more than anything; a wanting beyond the thrill of the physical, but there was something she had to do if her past and the camp and Manfred and Hyman and the resistance and her work at the kibbutz were to matter, were not all her pretty-little-rich-girl fictions, like the smashed cello and the rape about which she was no longer sure. Even the most wonderful real sex with the wrong person can be like a manufactured fiction, a distraction, an entertainment, an excuse, and she had to think also what was better for Kells. He spoke first.

"I was so . . . close to you. Like when we kissed last time in the car," he began. He sounded like a boy.

She forced herself to laugh.

"That's what we all want, Colonel Vardy. To get closer. To be real. And now you have got what you want, are you going to leave us alone? Are you please, please, please going to fuck off and leave me alone?"

PART THREE

I

KELLS COULD NOT say anything as he looked into Rachel's amused, perfect, impassive face and the ducks quacked on the lake. For him she had become a divine creature from Dante, the higher form of love he was seeking . . . Rachel lay smiling, staring into his eyes, hers so blue-green, framed by her red-gold hair.

He felt the whole world for her in that magical light that filtered through the leaves above onto her body. He opened his mouth, but his lower lip trembled as it had when he was a child. Her mystic beauty and that of the lake and the trees and the birds and the long lush green grass were in his head, shouting creation, and his words of love and shock and pain stuck in his throat, like witch's bread.

Her beauty made her words even more damning and impossible. He was such a fool. The duck calls reached a laughter-like crescendo.

Kells buttoned himself, picked up his hat, dropped it, picked it up again and strode, almost ran, off around the lake.

Shaking with anger, he got into his staff car, not bothering to search around for the dumb driver who would be smoking somewhere, and hit the Bakelite steering wheel as the big Buick failed to start the first time. In the end, the engine sparked into life with a backfire, and he left the country house as quickly as he could, head down, nearly hitting the sculptured stone gatepost.

Why the fuck had she said that to him?

Why the fuck had she done that to him?

That was a thing he had seen before. The folk who pretend to care about everyone really don't care about no-one.

He did not go to the base to pick up a flight, but turned onto

162

the small road that would take him to the highway leading east, that eventually went to Berlin. He hoped there was a jerry can of petrol in the trunk as he had no ration coupons and this would take him through the greater Russian zone. He tried to be hungry for banal practicalities to escape her teasing eyes.

Kells hit the steering wheel hard again several times and swerved towards a line of trees.

The clouds looming ahead looked as if they were made of dark slate.

There was a storm coming.

He felt himself shaking when he thought of her last words to him and the casual way she had said them. And he had not asked her one word more about Lucy, or managed to warn her about Hyman. But he knew that was phoney.

He wanted her.

The rain was splattering in large drops on the dusty windscreen.

Ahead, the storm flashed jagged forked lightning across the clouds between the black stands of trees.

He hit the wheel again. Why did she fuck him so wonderfully, if it meant nothing? What was he messing around with Rachel for if he already loved Gretchen? And where did that leave him with Betty who was buying marriage-contract soft-furnishing ball and chains? He had often marvelled in a self-congratulatory, superior way at the insanely complicated love lives of his men. How had this happened to him, and so quickly?

The windscreen wipers were not keeping up with the storm now.

The water was running down the screen in deep waves that altered the shape and the form of the forest and totally distorted the grey road, turning it into a river whose banks he was not sure of, while making the trees and the darkness behind curve and dissolve.

His nose was above the large steering wheel, almost pressed against the glass, water was coming through the door or the car floor and now and again the heavy vehicle skidded and gasoline slopped around in the jerry can he had not noticed on the passenger seat when he got in. The driver had remembered the extra fuel.

Yet Kells was still thinking of those steady blue-green eyes and that red-gold hair as she lay smiling by the water, a hand rested on a white-gold thigh.

"Are you please, please, please going to fuck off and leave me alone?"

The rhythm of her words, the cadence of her voice went back and forth with the wiper.

Please, click, Please, click, Please, click.

The words cut into Kells.

The road ahead had dissolved into failing light and the drumming of the rain against the bonnet was punctuated by the flashes of the storm. There was the sound of a huge explosion, as if the world was splitting apart, and he ducked instinctively. The sky above the pine trees was now the darkest black.

Then there was a flash that blinded him.

It was not a flash of fire but one of such searing whiteness that negated every shade in the forest and made the tall trees with their dark green pine needles vanish.

"Are you please, please, please going to fuck off and leave me alone?"

He had thought Rachel was nicer than that. He thought she had a beautiful soul. My God, he was wrong.

The lightning bolt had struck a tree to the left of the road.

It burst into flame.

He could smell burning in the air.

The red and yellow and black cut through the whiteness.

There was a smell like gunpowder. And the scent of struck flint.

He heard the crackle of fire.

Kells thought he saw a man dodge from behind a tree through the rain-smudged side of the windscreen.

Another tree was burning.

"Fuck!" he shouted.

The next thing Kells knew, the heavy black car was lifting

164

sideways, in slow motion that seemed to go on for ever, like in one of those fairground rides, when at first you go gently around and around in a little circular, spinning car, usually painted to look like a flying saucer, while the whole carousel goes around too, but then the music gets louder and both car and carousel spin faster and faster and gravity fails as the girls scream and the bolder boys snatch a chewing-gum tasting kiss, amid the fug of diesel and the smell of hot dog onions and burgers and the sound of trucks on the turnpike and the mournful bell of a nearby freight train in a dead-alive town outside St Louis, where you have taken your date for toffee apples and back-seat romance. Faster and faster and faster into the dream. The Buick hit a tree and Kells' head hit the windscreen and he was out.

When Kells came to, the car engine had stopped and there was a strong smell of gasoline and it took him several minutes to make sense of a sound. Someone was banging on the side window of the car with a coin.

He turned his head to look at the other side of the car. It was that side that had hit a tree and part of the snapped trunk had come through the door and into the car. If the car had hit on his side, had spun just one more time like a roulette wheel, he would be messy dead.

The coin-sound came again.

He did not feel fear. There was nothing there, only the muddled ache of shock. And, as always, he was one step away from himself.

There was blood dripping from his head.

The tapping was insistent and when he looked through the window he was amazed to see the smiling face of an elderly nun as the door was being prised open with a crowbar and he was pulled out by men in American uniform. They manhandled Kells and the nun back towards a grey-green bus and they only just got there when someone shouted, "hit the deck!" and the car Kells had been driving exploded.

Part of the forest was burning.

He remembered what Rachel had said about setting fire to the forest.

"Praise God," said the Sister, with a Scottish accent. "God wants you for something, young man. He has saved you from the fires of Hell. From the fires of Hell!"

A Russian officer had said something like that at the formal dinner that ended in a fist fight . . . But Kells' head was spinning. He was put gently on a stretcher and lifted into the bus. It was an ageing army vehicle and the nun was by him. They laid him down in the gap between the seats and she was there, praying all the time. There was another nun who prayed too, a pretty girl whose white hands were pressed together.

The girl had a very wide mouth and looked like a painting Kells had once seen in a museum of a Catholic martyr.

The bus proceeded slowly through the storm and the rain, leaving the fire behind.

The nuns, saying the Rosary, were lulling him to sleep.

He recognised the Hail Mary.

"*Ave Maria, gratia plena, Dominus tecum. Dicta tu in mulieribus et benedictus fructus ventris. Sancta Maria, Mater Dei, ora pro nobis peccatoribus, nunc, et in hora mortis nostrae. Amen.*" The older nun spoke in a high-pitched, lilting voice.

He smelled coffee.

He pulled his head up and looked towards the driver. The soldiers were brewing coffee. It smelt so good in that damp bus, as the rain drummed on the roof.

"Would you care for a coffee, young man?" said the senior nun. Her face was worn but her blue eyes were very kindly. The men at the front of the bus were arguing.

The younger nun fetched Kells a coffee, not just black, but made with milk, and he drank.

He had a headache and was bruised on his arms and kneecaps and, as well as the gash on his forehead that sent blood running onto his cheek, there was a small cut on his back where he had been hit by flying glass, but nothing serious. No one seemed bothered.

He did not like to think how lucky he was. A few seconds here and there and he would have burned to death in the explosion.

"So where were you going in such a hurry through a thunderstorm, young man?" said the Scottish nun.

Kells took another sip of his coffee.

"I am trying to get back to Berlin."

"I thought all you Yanks flew into Berlin? That's what the soldiers tell me?"

He nodded.

"That's what I should have done. I had a few things to work out."

The Sister gave a very knowing smile.

She had laughter lines at the corner of her eyes.

"It would not be impertinent of me to bet that this soul searching was not to do with how to organise the peace, but over a young and pretty lady?"

The other nun giggled. Kells had never heard a nun giggle.

"You are more than round about right," he said, using a phrase of his father.

"That's what they say in America, is it?" said the nun.

"That's what my dad says. He's full of old ways of saying things. We are from St Louis originally, but he is fascinated with the Rockies and the old west. He sent me to a boarding school way up in the Sierras called Los Alamos. There were forests up there . . ." Kells' head felt light and he was conscious he was beginning to babble but could not stop himself.

The soldiers from the front of the bus came and stood over him. One was smoking a cigarette even though it clearly said there should be no smoking on the bus. Kells was trying to focus, but the bang on the head had made him drowsy. He looked closely at the men and then realised what it was that was different. They had not shaved. They had regular army uniforms on, the badges of the Big Red One infantry division, but they had not shaved and did not seem to have an officer.

The older nun spoke: "Your father sounds a fine man. My name is Sister Annunciata and this novice is called Freda. So this girl who has taken your fancy is back there somewhere? The other side of the forest?"

Kells nodded. His head was really heavy now.

"She is at an old country house which has been turned into a kibbutz called Aviv, which means springtime in Hebrew."

Sister Annunciata sniffed.

"What is a kibbutz?"

Kells blinked. He thought a nun would know.

"It is a Jewish ideal community. A farming community. They are going back to British Palestine to set similar communities up and establish a homeland of such gatherings, a new Israel. After what happened in the camps. They are really idealistic young people, and this girl is one of them."

There was a long silence.

Then Sister Annunciata spoke in a low voice.

"Sweet Jesus. It would have been so much better for the world and all concerned if this girl and the rest of her vermin had all been put to sleep. My mother says the Irish and the Jews cause all the fucking trouble in the world. Ha-ha!"

They were the last words Kells heard before he passed out.

Kells woke with the rain pattering down on him in a small depression filled with pinecones and needles at the side of the road. He was conscious of the bus speeding away along the long straight road through the forest, but in the background was the sound of a siren. A two-note German police siren. The green and white police car with the siren and flashing light passed before he managed to lift himself up and fall back again into the puddle.

The siren sounded in every cell of his brain.

The water felt very cold.

He was naked. He was really naked.

They had left him almost nothing. His clothes were gone. His

168

father's wrist watch. His school ring. All his clothes and his wallet and his military ID. It was all gone. The small Walther automatic pistol that he had in his pocket of his jacket was gone too. Much fucking use it had been.

All they had left was his life and his ridiculous military hat, with its gold eagle holding an olive branch in one claw and thirteen arrows in the other, which lay, squashed by a boot, on the ground in front of him.

There was straw scattered all over the place too. He was not sure of the meaning of that.

By a tree there was blood on the straw and slowly, he got to his feet. There was an awful lot of blood, as if an animal had been butchered.

There was nothing for it but to start down the road and hope he ran into someone.

He picked up the hat and debated whether to put it on. In the end he did. He did not look any more ridiculous than completely naked and at least his head was warmer. In the end he was stepping out almost confidently, marching along, trying to whistle, and failing. There was no other traffic on the lonely road.

It took until nightfall, shivering, to reach a small hamlet where there was an inn. The door was locked and he banged on it and at first a small man who spoke only German would not let him in, even in his army hat, especially in his army hat. A woman he took to be the man's wife rushed out of the side of the house and ran off down the street and then came back with a very fat man.

"Why are you naked in our village?" asked the very fat man in English, but not in an unfriendly way.

Kells tried a smile. He was not going to argue the point because of the hat. It was summer, but he was freezing because of the rain and his nakedness.

"I was robbed," he said. Then in German, "*Räuber . . . ?*"

There was a furious explosion of conversation between the innkeeper and his wife and the very fat man. More slanty, rickety-boned, mediaeval people came out of the slanty, mediaeval hovels and began to join in and shout. A blanket was put around his shoulders.

The very fat man then grasped him by both arms.

"The gang on the road are not robbers. They put oil on the road and wait for cars to crash. They make butcher with their damaged victims and sell the meat in roadside markets. The gang is American. American cannibals. Like your army that eats our country. Why did they not eat you?"

It took Kells four days to get back to Berlin, courtesy of his hat, which the local policemen were impressed with and took him, clothed in overalls, to a small American base nearby, who were not. They stared at the hat a lot and then a major asked, "Who won the World Series last year, in 1944?"

There was a silence, and he knew if he got the answer wrong he would be arrested and things would get even more covered in shit.

"Cardinals appear when angels are near," he said, repeating a phrase of his father's, because if the red bird appears in your garden it is the spirit of a departed loved one. Kells wasn't big on baseball, but being originally from St Louis, he knew it was the Cardinals.

There was another silence.

"Shit, colonel, you are righteous American," said the infantry major and other officers then welcomed him as a brother and fed him and gave him a new uniform, money and a driver who took him to another base, who flew him in an empty Dakota to Tegal in Berlin. He was so glad to see the house on Schiller Strasse and the first thing he did was go into his study and pour himself a tumbler full of Scotch and kiss the Dresden figures one by one. The early morning was all so beautiful, and he sat outside in the garden and then went back in and refilled his glass. Every time he thought about waking naked on the road, he felt both embarrassment and breathless horror. He had no intention of reporting the matter. He imagined the cable:

NEARLY EATEN BY AMERICAN HIGHWAY CANNI-BALS PLEASE ADVISE STOP – MESSAGE ENDS

Joe could find him duplicate documents. He saw Gretchen's scarf on one of the chairs and was grateful she had not gone back to the ruins.

The flash of the storm was there when he shut his eyes.

He lit a cigarette and took another gulp of whisky.

There was a letter on the desk stamped State Department and counter-stamped CIA and signed "Allen Welsh Dulles".

It simply said: "Please stand down all operations until further notice. The city has been split more vigorously into the various national zones and this is a sensitive time that may not benefit from all but essential intelligence operations. This order is in particular to include operational 'loose ends' such as the so-called Operation Lucy."

II

HYMAN KAPLAN COULD not stop gazing at the pure white cocoons that were completely dry and ready to have the silk carded from them. He reached over and touched one with a feeling of excitement. With the nails of his thumb and forefinger, he began to pick at a strand of silk. To him this was such a wonder he almost felt like crying out as he sat by the table in the rearing room, where all around him silkworms were munching away greedily at the leaves on the rattan mats. He stretched the fibre of pure silk out to a metre. In the strong light on the desk, he could see the grub inside, killed by the boiling water. But what a death, to be transformed into something useful and more or less eternal! He wanted to show Rachel again; she had already seen the improving procedure many times, but she was up at the house with meeting after meeting, obeying his advice to the letter. He could not understand how it was that she loved him so completely and unconditionally. They were making love every day, especially in the morning when the sun came in the window. They were making love, even though he could feel the pieces of metal, like insects, like the Egyptian scarab beetle that is said to burrow into human flesh, little sharp-sided pieces of shrapnel, moving inside him as if alive, and there was blood in the toilet when they cut into his gut or his kidneys. There was nothing to be done. If he had to choose between making love to her on those crisp, cold sheets; her blonde ringlets spread all over the pillow like gold on pain of death, then bring on death! He had been there before and death did not impress him. Earlier he had walked with Rachel in the garden and they had looked up into the endless dark greens of the mulberry trees, their branches stained red with the fruit, as if by blood. He must stop such comparisons.

He was glad Rachel had sent the American away. There was a quality in the man's innocent stare that Hyman feared. He sighed. He must be grateful for what he had. Not merely grateful but ecstatic. He wished he were a poet and able to write how he felt about her, to shower her with verses. All he had for sure was what was in front of him, the silk. And there were rumblings of the past. He had had the strange dreams again of roaring crowds throwing flowers as he drove through a city in an open-topped car. These were mixed with dreams of being in a hole while there were explosions outside and his mouth and his nostrils and his ears were filled with dirt and the detonations seemed to explode within him. "My love, I am weeping blood," he cried out. But he never remembered being shelled or bombed, or his 'love', or riding through a city, or bleeding from the eyes. These most probably were a collage of newsreels and things he had read that intruded into his consciousness when he had tired himself out with the silkworms. Or perhaps even guilt at surviving, like the good rabbi said. Hyman tried to put these insurgent thoughts out of his mind. Perhaps in life there is only love and hard work to distract one from these devil thoughts and from pain. He feared the past that might force itself through the thin skin of so-called reality. He feared the magma underneath and the sick headaches he had having dreams he could not remember. He fingered the virginal cocoons. The ends of his fingers had not grown back and the nerves were still missing or damaged. He filled his mind with those pure white cocoons as he did with the smooth and tender flesh of Rachel, who put posies on his pillow, buttercups and cornflowers and hare bells, to scare away the bad fairies, she said. German fairy tales always seemed to have bad fairies.

He tried to think of nothing else but the purity of these strange white forms that would be now spun into perfect silk.

It made him smile.

Hyman Kaplan, who had no past, no family, no house or wealth, was the happiest man in the world. He was spinning his own future. He laughed. He felt a piece of the metal inside him move, somewhere near his spine. A sacred scarab was on the move, ferrying him closer to the afterlife.

He sighed.

There was only the now and a future accelerating backwards towards him, like a boat borne back by the current. He shrugged.

"*Ich liebe Sie alle*," he said to himself. I love you all.

III

A MAID CAME running out across the gravel drive. Rachel had heard a telephone bell lazily ringing up in the great house.

"It is the colonel, the American colonel, it is the third time he has rung. What shall I say?"

Rachel shook her head.

"Tell him I'm busy with a play. Tell him I am Iphigenia ready to sacrifice." The maid looked puzzled, but Rachel knew that the educated American colonel would understand. Sbe leant against one of the long tables that had been placed on the gravel overlooking the lake, smoking an American cigarette in an ivory holder. She wore a light green haute-couture dress with huge red flowers

173

and had painted her nails crimson. On her feet were high-heeled sandals, more treasure looted from the house. The delegation from Palestine were coming again today. She wanted to look her best for them. The American colonel was coming, after phoning and phoning, even though she had told him not to, that he was wasting his time.

The day was baking hot and the pollen from the lime trees made her sneeze as a large dragonfly whirred towards the lake in a blue-green iridescent progress. Two girls ran past her, girls who had been painfully thin only months before had filled out from the good food and fresh air and freedom and were laughing as if nothing had happened, though there was still a wonder in their eyes, as when first they saw and distrusted the old house and its deer park.

"A challenging play for those setting up an ideal community," said the rabbi, who had come up behind her. "Didn't being a priestess of Artemis in Tauris mean that Iphigenia's task was to sacrifice all male outsiders? In fact, all outsiders, after escaping the fate herself?"

Another girl, Laura, laughed. "It has a message, written in blood. It is about the equality of women and not to trust men." They all knew that Rachel had sent the American away and were glad for Hyman.

Under the trees at the far side of the lake, a choir sang. It was not a Hebrew song, but Bach's 'Leben Jesu', which floated across the water and the shouts of the swimmers. Around the lake, girls and boys in make-believe Greek dress, the Chorus from the play, stretched strands of silk from Hyman's cocoons. Hyman was down there too, laughing and smiling with them as he walked slowly with his stick.

All the young people loved him so.

She heard the sound of cymbals behind her and the butler came out, followed by Paul and a few others. The butler was extravagantly dressed in a comic opera German uniform from before the First World War, with an old helmet painted gold that ended in a little spear. There was a cheer when people saw him. Paul was attempting to play an old trumpet. Rachel thought she detected a change in

Paul, who appeared to have grown close to the butler; a man who, for all his showmanship, often shut himself in his room.

The sun was high and her thin body cast no shadow.

The interrogators at the camp had taken her shadow. Taken her soul.

Rachel still did not feel part of the feast or worthy of the kibbutz or the young lions who lived here. That's what the propaganda leaflets from Palestine called the young survivors: the young lions. She watched two girls making a daisy chain and putting it on a boy's head.

Beyond them the butler was winding the gramophone and unmistakable chords rang out across the picnic tables and the lake. She stood up. The shouts and the laughter died on the wind.

It was the "Old Pilgrim's Chorus," from the opera *Tannhäuser*, by Richard Wagner, the composer and antisemite worshiped by Hitler. Her father had said it was one of God's jokes to give such talent to such a shrivelled soul. Rachel loved Wagner.

"No!" shouted someone.

The small butler had already realised his mistake and, in trying to take the record off, knocked the stylus on until it landed in the middle of the choral climax. The intertwined voices were singing about heavenly Grace. *Gnäde*. Rachel still dreamed in German. Or rather, the people and creatures in her searingly romantic dreams spoke German.

A car had drawn up on the gravel beside Rachel, followed by another.

The delegation from Palestine got out of one, two young thin men and one swarthy and dark and much older. They carried brief cases. They looked at Rachel, horrified.

One of the younger ones said, "Why are you playing Nazi music?"

"No music is forbidden," said Rachel, as the butler took the record off and put on an ineffectual French composer. The butler looked very upset. At the same moment, Kells got out of a chauffeur-driven car behind the one of the Palestinian *Haganah* delegation.

"We are putting on a play for you. Then there will be a picnic," said Rachel. She could see the three newcomers thought this was wrong.

"I cannot believe you were playing Wagner," said the swarthy man. "We have come here to talk business. Our situation is critical and we come here and everyone is dressed like Romans and you are playing the music of a Jew hater."

Rachel said nothing. Music had been so important to her. But she no longer heard the rasping note of the cello that connected her to the past.

No art should be forbidden, and forbidding was a step along the road to banning and control.

When she looked up, she noticed that Kells had brought her an enormous bouquet of flowers. They were long-stemmed white roses. He knew their significance for the resistance. He started towards her. Luckily, the rabbi arrived first.

"If something is beautiful, should we throw it away because of who made it?" he said, beaming. "I have a very nice magnifying shaving razor that used to belong to the Nazi who owned this house. It is a thing of wonder I thank God for every morning. It helps me not cut my throat."

One of the young men stepped forward.

"And who are you? I had expected more respect for those who have been in the camps."

"Oh, I am only the rum-soaked rabbi. I'm not much use. Don't you remember from our first happy meeting?"

The rabbi assumed his sweet smile, turning his eyes upwards, first on one side and then the other. He always did this when one of the young people said something ridiculous.

"The rabbi was here throughout the war, fighting the Nazis," said Rachel.

"We all have enemies to fight," said the second tall young man, whose hand she noticed had been badly burned.

The first young man pushed him out of the way. He had a

purple-red scar on his face. All three were dressed in trench coats and hats, even on such a sweltering day, but were not sweating. All of them were thin, the two younger ones dangerously so, and very brown. The khaki coats were, ironically, British-designed and made. Her father had bought one and then thrown it out.

The man with the scar then said to Rachel, "Perhaps you will explain why you are dressed as a German whore? Perhaps you are not Jewish?"

"And the way you are dressed?" asked the rabbi, innocently.

To Rachel they looked like cabaret Gestapo.

She was angry. She was going to put her cigarette out on the man's purple red scar when Kells stepped in front of her. He was wearing a new and immaculate chocolate uniform with all his medal ribbons, and holding the roses.

"Sure hope I'm not interrupting. Golly-gee-wow! Rachel! This all looks marvellous. So do you, by God. Why don't you introduce me to your new friends? Are they in the play, too?"

The flowers seemed to take the anger from what was getting ugly. She turned to the men from Palestine.

"Please could you all come with us to watch our play? And then we will eat," said Rachel, who took Kells' hand. "Then I will take you on a tour of the community and explain what we do, and then you can give our young people your talk."

The rabbi beckoned the three men to go with him down to the lake where the theatre had been erected, and Kells was left by the car with Rachel, who was still trembling. She took the flowers from him and hugged them to her.

He took back her hand.

"Please do not say anything," she said, and he didn't."I am very sorry about what happened to you. In the forest. The rabbi told me. Do you want me to come to Berlin for more questions about my name on your Lucy list?"

He laughed.

"Not officially."

"What do you mean?" She was staring at him.

"They say I have nothing to do. I have been stood down and have probably got the sack or worse."

"But you are wearing the uniform?"

Kells shrugged. He had wanted to look like someone who knew what he was doing. He wanted to warn her about Hyman. He wanted to warn her properly about Lucy, but he did not know how . . . He just wanted to see her.

"They are still paying me, but I'm off Lucy, or anything else. I really don't know."

She moved up close to him:

"Thank you for the roses," she said, and kissed him gently on the lips.

He tried to take her in his arms, but she slipped away and he followed her.

"I . . ." he began.

She put her fingers to the lips she had just kissed and smiled.

"I know," she said. "But not now."

The jolly, perspiring mayor had come from the nearest village and there were several older men from the British and American administrations. Rachel walked down with Kells to a natural amphitheatre at the other side of the lake where the play was about to start. They sat down behind the front row, which included the three men from Palestine. She stared at their scrawny, red-brown chicken necks, and as the play progressed, those backs and necks had that stiffness of the truly, officially bored.

After the play, the visitors stood up and clapped politely. The play perhaps spoke too directly to the present. The older of the men who had come from Palestine, losing patience, went up onto the stage and addressed the crowd.

"I speak to you in English, which I know you have been learning with your Hebrew, because I will not speak to you in German. I only speak the language of small, colonial murderers. You have created a paradise here. We can create a paradise too in our new Israel. But the time has come to put aside all these games you have here. We are at war. I am sorry for all your histories and the things you have been subject to, but I will not say that again.

"Instead, I will quote the words of Richard Heydrich, the architect of the Final Solution at the Wannasee Conference, January 20, 1942: 'Under proper guidance, in the course of the final solution, the Jews are to be allocated for appropriate labour in the East. Able-bodied Jews, separated according to sex, will be taken in large work columns to these areas for work on roads, in the course of which action doubtless a large portion will be eliminated by natural causes. The possible final remnant will, since it will undoubtedly consist of the most resistant portion, have to be treated accordingly, because it is the product of natural selection and would, if released, act as the seed of a new Jewish revival.' You, the survivors, are those 'most resistant people.' You have been naturally selected. You are the new seed of Abraham.

"We are from the future. Your future. We are all members of the *Palmach*, the *Haganah* strike force. We are soldiers in a war and you will become soldiers too when you go to your kibbutz. You will not have time for Greek drama or silkworms. And I counsel you to be very careful of smiling Americans or British people bearing gifts, or providing food and houses. They only want to take you out of our fight. Underneath they hate you.

"I am angry, I make no apology for my anger. I do not want to see any more of my relatives have to walk meekly into the gas chambers and die screaming. Never again!

"We are still under attack, never forget that . . . The Nazis have been defeated, but there are Nazis everywhere. There can be pretenders hiding among you. I am not talking now of the British and their American masters. We unmasked an impostor at a kibbutz only the other day. Look carefully at the person next to you. Did you see them in the camps? When you get to Palestine we will sift the wheat from the chaff. That is why we are only allowing the young and strong who have not been involved in the resistance, and therefore open to compromise and treachery, to come to our new homeland. To become Judah's young lions. You will become Judah's young lions!"

There was a cheer, but Rachel was not clapping. It was always those who had never been in a war that so romanticised bloodshed. She realised, too, they were telling her she could not go to her Promised Land. She was devastated. Her dreams had been taken away by these sad little men. It changed everything.

Hyman was not present. He had stayed with his fat new silkworms munching at the trays of mulberry leaves. Amid the applause and clapping there was a more frenzied shouting and cheering, not from all of the young people, but enough of them, and Kells put out his hand to Rachel, who held it very tight.

IV

"I LOVE YOU Kells, I hate you, Kells . . ."

Gretchen was sitting in Kells' garden in Berlin, a growing scream inside her, as she pulled petals from a daisy-like flower.

She knew Kells had gone to see the girl called Rachel again. Gretchen remembered a slim nurse with red-gold hair at the press conference, and she was very beautiful. Too beautiful. She looked like a picture Kells had of Saint Lucy. It was stupid, stupid to feel jealous after all Gretchen had been through. But she loved Kells and had not said that to any man. No man. Not ever. That she loved him. The sea would come up and swallow all of the land before she said that to another man. The sea. All the water and whales and shells and mermaids would cover Berlin.

She imagined the capital letter 'I' on the paper that was in front of her on the metal table in the garden. I am going to write to him, she thought. I am going to write in English.

The 'I' had a powerful influence on her, like a narcotic, like the *kif* cigarettes smoked by the Moroccans who had been packed into a basement in the ruined street where she had lived. She started to write.

My Darling Kells,

I am going to tell you Kells, who I am. I am sick of pretending to be a person I am not and have never been. You think I am German. I think I am German. But I will tell you the real story. I have to. You know too that we both have to get out of here. What is Berlin to anyone? It is not worth another war. For a pile of rubble? For a flat with a floor that you can fall through? I liked falling through the floor with you Kells. The earth fell and the sky disappeared and we were still there naked and together.

I never used to think of myself as a person like this, as a woman who truly wants a man, who deserves love.

When I was working in the Foreign Ministry, I thought of myself as Deutsch, Deutsch, Deutsch. That I had to deceive to be loved. I had to act like that because my boss was protecting me. Sleeping with me, eventually, and then going back to his wife, but still protecting me, he said. My strict Christian upbringing by my mother, we were Catholic Christians, telling me lovely stories of saints and angels, was turned upside down in the shelters. My new faith was to protect my identity and stay alive, helped by the morphine needle and the Benediction of sleeping with strangers who could help me.

The lies overtook me and ate into me like fungus and lichen in a forest. Like lichen into a rock.

My boss in the Foreign Ministry knew who my father was and that he wasn't German. My papa was a ringmaster of a small circus that travelled from Cairo to Antakya and back each winter. He could juggle baby goats, three baby goats, black and white, and ride on a horse hanging upside down and swing on a trapeze and go into a cage with lions, though he was polite and a little scared of my mother, who was a tight-rope walker.

Never cross a tight-rope walker.

She kept my father from being too trusting and slack and drinking raki. She set his broken bones after accidents in the ring. She told fortunes and sometimes heard voices when she danced. One day she was told the future by her voices and would not come to Germany, where my father had been offered a partnership with a friend who had a bigger circus. She would not go, even though she loved him more than life. Her mind was set. He begged her, but she said she could not ignore what is written and what the voices told her, which was of sorrows and war. She stayed in Turkey to look after her brother's sons and wanted me to stay too. But I could not leave my father on his own. He often was in trouble. My father was a proud man and if anyone told him to go back where he came from he would look up at the sky and smile:

'The sky is mine.'

They would tell him that wasn't true and he would bend down and kiss the earth.

'The earth is mine. All mine,' he would say. 'It is everyone else's too, every living thing. And before you ask me, the sea is mine, and fire is mine also.' What he said made people annoyed, but he just smiled, and they called him a filthy gypsy, even though he bathed twice a day. My father would then smile even more, and magically, in his left hand there was his knife.

'This knife is mine too, come closer and I will show you it is also yours. I will show you where all things come from.'

Very few people took up his kindly offer, but one day two men ambushed him in a friendly way, exchanging jokes, suggesting a drink, before he could say the sky was his, or pull his knife from inside his purple waistcoat with heavy silver buttons, and he was taken to the police station, arm in arm, laughing, by the Gestapo, and never came back.

*They tried very hard to kill all the gypsies in Germany.
They would have killed me.*

*A policeman I knew, who I complained to about the arrest,
a senior policeman, then took me back to his own family, not
to abuse me, but to protect me. He was a romantic. It is as
common in the Germans as the 'flu or the clap and was one
reason why they were easy meat for the Nazis. The Nazis
knew all the children's fairy stories to scare them, and what
ordinary Germans wanted: epic hatreds, eternal love and
a little bread. The senior policeman, had been an ordinary
policeman but was transferred to the Gestapo and claimed
he had never interfered in ordinary Germans' lives. He lied
that I was his daughter by his first marriage. His second wife
was a simple soul who did not object. He never tried to touch
or kiss me at that time. When the war came she went to the
country and he was promoted very fast. I worked for him, filing
papers, working for the people who took away my father, and
when he moved to the front, he got me a job with a man in
the Foreign Ministry, a major, who said I would only be safe
if I slept with him, otherwise I may be denounced. And like
on the trapeze in the circus, I was a star performer. I had an
affair with him, but he was sent to the front. Before he left he
introduced me to an older man in transportation. I was sent
to work for this railway man. He found me a scruffy room
where I had sex with him and drank warm Apfel Schnapps.
It tastes pure as snow when cold, but warm you can taste all
the impurities. I hated his little, sweaty hands and fat body
and the smell of his prick. I hated the pig-iron taste of his
semen on my tongue that made me gag and swallow. I learned
about his trains in a deep anger and sent them the wrong
way. Trains that contained the arrested, the condemned, the
doomed. Jews, mostly. But on one I re-routed, hoping to help
the people escape, the train carriages were shunted into a
siding while the train was requisitioned for more vital work*

and many inside died of hunger and thirst and the cold. When the carriages were opened the rest were shot next to the railway line because they were unfit for work. That was the kindest thing, my boss said. I thought I would be shot when they worked out what I had done. Instead, many in the office congratulated me, and said if everyone acted like that there would be no need for camps. I was trusted because I was said to be the daughter of a Gestapo man and knew people in the Foreign Ministry. They took me to a bar to celebrate. That was when a tall, slim, soft-spoken German intelligence man, Walter, came into my life. He was already in the bar. He saw through me, knew what I had done. He seemed impressed I had the courage to survive the air raids and to send the trains the wrong way. I thought it was a trick to calm me. I knew I was going to die. I was put into a nice apartment and drank champagne with the intelligence man and I was even more convinced I was going to die when he kissed me. Afterwards, I would be handed over to the Gestapo, who would torture me and rape me until, tired of their sport, they would drown me in a toilet. I kissed the intelligence man back with a passion. He was good looking, a colonel too, working for General Gersdorff, but I already told you that, and Walter smelt nice, of lavender cologne, and his semen tasted salty like the sea. I was taken to restaurants and offices which were heated and started to learn the task of gathering information. Like a blinkered horse, I only thought of the road immediately ahead, fearing the whip and the slaughter man. I started to use the name Gretchen, the intelligence man's name for me, a joke about the Gretchen in Goethe's Faust, and my papers were changed to show I was German, and then changed again and again. I prided myself on being in control, on being like my mother, a strong woman, who took no notice of men. But it was no good. The intelligence man called Walter saved me, and I went to work for him under the kind General von

*Gersdorff. It was from Walter I learned about Lucy. He was
working for Lucy, as was the general. I was working for them.
I still I see a few of the people I knew and Walter knew in
Berlin, around corners, in cafes, hiding in the rubble like rats,
or ghosts, pretending to be foreigners, even pretending to be
Jewish and from the camps. I hear a step and turn and one
of them is there. A few managed to join the new police in the
chaos and would turn me in. Or worse if ordered. My papers
were lost in a raid, like Walter.*

That is the bad and the good and the bad of me.

I only have you, Kells. All I have is you. I love you.

*The sky is mine and tonight it is a warm pink. A bright
gold, warm pink.*

All my Love, Gretchen

V

THE FIRST LONG, lingering scream did not quite wake
Rachel.

It was followed by another and another. It was not a shrill scream
of fear or alarm, but a deeper more visceral sound of complete
hopelessness that comes from inside the human body, below the
nerves and sinews, veins and skin, from a cellular level. It was a
sound Rachel recognised.

Was it her imagination? Was she hearing the past. True or false?
Then she heard the sound of birds. Not the gentle dawn chorus.
A lot of birds were in the garden, crying out.

Rachel stared up at the cracks in the ceiling of the gatehouse in
the walled garden of the silkworm house. That's how she still thought
of it, in German, as the silkworm house, *Das Seidenraupenhaus.*
Yet more and more, she was speaking in English. They all had tried
to learn Hebrew, but it was slow. Hyman was asleep on his back,
as always, and the covers were pulled off her. He was not snoring

exactly, but there was a guttural noise in his throat. She reached out her hand. His body was warm. She had woken with a start. She had been in that half-dream state before waking, back again in those last days when she had taken the pistol of the surgeon commandant, Manfred, and had gone to the officers' quarters, as they called the place. Hyman had told her there was an image he wanted to tell her about in his dreams and she said she had an important matter to confide, also. He was such a fine man he was never going to talk to her again, not ever, if she told him. Tears welled up in her eyes. She wished it was all a dream. All her fiction. She knew many after the camps had decided that certain memories were like the morning mist, soon to disappear, imagined will-o'-the-wisps that served no purpose. She envied them.

Rachel wondered about what the American Kells would think if she told him. He suspected her, knew she had been involved in the resistance, and Lucy, but what if she told him everything of that last day? A part of her would like to look into his innocent blue eyes as she did so . . .

The scream came again and she began to get dressed, as quickly as she could. She stubbed her toe.

"Fuck." The Americans used the word with everything.

Another scream came from the garden outside.

She reached for the old leather boots she used for gardening and pulled them on. She put on her night dress and a sweater and went outside. There was a smell of earth and late roses.

The sky was beginning to get light and there was an August moon and she could still see the stars. The moon gave a glow to the lighter colours. To the corn in the fields. It was a magical light. There was no wind, but she heard banging from inside the silkworm house and upstairs a light was on, and someone was opening all the front windows and a girl in a night dress was throwing the mats of silkworms into the bushes. A few of the pupae had become silver-grey moths and tried an unsuccessful flight, swooping across the garden.

The birds were fighting over the worms. Gorging themselves and dancing with delight. In particular the shiny black crows.

"Murderers!" The shout was shrill and the crows cackled and rearranged themselves amongst their wriggling feast.

A girl ran out into the still moonlit dawn. It was Anna. She was in a white nightdress, barefoot.

She saw Rachel and paused. She began to move her lips, but the words stayed silent and she sprinted out of the gate and straight into the unharvested cornfield, tearing off her dress. Her naked body was pale and luminous against the corn. Rachel followed her and Anna was shouting:

"They shall not be killed. The white . . . The white . . . . Don't you realise the world is turning to white. The white! Is coming. It is exploding. I have seen a white fire. I have seen the white. We are all turning to white! It is a flash that you can see with your eyes closed."

Rachel ran after her.

Anna sat down in the middle of the pink-yellow corn in the dawn light, tears streaming down her face. She grabbed onto Rachel.

"We cannot kill them. We cannot kill the silkworms. They are like us, munch, munch. We are killing ourselves. Munch, munch. We are boiling ourselves alive. We are gassing ourselves! Don't you see what we are doing? What we who know so much are doing? To ourselves?"

Rachel slapped Anna in the face and she rocked backwards and forwards on her heels for a moment and then began again.

"I have seen the white. I have seen the future for all of us. It's coming. Do not worry, it is coming. You cannot hear me. I'm not talking to you. That's the problem. No one talks to anyone else. We say things, but we do not communicate. Because we do not want to."

Anna then began to cry like a little girl and Rachel hugged her. She hugged her tight and felt that she knew exactly what the girl meant. She was going to tell Hyman the truth about herself. I'm going to tell them what I did, she thought, in that cornfield, with the sun coming up, hugging Anna.

Anna spoke first, her words breathless.

"I know why I saw this vision. I did not help my friend. When they came for her, to take her to the other camp, I sat in the corner. Sat in the corner like a child and said nothing. She went with them, all the time looking at me. Looking at the other women in the room. But they were not her friends. I sat in the corner with my knees up, on the black floor among the cinder dust by the stove, shivering. I could not look at her. I could not look away from her. They said they were coming to take those who had been troublesome to the other camp. Everyone knew what that meant. It meant one thing and it was in her eyes. I remember thinking that the two men were so big and that their boots were so big and black. All it took for me was to cross a few yards and try to drag her away and they would have taken me too, and I would not be here now having these dreams and seeing the future. I have seen the future and it is gone in a white flash that makes your eyes run away in the gutter. Like raw eggs. A flash in which we will see ourselves one last time for the nothing that we are. I should have helped her. I should have helped Ruth, my friend. Instead, I sat there among the cinders. I deserve all that is coming."

She said all this quickly and Rachel listened as the crows gathered around them.

One hopped near and Rachel started and cried out. Anna's feet were bloody from the sharp corn stubble.

Rachel raised her hand and the bird went away.

"That's not being guilty, lovely Anna. That's being human."

"Her eyes were so fearful."

"Like yours are now. This is what the people who tortured you want. To make you feel responsible. To make you take their guilt. That's what they want."

She kissed Anna on the cheek.

"I have done much more terrible things than you."

Anna shook her head.

She sobbed and trembled and eventually got control of herself. A black crow hopped near in the sharp corn storks.

Rachel was about to say she slept with the surgeon commandant Manfred because that meant a job in the operating theatre. It helped her end the lives of those being tortured and who might betray secrets and the resistance itself . . . A swift pressure here, a knick with a scalpel, an injection of air, when left alone to clean up. She was going to tell Anna this, and then she realised it was too symmetrical and shorn of human fear and passion.

Or should she tell the story of what she did with the surgeon commandant's pistol, the Luger he had left behind? Was that only a story? She could see the heavy black pistol. Still feel its weight. She had checked it was fully loaded, the resistance had shown her how to use the weapon, how the action arch-backed on the top of the pistol and had to be slapped down. Rachel had walked into the officers' quarters and found two men still there, on one of the big horsehair settees with their uniform trousers down, fucking two naked nurses who worked with her. She knew the girls had no choice, but that was not the issue. One of the men had turned and grinned and said: "Another little lamb comes! The surgeon's whore!" in German. He and the second, fatter, more worried man, had been in charge of the selection detail for the other, final camp. They did not stop, their white bottoms pumping furiously. They were having their last bit of fun before fleeing. They probably had a vehicle hidden somewhere. She held the pistol behind her back.

She smiled.

They both then stopped and were looking at her.

They smiled.

She approached the settee and shot them both at close range in the head.

Never say a word, the resistance had taught her.

The two men slumped over the girls, bleeding from the wounds to their foreheads. The girls screamed and tried to push the dead soldiers off them. The nurses were only young, perhaps not eighteen. They had arrived the week before and one was called Martha and the other Dorta. They were smiling too now at Rachel, relieved. She could not explain to them. It was what they may have overheard from a patient, who later died, that was important, fatally important for them. She did not know the details herself. The less said, the less to reveal. That's what she had been told many times. She moved in closer still and shot Dorta in the head and Martha got free and hid under the billiard table on all fours, crying like an infant. All the time she was wailing and asking "Why?" and then collapsed into a foetal position, her thumb in her mouth, and Rachel gently put the pistol to the girl's head and pulled the trigger. There was a splintering of bone, splashes of blood and brain and the finality of the Luger's cordite fumes mixed with that of Martha's cheap perfume, given to her by one of the dead officers. Rachel had then poured a bottle of cognac over the settee and set it alight before going outside and trying to get as many girls as she could onto the road, from the camp to safety and freedom, weeping as she went.

Had that happened? In another version in her dreams the girls were already dead and the officers departed, and she was relieved that no one was able to point the finger at her for being Manfred's lover. She had loved him. And she was too horrified and untrained to do intentional harm in the operating theatre. Perhaps she clung to her mad fantasies to explain times that were beyond explanation.

"Everyone looks up to you," said Anna.

I cannot tell her I am a fraud. I cannot tell ~~what is~~ the truth, thought Rachel.

Had she done terrible things to protect her resistance group, and probably Lucy? Had she blindly obeyed the orders that came to her for, if not, it was all absurd and for nothing? While no one noticed anything odd about her, even Manfred?

The ghost of the killing remained inside her, sucking a thumb.

One of the crows bounced near her in the corn, pretending courage.

Rachel saw recognition in the black bird's blue eye.

VI

"WAKE UP, DARLING. Wake up, you are having a dream . . ."

Gretchen was in the large, German bed beside Kells, shaking him. In his dream it all made sense. He understood.

"You were talking about codes, and numbers and nonsense and Alice in Wonderland . . ."

He was grateful he had not been talking about Rachel or Betty or Lucy, but now he was awake and Gretchen was kissing him and the answer to the puzzle was gone. He had read her letter, fearing she was breaking off with him, perhaps leaving Berlin with another, then he was thunderstruck by her life and times, of how someone so German and sophisticated was really a circus gypsy acting the part, of collaboration and resistance, and her words moved him to tears. He had read the letter several times. He was sure her words were honest.

"I'll make you a cup of coffee . . ."

Gretchen got up and started to get dressed to go out and looked so lovely with all that hair and those great eyes that he had to have her, and she was just about half-dressed when he had to have her again. She giggled and said he had a problem, before they were completely naked once more, arms and legs beating furiously, but yet so intimately, against each other, like the silk moths, like the escaped silk moths he had witnessed at the kibbutz, flapping their wings against the window glass.

And then they were still, exhausted, folded into each other.

He certainly did have a problem. He was in love with two women.

In Berlin you could be in love with more than one person at the same time because all barriers had been smashed.

But he never thought he was making love to Rachel when he was making love to Gretchen. He felt Gretchen knew how he was crazy about Rachel, but either she did not care, or chose not to show it. He had once thought he was in love with Betty. He enjoyed being with Betty a lot, but that relationship was ruled by HOME and economics and was like an arranged marriage. This was different. Different as the war was to peace. Different as Berlin.

"Now I will try again to make that coffee," said Gretchen, getting out of bed, examining herself before a full-length mirror.

What he had with Rachel and Gretchen was off the scale. Candy Thunder. It was not always joyful. It hurt as much as it made him, or them, happy. Yet, for fleeting moments, he was alive again inside and in the universe and his way clear. They were his guides through hell and heaven, and amongst the ruins in Berlin he had started to glimpse the sacred and sublime because of Rachel and Gretchen, the earthly and transcendent love Dante touched on in his *La Vita Nuova*.

The paradox would never have revealed itself in the States.

"Let's go out tonight. Let's go dancing," he said.

"I thought you were being careful," said Gretchen.

He smiled. "I don't plan to die careful . . ."

Later that night, Kells took a long drag of a fresh cigarette on a street off the Ku'damm, saying goodnight to a drunken French major he had met at a party. Kells and Gretchen and Joe had all been out dancing. Gretchen had gone ahead to help Joe, who wanted to hail a taxi to another club where the girls were naked, but had clothes painted on them in edible dye. Unless the taxi ride was asked for in good German, the cab drivers would not take the fare, as the Russians and Americans routinely caused trouble and refused to pay. The three of them had been to a big barn-like club north of the Ku'damm which, despite all the restrictions, was still full of Russians drinking themselves lunatic stupid and fucking any girl they caught in the street outside. The band was good, though, and

Kells had danced and danced with Gretchen, while Joe made deals. The priest was at home reading Faust, which he pointed out meant "fist" in German. The priest was a good soul, but he always seemed to be unexpectedly there, like Jesus at the drunken wedding feast. Kells wondered if he was being observed, spied on.

He shook his head. Christ, was he suspecting the priest now?

Kells heard Gretchen's laughter ahead up on the Ku'damm. He was happy. The lights were painfully bright there, but not in the small street he was on.

He glimpsed a car. A blue Russian Gaz saloon moved level on the other side of the road. He caught sight of a man smiling inside. A face so white it looked as if the window was open.

The brick wall that he was standing against exploded in two puffs of red dust. Tyres squealed.

He never saw a gun, or heard a shot. Fragments of brick struck his face and he was bleeding.

He ran to the bright lights of the Ku'damm.

Gretchen saw Kells and put her hand to her mouth. She pulled at Joe's jacket.

Kells looked down. The blood was on the arm of his new raincoat. Joe turned from the taxi he had hailed.

"We gotta get you home. Get in the cab. Get in the cab. We're just going round the corner for now, you can take me somewhere later. My friend cut himself shaving. No, he's not in any trouble. Do we look like trouble? Take us round the corner."

But the taxi drove off, and Kells walked between the two of them feeling shocked and grateful. He had been shelled and shot at in war, but somehow that had always seemed like a great storm, lightning over the sea, the same smell of gunpowder in the air as if the world has been cut to the quick. This was different. It was personal when a man in a car pulled a trigger and missed you by, perhaps, an inch. Gretchen kissed him and held his hand.

She swore in German and then said a whole string of words in a language he did not know. He guessed they were gypsy.

Was this the Russians giving him another warning? Or was it Lucy? No one had been in touch with him from Washington.

He could taste a curl of blood in his mouth.

He was glad to see the front door of the large house where they lived. There were people ahead by a car under a street light and Joe tensed and his hand went inside his suit. Gretchen kissed Kells on the cheek.

"It was the same car as before," he said.

"Let's get inside," Gretchen said, pushing him along.

There were steps up to the door and all the time he expected another shot. He felt it in the skin at the back of his neck. He had to stop himself running.

In the hall they heard the sound of the priest calling from the drawing room.

"Hell, I thought this was late for me, but it's early for you. What have you done to your face, colonel? We'd better get some iodine on that."

It was Joe who attended to Kells' wound, delicately removing four fragments of brick dust from his face with tweezers and the iodine stung. Gretchen sat there and held Kells' hand. She had kicked off her high heels as Joe removed the last of the brick.

"It ain't gonna scar, so cheer up," said Joe. "I got news. I was going to tell you both at the dance, but there was too much noise. You know the burned-up guy you are not sure of? Wondered whether he was even Adolf himself, on account of where we picked him up? I know it's a long shot, but a Russian I know claims he has the dog that last belonged to Mr Hitler in the bunker. Can you believe that? The dog is called Wolf, of course. What I suggest is we go out to that Jew farm place and see if your man Hyman and Wolfie get along. Wolfie has a bad temper, but one prisoner they questioned said Wolfie and his former master were inseparable, like peas in a pod . . . At least he might be pally with a top Nazi? There are rewards . . ."

After Joe had gone, Gretchen and Kells both looked at each other and laughed. Joe had to be joking.

"That is a very bad idea," said Gretchen.

They were silent for a time and then Kells gently touched his wound and said, "Is it Lucy? Who did this? Is it Lucy's way of telling me not to look any further? Maybe I should contact them? Talk with them . . . ?"

"Please don't," said Gretchen, becoming fearful again. "Please don't. Promise me. We must go. You must get out. Can you get me a passport . . . ?"

"We are married, Kells. Married! *Mein Liebling, ich bin dein!*" Gretchen said, beside herself with excitement two days later, and threw a handful of rice into his hair as they drove out to Tegel aerodrome.

Kells was doing his best to get Gretchen to leave for the States now that she had a temporary US passport linked to his. She had the new papers he promised her.

He loved her. After the shooting, the only way to have her safe in the States was to get her onto his passport and fast. He thought this might be simple at the US embassy, but after waiting for hours, a smiling middle-aged lady said he should come back after the ceremony at the Sandesamt, the registry office, and wished him congratulations and gave him a packet of rice. He was going to argue, but the woman had the sort of determined American face that regarded such romantic matters as non-negotiable before an Old-Testament God. It was all so sudden Kells had not had a chance to talk about it with Gretchen. Even as they rushed to the Sandesamt, with her kissing him, he thought she would understand that the marriage in front of a city official, with two witnesses off the street, was the only quick way of getting the passport she wanted.

Gretchen had been getting more afraid for both of them. She was convinced that Lucy was trying to kill him. "Don't you understand . . . ? You work for Lucy, even if you don't know you are working for them. Then they kill you. That's why no one knows anything about them. That's how they are never infiltrated, or brought down. It is like a machine, with no one in control . . . The Americans just stand by and watch . . ."

When they arrived at Tegal, Kells took Gretchen to wait for one of the US Dakota flights that would ferry her to an English base and a plane to the States. To Washington.

Gretchen was crying by the time an airman came and said: "Can you go to the plane, folks." They then followed about twenty people, some military, most not.

The closer they got to the aircraft on the wet tarmac, the more emotional she became. It was raining hard now.

"I don't want to leave you, my darling . . ."

"It won't be for long."

He took Gretchen to the door of the plane. He kissed her and it was hard to make her let go.

"I will join you soon. I promise. I just must do things officially about my getting home. Soon as you land, ring the number of the friend I gave you . . . He is a good friend and trustworthy. He will take you to an apartment I have arranged. I love you . . ."

He left her waving on the steps in the wind of the props and the noise of the engines. She was wearing the suit he first saw her in. He had no doubt that she loved him.

When he reached his car, he saw the plane take off and followed the winking green starboard light up into the low cloud. She would be all right. He missed her already.

"Darling . . . !"

He turned and she was there. With the two-tone suitcase of her mother. She flung her arms around him.

"I am an expert at giving people the slip . . ."

Her eyes were enormous and innocent.

She could hardly speak and held onto him with both hands as he drove back into Berlin. She was so happy. She kissed him and kissed him on the cheeks, the little kisses of a happy child, many times.

"We are married, Kells! I never thought I would marry after all that has happened to me."

She then paused, breathless.

"I cannot travel to Washington now. At least, we must go out and celebrate our marriage. You must get me a new dress. We can go dancing. I must sing! We can be blessed in church. I love you, Kells!"

He felt giddy. He was now completely married to one of the women he loved.

"I love you . . ."

Kells had not told Gretchen he had sent a message to Roessler, stating that he wanted to meet, in person. That he had to know more. He regarded his cable to the Vita Nova publishing house, in what was described in his files as "a shabby, peeling painted old property at chemin de Longerale 2", as a rhetorical exercise, or trying to send a message to the beyond in a schoolboy séance.

But a cable reply came with fearful promptness:

NO MY GOOD FRIEND STOP I FEEL I ALREADY KNOW YOU! STOP WE WILL NOT MEET IN LUCERNE STOP WE WILL MEET IN GENEVA STOP BE AT THE BRIDGE OVER THE DEVIL'S GLASS. AT NOON STOP THURSDAY NEXT. UNLESS YOU ARE AFRAID STOP ALICE WAS NEVER AFRAID. STOP EVEN DOWN THE RABBIT HOLE STOP DO YOU WANT TO COME DOWN MY RABBIT HOLE? STOP TO MY TEA PARTY? STOP YOU MAY NOT GET BACK STOP MESSAGE ENDS

Kells swerved as Gretchen continued to kiss him.

"I love you, Kells."

"I have to go to Geneva."

She pulled away.

"Instead of Lucerne? They will kill you. Lucy will kill you . . ."

"Will she?"

But Gretchen, his wife, was crying.

VII

"I THINK ANNA is all right now."

Rachel was talking to the rabbi in her office and there was music in the background, swing music, from the radio, and they were waiting for the news at the top of the hour, hoping there was going to be news from Palestine, where there had been an attack on a British airfield by "Zionist terrorists".

"You said Anna dreamed of whiteness?" the rabbi mused, unwrapping a toffee.

"She said it was a flash of white. But it was not a good white. Like fungus in the forest, I suppose. It consumed the whole world. The whiteness of the cocoons. She thinks the killing of the silkworm pupae is symbolic of what happened in the camps. I have had similar thoughts to her about the colour white. Anna lost a friend she could not save. She was probably to be next."

The rabbi was nodding, staring out of the window.

He smiled:

"Not all white is good. We tend to think of white as good. Pure. I don't know if it is a racist thing. But don't forget there is the pale horse in Revelation, whose hooves echo in our own apocalyptic scriptures. Whiteness is nothing, and that is what I fear the most. No meaning, I suppose . . . No thought. What the Nazis thrived on. In Anna's case it is the guilt of the survivor, poor thing, what I advise . . ."

At that moment the dance music on the radio was interrupted by breaking news:

"This is the American Forces Network Broadcasting from Bonn, Germany on August 6, 1945. Here is a message from President Truman. 'A short time ago, an American aeroplane dropped one bomb on Hiroshima and destroyed its usefulness to the enemy. That bomb has more power than 20,000 tonnes of TNT. The Japanese began the war from Pearl Harbour. They have been repaid manyfold

198

and the end is not yet. With this new bomb, named Little Boy, dropped from a B-29 bomber, we have added a new and revolutionary increase in destruction to supplement the growing power of our armed forces. The white flash of a new age could be seen for hundreds of miles and, scientists say, on the Chinese mainland."

Rachel felt cold. Like when she had been told a dark fairy story as a child. "This is what Anna was saying." she began, astonished.

The rabbi had found a bible on the wooden shelves and was reading. He then read aloud: "And I looked, and behold a pale horse: and his name that sat on him was Death, and Hell followed with him."

One by one, other young people came into Rachel's office. They were silent and sat on the old silk-backed chairs and on the floor. They listened like Rachel and the rabbi to the large radio on the table by the fireplace.

Rachel felt they all realised that what had happened changed everything in the world, but it also brought back the past, their past, in intense detail.

One of the boys and two of the girls began to cry. Even among the most militantly Zionist of the boys there was a reverential silence. There was a radio in the drawing room downstairs, but Rachel was glad they had come to her office, with the rabbi. She knew very personally about the paradox of coldness and passion necessary to execute a fatal political act, but not on such a biblical scale.

"It is possible now to kill so many you do not like, who you fear, without effort, without even seeing them. You just turn them to dust," said a boy called David.

"They could kill all the Jews in the world in a second," said a girl, who switched off the radio, and ran out of the door and down the echoing marble stairs. A door slammed below. The silence returned.

They tuned in to a German station. A radio announcer, excited, revealed more of the details of the raids. More than the censor probably allowed. The bomber was a B-29 Superfortress, called *Enola Gay*. The bomber, on Special Mission number 13, was named after the pilot, Colonel Paul Tibbet's, mother. The young people in the room clung to the facts, to try to rationalise, but Rachel found the description in German unbearable. The announcer, to her, sounded pleased that a hundred thousand people had perished. Turned to steam and hot dust in an instant of holocaust. "With the fierce pressure of the blast, the air pressure in the area dropped precipitously, resulting in eyeballs and internal organs popping out from bodies." The industrial killing and the gas chambers of the Nazis were the past. Killing in the future was a bolt of white light. Rachel switched the dial back to the American Forces Network.

More responses were being broadcast about the bomb. "The entire population of Japan is now a military target . . . there are no civilians in Japan," said a U.S. general. Then there were others from Japan. "When I saw a very strong light, a flash, I put my arms over my eyes unconsciously . . . the whole city was destroyed and burning. There was no place to go." More chilling was a Japanese general who was quoted as saying: "Would it not be wondrous for this our nation to not surrender and to be annihilated, that it should become as a shattered jewel?"

Rachel had thought of Hyman's wounds as jewels.

The programme was then interrupted:

"And now we will pause for a little more dance music, folks . . . Let's do the cha-cha!"

Paul muttered something to several of the others, and with an angry glance at Rachel, he left the room.

"Will we still be able to go to Palestine?" said one of the girls, who had been comforting Anna, whose feet and hands were covered in bandages. They all knew the vision she had seen in her dream.

The rabbi smiled: "Oh, yes. That will go ahead. More than ever, now. These events will take a long time to understand. We must trust in the good of people. Try to think of the future, my dears and not of how this speaks to our past. Think of the future and it will be there."

Slowly, in ones and twos, people began to leave the room until only Anna and a few of the other girls remained. There was euphoria on the radio and Rachel turned it off. She found herself unable to get her breath. It was impossible for her, and she could see from the expressions of others in the room, not to appreciate the personal and racial implications of this new weapon, quite apart from the colonial. When she was five years old, she had seen a boy from her class tearing up leaves and putting them in a preserving jar. She had asked him if he was going to make jam and he laughed. He told her the leaves were from the graveyard, they were laurel leaves, and they gave off a fatal gas. He caught a butterfly, a Red Admiral, and put it in the jar and the creature fluttered and fluttered and then died. The boy watched every movement and Rachel had run away in tears. She had later dreamed of a jar, a huge jar, that the boys were trying to put her in, naked. She had never thought of that time until today. Even when she heard talk of the gas chambers and then read the evidence, she had not remembered the story of the Red Admiral.

The white light at the end of the world had brought the story into focus again.

A boy ran into the room. "They are burning down the silkworm house! Come quickly!"

Rachel lifted her hands to her head. She was terrified for Hyman. She ran ahead of the rabbi, around the side of the lake to the silkworm house, which was completely ablaze at one end all the way to the roof, exploding with yellow flame. She ran through the gate and into the garden. She opened the door of the lodge, but there was no light and no one was there. She ran out again and saw Paul and several of the other boys standing with torches in their hands. They were laughing and smiling and Rachel felt cold as a floor tumbled and there was a surge of heat and sparks.

Paul saw her and turned.

"Anna was right. We should not be exterminating anything."

"You idiots! Nazis burn things with torches. We don't. Where is Hyman?"

Paul shook his head.

"No one was in the house. We checked."

She completely lost her temper and hit him in the middle of the chest so hard she forced him back. She then ran for the burning house, but the boys grabbed her as the flames suddenly exploded up through the entire wooden-framed building and the roof fell in, scattering slates onto the mulberry trees.

"How do you know? How do you know?" she was shouting. "He can pass out at any moment. He could have left his wheelchair and passed out on the back stairs or in one of the store cupboards. Did you check them all? Did you check them all?"

Paul grabbed her.

"We checked everywhere."

"You should not have burned down the silkworm house," said the rabbi.

"I disagree," said Paul. "And I refuse to go to Israel to be a storm-trooper for King David. Not in a new world of instant genocide."

Rachel was about to scream at him, but one of the American guards came down from the main house. He stared at the fire and then at Rachel.

"I can call the fire brigade at the base, ma'am, but I think it would be too late. The old butler . . . The crazy old butler tried to hang himself. I think he is going to pull through. He will only speak to Paul. He left a note about generals and stuff, but I don't spreken ze German. He's up at the big house."

"Have you seen Hyman?" Rachel asked him.

"Can't rightly say I have, ma'am."

Frantic, Rachel went up to the house with the rabbi and Paul and about ten of those who wanted to go to Palestine. Behind them the darkness was lit by the flames. She hoped the walls would contain the fire and stop it spreading to the fields, but there was nothing she could do. She hoped against hope that Hyman was not inside. She knew he had gone into the house earlier to try and save what he could after Anna had ransacked it in the wake of her dream.

Rachel went to her office and Hymen was not there. She tried to calm herself. When she turned round she was face to face with Paul.

"Like I said, I'm not going to the kibbutz in Palestine," he said. "I want to stay here in Germany."

"Do what you like. We still haven't found Hyman."

Paul stood in front of her, staring at the carpet.

"A couple of soldiers cut the butler down from one of those big trees in the maze. They were in there having a smoke. He's still alive. Do you know that he is the army general who owned the house before the Nazis? Do you know what he said when I saw him? 'You are all so kind to me. It was killing me.' I destroyed the note that he left. And a few of the boys who strongly supported the *Haganah* men came and wanted to string the general up again and there was a fight. I told them they were fascists. I know they are not. I know I am not. But you can know something is not true and it can be true all the same. That is the lesson of the Hitler period."

There were tears on Paul's cheeks.

"I want to stay here. I want to help him. Am I going to be punished?"

She looked hard at him, he was trembling. Then she said, "Rebuilding Germany, the country that tried to murder you, will be punishment enough."

An hour later, Rachel still hadn't heard from Hyman. But when she hurried back to the sitting room, to her relief, he was there, comforting everyone. She nearly collapsed and leaned against a wall to steady herself.

She watched Hyman as he went to each of the young people in turn, standing firm with a stick, nodding and smiling, always confident and reassuring. He joked with a few of the tougher ones. "We should not take history so personally."

With others he appeared to be close to tears in his sensitivity. It was a sincerity she was quite sure of. She often woke in the night to find him wide awake. "Oh, you are awake too, my darling. I am worrying about Danny. The boy, Daniel Meyer. He is too much of a stay-at-home to go to a new land."

Hyman took everyone's history personally, and Rachel loved him for it and so did all the other young people at the kibbutz. In a way, he was as much a kindly leader of the kibbutz as the rabbi.

VIII

THE SEASONS ARE changing. It's September and the young people are calling me Papa Hyman and now I am the leader, the father, of the kibbutz when I want to be. It is a good feeling! Only now is the kibbutz getting back together after the shock of Hiroshima that led to the burning down of my silkworm house. I am not sure I will start again. That is a small matter. I was so glad to help out with the young people a little after the news of the bomb in Japan. Whether or not those, like Rachel and I who worked for the resistance, will go to Palestine is still in the balance, but, if not, I want to work with the young Jewish people here in Germany. To see them so broken and confused by the dreadful news on the radio is appalling. They know from bitter experience certain named individuals' capacity for savagery and cruelty, not beyond what I can imagine, but beyond what I can remember. The invocation of this anonymous bomb, dropped by a friendly force, the Americans, on a city where the houses are made of rice-paper, balances their collective vulnerabilities on the point of a red-hot needle. This is a threat to all of us. The theory of the bomb was later described on a radio programme as like a room filled with mousetraps with a ping-pong ball on the spring-loaded metal wire that comes down on the mouse. When one trap is triggered, its falling ball sets off another one and soon all the mousetraps in the room are set off. One atom is split and then a chain reaction follows. I do not remember ever being told or learning this. With refinements, said a scientist without irony, it could become a Doomsday weapon. I am flattered that they turn to me for leadership, like Rachel in such times.

Why does humanity, or some American generals, want Dooms-day? I do not know if I asked this question before, or if I did whether I asked it often enough. Yet in the face of all this, in the quiet of the night, I hold the goodness of those young people, the survivors, with me and view the future with such optimism. I do not care that they destroyed my silkworms. They were thinking, and that is enough. The young people's goodness makes me feel better because I still do not recognise who I am, deep down . . . I do like being in control, yet I have a frightening and absurd dread of power, the dreams I told the surgeon about. In the kibbutz I am the centre of my story more and more and it makes me anxious when my dreams are of the old Germany. In one I am looking out into a massive grey stone arena at the thousands and thousands of faces who have come to hear me speak. Why would anyone in their right mind come to hear Hyman Kaplan speak? I am on a high podium surrounded by red and black banners that are in a haze so that I cannot quite make them out. I am dressed in khaki. I am shaking, but it is not from stage fright or embarrassment. It is from passion and anger. The people are chanting yet again I cannot quite make out what they are saying. I start to speak. I shout and scream. I am a man, I say. I am a man and can only take so much on behalf of my people. I can only take so much and after that there comes a time to gird my loins and go into battle. I bring my fist down on the podium and the crowd go wild for what I have to say. I am seething with hatred against an enemy I have no idea of. Then I am shouting again and blaming everything on the enemy. It is not as simple as that, I say, making my voice drop for a moment. It is not as simple as that, and everyone stops to listen to my wisdom. I hope I am going to be more measured and polite. But no. You may think it is all a question of the enemy, I say, but I know the real enemy. I know the international conspiracy that is behind all this and the attacks on our beloved country. Our Fatherland. I know who is at fault. Tell me who is at fault, my children, my beloved? Tell your father who is at fault? The word then rolls back at me like thunder.

I am in a great stone-built stadium like those in ancient Greece. There are rows and rows of black uniforms and flags and banners. In the front are girls in pigtails dressed in *lederhosen*. Almost all of them are blonde and attractive. They are baring their perfect teeth in the collective anger.

I am hitting the lectern. I am beating the wood with my fist.

I am in a frenzy.

The hatred bubbles up over me like the boiling water on the cocoons and I scream:

"Kill the enemy. Kill the Jew. *Sieg Heil! Sieg Heil!*"

Hail whose victory? Who is this I am? The sky turns red. I wake. The words roll back at me as I sit up in bed, sweating. "The Jew . . . The Jew . . . Kill the Jew . . ."

"I am the Jew," I try to say, inside the angry man, inside me. The grub inside the cocoon.

IX

IN THE CENTRE of Geneva, Switzerland, near to noon in the last sunny days of November, Kells looked down at the deep, black churning pool, The Devil's Wine Glass, *Das Weinglass des Teufels*.

Great oily whirlpools sucked anything down from the surface. Kells threw in a cigarette butt and it disappeared. The corpse of a bird, what had been a pigeon, welled up from the depths and seemed to come alive, raise its head and open its beak, before being sucked down again. It was a place where water flowed out of *Lac Léman* to a river, and at other times went in the opposite direction. There had once been lock gates to stem the dreadful force but, such was the power of the water flowing in and flowing out, these had been long abandoned even in this, the most regulated of European cities. The dangerous pool was called the Devil's Wine Glass because it was always full. It was a favourite spot for suicides, his guidebook said, in that worryingly impersonal Swiss way. In the margin, in green ink, someone had written, Ha, ha!

There was a tug on his right trouser-leg from behind. He swung round and there was no one.

The sensation came again and he glanced around a second time.

When he turned back there was a male dwarf sitting on the white-painted wooden rail over the water. The man wore a grey trench coat and a blue fedora hat. He grinned and showed yellow, nicotine-stained teeth. He flashed a police identify card in a red leather holder. To Kells' astonishment, the man was a detective with the Fedpol police.

"Mr Roessler sends his compliments, colonel. You are invited to the Thursday tea party." The man spoke quickly and gently in French-accented English. He had a small, carefully waxed moustache. "We must hurry along."

"Where?"

"A chateau down by the lake. We will be taken in my car. I think we're already late. It doesn't do to be late for the tea party, which always starts at noon. I expect you are surprised I am originally from Southern India?"

"Not in the least," said Kells, politely.

The restaurant was not what he expected, but Kells was getting used to that. The small policeman's car stopped at a pair of iron gates, which were opened by a man in a frock coat and closed behind them. The car went up an immaculate gravel drive. He looked out over Lac Léman at a sunny, peaceful setting that had never known a modern war. Out on the light blue water, a yacht was making its slow, majestic way under sail.

There were large cedar trees in the gardens and snow-white ducks on a small pond.

The car stopped on pristine white gravel in front of a grey, French-style chateau with four towers, each topped with a conical slate roof. Kells got out of the car, which sped away. An attractive maid, dressed in black and white, came out and ushered them into a lofty entrance hall and, after Kells was searched by two military-looking waiters, the small policeman led the way up the stairs, positively skipping. There was hardly any light on the stairs and ancestor portraits were interspersed with bloody hunting scenes and antique weapons.

"I do like a tea party," said the small policeman. "It goes to the true meaning of our life. You can learn everything at a tea party. And nothing."

The maid opened a pair of twelve-foot doors and, from behind a lectern, a *maître d'* offered them a menu, which was blank.

The room was huge, a double-height ballroom, with floor-to-ceiling windows, one side overlooking the lake, the other a road going up into the mountains. There were three chandeliers, which were lit, but only one long table in the middle of the room, and at that table in an oversized, green top hat, sat a small man with the bush baby eyes and square glasses Kells remembered from the photograph in his Lucy file.

Kells took a step into the room.

He now felt real fear.

And astonishment.

He approached the table, which was set with silver and lit candles and on a silver pedestal in the centre was a crystal glass tea pot in which a single goldfish swam.

A waiter seated him at the top of the table by Roessler, the Mad Hatter, and Kells recognised the Mad March Hare and the Red Queen and the sleeping Dormouse, dressed in a golden fur suit, while across the table was a tall, elegant lady in a long silk dress and scarves and long gloves and a wide-brimmed silk hat.

She was perhaps middle-aged, perhaps older, but very beautiful in a high-cheek-boned, haughty German way, with strange, piercing eyes Kells could not tell the colour of exactly because they were so pale. She smoked a bright crimson cigarette in a black, ebony holder. The curling smoke matched the conspiracy of her smile.

Yet it was Rudolf Roessler who held Kells' attention. Those eyes, which had seemed so mild and harmless and ingenuous, now appeared to fill the event with enigma. They were hypnotic and playful, but Kells found himself being drawn into them, like a leaf into the whirlpool of the Devil's Wineglass. The man then raised his bushy eyebrows and beamed, an expression that not only lit up his face, but his whole body and the room.

Kells had not seriously expected a real tea party, even after what Gretchen had told him.

He knew how the use of nonsense in the codes was disorientating. What Kells saw around the table was beyond nonsense.

"Why is a raven like a writing desk?" The Mad Hatter spoke in English in a clear and melodious voice.

The Red Queen laughed, and pointed at Kells.

"He knows and he doesn't. Off with his head. It will help him think."

The small policeman was sitting on the Dormouse's lap.

"I am late," said an enormous White Rabbit entering the room. His costume was patched a little around the thigh. He then spoke directly to Kells. "I am late and if you don't watch out, you will be too. The late Colonel Kells William Bonney Vardy. Late. But early for your own funeral. Can you ever get things right?"

"Do not tease our guest. He comes seeking answers," said the Mad Hatter.

They all laughed at this. They laughed at this for a long time.

While they did so a waiter came to Kells' place and started to ladle soup into a golden bowl in front of him. It was chocolate soup, the smell was unmistakable. Molten chocolate around what looked like a female breast with a raspberry for a nipple. Another waiter then came and added a generous spoonful of whipped cream on the side. Another added a frosting of tiny, frozen woodland strawberries.

"Why is a raven like a writing desk?" repeated the Mad Hatter.

Kells took a spoonful of the chocolate. He then put the golden spoon down. The breast appeared to be real. The Dormouse woke and laughed. Kells almost ran.

Mad Hatter's Tea party

"He knows," said the Cheshire Cat, a woman in a very tight costume with black stockings and a long tail, who appeared from behind a curtain. Kells thought he recognised her from the files and he was sure the Dormouse was the MI6 radio operator, a Mr Foote.

"Put him out of his misery," said the Red Queen.

"Not yet," said the Mad Hatter.

Kells could smell, and still taste, the rich and bitter chocolate with the white streak of cream. He felt sick. Then from the bottom of the chocolate soup, tiny grey figures floated up, possibly edible but that looked like drowned children. Kells pushed the bowl away.

"Noooooooooooo!" shouted the Red Queen.

The others all looked angrily at Kells, with the exception of the Dormouse who, in the middle of doing the English football pools, had gone to sleep again. Kells dropped the spoon into the chocolate and it splashed on the serviette. A waiter immediately came and took the napkin away. Another came and took the bowl of soup. Another collected the spoon. All the waiters, Kells noticed, were identical. They had curly black hair and a southern Italian look to them. They each had a tooth missing at the upper left-hand side. As quickly as they were gone, they were back with light green jellies full of miniature arms and legs, and equally life-like gingerbread men, missing all their limbs.

Kells shuddered.

"Another arm, or perhaps another leg, Mr Kells? They are so lovely in this jelly!"

"He must not eat or even drink the tea," said the White Rabbit. "He must not. Until he knows, at very least, the reason for us having this tea party for him."

The March Hare laughed. "He would know everything."

"And nothing," said the Red Queen.

The Mad Hatter then cried out, seemingly with sheer joy, and gave a long sigh of satisfaction. By his side, on the table, was the same German version of *Alice Through the Looking Glass*, *Alice hinter den Spiegeln*, that Kells had used for "Beatrice's" book code. The giant, blue Himalayan poppies were unmistakable.

From under the table the elegant woman dressed in grey silk emerged. Distracted, Kells had not noticed she was gone. Hatless, she had a tousled head of short, ash-blonde hair. She now appeared much younger and wiped the corner of her large mouth and licked her red lips with a vulpine expression. Kells saw her eyes clearly. She had smoky grey eyes and, bringing her chair to Kells' side of the Mad Hatter, she squeezed his thigh with her long, strong fingers, in those grey silk gloves.

"Oh, do meet my tea party wife," said the Mad Hatter. "I am calling her Theodora today, after a sainted Byzantine empress, who formerly gave her all in a brothel. She is the nymphomaniac empress who the author thoughtlessly left out of the Alice story. A good story always needs a nymphomaniac in these modern, structuralist times. It is so enervating and democratically wrong footing don't you think, to sleep with any amount of complete strangers from Vatican counts and bankers to tram conductors and even brush up against chimney sweeps? I find all sorts of people sleeping it off in my bed and weeping quietly, still in desperate love. I often kill them out of sheer pity, an Act of Love I do not need to mention in Confession. But it has a purpose for Theodora, here. She indulges in the meaningless animal pleasure of sex with a legion of volunteers and then is able to ponder what female love is, in the most wonderful poetic quatrains, and weave that bitter sugar into our relationship and our understanding of the world. She is the harbinger of Dante's transcendent love in his *La Vita Nuova*, colonel, which we share your love and yearning for. And she has become so good at the disgusting and disgraceful animal side of things. She loves to surprise me under the table at these gatherings and always knows me by my vulgar taste in shoes."

A waiter came again and deposited what appeared to be a fried baby's leg on a golden plate in front of Kells, who remembered one of Lucy's units was code-named Dora, and that Roessler's actual wife was named Maude.

"I am sure my tea-party wife will sleep with you too, if you remain still long enough."

"Twinkle, twinkle, little baby," said the March Hare, eating his baby leg.

"But I'm late and this does not help explain the question of Time," said the White Rabbit, taking out his watch.

"His wife always has time for me," said the March Hare.

They all laughed.

The Mad Hatter leaned towards Kells.

"In the first days of the recent stupid war, this old family house became a restaurant after the owners died mysteriously. Many deaths in Switzerland are mysterious because we are a private people. Money was flowing back with all the cowards of Europe and the restaurant clients did crazy stuff. It became the scene of incredibly refined and sophisticated culinary pornography. A fourteen-year-old girl was eaten arranged on a platter, among seasonable infant vegetables, as if she were asleep. A Michelin three-star chef cooked her, very slowly and carefully. She was drugged and alive for much of the process, it is said. Imagine that? The eventual pain. The embarrassment. She had long eyelashes, and her eyelids were dressed with pomegranate syrup and mimosa flowers. She came with a powerful man she had a disagreement with. You could say she disagreed with something that ate her."

The Red Queen hooted with laughter until she wept and beat the table with her left shoe.

Kells prodded the leg in front of him. He had hoped it was a disguised confection of pure sugar. But it was, indeed, a leg. One waiter took it away, with another arguing with him, as Theodora bent down and playfully bit Kells' thigh with her large white teeth. Gloveless now, her nails were long and red. Embarrassed, he drank a glass of wine that had been put down by him that did not taste like wine, but blood, and he wished he hadn't. Two little girls, they could not have been more than nine, dressed as green mice, came into the room in ballet shoes and began to dance suggestively, turning and wiggling their little bottoms. They both winked at Kells.

"I murdered Time, so they say," said the Mad Hatter.

"That's what it says in your excellent Alice edition," said Kells, trying to sound in control.

"Time is a relative."

"Time is relative," corrected Kells.

"No, the man I killed was my half-brother. For me he had come to signify time. He was so boring. It has nothing to do with this spy nonsense. But relativity has," said the Mad Hatter.

"Bang!" roared the Red Queen.

"So the only way to stop the end time is to . . . ?" asked the Mad Hatter. "What can be in both enemy hands and none by its nature?"

"Murder," said the White Rabbit.

"Of a new and different kind," said the Red Queen.

"I do love riddles," said the Dormouse.

Both waiters then brought golden plates of live snails whose shells were exquisitely painted to resemble human eyes. The eyes crawled off the plates and around the table.

"What has a raven in common with a writing desk?" asked the March Hare, crushing several snails with his fist.

"Mr Kells thinks he can still solve problems just by looking at them. But the eyes can deceive," said the Mad Hatter. The hat on his head had seemed to grow larger, higher, greener, shinier. "Perhaps he can produce a few notes. Dangerous notes for us. Like the Raven. Like the writing desk."

"Rubbish," said the Red Queen. "It will not just be a few notes. A man I know well in Wengen has a raven who can recite the sacred Mass in Latin!"

"Nonsense!" shrieked the March Hare.

And a food fight began.

All at once Theodora stood up and stepped elegantly away from the table. With a movement of her shoulders she shrugged herself out of the grey silk dress, which fell down to her high heels, and stepped towards Kells. His mouth quivered, though none of the others at the table seemed to notice. Her breasts were not large, but her areolae were and her nipples erect. She had no pubic hair. It was shaved quite smooth and he stared at the folds of her labia.

She wore grey, silken high heels. Her long but very strong hands reached out towards him. Her eyes were amused, and for an instant she was an oasis of sexual reality at the Tea Party as the March Hare and the Cheshire Cat tried to make the Dormouse drink a tea pot full of what smelled like whisky when he refused the glass one with the gold fish. The Dormouse was choking as the Cheshire Cat turned towards Kells and pointed a finger. It was not her finger. She had taken it from her chocolate soup.

"This one knows a lot. He knows too much."

"Off with his head!" demanded the Red Queen.

"We could lose ours," said the White Rabbit. The man's nervous darting stare always ended up fixed on the nearest door.

"The Yank knows far too much for his own good and ours." The Cheshire Cat's very English, very shrill upper-class, female voice was not playing a character, for that sentence at least.

"Oh, we should not trouble ourselves. All the poor boy wants is knowledge," said the Mad Hatter.

Everyone laughed again. The Red Queen laughed so much she fell off her chair backwards

While they all were laughing, Theodora, naked except for her high heels and a string of pearls, took Kells' hand and led him in a slow and dignified way out of the room and through a door a waiter opened. They climbed a cold stone staircase. Somehow, as he did so, she wrapped herself around him, like her cigarette smoke.

She reached out and turned a polished brass knob on a narrow green door, which opened into a bedroom. Her perfume hung over the staircase and for a moment, it was probably an illusion caused by whatever Kells had drunk, which had dulled any hesitation he might have had, she seemed to be inside him, inside his head, inside his soul. It only stopped when he noticed a six-figure concentration camp number tattooed on her blue-veined arm. She saw he was staring at the tattoo and brushed her lips against his and smiled and pulled him into the room, which smelled of roses and floor polish and Swiss cleanliness. She seemed always on the point of laughter, but did not laugh. The room was dizzyingly tall with a great, double, four-poster bed in the centre and two narrow windows that looked out onto *Lac Léman*. She led Kells towards the bed.

Kells did not say anything. He could not say a word. Her body was thin and angular to the point of starvation, but he could not keep his hands off her. His erection was so hard it hurt as she rubbed her lips against his again.

"I am not Alice and this is not make believe, or Wonderland, or through any Looking Glass," Theodora said, in her deep, German-accented voice as she started to take off his uniform tie. "This is not one of your casual Saturday night drug-store encounters, Colonel Kells Vardy. Nor your stupid war. I have rules and standards. I was brought up to have the highest standards, colonel. This is real. This is the Thursday Tea Party . . ."

Afterwards, even though he felt so weak he could barely dress, she dragged him down to an old pre-war black Mercedes and with Roessler, now changed into a grey suit and tie, they drove out of Geneva to one of the small, faceless villages that bordered the lake, made pretty for tourists. They walked briskly to a neat harbour and went out on the water in a little speedboat, all rich, varnished wood and shiny brass cleats and wheel, that Roessler drove sedately, as if at a Venetian funeral. They did not go far and then returned and sat in the sunshine outside the only open restaurant. Roessler ordered them all a Campari and soda with a slice of orange.

"Do make sure that it is a thin slice of orange," he said to the waiter in precise, Académie French. *"Assurez-vous qu'il s'agit d'une fine tranche d'orange."* There was not a hint of a German accent.

"You must excuse our amateur theatricals with Alice, Kells. So we put on the Tea Party to show we have all gone completely mad. The costumes were left behind by the Royal Shakespeare Company on a tour of Swiss schools. Lucy is her own creature these days and she won't kill us if she thinks we've gone mad. You do understand?"

"I do."

Everything was so civilised now, but Kells looked about him and he could feel there was a slight nervous tic beneath his lower lip at the left-hand side. The sun vanished and then re-appeared from behind high, white clouds. The bitter drink twinkled in the light. A waiter brought a basket of bread, which Theodora fed to the swans on the waterside. Roessler took out a gold cigarette case and offered Kells one and then produced an equally heavy gold lighter. The yellow metal flashed. Theodora was too interested in the swans.

"I do love the business with the so-called Hyman and his silk-worms. And how you became involved with this burning man," Roessler said, after exhaling a lungful of smoke. The cigarettes were Greek, Muratti Ambassador. Kells had a friend at university who smoked them to appear sophisticated.

Roessler continued, "Do you realise that silk was used in the detonators of the atomic bomb that was dropped on Hiroshima? Probably from relatives of the French silkworms at the Aviv kibbutz. So many links to mass slaughter? Almost as if someone is playing an elaborate joke? Is Lucy a joke? Perhaps the entire recent world war was a joke. I wonder that often during Mass, about our mortal life in general and, believe me, the devil is as confused as anyone. We are such ridiculous creatures. Demigods who ejaculate and defecate and whose deeply human and flawed moral compass always leads them in the opposite direction to the truth, to another pert bottom or sack of gold, or worse still, a war."

He theatrically inhaled and exhaled a lungful of smoke.

"My God, is that a drop of blood on the table from the cut on your mouth? And if I am not mistaken, there will be an honourable scar on your penis too, from Theodora's sharp teeth. After a day it will look like syphilis. Tell your girlfriends not to worry. All she has is a harmless mouth infection she contracted in Dachau before we got her out. She perfects her sexual arts for when she finds her true love again. She was terribly betrayed, you know. By her true love, of course."

Theodora did not turn away from the swans.

Roessler blew another cloud of sweet smoke.

"Switzerland appears so safe today. That is the illusion. This was the state that supplied the mercenaries to Europe, to the Medici and the Sforzas. They supplied the poisoners and the torturers. Then Calvin created the three-person cell structure used in espionage today. There is darkness behind the picture postcard. So much darkness. Is the new Lucy a magic trick to distract us from what is really happening? Most religions have their mysteries, truths and secrets, all of which are totally meaningless. Do you want me to tell you how the secrets of the plutonium bomb were passed to the Russians? You must have been told about that? Where would that get you, Colonel Vardy? My dear Kells . . . I see I have got your interest. You have dropped your cigarette . . . But was it perhaps meaningless in that the Russians are still ten years behind the land of Mickey Mouse? I do love that badge on your coat . . . And even possession of such knowledge would be justification for the more lunatic American generals to sound the charge . . ."

Roessler paused as a waiter brought a plate of olives.

"You also want to know the true identity of the man you call Hyman at the Aviv kibbutz. You may find that is far from what you expect. I would like to see their maze. It is hundreds of years old. Imagine all the souls lost in between those leaves, and what innocence brought to an end. My advice is not to take Lucy so personally and maintain a sense of humour and decorum. You might come and live with us. We are not operational anymore. You must believe that. You can always get that sweet German girl, or is she Russian, or gypsy, out through Switzerland. The other one too. Sweet Rachel. What exhaustingly pleasurable times we would have!"

Theodora was now feeding a swan, by hand.

"*Liebling!*" She stroked the large bird's head.

"We did exactly what we intended to do against the Nazis," said Roessler. "And as for now, what did that insane German philosopher say? Nothing is true. Everything is permitted. If you try to know the truth about Lucy, about what Lucy is today, then you will die. If you find the meaning of Lucy, you will die laughing."

Roessler then laughed and Theodora turned and laughed too. They laughed and laughed and the sun flashed on the water as Kells raised his bitter drink to his bitten lips. Theodora then jumped up with more bread to feed to the swans and she said.

"*Ich liebe Sie alle . . .*" I love you all.

X

KELLS SAT AT his desk, staring through the open French windows into the garden. He had not expected what happened in Geneva. "*Ich liebe Sie alle . . .*" I love you all, echoed in his head . . .

He had asked Theodora where she had heard the phrase, but she did not answer and neither did Roessler, and after he had finished his drink, a taxi was called to take him to his plane. He was not completely scared until he landed at Tegal, where he kissed the ground. It was December now and Christmas was coming. There was even an artificial green tree with decorations in the corner of his study that Joe had provided. Joe liked Christmas.

His lip hurt and, even after stitches at the tiny hospital at the airport, might never be the same again. "It will scar," said the women doctor, triumphantly. Theodora liked to bite. He did not mention his penis. Gretchen had chosen not to see that part of his rawness, or the scratches on his back from Theodora's long nails. Gretchen had immediately taken him to agonising bed and she had hugged him and hugged him, relieved he was alive. "We are married. You are my man . . ." Then she said simply: "Now they will come for us, my love."

But no one had.

Kells stared at one of the pieces of intelligence intercepted from

218

Lucy in the State Department file from 'Beatrice'. After Geneva, the vagaries of the absurd codes seemed almost approachable and the next moment the opposite. He had read of how some unbreakable absurd codes were set just to drive the code-breakers mad. He then reached into his jacket pocket and his hand felt the smooth surface of an envelope that had not been there when he put the jacket on that morning to go to the news stand. Just like before. He took the envelope out and opened it with the paper knife on the desk.

There was a message inside he immediately recognised as created using the *Alice Through the Looking Glass* simple book code. At first he felt relief as he did the schoolboy exercise. Then he stood gazing at the words for a long time. Simple, fatal words.

"Immediate Kill Order: Rachel and Gretchen."

It was ridiculous and he was going to ignore it. Was it a joke? Was it from Roessler? Why is a raven like a writing desk? We all crave a guiding note or two and rarely get one . . . Or was it his own people trying to trick him into revealing he was working for Lucy?

Below the kill order there was another line which he de-coded.

"Recommend Target to your contact."

He swallowed hard.

Kells was meant to set someone up to be killed. Another target. And who was his contact? He did not have a fucking contact. These notes formed a fatal chain letter.

If you obeyed the orders, it was natural to think you would be spared. Unless someone who you may have never met recommended your demise, because you were part of the self-cancelling group. Kells shuddered.

There was a knock on the door and Joe entered in a well-tailored, dark-grey suit.

"Hey boss, what's up? Those codes will drive you looney-tunes! I got an idea. Remember the dog I told you about before your trip? It's very available and can answer the sixty-four-thousand-dollar question about if the man at the Jew farm is Hitler."

Kells lit a cigarette. He poured a Scotch and one for Joe. He poured another for the priest who had just come in, who shook his head at the offer, but took the glass. The curtains at the French windows billowed in the wind.

Kells sighed. He had never believed in the dog idea.

"I'd forgotten about the dog."

"Hitler's dog," corrected Joe. "Wolf. If you turn up Hitler, you will be back in with Washington and your intelligence bosses. For sure. Think of it as a Christmas present."

"Adolf was very fond of our canine friends," said the priest. "He even sent Germans to the camps for abusing animals."

There was a silence.

"Yeah. The dog's the real thing," said Joe. "The Kraut who sold him to the Russian who has him says the dog so loves his master he could pick Adolf out in Grand Central Station at Christmas."

It was then Kells noticed that Joe was bleeding through a bandage on his right hand. Joe nodded. "Yeah, like his master, Wolf can be a bit emotional. He bites the flying fuck out of everyone that's not his master's good friend at very least. So I say we take Wolfie up to the kibbutz and see if he bites or falls in love again with Hyman the burned up Jew. Leave it up to the wuf wuf, I say."

Kells lit a cigarette. Lately he had begun to question reality itself.

There was a wolf-like howl from the garden.

"You put him in my garden?"

"Relax," said Joe. "I gave doggy the morphine. He's blown out of his vicious, stormtrooper mind. What say we get the car and drive there? I wanna see their faces if it's true and that nice guy with the caterpillars is really the devil. You never know, do you? I don't believe this loss of memory stuff. I can remember all the shit I ever done wrong, ever."

The priest smiled: "I can attest to Joe's incredible memory for his sins. I also found out that Adolf means 'majestic wolf' in Old German, and Wolf was one of the *Führer's* nicknames."

Kells was thinking of the kill order. The world was spinning towards madness.

The dog was an Alsatian Shepherd dog, but to Kells it looked like a wolf. He had once seen a real wolf run over on the highway in Wyoming on one of his father's fishing trips for lake dwelling Striped Bass. The Wyoming wolf was away from the pack and starving and did not look a threat to anyone. A fat man had tried to take a souvenir of the wolf's canine tooth with a stone and a penknife but had given up when a truck passed and messed up the corpse more. Wolf, the dog that Joe had bought, was twice the size of the Wyoming wolf and very powerful. It took the three of them to carry the drugged creature and tether him to the back seat by one of the doors and a hanging down strap. Wolf was growling the entire time.

"Come on, Wolfie. Whosa gooda boy? You wanna see your master? *Der Führer? Ein, Zwei, Drei?*", said Joe.

The dog lunged at him and snapped its jaws, but missed.

"At least that proves you're not Hitler, Joseph," said the priest, taking a drag on his pipe.

They drove for many hours, through the dark forest where Kells had been left naked, and Joe occasionally topped up the morphine. But when they were getting near to the house, Wolf started to wake up. The strong dog smell was overpowering. The dog's barking and growling filled the car and its pulling and thrashing caused the heavy automobile to rock and swerve and skid as the priest drove.

"Give the dog another needle," shouted Kells to Joe in the back.

"No, Wolf has to have all his faculties about him to play detective," said Joe. "I gave him a pep shot, a bit of speed, to make sure. Like maybe what they gave to Hyman."

"Perfect," said Kells.

They stopped on the gravel drive of the kibbutz and the dog was struggling fit to lynch itself, when Joe cut the hanging strap with his switchblade, but missed when grabbing for Wolf's collar. The priest had already opened the driver's door and the dog, now ampheta-mine-awake to every hair and nerve end, leapt into the front of the car and knocked him over and was off, racing towards the lake. All three of them ran in pursuit but could not keep up. It was getting dark.

"Hyman lives down there. In an old lodge. The bigger house where he kept the silkworms burned down. But they saved the lodge," Kells shouted, as they all ran faster. He was concerned for Rachel. What on earth was he going to tell her?

"There was another thing about the dog," said Joe.

"What?" snapped Kells.

"I was told he's been trained to hate Jews the most. He was put in a sack when he was little for six days and beaten and then they got a Jew boy with side curls to let him out."

"Great, Joe. So we bring it to a kibbutz? Fucking outstanding."

"What I do?" asked Joe.

It was then they heard the gunshot.

They found Hyman sitting under his favourite mulberry tree in the walled garden. In Hyman's good hand was a pistol. In front of him was a dead Wolf.

"The dog went for one of the boys from Palestine, Ehud, who I was talking to about the new Israel. Do you know who the dog belongs to? My friend here dropped his gun when the creature went for him. I picked it up and had to shoot the dog."

He made it sound easy.

The youngest of the three men from Palestine, Ehud, was by the dead dog, moaning and bleeding onto the grass from deep bites to his hands and left leg and agonised face.

The priest smiled. "Why don't we go up to the big house and get some medical supplies for your friend here."

Hyman bent down to tend the injured man and Joe did not speak until they were the other side of the garden walls.

"Now we are in the money! There will be a reward. Look who the dog bit," said Joe.

"Not quite yet," said Kells.

"I concur," said the priest, with a careful puff of his pipe.

"The dog liked him. Before he shot him. He's the Nazi," said Joe. "Wolf half killed the genuine Jew."

The other two shook their heads.

"That may be so, but we can't say that," said Kells. "We set the balls rolling that got Hyman here. Think about it. A secret US intelligence combat operation put Adolf Hitler in a kibbutz dedicated to becoming the spiritual heart of the new state of Israel?"

Joe shook his head. "Life's complicated sometimes."

The priest sighed.

"The only proof we have is the dead dog. An insane dog. An insanely violent dog, even by Nazi standards."

Joe looked uncharacteristically mortified:

"I sad now. I very sad."

Kells motioned for the others to draw closer.

"If anyone is going to question Hyman about this, that person must be Izzy the rabbi. Everyone respects the rabbi. If he thinks that Hyman may be Hitler, or at least a top Nazi, on the evidence of the dog or our other evidence, then that is a beginning. C'mon, let's go tell the rabbi. Only him for now."

The rabbi pressed the fingers of both hands together for a long time. He then rubbed his temples with his finger ends. He was prone to migraine headaches.

"You are telling me that Hyman Kaplan is Adolf Hitler?" he said, not smiling. In the quiet of his office, the ridiculous situation with the dog was suddenly underscored with seriousness and dreadful loss.

They all nodded. Kells was surprised how calmly the rabbi took the news. The rabbi stood up and sat down and put his head in his work-hardened hands. One look into the man's sympathetic but very sombre eyes ended the idea that this was any sort of joke: "I know you have suspected this for a while, Colonel Vardy. The surgeon told me of this, concerned for his patient. He thought it was due to your stupid sexual jealousy. Yet, if we take everything together, all your evidence, I must investigate. I will inform Hyman through Rachel. We will see what he has to say. Now, please tell me all you know, Colonel Vardy."

The words hung in the dusty air of the rabbi's small book-lined office and Kells wondered if he was about to regret what he had done.

XI

RACHEL HAS TOLD me the news that I, Hyman Kaplan, am suspected of being Adolf Hitler and the accusation turned me upside down. I sensed that Colonel Vardy has suspected me of being an imposter for a while, but then there are the dreams, always the dreams. Dreams of riding in open Daimler cars in front of adoring crowds. Then there is where I was found. And the men who tried to kill me. And a man who talked with Kells in Washington, Rachel said. How can a human being be responsible for all that fire and death? The war. The Holocaust. I feel I have stepped outside myself and want to run from the monster I am looking at, disguised as the much-loved Hollywood star, Clark Gable and Doctor Hyman Kaplan. If I had a firearm at this moment, and I do not say this lightly as Hyman Kaplan, I would blow my remaining brains out. My undamaged hand is shaking.

But there is a hidden man in me, underneath my assumed identity, who is not so good perhaps . . . I have known for some time that I must have been a terrible person. And in those Berlin ruins on Walpurgis Day anyone alive must have been a terrible person. I feel guilt. I have tried to rationalise my thinking this way, persuaded by Rachel, in that most of humanity is conditioned to think like this, be guilty, make up untrue narratives to fit that guilt, because of the various religious sects and dogmas that reinforce social control. We all carry guilt. Worse than that, preformed images and structures become written into the cells and neural pathways of our brains that trick us. Images of heroes and villains that rise up like clanking ghosts ever chained to us and we do not see, or miss, the truth, even about ourselves, especially about ourselves.

Selfishly, the most awful thing is the effect my unmasking will have on all the good young people at Aviv, and on my dear love, Rachel, even though she says it will not. She is so wonderful. I tried to explain to her about my dreams and how I appeared to be enjoying myself in them. It is one thing to look like a monster and to have that appearance disguised, that image improved; it is another to realise that, yes, one is the monster that has killed eighty millions in a world war and enjoyed every second. Even if I am not the monster himself, I may have been amongst those who obeyed him, his lesser demons.

Within me I know there is a man inside who wants and takes. I wanted Rachel and have taken her. This man does not feel guilt.

He might even be amused at being mistaken for Adolf Hitler.

XII

RACHEL CAME BACK into the room. She was very angry. "This is ridiculous," she began to say, but saw the expression on Hyman's face and the tears in his good eye. There was nothing to be said. "We must go up to the house. They are waiting."

"Yes," he said, and there was a silence for a very long time.

They both walked slowly past the lake and up to the house. Hyman did not speak until he was standing in front of the desk in Rachel's office, looking at a very sombre rabbi. Kells stood at the side of the room, by the fireplace with Joe and the priest.

"Are you going to turn me in? Do other people know?"

"A handful."

"In authority? People in authority know, but they do nothing?"

The rabbi sighed. "The world has turned. It has moved on, as you see here. Adolf Hitler is dead, the newspapers say so. I do not think you are the man who did those things. Who tried to exterminate my people. Even if it was Colonel Vardy who named you Hyman Kaplan. Perhaps, if you were this man, you wanted to kill everyone. But you failed. If you are him, from the details I know from Kells, you probably failed in the suicide attempt and were thrown into a shell hole, dressed as a Jew. When you were dowsed in petrol and set on fire, you leapt out of the pit and were set on fire again. Your naked universal image stopped a battle in its tracks. But only because you represented the suffering of all. For, unlike Napoleon, not even a lunatic wants Mr Hitler back. No one. Not even the most fervent stormtrooper, who would prefer to get drunk and sentimental over Adolf's memory than have the loser back. That sort of insane nationalism is, and must be, over. There are ruins, atrocities, but you cannot even, I think, lay much claim to them, if you are him. You were the mouthpiece of the horror, but the horror would have found another mouthpiece, another corporal to scream its fears through as dark dreams. And now you have found yourself happy and respected in a better place your former self might have thought utter Hell. If you were Hitler, you are no longer. Funny, eh. Jewish humour, I'd say."

Hyman bowed his head:

"Yes."

The rabbi fiddled with a piece of paper on the desk. Rachel was about to interrupt, but the rabbi spoke again.

"In the old days there was a dichotomy of the soul and the body, the ghost and the corporeal. Not a corporal. Now we are so scientific, we do not believe in such things. But I think at Aviv, whoever you are, you have had a glimpse of what heaven can be and how that sublime grace differs from the grey material world, and the world of marching jackboots."

There was a longer silence.

"Will I be turned over to the Americans?"

The rabbi shook his head. Rachel was staring at Kells and thinking how guilty he looked. The rabbi put one clenched fist on the desk's ink blotter.

"For a trial? What purpose would that serve? Except to let the antisemite colonialists of America and England signal their spurious virtue. The enormity of the crimes we are talking about should not be treated like motoring offences. Only our new homeland through the kibbutz experiment and finding the real causes of this Holocaust concern me. Not executing more people, and then doing the same thing again."

For once the rabbi's voice was loud and almost brutal.

Hyman stood up and then sat down. His hands were trembling. "So you must kill me."

No one spoke. Then Hyman said.

"I will not be as much use as the silkworm cocoons when I drop them in boiling water. But you might use me as fertiliser around the mulberry trees."

Rachel was about to say something, but the rabbi held up his hand:

"I would most certainly have killed the man who it's said you were, if there is any truth in this, but now I see hope. I see hope everywhere. Whoever you are, you are not the man you were. None of us are. As I said, the world has turned."

"So what is to be done with me? What if I hand myself in?"

Rachel poured Hyman a glass of water from a decanter on her desk.

"There is no proof. Not even for yourself," said Kells.

"Then why accuse me?"

The rabbi nodded, looking down at the desk:

"Rachel is devoted to you. She loves you. You love her. Her arms are your shackles. She is the bullet through your heart. You love her and have to make her happy. That would completely reverse all your plans and will to power, if you were Hitler. That would be a terrible punishment for a dictator."

Rachel was staring at Kells.

"We are trying to build a utopian community here and, Colonel Vardy, you come and make these accusations with a ridiculous, antisemitic dog," she said in quiet fury. Whatever Hyman himself thought, to Rachel there was not even a remote possibility of his being Hitler. Instead, she stared at the three Americans as if they had committed unimaginable crimes, as if they were Nazis.

Hyman looked across the large desk at the rabbi.

"Now you are joking with me. I am not to be punished? For my enormous crimes?"

The rabbi shook his head. Joe was about to speak, but Kells trod on his foot.

"The question must be, did you commit them? Or are you innocent?" said the rabbi. "The truth matters in the world after Adolf. We cannot rely on the last attack choice of a brutalised dog, but the suggestion has been made. And is it right to convict a man who has forgotten completely the identity he is accused of . . . Perhaps we will send you to South America. There you will use your considerable organisational talents and charm to set up communities for those who cannot bear to live in Europe anymore because they fear noisy men and dogs."

"That is too generous," said Hyman.

"And it must be soon. You saw our brothers in the *Haganah*. They are not as . . . spiritual as I am. They would demand vengeance if you were denounced by a woodlouse. It would all get in our way. Of our new state, of everything. The publicity. I care about that more than maybes or possible pasts."

A smile creased the side of Hyman's face. "The devil as distraction?" he said.

"Yes. If you like," said the rabbi.

"So my punishment is to live with my demons?"

The rabbi stood and his voice was loud.

"Forget your demons. There are no demons, just yourself. It's not about you. It's all about you. No, your task is to love Rachel and provide homes for the homeless in a foreign land. There will be no time for demons or drama or self-pity, whoever you are. If you are who you think you are, all your false gods died in the fire that burned you. Leave them there. Trust the small voice inside you to make all the thunder you need."

"How can I . . . ?"

The rabbi sat down again and took out a packet of cigarettes and lit one.

"You already have. At this kibbutz," he said.

"Thank you."

The rabbi laughed. "No one is to be thanked. This is not a thanksgiving."

"*Ich liebe Sie alle*," said Hyman. I love you all.

"I know you do," said the rabbi. "That makes all this, you accused of being Hitler, much more of a problem, don't you think . . . ?"

The door of the committee room was then flung open and the older and one of the younger men from Palestine burst in, their faces angry, followed by David and Jacob and Anna.

"We understand that the kibbutz secretary is being accused of being Adolf Hitler after a dog was set on our friend Ehud. With great courage and presence of mind Kibbutz Secretary Hyman Kaplan shot the dog . . . We demand that the Americans who brought this dog be removed from Aviv immediately and these ridiculous accusations be dropped. Shame on you, rabbi!"

The rabbi held his head again. Rachel heard raised voices and went to the window. A small crowd had gathered and American soldiers were keeping them away from the steps and the front door of the house. She noticed how Hyman's demeanour and expression had changed. He was standing taller, his chest puffed out. The mood was raw and angry. Rachel saw Kells pull the two men who had come with him out of the room. Below the crowd chanted.

"Hyman! Hyman! Hyman!"

XIII

"*FROHES NEUES JAHR*," Happy New Year!" said a smiling, drunken stranger when Kells went out to get a pack of cigarettes.

The man was premature. It was still New Year's Eve with a dusting of snow on the pavements and Kells was late seeing Gretchen. He had telephoned Rachel several times, but she did not return his calls. He and Joe and the priest had been lucky to fight their way to their car in one piece and only because Joe had stopped and turned and covered their retreat with his gun and his fatal smile. The American guards were confused and the crowd then surrounded and began to drum on their car. The corpse of the dog was thrown at the car and bounced off the windshield and slithered down the hood. Only when Hyman came out, raising his good arm and calmed them, was Kells able to drive away, tyres skidding and throwing up gravel. Hyman was in control of the kibbutz now, where he always wanted to be, but of course he was not, and had never been, Hyman Kaplan.

Gretchen had gone to meet a girlfriend at the Café Kranzler. Kells took the envelope containing the overdue kill order out of his desk. He was going to ask her what to do. Whether to run. Just to abandon everything and leave. They were going to a party with his State Department contact.

The phone rang, it was her husky voice.

"Meet me where we met before. Don't worry, there are soldiers and police everywhere," she said quickly, before ringing off. She sounded in high spirits and the street she meant was off the Ku'damm, in a lattice of bombed but safe avenues. He was about to leave when the priest came in with Joe.

"I have been talking to Joe after such a peaceful Yuletide about how I can hear his Confession," said the priest. "I can hear yours too if you like?"

230

Kells was surprised. He looked at Joe to make sure what the priest had said was not a joke.

'That sounds . . . ambitious. But at this moment I have to meet a State Department contact and Gretchen. Thank you, Norton."

The last time Kells had been to Confession was before he had been sent overseas and the family priest had talked mainly about honeysuckle cuttings he had sent to Kells' mother and never to engage solitary women in conversation on foreign tram cars as they were a threat to America's national security and moral hygiene. Kells had secrets now he felt hard to confess to himself, let alone God or somewhere as public as the kingdom of heaven.

Then Joe said: "Shouldn't we make a report about Hyman and the dog, boss?"

Kells swallowed. What may have seemed a good idea once might not be received so well by the shiny new, button-down CIA. He wondered what had caused this sudden earthquake in Joe of well-concealed piety, but he knew he and the priest had been talking long into the night about incidents when Joe worked in Chicago.

Kells smiled. "Please leave it to the rabbi, for now," he said, and then more or less ran the half-mile to see Gretchen, almost knocking down a one-legged man in a cowboy suit advertising a John Wayne film *Dakota*, about a land grab, to be shown in the US sector. It made Kells think of his father and Billy the Kidd and that he should call.

Gretchen was standing against a wall. All the plaster had been blown off the brickwork and it was raked with shrapnel and bullet holes.

The baby smoothness of her skin stood out against the rough surface.

She was carrying a red umbrella. Bright, crimson red on the grey-ochre of the street. She was wearing a new, black market red coat. She waved immediately, the dimple of her smile showing.

That's what he liked about her. She wanted to have fun.

He was halfway across the street when he heard a screech of tyres behind him.

She was pointing up the road past him and her mouth was open in a silent shout.

He half-turned and saw the blue Russian car.

That was all he saw, before the car hit him and he had a vague remembrance of going over the bonnet, sailing up into the air, weightless, as if powered by a big wave. This was the biggest wave ever.

Candy thunder.

There was no pain.

He looked out for Gretchen. He tried to shout. He thought he saw her red umbrella in the road. Where was she?

He was flying. He never, ever, seemed to land.

There are things worse than death.

Kells woke up and blinked and immediately knew everything was wrong.

The smell of new wet plaster was very, very strong. Kells remembered when his dad had the old house re-plastered. The smell was there for weeks.

Had a bomb gone off below the partially mended houses nearby? There was always that smell of plaster when houses are blown apart. Was Gretchen all right?

He still did not feel any pain, in fact his head was surprisingly clear. He was not in the street. He was in a white room, totally white, white tiles and newly painted white walls. He was in a hospital. He smelled the antiseptic and the bleach and the ether and his head was back on a wedge of pillows. He peered down the bed and the sheets were held away from his body by a frame. They were so clean and white and starched and came up to his chin. He must look as pristine and virginal as one of Hyman's washed cocoons at the kibbutz, in the old stone lodge that housed the silkworm farm. It was a strange thought, but he could not shake free from the picture of all those cocoons drying on dishcloths, transformed into a stronger and eternal state of silk, to be woven into a lady's gown

232

or headscarf. He took a deep breath. There was a chair and a table in the room. They were also white. An overhead bulb in a metal shade gave out a pure white light. He was in hospital, but he could not hear the sounds of the hospital, the crash and banging of the trolleys in the corridors and the shouts and laughter of the nurses and the orderlies, or the occasional scream. The white curtains were drawn at the one window at the side of the room, even though it was day. A blood transfusion tree was at the side of his bed.

Did he remember being taken to the hospital? He tried to, but his brain was as blank and tranquil as the room.

He felt a panic-edged euphoria. He tried to move his right leg, but the drug they had given him made him feel he was floating. He felt he was surfing on a great yellow wave, not towards the shore, but in the other direction, towards the setting sun. The rush of the sea magnified in a million tides and rollers in his veins.

Then, back in the white room, shivering with cold fear, he thought of watching Hyman in a white bed in a white room, so badly burned everyone thought he was going to die.

Was he, Kells, going to die, without the priest hearing his Confession? Who had done this?

"¿Quién es?"

"Who is it?"

The last words of Billy the Kid.

He must have passed out because when he awoke he was in a different large white room and a tall man in surgical scrubs was looking at him, worried, from the bottom of the bed.

"I want you to listen to me very carefully, son. I am your surgeon. There is no easy way to say this. You were hit by a car and taken to a hospital in the Russian zone. They claim they did not operate on you, although there was an operation on a sepsis victim. There is a man who died of sepsis in that hospital who was not given an operation. His legs were due to be amputated . . . Your legs . . . Your legs have been amputated, and so have your arms . . . Simply, you were muddled with the sepsis patient and the Russians put you in a plaster cast to aid recovery, which I am told in a written note is their way. Your cast is full-size as it is built round a protective lining and that is the only size they have. There are tubes for bodily wastes and blood transfusions. There may have been damage to your neck and vocal chords, but we expect you to be able to recover your voice, if only in a whisper at first. You were not harmed badly during the accident beyond a few cracked ribs. The Russians say they did not do this to you intentionally. I'm really sorry to have to tell you this. Such is the nature of the amputation it may be hard, but not impossible, to fit prosthetic limbs. It is impossible for me to examine you as you have been almost completely cocooned in plaster, which we do not dare open while your wounds heal. That too was made clear in the note from the Russian doctors."

Kells tried to raise himself from the bed and his neck scratched against the cast.

The surgeon's gentle voice continued.

"I've given you a shot. Unfortunately, I've to go back to the States because my wife's mother is getting married again. I'll be back in a week or so. I don't usually work in Berlin. We'll be sending in a psychiatrist to help you . . . I think you should accept that help."

Kells looked up at the earnest face of the man.

He was thinking of what the Mad Hatter said at the tea party:

"Another arm, or perhaps another leg, Mr Kells? They are so lovely in this jelly!"

Kells' every thought, every breath, became one long scream.

A day later there was an attractive woman psychiatrist in his room holding a clipboard. and he watched her, exhausted. He had once broken his arm and had it in a plaster cast for a whole summer, and the much-signed cast had itched and itched. This was far worse as he felt spasms of cramp, even in his lost limbs, which the nurses told him was normal. The psychiatrist's grey-white woollen skirt was short and tight. Her lipstick was very red and her dark blonde hair was tied back with a band.

What sadist had sent an attractive woman to a man without arms and legs in a plaster cast?

"Now, tell me again, slowly, sir. You were trying to tell me just now that your German Shepherd dog told you that this Jewish man called Hyman, who you had rescued on the last day of the war in Europe, was really Adolf Hitler? Did the dog speak to you directly? Please try to articulate, colonel, I can lipread. Or was this some code involving the tapping of paws? How did he communicate to you that the man was Adolf Hitler?"

Kells looked at her bewildered. He tried to manage a whisper.

"The dog was called Wolf."

"I thought you said the man was called Wolf?"

"No, the man was called Kaplan."

"I thought you said the dog identified the Jewish man called Hyman as Adolf Hitler?"

"Yes."

"So who is this Hyman?"

"Hyman Kaplan is what I called the man who I saved in Berlin. I was looking for a man called Hyman Kaplan . . ." Kells found speech very difficult.

"But the man who you saved was not Hyman Kaplan?"

"I was told later he was the *Führer.*"

"By the German Shepherd dog?"

"No. First by a German prisoner in the State Department and then, in a way, by Hyman himself. He had dreams."

"And the dog?"

"I got hold of the dog. He used to belong to Hitler."

"And he recognised him?"

"You bet. He went all slitty-eyed crazy. He bounded straight up to him. He bit a militant Jew from Palestine who was standing close by."

"Hitler?"

"No, the dog. Wolf."

The woman was frowning over her pad and writing fast.

"Can you say the last word again, please?"

"Wolf." Kells felt he was shouting, but what came out was a croak.

"So the Jewish man, who was not from Palestine and who you accused of being Hitler, confessed to you that this talking, antisemitic dog was his? Is that what happened?"

"No, he could not remember. He could not remember anything. Anything from before we found him. You have it in your notes."

The woman stopped writing.

"I think it best that I write this up for Mr Dulles and bring it back for you to sign."

Kells tried to raise his head more and failed.

"You don't understand. There were dreams involved, of swastikas and rallies."

The woman sighed:

"I'm sure there were. You have had a tremendous shock, sir, with what has happened. And you were in combat for such a long time. But the war is over and we can't just keep fighting it, can we? The medical facilities in Berlin are less than perfect. But if I were you, I'd think again about this talking-dog story. Then there is all this disgusting business of a Mad Hatter's tea party at which you say members of a former espionage ring called Lucy were present, not to mention a woman with loose morals. Did she talk to you?"

"Not that much . . . She bit me."

"Well, you have only yourself to blame, colonel. You were told to stand down by Mr Dulles personally."

"So you are not just a shrink?"

"I am a psychiatrist, but we all are patriots."

"You work for Dulles?"

"That is neither here nor there. Many of our people involved in even a minor way with Operation Lucy have died suspiciously and Mr Dulles is wanting to charge the culprits with treason and homicide in the first degree. The Lucy group cannot be found in the fancy dress form you describe in Lucerne or Geneva. The individuals you name are respectable publishers who, indeed, publish a German version of *Alice Through the Looking Glass, Alice hinter den Spiegeln*. But the Lucy we are concerned with is very dangerous. And I would think again, Mr Kells, if you plan to deceive the United States government. Mr Dulles' investigations touch on our vital atom secrets. We may well be on the verge of another more terrible war, which we must win. If there is something you are not telling us, or there is someone you are protecting, a girl perhaps, you only need to consider your condition. Your arms and your legs have been removed. Friends have not done this to you, colonel. Speak up, Colonel Vardy. You are a decorated hero and an American. You cannot just think of yourself, or your lost arms and legs, at a time like this."

After she left and shut the door, Kells cried for a whole hour.

The tears ran down his cheeks and there was no way he could wipe them away. It was futile. The tears only went into the sarcophagus of a cast and itched like the seeds of roses they used to put into each other's beds at boarding school. So he stopped. A nurse came in and gave him a shot of something in the blood transfusion tree at his side and he drifted off into a welcome sleep. At first it was more of a daydream than a sleep. He was in a large open car, an old Mercedes, speeding through unfamiliar countryside at the height of summer. The car slowed as they came upon a village and there were people waving at the side of the road. Girls threw flowers into the car and everyone was happy. He was happy and waved back and saluted them. He was full of joy that all his plans were coming true. His dream became increasingly vivid and there was more detail, even down to the toothless grins of the veterans with their medals, and girls in traditional German costume with flowers on their bodices. A posy of marigolds was thrown into the car and he was overcome by their mysterious sanguine smell on the crisp morning air. There was not a doubt in his mind or a cloud in the sky. He sat down and there was a mirror on the seat in front. He was looking at the smiling faces of Adolf Hitler and the new CIA head, Allen Welsh Dulles, who spoke: "We all have problems with women from time to time, Colonel Vardy. Let us confide the secrets of my success ..." They went into a Hollywood musical song and dance number.

> *Sex, sex, sex, it's as easy as ABC ...*
> *Sex, sex, sex, take it from him and me ...*

Kells then began to wake, or the dream moved to the room he was in.

Across the room were two mice in ballet costume.

The two sexually precocious little girls who had danced at the Mad Hatter's Tea Party in Geneva. He was overcome with terror as they danced around the room, getting nearer and nearer to the bed.

They danced beautifully.

When they reached his bed, they knocked on the plaster cast with their little fists where his arms and legs had been and laughed. They laughed and laughed and laughed. Not a human laugh, but a squeaking laugh as one might expect from mice.

At that moment he fully realised for the first time that his arms and legs were gone for ever. They had been cut off. He had been punished for trying to find out too much. Or was this a punishment for all the bad things he had done in the war? The fact that he had not cared enough? That he was as much a part of the slaughter and extermination as the man he had called Hyman Kaplan?

The little ballet mice danced closer.

One threw a handful of wriggling green silkworms onto the bed.

The other tossed several white cocoons.

They pointed at him and began to sing.

> *"Water boil, water boil, soon you will be dead!*
> *Water boil, stop toil, we'll unravel your thread,*

You've been greedy, so let's spin you into silk
For we are needy, for gowns white as milk!"

The two little girls with their mouse masks bent over him and he attempted to roll and throw himself, heavy cast and all, off the bed. Only he could not move, and they danced and laughed more. One of them fingered his Mickey Mouse badge on the bedside locker.

"Pull my drip out, you sadistic little fuckers," he managed to hiss.

He wanted to bleed. He wanted to die. Anything was going to be better than this. He screamed at the top of his voice, but all that came out was a strangled whisper.

The girls ignored him and danced back to the other side of the room and then they were gone. The two little ballet mice were gone. The fat silkworms and the white cocoons they had put on his sheet were gone too.

But Kells was still there with what was left. Himself.

He had never realised quite how fucking painful that was until now.

The door to his room opened and a nurse, an American nurse he recognised, came in carrying a large aluminium bowl of steaming water. Like the ones for the cocoons at the kibbutz. She was smiling.

"Look what we've got for you," she said.

Kells put back his head and howled.

XIV

"COLONEL VARDY HAS always been attracted to me, Hyman, but I never thought he would try anything like this," Rachel says. She is still angry about the dog.

Today is a bright morning at the kibbutz and I have been in a state of shock after what Colonel Vardy told the rabbi and the small riot that followed. At first, I was strangely convinced that what the American said was true, totally true. It is part of human nature and a religious upbringing, if I had a religious upbringing, to think we are sinful. To think we are the devil. Rachel says in my case it is survivors' guilt, and I cannot believe the stories she has told me of what she did in the camps.

I do not want to think like that. I have been so happy. I want to dance. I want to dance to the moon. I want to cha-cha among the stars with Rachel.

Then I think again of being accused of being Adolf Hitler, and how even that has worked to my advantage.

And, from what I have seen, even in the short space of time I can access as memory, I am sure that every man is capable of the barbarity that was practiced in the concentration and extermination camps, capable of the hubris of thinking themselves superior to others; any one of us who is part of a state, or pays his taxes and supports the wars of politicians can say: "I am Adolf Hitler," with a degree of truth, in that he stops being an individual and joins the wolf pack.

We have been sent for again by the increasingly busy-body rabbi. We both go in and sit down.

"Why do men do such things? Become dictators?" I ask. I do not like the man as much as I did. He forgave me far too easily if I were Adolf Hitler. The men from Palestine think he is too liberal and weak. He coughs.

"I once saw it referred to as the Lucifer paradox," he says in his pompous way, lighting a cigarette with an old wheel and rope lighter and coughing more. "But their bargain is with the world and its power, and not God or his servant the devil. These are men who are dazzled by creation, overcome by the beauty of the earth and humanity. They are revolted by the sewer of political life, but have to use politics to seize control of that creation for all. Their child-like wonder goes sour precisely because they have made it political. That is the paradox. They have rendered paradise flawed and human. In the end they find only logic and personal ease in destroying everything. The more innocent they start out, the more vicious they become. To such men their atrocities are an act of frantic and frenzied and virgin love."

"An Act of Love that can send children to gas chambers?" I say.

The rabbi nods gravely. "Exactly. Such is the passion of the child in man," he says. "Such is the anger of once-good children."

Then I say, "Sometimes I think that mankind will kill each other off. That we are suicidal creatures, designed to eliminate ourselves."

The rabbi laughs.

"No, my friend. We are not that clever. Part of my hope for man is that we always make a mess of things. Even the Final Solution was not final. I am still here in Germany drinking kosher rum . . ."

I wait a moment and then say to him. "Or do you think it part of God's purpose to have the bad as well as the good? Yes, there are limits, as the recent past shows. But to create anything there often has to be destruction. America would still be using stone axes if the colonists had not gone out there and taken the land. All the art and science of the country that protects us would be lost. We have to guard against anger and the fanatic, but surely we must help ourselves to what is there?"

"But that is colonialism, of which the Nazis were only the most bellicose example in high-fashion uniforms . . ." The rabbi does not finish his sentence. Two of the men from Palestine walk in, followed by David who helped with my silkworms.

"Rabbi, we are here to inform you that at a meeting earlier this morning with the Kibbutz Secretary, Hyman Kaplan, and every other member of the committee, it has been decided that your outdated ideas are no longer wanted in this Kibbutz Aviv, which is dedicated to the establishment of the nation state of Israel and nothing else. We thank you for your work. But your misplaced liberal teachings may be confusing the new settlers. Everyone agrees. Paul, who shares your views, and the former Nazi general who owns this property, are going to Bonn in a truck this afternoon. Can you gather your belongings together and be on it, please?"

The rabbi stood. He was about to say something, but his shoulders dropped and he shook his head.

"You knew about this all the time, didn't you . . .?" he says to me. "I know who you are, now. By Jehovah, I know who you really are . . ." And then he left in silent tears.

XV

"CAN YOU DRIVE us to the railway station?" said Rachel to one of the American soldiers. That morning the fields had been covered in a thick January frost.

"Sure thing."

"We are going to Berlin."

The American guard, who had lost his arm below the elbow and had the sleeve of his jacket neatly sewn and shortened, drove them the ten miles in an open US jeep, despite the drizzle.

Rachel wore her best coat, luckily a green one, with her green dress. And a matching green felt alpine-style hat. She had taken great care with her make-up and had borrowed a new pair of silk stockings from one of the other girls. She hardly recognised herself. She took a deep breath of the morning air. It had not really dawned on her before the grating sound of the cattle grid, a noise which was close to that of a machine pistol, that this was the first time she had been any distance since she came here, months ago. The work and those around her had been so intense and demanding and now everyone at the beautiful old house, and it was beautiful, whoever it had belonged to, was in even more of a rush, a pell-mell, headlong panic, preparing to go to British Palestine, to an Israel, the mythic promised land, a land where they were all going to be happy and safe forever. She wished she and Hyman could go.

The surgeon in Berlin had not said Kells was near death, but she was familiar with that tone of voice, when doctors suspend science and take on the slow and measured tones of priests. He had been in hospital for two weeks.

A sleety rain started as they got to the station.

"Call ahead and we will pick you up on your return," said the driver. "Good to have people to talk to. Be careful now," he added, without irony, even though she had said only a few words.

They watched him drive the jeep away and Hyman opened his umbrella with great formality and held it above Rachel's head, as if she was a princess. No one had ever treated her as Hyman had these past months, not even her dear father. She put her arm through Hyman's and held him close.

"I have been talking to the Americans about getting more silk-worms," she said.

"Oh, it does not matter."

"It does. Paul and his friends shouldn't have done that. Burned your work."

Hyman made no reply as they walked up and down the platform, which glistened in the winter sunlight. Up the line, under a bridge in a cloud of snow-white steam, they both saw the black engine pulling the train that would take them to Berlin. The air smelt of coke soot from the train's boiler. The two syllables of her fatal city turned over and over in her mind. She was trembling.

When Hyman spoke, his voice was kind and gentle: "What matters is that those young people get on their way. Get on their way and make things better and mend the world."

The journey was not an easy one for Rachel. Even before they entered the Russian zone, there were all manner of unexplained stops and then official halts and checks by men in shabby uniforms who had the air of bus conductors promoted to generals. The blinds were pulled down so they could not see out and she had the desire to go into the corridor, open one of the carriage doors, throw herself off the train and run into the woods.

She had been on a train going east before.

The compartment door snapped open and made her jump.

"*Papiere, bitte.*"

Their papers were checked and their luggage searched again. The soldier was disappointed when he saw they had American military

243

documents and temporary passports. To appear calm, Rachel took out a compact and powdered her face.

"Where are you travelling, *fräulein?*" demanded the Russian soldier in German. "Are you travelling alone?"

"We are going to Berlin," she said very slowly. The Russian's brown uniform was pressed close to her and smelled of boiled cabbage and urine. The second soldier had a machine-pistol.

"We smashed Berlin," said the Russian. He lowered his right hand until it was almost touching her face.

"Then it should be easy for me to find the hospital I'm going to in the American zone."

The soldiers left and Rachel swallowed. There were stories which she had been told by the American soldiers of women, even married couples, being raped on the trains in the Red Zone.

Zoo Station in Berlin was much the same as she remembered. The bombs had all missed, but she could not believe her eyes as she stared out at the rest of the city, once so solid and seemingly eternal. Entire streets were in ruin or missing. Expensively decorated rooms hung in mid-air above the pavements, with tables and chairs and in one case an immense chandelier in a ballroom without a floor. There was a fog of dust in the air after the countryside, and everywhere there were rolls of new barbed wire and soldiers. There was a smell of boiling split-pea soup, and beneath that the smell of the rubbish dump, of human rot. Underneath the bricks and plaster were thousands and thousands of bodies in a city that had once never stopped dancing.

It was strange to feel so sad about the destruction, when those in the city had murdered her family and nearly her entire people.

Berlin was still her home. The destruction made her abyss of loss even more real.

Hyman went to hail a taxi, but Rachel shook her head.

They were nearly swept aside by a rush of people who had got out of a bus.

A man shouted. Rachel saw a big, black, Mercedes taxi.

"Come on, Hyman. Don't frown so. This is our ride."

The man took them to the American hospital, without a word. They got out of the car and Hyman was about to pay.

"Now, you go inside. They gave me dollars to settle this," said Rachel, and she watched him walk stiffly towards the doors of the hospital. There were shrapnel marks around the entrance where a queue of shabby men and women, in threadbare shadows of their once best clothes, ghosts in make-up and neckties worn for the first time in years, had come to try and see a doctor or relative. They did not look at Hyman, who even with the face of Clark Gable, was invisible now in the starved and destroyed city, whoever he was before. One family, a well-dressed couple and three children, were sitting on an expensive silk-covered couch, looking at a duck trussed at their feet and a bottle of Schnapps. Hyman was walking well now, though his eyes had looked so sad since they arrived at the station. He was not scared, only sorrowful, like she was. He held the small case he had brought with him.

When Hyman had gone inside, Rachel paid the driver. She needed a few moments to collect herself.

In her handbag was a pistol. The one Hyman had used to kill the dog.

Rachel had received a phone call at the kibbutz that had made her feel very cold and confused. It gave a password and target and means and date. It asked her to provide another target name in the near future. The woman then rang off, as was resistance procedure. She had used the words, ELIMINATE TO FREE, a resistance phrase. Rachel had been so breathless and frantic that she nearly forgot the date, scrabbling for a pencil to write things down. Did this mean she worked for Lucy in the camp? That her memories of killing people on the operating theatre were not the twisted fantasies of a survivor? That she had killed the two girls?

She got out of the car and the taxi drove off and Rachel walked a few steps with great purpose. She had orders and understood the need for them. She had to obey or what she had done, must have done, in the camps was meaningless.

XVI

"NO, IT CANNOT be so!" I, Hyman Kaplan, say, out loud, as I look down at Colonel Vardy in the white room, on the white bed in a white plaster cast. When I first heard of his accident, I felt the thrill of *schadenfreude*, but now I am shocked. The notes at the end of the bed state his legs and arms have been amputated and that he is in the oblong plaster cast of dimensions measured to the millimetre. The nurse says, "We are giving him morphine, but you do not have long. He is very upset. It was a car accident."

I take a deep breath and nod, though I doubt it was an accident. I almost weep for the poor man, my rival in love, who is never going to recover. Involuntarily, I reach out towards the bed.

"Please do not touch him. Keep away from the bed," says the nurse, and leaves me there. Kells' handsome face is undamaged and he is looking at me with a complete hatred. An American hatred. The sort of hatred Americans have when their bright, childish dreams are taken from them. I look away. His blue eyes are boiling with anger, as if somehow I am responsible for where he is. A tube from a plasma bag connects to a drip and snakes into the sarcophagus of plaster by his left shoulder. He is only a torso. A stub. I remember I once saw a boy pull all the limbs off a crab at the seaside. *"Er kann jetzt niemanden kneifen!"* "He cannot pinch anyone now." It is a sudden and surprising memory of a childhood I do not remember at all.

Kells is as helpless as the crab, and then words pour out of me.

"I have been so happy since you saved me . . . I owe my life to you and my deep and lasting love of Rachel. I know you had warm feelings for her, and I ask that you be happy for us now. I am sure you are exhausted from the war and all your work in Berlin and you did not mean those hurtful things you said to me . . . We will not be going to Palestine now, because we must not let anything stand in front of the idealistic dream of the young people, and it may be that you have written a few words down, or spoken of your suspicions about me. Imagine a man going to the new Israel and being accused of what you were trying to accuse me of with that dog. I do not have the strange dreams any more either. They are gone. If I was responsible for so many deaths and so many tears, do you not think I would know about it in my soul, in here?"

I tap my chest. Kells bares his very white American teeth and his tongue rolls out. I catch the word "kill," and then a drooling jumble. Slowly, Kells almost appears to relax and after a silence says, "I have your dreams now, you Nazi motherfucker!" before his speech becomes incomprehensible again.

I approach the bed and I see, to my surprise, that there is a silkworm on his locker. By a Mickey Mouse club badge. It is on part of a mulberry leaf and the insect is large and fat and should not be in here with a man without his arms and his legs. It may easily get inside Kells' plaster sarcophagus and cause itches and tickles that would be maddening. It must have been put there by a person who knows of my work at the kibbutz. Of my work before the war. I must be seeing things. I have been working too hard. And then came the accusation. I am mesmerised by the creature and reach for it when the nurse, who had silently returned, pulls me sharply away:

"No, sir! Do not approach. He bites, don't you colonel? He's been saying silly things about being Hitler's dog and so he has to bite folks."

Rachel then comes through the door behind the nurse and, with a flick of her pretty head, gestures that I should leave. The nurse is explaining why the Russian doctors operated. It is something to do with septicaemia. The nurse can see how emotional poor Rachel is. The look on her face is one of horror and she cannot properly get her breath.

"Please wait outside, Hyman. And you please, nurse. I want to be alone with the colonel. We have private business."

I want to stay and comfort Rachel because I know she is upset.

I turn one last time to the bed and Colonel Vardy screams. It is a scream from Hell.

XVII

AFTER KELLS' SCREAM, Rachel stared at the bottom of the bed for a long time, at the ironwork, how the structure fitted together. She swallowed. She was trembling. She read the notes and tears came to her eyes. She had not expected this. She was not told of this. The white sheet on the bed was neat and tucked in expertly to make hospital corners. The sheet on the frame over the truncated body in the cast had been freshly laundered. The room was almost identical to that in the American hospital where she had worked, where Hyman had recovered after his operations. She then looked into the face of Kells, into the blue eyes that were staring at her. Here was what was left of the young American colonel. Her hand was on the gun inside her green hat. The hospital was near one of the most bombed areas, which the American sappers were clearing. Every now and then there was an explosion. If she fired through the felt of her hat, the pistol's gasses' exit velocity would be reduced and the sound would be absorbed in the levelling of the buildings that had already been bombed. She had considered putting an American condom over the end of the barrel, but the gun was too small.

Despite herself, Rachel laughed. In other circumstances she and Kells might have been together. The hero and the pretty cellist. How could he know what sort of world he was entering? The face, shaved and pink on the pillows for all the war it had seen, or avoided seeing, was still the face of a child. The colonel had always been in an army, and never on his own. That was the real test. When you are on your own. When it's just down to you. One's own demons are worse than any enemy.

Rachel knew it was going to be very hard to kill Kells. Was he such a threat to the Lucy organisation now the war was over?

Kells' expression had changed from that of complete hatred for

Hyman, when he was in the room, to one of almost pleasure at seeing her, mixed with resignation. Rachel had seen the same resigned expression on the faces of the two girls she had been told to prevent talking in the last days of the camp, when they should have been free, gone with her into the countryside, picked daisies laughing in the grass, the orders from the resistance, probably straight from Lucy, coming in a morsel of bread from a prisoner she had never seen before, bitter words to be immediately swallowed. It was not a fantasy. She had not made it up. She was to shoot the two young girls who had gone to the officers' quarters and who were probably going to be killed anyway, but may say too much before they were. In the memory that she had tried to dismiss as unreliable, they had attended a scientist who had been tortured and was sent to the infirmary so he could be patched up and interrogated again. Luckily for everyone concerned, the scientist had died, but not before he had raved about his work and about Rachel's network. And someone else heard and had told Lucy.

She was sure she must have heard the word Lucy before Kells talked to her about the operation.

You never knew where or who Lucy was.

Rachel hated all this, and even wondered if her initial arrest in the ambulance had been set up by the network, to get her into that particular camp, where being part of the resistance meant she started working for Lucy. It was a raw, paranoid thought. Her father had been involved with the fashionable, artistic underworld of the resistance. Had her own dead father used her? To appear totally committed to his friends, not knowing who she would end up working for? Was she going mad?

Rachel's finger was on the trigger of the pistol in the hat. The ridiculous green hat.

The pistol was real.

When, in her elaborate memory of the event, she had killed the two officers and then the two girls on the last day at the camp, the Luger was heavy and awkward and felt like an artillery piece. The commandant surgeon, Manfred, had told Rachel where he was going to leave it before he fled. He had given her a little kiss on the cheek, like a brother or a friend, and then a passionate one as the lover he was. She had found herself hoping he got to safety and his wife. She knew that was true. Then she saw the Polish nurse Martha under the billiard table, sucking her thumb. She had put the pistol against the girl's head. Again, Rachel heard the splintering of bone. Was that true? Had she been ordered to do that? It now seemed so.

Kells was trying to speak. Rachel stepped nearer the bed.

"So, this is goodbye?" he managed.

"Yes."

"Did your people do this? Lucy?" Rachel thought he meant the amputations, she swallowed. It probably was not known how much Kells knew.

"*Ich kenne keine Lucy* – I know no Lucy," she said.

She looked Kells straight in the eye. If she placed the muzzle of the pistol gently under the plaster, the nurses would think at first he had perished from his internal injuries or septicaemia.

Kells was talking fast.

"The Lucerne people. You know who I mean. I went to see them. Is that why you have come to kill me? Please kill me, Rachel. Did they do this? Was that the reason for all the sugar arms and legs at the tea party?"

She shook her head very slowly. She had no idea what he was talking about. His words sounded so absurd. She had no contact with anyone in Lucerne. She wanted it to be over.

"I never expected you," he said.

She had a tear in her right eye. He maybe was emboldened by it, but her face was firm. She should not have started to talk to him.

"Are you going to Palestine, to Israel?" he asked her.

"Not now. Not after the ridiculous business with your dog."

"I see. Where will you go?"

She knew he was playing for time. She leant over the bed. She pushed the muzzle of the pistol down the cast, against his flesh.

There was the smell of his body mixing with that of the fresh plaster. He did not struggle. His eyes were pleading, but she did not know if he was pleading for life, or in this awful state, death.

Rachel's hand was shaking, but she had to do this. She mustn't put the many at risk because of the American colonel. She did not know who Lucy were. She always had to trust and believe. Like everyone.

"Please forgive me," she said, her finger tightening on the trigger.

At that moment, the door burst open and Gretchen and Hyman came into the room.

"Stop! Whatever you intend, please stop, Rachel," shouted Gretchen.

She moved quickly forward so her outstretched left hand was almost touching Rachel's green coat.

"We must get Kells out of here! There are documents inside the plaster cast relating to Lucy that I obtained for Kells from my Russian contacts. I cannot tell you how important this is. We are on our own. We have to get out! Disappear, fast. Shoot him in that cast and we will never get those documents. They implicate us all."

Rachel was staring at her but did not move. Gretchen turned to Kells.

"You have not lost your arms and legs, Kells, my love."

"What . . . ? What the fuck did you say?"

"Your side, the Americans, all sides, were trying or planning to kill you. I had to get you away. A circus deception . . . We are all disowned and hunted. Your side suspects you, as does mine, as do the people who run Lucy and are behind Lucy. Rachel, too, is a loose end and it goes without saying what might happen to Hyman, from any side. People already tried to shoot him. The Americans think we are Lucy, and Lucy thinks we are with the Americans. It is all fatal. We are alone and naked. They intend to kill us all."

Gretchen paused. Rachel turned the pistol on Gretchen.

"I always wondered what you looked like, Rachel. I am Gretchen. I am Kells' wife . . . I think I know who you are. We both love Kells."

They stared at each other.

Gretchen gently extended her hand and put her index finger, with its nail painted bright red, over the end of the small automatic.

Time and death seemed to swing in the air.

Gretchen then shouted, her lips quivering, "This must stop! I have come from Kells' house. I found Joe and the priest. It looked as if the priest was taking a Confession and both are shot through the head. The housekeeper too. Her head was hacked off. Whoever did it wrecked the place. Here is Kells' copy of *Alice Through the Looking Glass*, if you don't believe me." She took the book from her coat pocket with her right hand. The big blue poppies towered over Alice.

For several minutes it was as if Kells could not get his breath. "I can't feel my arms and legs," he gasped.

"You will. The Russian doctor very carefully deadened the nerves," said Gretchen.

"So you are with the Russians?" said Rachel.

"Not now," said Gretchen. She put the book back in the pocket of her coat and took off her fluffy pink beret. She did not move her finger from the muzzle of Rachel's pistol.

Gretchen smiled at Kells.

"Kells loves you, Rachel. You love Kells."

Rachel was furious for a second, with the truth she supposed, like the tantrum of a little girl, and then stepped away from the bed. She put the gun in the pocket of her coat. She felt faint, she was so relieved. It was all madness. Now she, Rachel, was under the billiard table with her thumb in her mouth like the Polish girl. And someone would be coming for her.

Gretchen dropped her hand.

"We must get Kells out of here to a place I know. There is a safe house. It's a safe house in an uncleared zone where some musicians were living. We must go there now. There's not a moment to lose." Behind her an orderly came into the room. He had a circular saw, which he plugged into a wall socket.

"You got the money? I can get in big trouble for this. You know, big trouble," said the orderly.

"Betray us, and you will not know what big trouble, or anything else is, anymore, ever," said Gretchen, very coldly. The man turned pale and nodded and went to work.

Gretchen removed the sheet from Kells, exposing his encased body. "Those Ruskies know a thing or two when it comes to plaster casts. This is an Acropolis of a cast. You should have all written your names on it," said the orderly and set to work on removing it with his saw.

The buzzing went on and on and plaster dust filled Kells' nose and eyes, but he did not seem to care. Gretchen stroked his hair. The giant cast was pulled apart by Rachel and the orderly in a sudden theatrical way, as if a deer's stomach had been opened by a hunter's knife. A pile of papers tumbled off Kell's chest. Many were marked TOP SECRET. The orderly was about to say something but then stopped. He took a roll of dollar bills from Gretchen and went to the door. "Best forget everything," said Gretchen. "We will find you," but he was already gone.

"His arms! His legs!" shouted Hyman, very pleased. "It is a good magic trick!"

Rachel bent down and picked up a piece of paper.

"There's a letter. Written by hand."

"Read it please," said Kells.

Rachel read:

My Darling Kells,

I am sorry you have been trussed up like this, but I had to make several bargains to get you clear. I hope you are not too mad with me. We never know how things will change and what is coming. Do you remember the time when we fell though the floor after making love?

All my Love, Gretchen

Rachel tried to laugh, and failed. She burst into tears. Gretchen hugged Kells and kissed him on the forehead.

"The letter was if I didn't get away from the Russians," Gretchen said.

Kells took a deep breath. "I feel . . ." he began in a croaky, reedy, feminine voice.

"We have to go, right now," said Gretchen.

They all saw he was trembling, and his flesh, liberated from the plaster, looked clammy and grey.

Gretchen reached for her large bag. From the bag she took out a blue dress and a blonde wig and put them on a table in the room. She then took out some black court shoes and stockings and underwear and even a lipstick. She laughed.

"Please put these on, my darling. You'll not be able to walk. We do not know if they will still be looking for you. They'll not be looking for a well-made American girl in a blue dress in a wheelchair."

Kells nodded. He let Gretchen clear away the plaster and dress him. He attempted to laugh along as she put lipstick on his lips.

"Rub them together, darling. If anyone asks, your name is Lucy, Lucy Kessler," said Gretchen. "Doesn't Lucy look so good?"

PART FOUR

I

IN THE SAFE house, Rachel was daydreaming erotically about the burning man, blue and pursued by his own yellow fire. He was inside her, and her mouth muscles fluttered and the flesh on her cheeks quivered while her pupils dilated and her irises turned up, almost disappearing under the long eyelashes of her upper eyelids, as they always did, and her thin body contorted and bent and whiplashed as if by an electric shock. Then she fully woke with a cry of orgasm in a house that was silent but for the ticking of an old clock; a place where she hoped no one would find the four of them, like a gingerbread refuge in a fairy-tale forest.

Yet part of her wanted the wolves to find her and her gingerbread. Another part never wanted to leave her personal forest, haunted by the past. A place of terrible certainty in an uncertain world. Of orders and order. Reality was more complicated. She even had fantasized about Hyman being Hitler. But Rachel preferred the burning-man version, born out of the desolation that was inside her and destroying her vile body with his Gabriel flames.

The dark of dark sex had been the only possible affirmation of her existence. She had not escaped at all from the camp, from the vicious men in black uniforms with swastika armbands who she desired, because she was no different or better. Now even that twisted solace was fading, and she alone carried the burden of all she had done, its weight pressing on her shoulders as she sat in a dusty armchair and looked out of the front window of their "safe house" onto the grey, wooded lake on the outskirts of the city at Charlottenburg-Wilmers-dorf, the *Teufelsee*, the Devil's Lake in the Grunwald.

She yawned and stretched and froze completely awake as she thought of how she had so nearly killed Kells. So nearly obeyed the orders of Lucy. If the orders were from Lucy.

The white stucco mansion of a merchant had been built in the nineteenth century, a villa with green roof tiles to complement the shutters, and even green iridescent tiling on the front wall. She remembered going to birthday parties in this section of Berlin as a child, playing musical chairs and passing a matchbox from nose to nose, oranges from under chin to under chin. The house made her think of her father, and she had often played her cello enthusiastically, but badly, for friends after the children's parties. There were eight bedrooms, a huge cedar tree in the back garden and, oddly, a mulberry tree in the front. Its trunk was painted white and the leaves still far from starting to unroll themselves from the buds. It was as if the silkworms were following them.

Munch, munch, munch.

Ravenously eating what was left of their lives. The front garden's large pergola led straight onto a cinder-track-like road, with a sandy beach on the other side and then the lake itself. A couple of hundred metres up the road, was a burnt-out Soviet armoured car, stripped of every useful part, rusting quietly by a clump of elderflower trees that were coming into leaf in front of a fading red star. Another skeleton of a tank already looked like a fossil of a dinosaur she had seen in a museum, after a shell had set off the ammunition within, leaving a head and ribs of metal. This was the American sector of the greater city now, although no clear lines had been drawn.

In the low grey clouds, the gods looked down and waited for the next war.

On the beach were several typical ancient wicker settees with everlasting flowers garlanding the armrests. The large houses in the area once had a reputation for decadent parties with nude bathing in what had been a glacial lake. The flowers, blue and white and pink, were woven into the wicker with wire, covered with a green felt material; settees that had seen some of the wilder parties, no doubt.

Rachel remembered swimming naked in one of the other lakes after a party.

She remembered the false gaiety and the forced enjoyment. She remembered a teacher telling her that the lake was the home of a very rare fish, the Bitterling, from before the last ice age. There was even a Bitterling Society, *Bitterling-Gesellschaft*, and Rachel wondered what had happened to its members during the war. Was the *Bitterling-Gesellschaft* for or against National Socialism and the Final Solution? The lake was deserted now, as if what had followed the last Ice Age had not happened.

The villa with its green shutters and a whimsical, Italian air, did not look like part of Berlin, of the war and the Nazis at all and it had not been damaged, not a single scratch or bullet hole spoiled the ornamental plaster. It stood almost on the lake, while all the other villas further back had been levelled to rubble. It did not have much in common with a red brick structure on the far side that might have been a school. Its red-brick chimney made Rachel pause. She took a deep breath. Brief exploding images from her own recent history, of the camps, of air-raids with white searchlights in dark blue skies and concussive explosions flowering from the earth, intertwined with the placid landscape around her, like the old rolls of rusting barbed-wire that were now partly overgrown with brambles. She hoped the house might be invisible to such horror, and to those still intent on finding them and murdering them because of their involvement with Lucy.

Once good, Lucy had turned bad to survive.

Like in the Holocaust, Frankenstein structures had replaced human thought and become self-perpetuating.

She wished she could talk to the rabbi. But now it was impossible, and she feared for him.

Rachel's father had met his society resistance contacts in the *Waldensee*. The house was from a gentler time and just looking at it moved her. It had, Gretchen said, been owned by a cultured man who had given money to the cause of Israel, but had been arrested for trading in fake penicillin. Three black musicians from a jazz band marooned from before the war and harassed by the police had been living there and that's how Gretchen knew of the place.

One guarantee of privacy for the house, and indeed the lake and the whole forested area, was that it was heavily mined and had not been cleared. There were posts with neat, Germanic skulls and crossbones and underneath the word MINEN.

Another large sign saying DANGER had broken in two and was splattered with shrapnel, and there was only one road out and in. They were safe but trapped in a cul-de-sac.

Gretchen said the black musicians now had a place by the small club for 'lady-boys' they played at, called The Katzenmutter Club, or The Mother Cat at Holzmarktstraße, down from Alexanderplatz and by the River Spree. There were several dreamy posters of men dressed as women and women dressed as men pinned up in the hallway. To Rachel's surprise, Gretchen had sung with their band when it played at another house on a lake nearer the city.

Rachel did not trust Gretchen.

A flight of ducks landed perfectly on the water, wings arched, feet extended.

The slightest movement outside disturbed her.

A growing sense of inertia, like dull toothache, had come over them in their isolation. The kibbutz, which she passionately missed, was a world away. All that was gone. Like her family before.

For three weeks now the four of them had been in a state of shock. They all sat either by the window or out under the pergola and watched the lake until in the evening the cold air stung their faces and their bodies should have glowed, glowed with the realisation that perhaps their war was over.

Time did not so much stop as speed by, ignoring them. Only Hyman lit the oil lamps, cooked food for them on a wood stove and kept the house going. Rachel wanted to talk and felt the others did too, but few words came and, like the mines, there were many subjects to avoid. They were forced to look so very closely at each other and themselves. The realisation had dawned on Rachel that they had all been part of the monster, Lucy, that was pursuing them.

Rachel was glad she had not been able to kill Kells.

But she had intended to kill him and the others knew that.

How had Gretchen been so brave? Rachel was simultaneously in awe and jealous and suspicious of the fact.

She still was not sure who had tried to kill Kells with the car. Gretchen had admitted to orders too. Had Gretchen known what was going to happen before her trick with the plaster cast?

Rachel had papers that belonged to a girl at the kibbutz called Ulrike, who was going to the kibbutz in Palestine. Ulrike now only had a copy of them, done by Rachel's *Haganah* contacts only last week, who specialised in duplicating such American-issued German papers. She had hung onto them in case she had to disappear after killing Kells.

Rachel had become a German citizen again. A fake one. Who exactly were "her people", her *Leute*, now, beyond the others in the house? Gretchen was a fake too and she doubted if her marriage to Kells was in any way legal.

At the side of the house was a garage and a car, a French Citroën saloon, which was undamaged, but when she tried the key, which was in the dashboard, it refused to start.

Rachel was about to get up from her chair when Hyman came into the room and limped quickly up to her, without his stick, a book in his hand. He theatrically breathed in the air from the lake, and Rachel noticed the birdsong. Hyman was the only one trying to keep cheerful, like the birds. He had taken control and was doing everything at their new home. He worked so hard he made her feel dizzy. She did not want to work hard anymore.

"I must tell you this, Rachel," he said. "I read in an old book in my room that this lake is meant to be haunted by a knight who, hunted down for his honesty, is granted a wish to disappear by an old man. The only trouble is the old man is the devil and the knight, in return for his wish, has to tramp around the lake for all eternity as a pale and ineffectual ghost. Can you imagine! A ghost is the very worst thing a German can be, even in a place of such beauty. There is no work here. Nothing to do, or achieve, or build or conquer. Just to be. For all time. No chance not to be. I bet the knight is not such a good soul now. I think it is a cynical German warning about best intentions." He laughed.

Rachel lit a cigarette from a packet on the table, and stubbed it out almost immediately and lit another. She felt at one with the murky twilight of the room, where the curtains were already half drawn. She had to force herself to reach out and flick the ash into the ashtray.

"Yes, we have disappeared. We have become children of war. Refugees. Everybody is a fucking ghost."

An early spring fog persisted on the small lake and she felt it seeping into her. She stared out across the water into the mist. The world beyond was too complicated and frightening.

Hyman looked at her with a loving smile and shook his head.

"No, my love. I think you are wrong. A few of us have escaped and are still escaping. Like those silkworms that hatch into moths in my paper. If I am indeed the man who wrote it. You remember? 'Scenes From The Sexual Life Of Escaped Silk Moths In Springtime by Hyman Kaplan, Berlin 1938'. It goes something like: however efficient the security of the silk farm, however modern and industrialised the process of killing all chrysalises for the maximum production of silk, by gas, heat or boiling water, there are always a few moths that escape and fly free, becoming creatures of strange beauty and promiscuity. Freedom's miracle."

II

"I THINK I will go and find out what makes the boiler work better," I say, picking up one of the unlit oil lamps from the large table. "It is cold in the night. I still have a lot of those fascinating papers to go through from Colonel Vardy's plaster cast, and I would like to finish what I have started," and I get up, leaving Rachel staring at the lake, and I turn the porcelain door handle and go out into the hall and close the door quietly behind me. I have both a curiosity and dread about what is in the papers. I am in search of myself. I light the oil lamp at the bottom of the wooden stairs. I sit down on a rickety chair. With a metal hook I open the door of the old, solid iron boiler furnace and a welcome blast of heat and a reddish, dancing light spills out into the room. I have given myself the task of sifting through the intelligence, as no one else wants to very much. Rachel seems unable to do anything, unwilling to let go of her past, and Gretchen, who I like a lot, spends all her time with poor Kells, who still insists on disguising himself as a woman after his horrible experience in the plaster cast and Rachel, who he loves, coming to kill him.

Gretchen is worried Kells may kill himself. She caught him with a razor blade held to the artery of his throat, under his ear.

It is strange that whenever there is the most absurdity, we are immediately borne back to the most real.

So many papers from Gretchen's mysterious Russian contacts were packed into Kells' plaster cast. They are piled in the basement. Intercepted messages from and about Lucy by various intelligence services, including their own, the Soviet, the German, the British, the American and ones I did not expect like the Swiss, the Romanian, and even the Holy See, The Vatican. I find this all most extraordinary. I had no idea the Pope has, or needs, a secret service, if one assumes he is in communication with an all-seeing God. Much is not in code. but anything relating to the present purpose and aims of Operation Lucy remains in the Colour and Nonsense Codes that defeated Kells, which on one of his better days here he told me about. He really does not care anymore. I sit down again on the chair and take out an English Woodbine cigarette from its exquisite blue green packet, the shade of a duck egg. There are tins of boiled sweets and cigarettes, British army rations, down in the cellar, that the negro musicians forgot about. I take a long pull on the cigarette and blow the smoke out through my nose, not even coughing I am so well. I then pick up a paper from a jumble on the stone floor. I think I spot something.

There is even a telephone number for Roessler, Lucerne 666, with whispers of Lucifer and Faust, and showing a dark sense of humour. Yet in the encoded intercepted orders to Lucy agents the word TOPSECRET is written joined together. "*Scheiße!*" I say, out loud.

Simplicity may be the key.

TOPSECRET has nine letters. The colour codes are arranged in squares of nine. I snatch up one of the pieces of nonsense from the floor, and in a small notebook write down every ninth letter with a pencil stub I have in my pocket.

The first piece of nonsense I try it on does not work.

The next makes me sit back smiling and open the stove and watch the fire and the red-hot logs burning and falling into each other. The nonsense piece, after a sequence of colours where red is dominant, possibly meaning urgent, but ends in brown, perhaps denoting the military, begins: "*Billy P was married at about . . .*" which if one takes the first and every ninth letter is bmb, an abbreviation for bomb in simple shorthand. The whole message runs "bomb plutonium formula delivered to K from L, with love."

Another is for an initiator or detonator, partially made of silk, used in the atomic bombs on Japan. Always the silk!

A long uncoded Russian memo, fortunately in German, from their intelligence, reveals that the K in the Lucy communications is Igor Kunchatov, the head of Soviet atomic bomb research. It seems that the Soviets had been unsuccessful in obtaining enough uranium to make a bomb, after which information was passed to Kunchatov from Lucy, through the Russian secret service, the NKVD, giving details of how one can be made using a synthetic compound called plutonium. They were given a helping hand to be the next great enemy. Pluto is Mickey Mouse's pet dog in the Walt Disney cartoons. The American soldiers at the kibbutz had their comic books. It was the only thing many of them read.

A Swiss Bureau Ha memo speculates that the British spymaster, Eric Liddell, was the one who passed the plutonium secrets and details of the silk trigger mechanism for a bomb. The Swiss say that Liddell had done this working for the old Swiss Lucy, not the British, and had been recruited to Lucy after his discovery of the Japanese plan to bomb Pearl Harbour had been ridiculed by Edgar Hoover, the head of the American FBI. Liddell, a very patriotic Englishman and holder of the Military Cross, feared an invasion of Russia by America, or even a freelance operation involving one of their more lunatic generals like George S. Patton or Douglas MacArthur, using nuclear weapons.

Then, I nearly drop the papers I am holding.

Guy Liddell, the Bureau Ha memo states, is the second cousin of Alice Pleasance Liddell, who was the model for Alice in her friend Lewis Carroll's, *Alice's Adventures in Wonderland* and *Through the Looking Glass*, the latter being a book published by Roessler's Lucerne publishing firm, Vita Nova, and the basis of the book code initially used by Kells. My God! I learn from Kells' notes that Roessler's code name is Lucy and why the Lucerne group dress up as *Alice in Wonderland* characters and have strange tea parties.

Their work, with every good intention, was to stop another, more horrible, world war. But it is not what I am looking for.

My back is hurting, really hurting, so I walk around for a while.

From what I piece together, a new Lucy has taken over lines of communication in intelligence services and former resistance groups, often operating agents without them knowing who their real boss is because of the trade's passion for security, and then killing off those who work for her, so her secrets never leak, and replacing the dead and silent agents with new blood. Or is it even worse and the murderous corporation of Lucy is headless and on automatic, a doomsday weapon more personal and intimate than the bomb, watched over by the Americans . . . ?

There are lists and lists and lists, provided most often by the Gestapo, of trade unionists, communists, resistance activists, those who probably are best culled in the name of taking the American Dream worldwide. To allow the triumph of the car in the driveway, Hollywood, hamburgers, Rock n' Roll and Mickey Mouse. Lucy is now doing this, the papers say . . . The continued existence of Russia is an asset, life there was completely miserable even before the war. I laugh. No invasion or atom bombs necessary. A new world order has already happened in the young minds . . . And the human mind knows no frontiers.

There is a picture of a blonde-haired St Lucy, looking very like Alice in Wonderland, with candles on her headdress. She poked out her own eyes rather than obey the Romans.

The new Lucy, and who is behind her, if anyone, is becoming a threat to every side. She is out of any government control and is possibly why Gretchen's Russians gave her copies of the papers because, like her, they discovered after the fact they were working for Lucy, something that might get them shot.

A spark jumps from the boiler's furnace.

I sit down again hard. I have let the fire burn down and put on another log. I close the furnace door. I reach down for a bottle of Schnapps and a glass by the side of the boiler and take a small measure.

The spirit warms me as the fire catches and I open the door again, letting the red glow colour the room. A short communication from the Swiss Bureau Ha confirms that Hyman Kaplan was tortured to death six months before the war ended. His record in the resistance is boringly impeccable. He did not betray a single comrade, the fool. I read also in Kells' personal intelligence log how poor Gretchen and Rachel were used, but it is short on entertaining detail.

There is a State Department translation of NKVD, Russian secret service, transcripts on Hitler, that evidenced death. The memo noted that *Smersh* had retained Hitler's lower jaw, for a pencil holder.

I then begin, not with any great hope, to search the uncoded papers for who I might be, if not Hyman or Hitler. I light another Woodbine. There are noises above. The lovely Gretchen and Kells are arguing. Love creates its own violent politics; more love-struck citizens are killed by their bed-fellows than by a political party, army or nation state. Once human beings try to create any representation of their wants, from the Catholic Church to Communism to an innocent building aid like dynamite, we step through a Looking Glass and nothing is the same and our good intentions are most often reversed . . . Love . . . That is so funny . . .

III

"PLEASE, MY DARLING, get undressed and get into bed. And take your wig off. It is a cold night but you will still be too hot and you will wake me. I do need to get some sleep, my darling, I really do. I understand you. I really do understand. About changes," Gretchen said.

"You fucking don't."

Kells was sitting on a chair looking out at the lake. He had placed the chair by the window when they first arrived and sat there night after night, fully clothed in the blue dress he had fled the hospital in, watching for people coming, or just watching, hour after hour. To start with she had been able to undress him and wash him in cold water from a bucket and get him into bed, but now he was much worse. He wore her lipstick all the time. The room was full of cigarette smoke. The only way of confusing whoever was coming for him was to keep wearing the dress, he said.

"I need to keep this dress on."

"My darling. Come to bed. Come here. I love you."

In one sudden movement, Kells got off the chair and threw it across the room, smashing it into the door.

Gretchen thought the noise would bring the other two upstairs, but she heard nothing. Hyman and Rachel stayed where they were. Gretchen was scared, but she got out of bed. She was naked and shivering. She put her arms around Kells. The light outside the window had almost faded now. His body felt cold.

She kissed him first on one cheek and then on the other.

"Come to bed, my love. I am here and I am your wife and no one knows where we are. No one. Get into bed. Get into bed and let me warm you. What has happened is terrible and it is my fault. But it is better than being dead. You have disappeared. There was a body in a Russian hospital with your name tags on it. We have disappeared."

She manoeuvred Kells to the bed and sat him down. She took off his shoes. First the right and then the left. But when she started to take of his dress he shook his head.

"You don't want that nice dress I washed yesterday to get creased again, do you?"

Reluctantly he let her take it off and she got him between the sheets. He still had the bra and panties on and she hugged him to her.

"What are we going to do with you?"

"My name is Lucy," he said.

"Yes, of course. You are Lucy."

She thought he was going to sleep when he said, "Don't be fooled. They are coming for us. They are coming to kill us all. Better to be someone else. That's the trick. Then they cannot kill you."

His breathing became calmer. Then he said, "Rachel was going to kill me. Maybe you tried to kill me. Everyone is trying to kill me. That's the war for you. Nothing means nothing. *Macht Nichts* . . . Fuck it."

He put his hands around her throat and squeezed and there was nothing she could do. Not even scream.

She began to black out.

Then he relaxed his grip and began to fuck her, hard and then harder, and he came with a shout. He put one arm across her and went to sleep. To immediate deep sleep, like a child. She felt the strong breath from his nostrils against her cheek. She watched him for perhaps an hour, still terrified, still loving him beyond reason, and then went to sleep too.

IV

I DO NOT hear any more crashing from upstairs, so Gretchen must have calmed the increasingly demented Kells. Down in the basement, my bunker, I am not finding anything relating to who I may really be. Or am I overestimating my importance? Then I turn up a file with a name that does not cause an exact memory, but which I have a feeling about. In the Swiss communications, a final, red-lettered pile, I find the name 'Putzi' – short for Schnuckiputzi, or sweetie-pie.

Harvard educated Putzi, born Ernst Hanfstaengl in Munich, was a member of the university's socially prestigious Hasty Pudding Club, and well known as a socialite and gifted pianist in the roaring Twenties in New York, where he befriended Charlie Chaplin, Randolph Hearst, both Franklin and Theodore Roosevelt and became engaged to the lesbian novelist Djuna Barnes. Not an ordinary Nazi resume.

In the Thirties in Germany, I surmised, he might have gone to the same artistic Berlin parties as Rachel's father. Putzi became a close friend of Hitler, who described him as his personal pianist, and he was Hitler's son Egon's godfather. Putzi loved the new black SS uniforms and even penned marching songs based on Harvard football anthems for the Hitler Youth and invented the chant Sieg Heil. Unfortunately he flew too near the sun and fell out of favour with Joseph Goebbels and the British fascist Unity Mitford, who suspected him of not taking the Reich and National Socialism seriously enough after he wrote a very accomplished but rude song Mein Schwein, in the manner of the English entertainer Noel Coward, about Hitler falling romantically in love with a pig. They denounced Putzi as a possible double agent when, as yet, he wasn't. In 1937, working for German military intelligence, he was taken up in a plane and told he was going to be dropped into Spain as a spy, but the pilot, when they were in the air, confided at the last moment he would be dropped over Republican, not Fascist, lines, which would have meant a long and creatively Spanish painful death, as his hangdog face was familiar from the newspapers and newsreels. In fact, the plane only flew in German airspace, before being recalled, and Putzi was returned to Leipzig and thought to have learned his lesson about being too talkative. He had. Poor Putzi, fearing he was about to be murdered, was so scared he fled to Switzerland, confessed all to the Bureau Ha, and went to work for the Americans, in particular the State Department's S Division, thanks to his friends in the Hasty Pudding Club and Franklin D. Roosevelt connections, advising on psychological warfare against Hitler for the Office of Strategic Services.

This almost makes me laugh, but there is more, which does not.

Putzi had left behind a very close friend, Anton Brauner, a man who 'loved' both men and women and had many affairs and was described as charming and irresistible, but was coldly incapable of love. Anton often tap-danced when Putzi played the piano.

A Russian intelligence document states that Putzi and Anton encouraged members of the Jewish community to think they were safe under their patronage, and got them to rat on their friends, before having them sent off to the camps.

I even find a picture of Anton Brauner, under a cherry tree, perhaps in the Tiergarten, wearing an expensive grey fedora hat. He has the happy half-smile of a soul at peace with itself. A man who knew what he was doing, which is made very clear in a memo from the Bureau Ha. "Brauner targeted women on their own, whose husbands had either fled or were already in the camps. He and Putzi betrayed them to the authorities and then took over some, or all, of their property. Anton Brauner, in particular, seemed to relish betraying his lovers, although he may not have intended to betray them all."

In one case a Munich sewing-machine heiress was targeted by Anton, who persuaded her to give him a precious painting, *Portrait of a Young Man*, by Agnolo di Cosimo, a sixteenth-century artist known as *Bronzino*, in order to buy her way out of the country. The painting ended up in the hands of Gerdy Troost, Hitler's interior designer, and the woman was picked up and murdered in the Kaunus concentration camp. There is a confident arrogance in *Bronzino's Portrait of a Young Man* that is very like the photograph of Anton.

It is not made clear by the Swiss, but I am in no doubt that by 1937, Putzi and Anton, both men of sophisticated, international sensibilities and immeasurable moral ambivalence, may have been passing information to Roessler in Lucerne and becoming part of Lucy. Both were, as they say, hedging their bets, and the Swiss claim that from 1944, Putzi was working for the British MI6.

The image of agents being nurtured and then culled is again like my silkworm harvest. An absurdity worthy of *Alice Through the Looking Glass*. Or the camps.

In a separate Gestapo file, all on its own, is a letter from Anton Brauner to a lover called Ilsa, an actual letter, handwritten not typed, containing small fragments of a white flower, thought to be the remains of a gardenia. From this charming man, 'incapable of love', or so the Bureau Ha had said. The letter quotes an English poet, Coleridge: 'If a man could pass through Paradise in a dream, and have a flower presented to him as a pledge that his soul had really been there, and if he found that flower in his hand when he awoke – Aye! and what then?'

My hands are shaking.

I do not make jokes about love now.

The surgeon told me I was clutching the petals of a white flower when I was found.

The letter did not seem to be that of a philanderer, but the tortured, over-sugared prose of a doomed lover. It goes on: 'When they take us, we must look back to the snatched joy, the divine spark (the German was rendered as Schiller's phrase *Götterfunken* from his *Ode to Joy*) that we had, that no one can take from us. I have your sacred flower . . .' I find it hard to imagine myself writing such a letter. From what I have read of Schiller's words, he seems a dangerous fool. Like Kells' musings on Dante.

At the end of the letter the name of the woman is in capitals ILSA, in probably an intelligence operative's pencil, and then spelt out as, *Ich liebe Sie alle*, I love you all.

I love you all.

The very words that had come from my lips after running up a pile of rubble on fire were *Ich liebe Sie alle*, I love you all. They were words I said often at the kibbutz. My words.

In the papers there is an order from the new Lucy that I decipher, using the nine-letter code, referring to Brauner. It simply says: 'Burn Mr Brown, without trace.' It uses the English, Mr Brown, not Brauner.

Another memo from the Swiss Bureau Ha, speculated that Anton may have been interrogated at Gestapo headquarters near Hitler's bunker on the excuse that he was spreading defeatist rumours, after terrifying the wife of a Norwegian diplomat with a story, possibly in jest, that the Germans had planted their own doomsday device, more likely to be tabun nerve gas than something from the failed atomic weapon programme, under the rubble of Potsdammer Platz, in Berlin.

Putzi, Hitler's favourite piano player, was by then working for the State Department, the British and Lucy. So on that last day in Berlin, Kells and his unit may have been under Putzi's advice if not orders, as a State Department memo said he was concerned with Nazis posing as Jews.

Lucy had gone world-wide.

And as the real Hyman Kaplan had worked for Lucy, Putzi would have wanted him dead. Perhaps to protect himself and other former Nazis at the top of the new Lucy. A Lucy increasingly under the gaze of the Americans and Allen Welsh Dulles' CIA.

I take another glass of Schnapps, sipping slowly this time, staring at my missing fingertips and pondering how quickly once-saintly Lucy has gone to the bad. To Lucifer.

And I am not quite part of it all. More a shabby criminal. A jackal at the feast.

Except for that flower.

I wonder where Ilsa is, if she is still alive? Or, had I sent her to the camps? Had I been given back the flower I sent to her by my kindly Gestapo torturers on that last day, one or more of them working for Lucy? Or just out for jealous revenge. I imagine the fierce lights and a fragment of dried-up white gardenia being put into my bloodied hands across a rough wood table. My tormenters would relish my tears and the way I gathered every desiccated piece of blossom I could into my hands and howled. They had found my flaw. A man without feeling or honour had fallen into a flower-filled pit of adolescent love. I can see the glee in their dead pig eyes, hear the interrogator's voice.

"So you're human like the rest of us, Anton . . . Not so clever now, are we . . . ?"

After such agony, it was no wonder the bullet to my brain and the fire did not kill me. I did not let go of those few petals, even as I burned. I did not obey death.

If I am Mr Brown, Ilsa must have been important to an extremely bad man for that flower to survive the largest battle on earth and all that fire. But the flower did. And so did I.

The new Lucy must want me far more than the other three. They may still believe I can tell a tale.

If I am Mr Brown, I must at a certain point leave my dear friends Gretchen and Rachel and Kells, if I love them. And I do. But if I am Mr Brown, am I capable of loving them and leaving them? When I can have them all?

The flower, and the letter, are the only things I do not put into the furnace.

The fire burns yellow with a whoosh of familiar flame.

V

"I WILL WALK to the city. Into Berlin . . ."

Two weeks later, Rachel realised the house was totally out of food and it partly woke her from her listless inactivity. Her numbness. It was a problem she could solve. There was not a single thing left in the sepulchral larder off the kitchen, which was as cold as a refrigerator. There were no tins, or rice or flour.

"I will go into the city," said Rachel, putting on her coat.

"How will you get there?" said Hyman, who had risen late and been very quiet. "I do not think the car works, even if it has petrol."

"I'm going to walk. I have to go somewhere, or I will go mad. No one has come for us. We are ghosts. But even ghosts have to eat. It's under four kilometres to a shop I know. If it's still there. I came out here before. When I was a little girl."

Gretchen had come into the room with Kells, who still wore the blue dress, but without the blonde wig, which Gretchen was carrying in both hands, like a crown. They both had stopped, frozen at the phrase "little girl".

Rachel had heard the violent arguments and prayed for Kells to get better. She had tried to comfort him, but what she and Hyman said had no effect. Gretchen was the only one he trusted, and only then as 'Lucy'. He became dangerous and angry when he was not fully 'Lucy'.

"I can do with the walk," said Rachel.

"It's not safe. We may be being watched," said Hyman. He looked white and she knew he had come to bed with the dawn. Since he had read the papers, he often spent the night in the boiler room, drinking Schnapps. His mood constantly changed.

"Have you been reading the documents again?" Rachel asked.

"Oh, yes. Those papers. I will try to crack the code, Kells. I mean, Lucy. Most of it is about hilarious disasters . . . Some of it is beyond sadness . . ."

One minute he was cheerful, in charge, the next sombre. He avoided discussing the papers, yet still tried his best to keep everyone going.

"If Lucy, or probably the Americans or the Russians, knew where we were, we would be dead," said Rachel, with a shrug. "We need food, even to be murdered."

Hyman put down the book he was carrying on the table, and they all stared at Rachel, who had washed her hair and dried it into tight strawberry-blonde curls that made her look far younger than the authority she had assumed at the kibbutz. She, too, realised what she had said, "When I was a little girl . . ." and the age of innocence that invoked. And she heard the impossibly sad notes of her cello again, and the melancholy of the lower notes seemed to flow from the violet blue sky and the green and grey reflections in the deep lake, as the bow rasped between freedom and the past.

Gretchen came across to her.

"I'll go with you," she said, putting her hand on Rachel's shoulder.

"I will keep Lucy here company," said Hyman, smiling at Kells, who was staring at the floor.

Rachel and Gretchen collected two great canvas shopping bags from the pantry. There was a trumpet they intended to take back to the boys from the band at the Katzenmutter Club. There was also an envelope of money, dollars and Occupation Marks, that had been entombed in Kells' plaster cast with the papers, but the envelope had been opened and, she guessed, halved. What kind of thief steals only half the money? They both put on headscarves that Gretchen had, to blend in. They stared back at the house with its holiday air, and then began to walk around the lake to the road into the destroyed city.

After about a kilometre, past abandoned cars stripped of their wheels and upholstery, the sun was climbing in a blue sky and the day was getting warm. A man then wolf-whistled and they were challenged for papers by an American patrol, but the boys smiled and strode on, their black ankle parachute boots creaking.

Rachel often looked back, but no one was following them.

"Hyman is such a fine man. He is always concerned about us," said Gretchen.

"He is a good man," said Rachel. "I have never had doubts about him."

They walked on.

"You do not like me much, do you?" said Gretchen.

Rachel did not reply.

"You love poor Kells, and I do too." Gretchen almost shouted. There was a real agony in her voice and an honesty in the desperation of her love stripped bare, as they stood by a ruined shop near a burned-out crab-shell of an army truck. Rachel could see the bruises on Gretchen's neck.

She stopped and faced her. "Even now?" she asked.

Gretchen's lip quivered.

"Especially now. More now. He needs me. He is sick. He needs us. No one can tell us *scheiße* anymore, can they? How to behave. They were no rules in war, why should we go back to pretending there are in the peace? No one can tell us *scheiße*. Shit. What to do. No one," she said.

They both laughed, and Gretchen threw her bag in the air and the old silver trumpet they were taking back to the band fell out. She put it back, like a guilty secret. Then they laughed some more.

The closer they got to the city centre, the more the destruction. It was the first time Rachel realised exactly how much of the city had been burned and pummelled and blown apart. She had been blinkered with the task of killing Kells when she went to the hospital. A formal dining room hung in mid-air as if waiting for a maid to appear and a meal to be served. There were silver candelabra on the table, but the room was too high and too unstable for looters to attempt a theft. It hung forever in anticipation of the soup course.

In another house a bath was supported only by its plumbing.

Again she felt the contradictory emotions of love and hate for her cannibal city.

As they went further, there were little pockets of frenzied activity. There were people riding bikes and pushing barrows full of potatoes or retrieved fireplaces in old prams. One man, his face on the edge of despair, his trousers those of the *Wehrmacht*, was pushing a stuffed bear in what must have been a pram for twins. The bear appeared to have a smile on its muzzle. On a corner of a street that had not been hit directly by the bombs, Rachel found an old Chinese market shop, one of several, which she knew from before the war. Outside the shrapnel-pocked shopfront was a table neatly arranged with four Red Cross parcels, five large potatoes and two eggs. An old lady sat inside the desolation of the shop on a rocking chair, in exactly the place she had sat before the war, reading a Chinese horoscope she had once shown to Rachel. She smiled slightly. Her son behind her smiled too.

"Don't eat fresh meat. There's still too much of it around," said the son, coughing and laughing. "Look at paper."

He thrust a sheet from a German newspaper in front of them. A sub-headline read: "The number of incidents of the use of human flesh in cooking decreased this month to fifty-six, say police." The man then went inside and brought out a small pram filled with American rations for which Rachel bartered, but still paid a fortune in dollars.

"Come tomorrow. But no meat! You could be eating *Helden*. Heroes. The Allies farm them in camps like cattle," said the son, while his mother shook her head. "Where you go now?"

"The Katzenmutter Club."

"Ah, the pansy place. Don't go down there today. There is shooting. Soldiers pick up black marketeers. Shoots them against wall outside. Bang, bang, bang. More hamburger! You can get shot for having a bread knife. Worse than before. *Macht nichts*, never mind." He laughed, and winked and coughed again and spat. "You can leave that trumpet with me. Pick it up next time, for sure." Rachel handed over the trumpet. Despite the son's sense of humour, she knew he was mostly honest, and would not engage with the authorities as, like her, he officially did not exist. Another ghost. She wondered why the Nazis had never interfered with the Chinese. Perhaps it was that someone had to run the shops and write the horoscopes.

Rachel and Gretchen pushed the pram home, like a recently married couple, sharing a bottle of impossibly luxurious dark and milky Russian beer. They glanced around, often. No one followed them, no one stopped them. A smell of rot and decomposing flesh blew from a nearby cellar.

"I will try and help more with Kells," said Rachel.

"Thank you," said Gretchen. "We are alone. The four of us."

VI

"GOODBYE HYMAN!" RACHEL shouts to me. I stand at the window and watch her go with a feeling of excitement and arousal rather than jealousy.

A month after she first went into the city with Gretchen, Rachel is out walking with Kells, hand in hand around the lake. Kells is much calmer and has on a woman's coat, but also his wig and a dress and the outsize women's shoes Gretchen gave him in the hospital. The coat was with the stuff the musicians left. Kells seems happy, and no one has tried to stop him wearing what he wants. It does not disturb me and I wonder again about my own previous identity and the distinct possibility of being the loathsome Brauner/Mr Brown, after my discoveries in the boiler room. How many other idiots were running around that wasteland on fire with dried gardenias in their hand, saying 'Ich liebe, Sie alle,' I love you all? I am surprised I do not feel more unsettled at not telling the others.

I watch Kells and Rachel pick their way carefully around the side of the grey water as I smoke a cigarette in a holder I found in the house, hoping Kell's heels do not get stuck in the sticky mud half-way

276

round, next hoping they do, and then I turn and see Gretchen is reading a pre-war American movie magazine.

I blow a ring of smoke, which I do not usually do, and was not aware I even could do. I tell myself I do not feel guilt at the possibility of being the horrid Anton, but rather a strange, new elegance of spirit, and a certain triumph, if I am him, of having re-invented myself as the good Hyman.

"Gretchen . . . would you say I am a good man?" I ask her.

She looks up from the magazine with that gorgeously seductive, blowsy, laziness of hers.

"We all think you are good, Hyman. You are the best of us."

I feel myself attracted to Gretchen in all the usual ways, her wide lips and raven-black hair, but even more so if I think of myself as 'Mr Brown'. The well-meaning, sainted Hyman would, of course, never attempt or contemplate Gretchen's seduction. Perhaps, as the sainted Hyman, I should drive Rachel and Gretchen and poor Kells away from me by proposing we explore more sexual contact with each other, the free love, *Freie Liebe*, Rachel says was so fashionable in Berlin before the war? Human kind are not the most capable of animals when it comes to the emotional distance of coping with multiple partners. I sigh. I never sigh. Did Mr Brown sigh? There is a definite pubic quality to Gretchen's eyebrows as I gaze at her. There is a darkness about her, and therefore a kind of light.

Light does not shine in light, the troubling message of Lucifer.

Gretchen is also possessed of a timeless certainty. The certainly of an individual whose sublime and mystical knowledge owes precisely nothing to the great religions.

If I am Mr Brown, I will enjoy seducing Gretchen. Perhaps she will murder me by shifting a piece of metal near my spine. I am almost convinced this is a scientific endeavour.

"Why don't you sit down and have a drink with me?" I say, and she goes and gets two bottles of cold beer from the pantry and large, salty pretzels she and Rachel bought at the Chinese grocery.

Standing close to me, my cigarette smoke mixing with her

perfume, she slowly pours my drink into the glass and the head foams and spills over onto the bare wood of the table. She smiles and then pours hers and sits down by me. The glass above the froth is slightly steamed on account of the liquid's coldness. She raises her glass and takes a sip as if we are a normal German couple. There is a trace of beer froth on her upper lip. The trouble is, as Hyman I have come to love Gretchen's moral strength, and the fact she knows and understands all the *Dunkel Winkel*, the dark corners of the city and does not judge. I have come to love her, and that weakens the worst scoundrel's intent.

The sun comes from behind a cloud and the light from the window catches her hair and a dimple in her cheek curls above her smile, and I become more and more aware of a haze of perfume and face powder and the softness of her body.

VII

"I KNOW SOMETHING that may interest you. The big secret. The biggest . . ." Gretchen said looking at the quietly smiling face of Clark Gable, and the man she knew as Hyman. She smiled back.

"The big secret? About Lucy? Tell me," he said.

"Not about Lucy. About you . . ."

"What then?

"I know the day you are going to die. The hour. Let me whisper it to you . . ." She leant towards him and then sat back in her chair.

He was smiling now. That knowledge usually stopped men in their tracks like a sledgehammer.

Yet it did not seem to upset the man she knew as Hyman. His mood was dreamy and detached. Possibly because he thought he had already died once when Kells found him burning.

There was nothing of the hospital about him anymore. She had never seen a man more straight-backed and alive. Yet, in the last days he had seemed more sophisticated somehow, more aloof. He was obviously trying to plan their future. He looked very much like the American actor in his movies and she had been a fan of the movies. Hyman's moustache had become more substantial and covered the scarring left by the plastic surgeon on his upper lip. He had white scar tissue down the side of his face, as if he had been struck by lightning. He looked at her with interest and a new charm.

Gretchen remembered the old woman who told fortunes before and in the intervals during the circus, standing back from one man, a bus driver, who had the same lightning-bolt scar tissue mark, somewhere in Alanya or Adana . . . The old woman's booth was decorated with pictures of Tarot cards and real marigolds, which have a pungent smell and kept away flies. But the old woman really had a power. She knew when a man or woman was going to die, and told Gretchen the secret of it one day when she was drunk on raki and sherbet. The old woman did not want to tell the whole secret, even to herself, but the magic had to do with thinking of a colour, suggested by the aura of the individual, and then concentrating on the face of the person. You asked them the date of their birth, and then the second date to come into your head was the date of the person's death. It only worked if you had the power, but simply to go through the motions scared people. Gretchen already knew the date of Hyman Kaplan's birth from a newspaper article about the 'burning man' Rachel had. Gretchen also knew that Kells had thought that Hyman was Hitler, and that date was April 20. Yet, Gretchen doubted that the man drinking beer with her could be either of these. It was a feeling, and that is the best way to the truth. So she estimated a year and a season and then trusted herself to come up with a date, after examining Hyman's palm. She thought of the woman in her booth and the way she fed stray cats and how women would go to her if their husbands fell sick. The bus driver with the mark like lightening at the side of his face said she was a fraud and threw small stones at her and pushed down her booth and laughed. For free she told him when he was going to die, the day and the hour. A week later the bus driver was found dead in his bus with a marigold in his mouth. The bus had been struck by lightning.

Hyman was staring at her in the way men do, as prey. He did not feel to her like an evil man, though there was a power about him and recently a yearning, or sadness. He may have been a follower of Hitler, and men who had followed that dictator had killed her lovely father. She saw her father whittling at a stick with his big knife.

"They will never take me alive. They will never make a monkey out of me."

She thought of the colour orange when she thought of the man in front of her and his estimated birthdate. She came up straight away with the date of his death. Then the hour. By all the laws of her family and people, she should kill him if she thought him a former Nazi. She could kill him. There was a knife in her bag, and Rachel had put her automatic pistol in a drawer. The knife in Gretchen's bag was a vegetable knife that had almost been sharpened away. She could shave a pig with that knife, or cut the animal's throat. She had used it to cut Kells' hair.

Yet, this was not the day Hyman was going to die.

"Where are you from?" he asked her.

"Here. And there. And not. And nowhere," she said.

"Where were you born?" Hyman leaned back in his chair. She thought the name had never suited him.

"In the circus. I told Rachel. You know that. From Kells perhaps? I think you know everything." She laughed. Entertainment had become an instinct with her before the war, both as a woman and a performer.

He laughed too. "Perhaps you could have got out to America."

"They would have found me out. Even the Americans don't like gypsies."

"So you didn't try?" He moved his hand close to hers on the table. "I cannot believe that you are not adventurous. I said that from the first moment I saw you at the hospital. You were magnificent. I said, here is a woman who likes adventure."

He was a clever man. She said nothing and lit a cigarette.

He stared at her for some time, stared at her hard and then said, "You wanted to remain in Berlin in the end, now that the war is over, because you wanted to remain with Kells. And now you have a marriage certificate. You are a little in love with Kells, and he is a little in love with you, you think it can only be that, because he is a little in love with Rachel, and has still not learned to love himself. Even a little. I'm not so sure he loves me at all."

She smiled.

Hymen took the cigarette off her and blew a ring of smoke and handed it back. "I know Kells is curious about everything. When you get a curious American, nothing much stops them. That's why he became obsessed with these codes and the Operation Lucy. Dangerous work."

She shrugged. "I think now he is terrified. He doesn't know who he is anymore." She blew smoke at Hyman. "He thought you were Adolf Hitler . . ."

He did not look shocked. He knew she was teasing him.

"I think that was because he was in love with Rachel," he said, and put his hand on hers, a wistful expression on his face. "The stupid business with the dog. In the circumstances I don't think I can ever truly know who I am. I may be the devil."

"Maybe that's why you did not burn."

His hands were warm.

"Perhaps, Gretchen, I should hire a troupe of your circus clowns to play out the probable scenarios. They say the *Führer* attempted to shoot himself in the head. I still, if the doctors are to be believed, have most of one bullet, a low calibre bullet from a lady's gun, in my head. They say the *Führer* was burned and I can attest to that, I remember burning. I remember being a human flame with a ridiculous erection. I do not remember before. I do not remember anything before last springtime. I have been through gates no one should go through and have come back and am still here. And I say, I love you all, '*Ich liebe Sie alle*' I detect no reason, of course, no purpose in all this, except to have been swept along by a river of pure power, that force of wanting, which is everything in the world, and now I am beached here, with you, Gretchen, at the side of this lake. I am not mad because probably a lucky accident to my brain has divided me from madness, or knowing who I am. I am simply who I have invented. My idea of Hyman Kaplan . . . I am what I imagine myself to be now, an ordinary man. Perhaps a new type of man. Say what you think I am . . ."

He lifted his hand and put it on her shoulder.

She looked into his good eye. He was, she thought, sincere.

"Do not feel guilty," he said. "About the past. It no longer exists in any true way. There is no point in feeling guilty."

She had cured herself of feeling guilty long ago. Guilt does no good.

"No," she said, very quietly.

He took her hand in his, and said, "Do you not feel guilty for what you did, Gretchen? You do remember?"

"Did Kells tell you?" She pulled back from him.

"I do not think he knows everything, does he?" said Hyman, putting his hand back on her shoulder.

She was silent. It was like talking to one of the family elders or a priest. She recalled the smell of summer roses in a vase, blousy roses teetering on the edge of death in a wooden caravan.

Hyman smiled.

"Your father was taken away to the camps. To the gypsy camp at Auschwitz. The camp that was totally destroyed along with every single person there on August 2, 1944. Yet, you worked for the German railways, organising transports, and German intelligence. I read this in the files . . . I can imagine the work. Clean and indoors. I can imagine your bosses. Perhaps they threatened to kill you. But I think not. Why did you work for the Germans? For the Nazis. For the enemy?"

It was the charm and the directness. She felt tears come into her eyes.

He reached into the pocket of his jacket with his right hand and offered a handkerchief. "Dry those eyes. There is no use for self-pity."

It was the same way Walter, the colonel in intelligence, had talked to her. Like the fortune-teller, he knew everything. There was the sudden, definite change in his voice. At first he just talked to her, talked to her for days about everything and anything and her ambitions, until in her head his voice replaced even that of her father. Walter had got inside her as easily as if he had opened a door. What Hyman said about power was true and it made her now very afraid.

She stubbed out her cigarette in a big glass ashtray. "Did you read all the papers in the plaster cast?"

Hyman seemed to ignore her words. Instead, he moved forwards and kissed her on the cheek. He then licked her cheek and she let him. She began to tremble.

"It is good to think we can help each other, Gretchen. In our small group. My spirit flows into yours, yours into mine. It makes us less on our own. In the face of such power. In the face of such absurd, naked power."

Gretchen felt breathless, as if her chest was being squeezed. It was as if he knew everything and could read her mind. He was holding her right hand now.

"What did you do? A pretty girl in an intelligence operation?"

She did not reply for several minutes. She could hear birds singing in the trees outside. She could hear in particular the song of a blackbird.

"I was introduced into the company of certain men."

"You had to seduce men?"

She did not answer.

"And you got up in the morning and the sun rose and you went about your business and everything was the same, just better and with food. Sometimes you enjoyed yourself, then more and more. After a while it all became part of your life and, possibly, you still slept with the man you worked for, this Walter. Who tried to stay in touch in the peace? He and his friends?"

"Walter was killed in the bombing," she said.

It was true, she often had a very good time with many of the men she befriended. A better time than she had had with anyone before. It had been like that with Kells. It had gradually changed into something even better.

"Perhaps you really love Kells? More than life itself?"

How did he know what she was thinking?

"He loves Rachel, as I do," said Hyman. "Love. What's in a word? That does not matter, you know. That he loves Rachel. We know that convention, when it is based on property or ownership, is the worst place for invention. For freedom. Anything that stops us exploring the world more is wrong. Anyway, we should not vex ourselves about what has already happened."

They were silent for a moment.

"She is very beautiful. Rachel. She is perfect," Gretchen said, and took a sip of beer.

"So are you. And married to Kells."

She turned up the side of her mouth, showing a dimple. "But you don't mind? That Kells loves Rachel?"

He laughed.

"Mind? On the contrary. How one conducts oneself in such matters is a test of character. Perhaps the ultimate test of character. There are certain things we must not interfere with among those we know. I speak as a man already dead once and soon to be again. A man suspected of being Adolf Hitler, even though I look like Clark Gable. Perhaps a piece of shrapnel will shift in one last tango and I will die the next time I get up from this chair. Or the next time I make love. I do not care about irrelevances. I care about being one with you all."

The clock ticked. She had not noticed it before.

"They may have gone into the city in search of more food. Rachel and Kells."

He nodded.

"When do you think they will they be back?"

"If they go into the city they will be late. I am sure they will be careful." He was smiling at her and patted her hand. He stood slowly. "There! I am not dead!"

She looked up and felt a trembling warmth towards him. She wanted to hug and comfort him.

"You are beautiful, Gretchen. I think I will go and lie down."

She took his arm. She took his arm automatically, and then led him to his bedroom on the ground floor, where a dress belonging to Rachel was on the chair. She liked Rachel, and had the strong sense she would not mind. There were no rules now.

Hyman stopped and smiled. "Do, please, help me undress. I love the cold feel of these linen sheets on my body. I think that is a cold that everyone likes. Such deliciously cold sheets! I think you do too. The cold of new, crisp sheets in an unknown bed. Didn't the poet Goethe say there is nothing like the feel of good, starched linen in a bed that is not your own? Come here, Gretchen. Please give this old wreck a hug."

She did exactly as he asked, and wanted to do so. It was the same when she had slept with the man called Walter from the intelligence service. She had been his prize all along for recruiting her for the passing on of messages. The reward for a bargain. All engineered by people she never met. It had made her feel good and bad just like now, with this strange, wounded man with the off-centred face of a film star.

She stood and he began slowly to undress her. So slowly. She knew now she had been right that he was someone else entirely, not Hyman Kaplan, nor Hitler. In another life he had done this for money or pleasure or both. These were not the actions of a man who studies only the sexual life of silk moths.

He unbuttoned her white blouse and kissed her breasts above her bra, before removing that, more deftly than any man she knew. He took her nipples in his mouth one by one, his hands around her waist, and she winced with pleasure and cried out with her head back. He undid the belt on her black skirt, undid the side buttons and let it fall to the floor and stood looking at her in her laddered stockings and suspenders. She lifted her feet out of her shoes and then he pulled down her black lacy French knickers, a present from Kells, and his hand was on her pubic hair.

She moaned, and then began to undress him. His scarred body was hard and so was his prick as she took him into her mouth, and he pressed her head to his flat belly. He then pulled her up and they snatched up their clothes and went upstairs to the room she was sharing with Kells. He pushed her down on the bed and was licking her and she screamed and screamed again as he was inside her, and coming. To her surprise he did not stop making love to her, again and again until she felt exhausted.

Her mascara ran onto the pillows.

"You think I am a good man?" he asked.

VIII

IT IS WEEKS, perhaps a month, later and I am still not sure whether I seduced Gretchen as Mr Brown, or love her as Hyman.

It is a bright morning and I smile and watch Kells, who now is 'Lucy', as we walk into what is left of my city. At first I thought Kells would snap out of his fear and his bouts of violence with Gretchen, but he hasn't. We go slowly because of Kells' heels and are following Rachel and Gretchen, who have gone before us to the Katzenmutter Club, as the owner wants Gretchen to sing. She says she cannot bear to hide away any longer, perhaps the Lucy killings are over, and anyway we need the money. She is singing again. She sings sometimes as she is making love, and this is a glorious sensation as if I am feeling the stars in the universe move through the vibrations inside her, and that is something new to me, even if I have lived before as a shit like Mr Brown.

'Lili Marlene' is the best, and may kill me.

The Katzenmutter Club has moved location at times, but I am sure I know where it is from Gretchen's directions, in a damp basement by the River Spree. Kells is not content with just dressing all the time as a woman now, and is copying the mannerisms of Rachel and Gretchen, little glances or gestures of the hands, even though he has spent separate nights with both of them, kissing and caressing them as a woman, but penetrating them as a man, a lesbian relationship, but with a real flesh and blood prick, not a black leather substitute. How do I know such things? Gretchen confided this, and I am fascinated. Gretchen tells me more than Rachel, though I see Kells becoming Lucy excites Rachel too. He is not violent towards her because, I think, he knows he will never be sure of what she is capable of doing.

Gretchen has braided Kells' wig, and with his scavenged blue wool dress on, he looks like a schoolgirl, albeit a six-foot, awkwardly broad-shouldered schoolgirl. We are meant to be shopping for essentials, but I say, "Why don't we walk in the Tiergarten? Lucy . . . ?"

As we pick our way around the broken paths towards and then back from the ruins of the zoo, an expensively dressed older woman in full make-up ambles past us and stops. "Your daughter looks so lovely, and how she has grown in the peace!" she says.

"You have no idea how!" I laugh, and the woman laughs too.

On the approach to the zoo for a second time, Kells halts, agitated. When he speaks, his voice is that of Kells, not Lucy.

"The last time I was here, the paths were burning. Like rivers of fire. There was a flack tower over there. It was as big as a fucking castle. It's gone. Not a brick. I wasn't scared then. I didn't feel anything. There was just a veil of nothing . . . I'm scared now. Properly shit scared. There was an Egyptian temple . . . I feel . . . I'm scared of everything now. All the time."

I take Kells by his arm. "The last time I was here, I was burning. Considered dead."

Then we are silent. I watch him taking long breaths, as if trying to make sense of the new air.

We search where the trees give way to rubble, trying to find where we had first met, like lovers in their favourite park, but do not find any trace of a statue, or parts of such, that might be Frederick the Great. The city is tidying itself, but not everywhere. Below one pile of rubble is a naked human leg, uncovered and torn by dogs, but still wearing a high-heeled shoe.

"Come away."

I put my arm around Kells' shoulders.

It is a gentle yet definite movement, as when one takes hold of a young, trembling bird that has got into a house, and we go in the direction of the Ku'damm and the Ka-De-We, and I am surprised to find the Café Kranzler I had been told of intact and doing a good trade. A well-dressed *hausfrau* is eyeing me while eating an eclair, with obscene passion, A smiling waitress in a uniform that is two sizes too big, her thin waist the result of living on cabbage soup and nettles, serves us. Her accent is too refined for her job. Before the war she was most probably a customer, not a waitress. She stares at me and for a moment I think she is going to ask for Clark Gable's autograph.

"My mother used to make this. This is better. Mother's was like concrete and you could throw it like a discus at the cows in a field near where we lived," says Kells, on his second helping of *Schokoladentorte*. He is now speaking in the low volume, scratchy, high-pitched voice he has adopted with the dress as Lucy, and partly the result of the plaster cast. His eyes are excited, but his voice lingers with a certain panic on the word "better".

IX

AFTER THE WALK past the battered houses of the River Spree, Kells hesitated, and then with Hyman went down the steep and rough, black-painted stairs into the basement that was the Katzenmutter Club.

There was the usual Berlin club smell of damp and mice and plaster dust, mixed with real coffee, toasted tobacco, cheap perfume, sexual adventure, face powder and the sour-sweet smell of Schnapps. At one side the ceiling had come down, and there was a little pile of exquisite plaster angels. On the walls, here and there, were tiny, two-inch framed pictures of cats, some in bowties, some in top hats. The place may have been a theatre or a cinema before the scythe of war demanded entertainment that was live and kicking like a mule. There were balconies with more plaster angels and flowers and dark spaces behind, where there were hints of movement and groans and occasionally orgasmic shouts.

Two skinny girls, schoolgirls, over made-up, stood at the bar silently, gazing at the door for custom. They were real girls looking for soldiers and dollars. They wore once fabulously expensive dresses looted from the ruins. There were needle tracks on their arms, probably from occupying forces' medical packs. Any soul behind their eyes, at the bottom of the well of stolen make-up, had probably died with their fathers on the Russian Front.

Another girl walked through the bar to a door behind the stage smoking a cigarette, wearing nothing, swinging her pert bottom, her breasts bouncing. Her skin was white as bones in the desert. Her pubic hair was dyed bright crimson. Hang Eleven, as the nude surfers say. Candy thunder.

She was part of the cabaret, thought Kells.

The cabaret was there to encourage the much-needed sex, Gretchen had said. The warm flesh to warm flesh affirmation of the triumph of life over death needed by those at war. The pulse they had to get a finger on. One last time.

Before flesh came apart.

Before the blood ran, and the tomb opened.

Kells understood that. That's why he had to be 'Lucy'.

To take time out.

He nearly fled and covered his face with his hands.

The two teenage prostitutes drank coffee, but never stopped looking at the stairs. The next soldier down might whisk them away to Kansas.

The precious coffee doubtless was brought by the club's visitors, often timid and curious men from foreign armies, guessed Kells. A sailor in white uniform was collapsed under a table, while another much bigger sailor with a ridiculously small cap on his head, sat cross-legged on a white marble-topped table, staring into infinity. Cobweb-hung bottles stood to attention on dark and grimy shelves, while here and there were heads, some broken, of pot dolls, looking out with manic, long eye-lash framed blue eyes. Only a few of the dolls were whole. A third sailor, in white bell bottoms and a small blue hat, but stripped to the waist, his rib bones and stomach muscles perfectly defined, was weeping silently. At another table a boy made up as a girl, but in male evening dress, looked into the fake eye-lashed eyes of a boy dressed carefully and exquisitely in a short, peach silk party frock and white silk stockings. The latter were too good to come from the liberating invading armies. The boy in the suit had the easy manners of money. There was a large engagement ring on the boy-girl's finger and on the table were red roses and a bottle of champagne and two glasses. Hyman wished them well with their dreams. Their dreams were just as viable and likely to be achieved as any government's in the ruined city.

A broad, fleshy man with a magnificent head, like that of a Roman emperor's statue, emerged from the darkness behind the bar. He did not look at all German, but like a man who organised things at the church when Kells' mother went to Mass. His mother's friend was a bank manager, with the ever-amiable smile of a man in charge. The man behind the bar had the same smile but wore two grey cat's ears on his shiny head, his face plastered expertly with grey make-up and stick-on whiskers. Over his shoulder hung a furry tail. He pointed the tail at Kells.

"I want her!"

Thus Kells became part of the cabaret too.

X

I, HYMAN KAPLAN, applaud warmly as the Mother Cat continues to speak, "I want this new beauty up on my fucking stage, now. Now! To sing with the other two. To sing with the other two beauties. She is perfect. Absolutely perfect, darling."

The Mother Cat speaks in English. Perhaps he has been warned of our impending arrival by Gretchen. It is honeyed rich, patrician, precise English that suggests a lifetime in the London theatre. It is then that I see framed black-and-white photographs behind the bar, among those of the cats. I recognise the large, oblong face of Putzi, pictured in his tailored black SS uniform next to the British socialite and friend of Hitler, Diana Mitford, a photograph I had seen in the Bureau Ha file. In another, Putzi is in riding clothes with Mr Brown, Anton Brauner. A third, much larger print is of the backs of a man and a woman holding hands and looking out from a balcony over a country estate in the snow. You can see they are very relaxed and fond of each other and may be in love. I am sure that the man is Mr Brown, Anton Brauner. The woman, a very tall lady with a long, ivory cigarette holder, has short blonde hair. Who is she? Could this be Ilsa? I have no memory of her. But Kells told me about meeting such a lady in Geneva with Roessler. I ask about another photograph first.

"They look a group of rascals," I say in English.

The photo is of a group of shifty-looking men, acting tough.

"Rascals? The fat one is Revolver Heini, next to him is Butcher Hermann and Yankee Franzi and Mad Dog Schultz, among other Berlin apaches. That was before the Nazis killed them all at a formal dinner to which they were flattered to be invited."

"Do you know who those people are? In the other photographs?" I ask.

"Oh, that is a man called Putzi with Diana Mitford. A good pianist, Putzi used to come to the old club, before fleeing the *Reich* in fear of his life. He was just a chancer. He loved jazz. The younger man is Anton, whose sadistic antics probably guaranteed Putzi's downfall. Anton was a total shit-bag, who loved boys and girls and no one."

I want to ask more about Anton, but know it would arouse suspicion. "And the girl? Who is the girl? The woman? In the snow?"

The Mother Cat shrugs.

"How should I know, dear? I don't do women. Nobody was around Anton for long. They say he was from a rich family and could have got out of the city, but he stayed. One of those inbred *Ruhr* steel families, I think. He enjoyed himself. He was a very dangerous man, even in Berlin, which was full of dangerous men. Vipers! He was a man who loved to destroy. And the Nazis allowed him this *Faust* bargain even if he did not have a soul to give them. Instead, it is said, he turned in his mother to the Gestapo, for helping Jews. She had had a Jewish lover. He turned in his friends and lovers. I keep that picture there to remind myself how kind and gullible people can be to utter shits. That younger man is the most evil person I have known. That is saying something in Berlin. He liked to harm for no reason. It delighted him. Cruelty for its own sake. He personified the regime. He was so clever. So beautiful. A beautiful man. I do not like to talk of such a man, even now. He was always telling people he loved them all."

"What? What happened to him?" I say, staring at the photograph, my right hand pressed against the bar to stop it shaking.

The Mother Cat smiles:

"My, you have gone quite pale, my dear. I did not mean to shock you. Oh, I think sweet Anton was killed in an air raid. Or by his delightful friends. The SS and the Gestapo kept places like this open so they had an excuse for killing those denounced as puffs and pervs. If you came here you were obviously bent. In particular they hated the third sex, a person who is in between, fluid, not easily labelled. The Nazis loved labels. But in the last days no excuse was needed. They no doubt thought Anton was doing too well. Having too good a time. Yes, we were and we are the home of the third sex, *Das dritte Geschlecht*, DDG, free from the patriarchy of Adam and the subjection of Eve. We are open to all and everything. We are the essential democracy of pleasure the Americans and the rest of the world fought for. We are evolution. Then and now. There are no queers, bum-fuckers, chocolate shunters, penis strapping lesbians, tit men, lady damsels, young delectables, pansies, pansy pickers, willy wolves, nor an endless horizon of gloriously filthy in-betweens, even beyond the sublime prose and imagination of the Marquis de Sade. There is only sex, darling!"

The Mother Cat pauses after shouting the last words over the band, and takes a drink from a very small glass in his large fist.

"This is what I mean by the third sex. This is the world of the third sex. The Nazis had the Third Reich, we have the Third Sex . . . Anton Brauner was not really part of this world either. And he went beyond even most Nazis in that all he wanted was to hurt. Down here the ball continues, while upstairs is the wasteland he craved. The smashed streets of Berlin would be a paradise for him. Hell as heaven."

XI

KELLS WAS NEAR the stage, excited, breathless, but then lost his confidence and put his hands over his eyes. In the gloom, beyond stacked chairs and tables and almost as small as the bar at the far end of the room, the stage was next to a bent gilt palm tree. Through his fingers he saw that Gretchen and Rachel were now by the footlights and, angry with himself, he pushed past the tables and chairs and up the steps onto the small platform, painted black against black walls. They both kissed him immediately on the cheek. A piano he had not noticed started to play and the two girls went into a dance number as he stood there, both amazed and helpless. Rachel learned quick. Then Kells was terrified again. He really felt scared. He could not fucking breathe.

Yet, he felt, felt the world again, and that made him elated.

He tried to follow the steps of Gretchen and Rachel, and the third sailor stopped crying and started to laugh.

On stage they sang. *"He's a boogie-woogie bugle boy from company B!"*

The man at the bar with whiskers and a tail clapped loudly.

"Enough! The Mother Cat loves you! Next."

Kells saw that Hyman was clapping too. A black man, who was obviously a friend of the band, emerged from behind the back curtain, while the trumpet player, a saxophonist and a drummer began a lazy tap dance number. The black man fell over twice and even Kells realised the man was not so good and possibly on narcotics. But what really surprised him was that Hyman had got off his bar stool and that his good foot had started to move with the music. As if he was trying to show the man. It was absurd: a white cripple trying to show a black man how to tap dance. Yet Hyman began to dance, and he danced well.

"You get up on stage," said the Mother Cat, who had left the bar and stepped up on stage. The Mother Cat now spoke German.

Hyman obeyed. The Mother Cat had that type of voice that demanded total obedience.

The stage manager took off Hyman's overcoat and draped a jacket around his shoulders.

He was brought a pair of tap shoes.

The band resumed their seats and started playing.

Kells watched in awe as, somehow, Hyman managed to dance up and down the stage, carried on by the music. Kells did not think tap dancing was possible or a good thing for Hyman.

"He looks like Clark Gable," said a soldier at the bar.

"He can fucking dance," said another."

"Enough," said the Mother Cat. "You are on tomorrow night, Mr Gable." The Mother Cat was speaking English again.

When they got back from town, Hyman stood over Kells, who was sitting on a dining chair, bony knees together, smoking a cigarette from a holder. Gretchen was due to sing at her old club off the Ku'damm and pick up her wages. Rachel had stayed with her. They were taking a risk, but the manager would give them a partial lift back.

"You are different these days, you know," Kells said to Hyman. He was using his Lucy voice.

"How so?"

Kells thought for a moment.

"You seem to have taken command of us all, but not in that kindly professor way you had at the kibbutz. You are more charming. And there are other things. Look at the way you are holding your cigarette. You never used to hold a cigarette like that between your thumb and forefinger. If you smoked at all."

Hyman looked at his fingers and the cigarette and shrugged.

"Well, we all have changed, haven't we? You are wearing women's dresses more and more . . . I correct myself . . . in fact, all the time. Should I always call you Lucy?"

"Please call me Lucy. I like it when you do."

Hyman laughed. "Now that is funny. Lucy."

"It is. I'm a joke. In getting everything wrong, in following all the wrong trails. I don't know shit or what I am doing here . . ."

"Does anyone?"

"Did you find any explanation in the files?"

Hyman shrugged. "Not a great deal in the uncoded section . . ."

Kells did not care about the files. He did not want to see them. He did not believe in truth or evidence much anymore. *Macht Nichts* . . .

"What's my fucking mother going to say?"

The ash fell off the end of his cigarette and for a second he felt he couldn't get the air down into his lungs. His world had become beyond insanity.

"She'll like the peace," said Hyman. "Mothers do."

"That's to be seen, and for how long? In the meantime, I can tolerate deviations in my own behaviour and sense of self. And I'd rather be Lucy the next time the bad guys come looking for Colonel

Vardy. It's safer to be a woman. Perhaps you do not want a woman? You seemed at home in the club. I didn't know you were bisexual?"

Hyman smiled and raised his eyebrows. "I'm not, *liebling*, I am just so very fond of you."

Kells laughed.

Hyman continued, "We have become close, yes? Come here. I do not want anyone to tell me who to be. Come to me, why don't you? Let me kiss you. We should not stand here like two unlit candles on an altar. This closeness is real. Perhaps it is the only thing that is real. And in these matters I think you are not a total innocent."

Kells shrugged. "No, I am not."

Hyman stroked Kells' knee.

Kells sighed. "My mother used to dress me as a girl. She had lost a baby girl. She was very happy when she did that and so I used to put her clothes on if I was feeling blue. Then, to make a man of me, I got sent to the Los Alamos Ranch School near the Sangre de Christo mountains."

He sang: "'*Far away and high on the Mesa's crest/ Here's the life that all of us love best. Los Al-amos!*' Los Alamos is so called after the Cottonwood Trees that grow on the Parajito Plateau. They tried their best to make a man of me."

"They did," said Hyman, his hand under Kells' dress.

Kells smiled. "Very nearly they didn't. I was always a girl in the school plays. I was much more fun and confident and out-going and liked as a girl. I got into fights as a boy. I was the lead, Dale, in *Top Hat*, the Ginger Rogers part. You know . . .

Heaven, I'm in heaven
And my heart beats so that I can hardly speak
And I seem to find the happiness I seek
When we're out together dancing cheek to cheek."

Kells moved to imagined music.

"My dress and hair and heels were perfect and, aged thirteen, after the dress rehearsal I was taken to the school's photographic dark room by the art master, who was the show's director, who pushed my cock back between my legs and then told me to press them together, so it looked like I had a cunt. He was so gentle. He took his trousers down and I sucked him. But I had to keep my dress and heels on. I wasn't there as a man."

"No," said Hyman. "Perhaps you will do that for me?"

Hyman carefully pushed Kells' dress up higher and pulled down the lace panties the American was wearing to an inch above his knees. Kells felt breathless as his erection was gently pushed between his legs and he closed them again as he unzipped Hyman's fly buttons. The man's scarred cock was in his mouth only a moment before it grew and grew like Alice, and there was a flood of semen. He swallowed. He pulled away and looked at the burned stomach and side and the tops of the legs. Kells was embracing in living form the ruination he had caused in the war.

Hyman then pushed him slowly back onto the bed, face down, careful not to pull Kells' panties further down, and with difficulty, but great care, entered his anus.

The burning man was inside him.

Afterwards, on the bed, Kells realised he had been fooling himself all day. All year. For a long time. For all of his life.

He realised he had just done things that were obviously within his nature and he felt quite at peace with that, which astounded him. He even was okay with the suspicion the man he had made athletic love with could still be Adolf Hitler, even if his face looked like a lop-sided Clark Gable. Kells doubted that very much now. There was a nervousness, a social hesitancy in Hitler, in the newsreels, that Kells recognised in his former self, but not in the man who was now making coffee downstairs and whistling cheerfully. There was something too assured, too sexually preda-tory, possibly even too demonic for the man whistling to ever be Hitler.

A man of such appetites, such tricks, did not need to invade Poland.

Kells turned over on the camomile pillow. That was a cheap shot, Poland, but all in all the man who was not Adolf Hitler, who had fallen into Kells' life after being burned alive, who "loved" the two women Kells also "loved", was a truly remarkable man. Was it possible as in Dante's *La Vita Nuova*, to use this physical love, in its courtly guise, to bring about a higher love that helped all mankind? Kells used to hope so.

What disturbed Kells most as he lay there on the bed, his asshole hurting, was his own former refusal to experience the war in any real way. He had seen the dead. He had felt the heat of the bombs and the shells, but nothing had touched him. He was like a golden-haired child walking down the aisle of a burning cathedral.

He sighed. He lit a cigarette. This was real. He could not deny this. Hymen's ejaculation was running down his right thigh, on a damp bed in no-man's land, with a black bra that did not fit well, fastened around his chest. His crime, as great a crime as any in the war, was not to experience the experience, not to let the atrocities burn into his head, to change him. He had stood aside, like the most wretched in Hell, like the Coward Angels, who neither chose God nor Lucifer. Kells had preferred it all kept behind plate glass.

He was not alone.

The everyday mass killing had meant nothing to most people he had met in the American Army. He knew this because he was one of them; he had driven oversize cars and eaten hamburgers in diners on desert roads to nowhere, or watched the surf on empty beaches. Yet, he had been in battle and walked in the blood of friends. At the same time, he was not there at all. He had seen the elephant, as the old veterans say. But he had not felt a thing. Candy thunder, but without so much as a toe in the ocean. He must feel more. He must feel each moment until it hurt, to salty tears. He did not even mind if it was pain like the one in his ass.

Every day was new and unique and would never happen again.

"Look at it, kid. Take a mental photo. It's never going to happen again like that," his father used to say of a particular sunset.

It was important to experience fully the bad, as well as the good: beauty and horror.

Hyman was whistling louder and coming up the staircase with the coffee. Kells could feel the male weight of the man's boots on the stairs. "Well, that was beautiful, yes?" Hyman, the burning man, said. "You have no idea how such tenderness moves me. No one can be bad when such things happen. I think the future is going to be different. Different and wonderful."

Kells put out his cigarette. He took the cup of coffee that Hyman passed him. Kells had loved every moment and not just the physical. The four of them were now entwined in Dante's transcendent love.

He relaxed and started reading a movie magazine, hoping to get something they could use with the three singing girls act. Instead, he found a piece on Clark Gable, who had received a medal for being an intelligence photographer and gunner on a bomber.

"You know one of the band, Mo, suggested you do a comedy spot? And the Mother Cat?" Kells said.

"I don't think that is a good idea."

"Here's an article on Clark Gable you may be able to use."

Hyman smiled. He took the magazine from Kells and sat down on the bed. He nodded. "This is very interesting. Perhaps I will go to Hollywood. Wasn't that your nickname in the army? I love Hollywood."

They both laughed.

XII

THE NEXT NIGHT, when Rachel, Gretchen, Hyman and Kells as Lucy arrived at the club, it was closed. A man came up to them and said there had been a raid and to ask in two weeks at the Café Kranzler and not to go to the other club Gretchen sang at.

But two and a half weeks later, the Mother Cat was waiting. "I have just what you want. I have what everyone wants. Go and put this on downstairs. I know what you want, Hyman. You want it all, my dear. And I am sure you will get it."

Rachel went first down an iron spiral staircase into the dressing rooms where an old Chinese man was sprawled in a leather armchair, covered in chop suey. 'Artistes' made up in front of two mirrors sectioned off by wooden screens, held together with tape not well disguised by pictures from *fin de siècle* pornographic magazines and those of Hollywood film stars. Kells hesitated and Hyman directed him behind the furthest screen. The Chinese man then woke up with a broad smile on his face and Gretchen gave him several Occupation Mark notes as a tip.

Hyman turned to Gretchen. "I will put the make-up on Kells, our little Lucy. He's much too nervous. Do not worry, Gretchen, I'll do it most correctly. You look after dear Rachel."

Behind the nearer heavy wooden screen, Gretchen and Rachel began slowly to undress, with a laugh and a shiver. Gretchen took out what was left of a bright red lipstick and applied it to Rachel's full lips.

Rachel broke away, and shouted to Hyman who was now with Kells. "Perhaps Kells wants to be a boy again!"

Kells said nothing.

"I think girls have more fun," said Hyman.

"Do you really think so?" said Gretchen, starting again to apply the lipstick to Rachel, who stood before her in her underwear, barefooted on the gritty stone floor.

"Oh yes," said Hyman. "It is the classical story of Hera. There was a debate in heaven after Zeus, who was having many extra-marital affairs, excused himself for not having as much sex as before with Hera, on account that women had more pleasure from a single sexual act, whereas a man needed a greater quantity. There was then a great argument on Olympus, which was settled by the prophet Teiresias who, seeing two snakes mating, had killed the female one and was then forced by the gods to live as a woman for seven years, becoming an extremely beautiful prostitute. Teiresias said women had nine tenths of the fun and men only one."

"But Kells was a soldier," said Gretchen.

Behind his screen Hyman said, "So was Teiresias, in the Roman histories. Perhaps such transitions are easy for Kells. Perhaps he has another self. A female self. The dominant self. Like Alexander the Great."

"Take off your blouse," whispered Rachel to Gretchen. After being on stage, Rachel's confidence had returned. "Take off your blouse," and Gretchen did so, it was easy, there were only four buttons. Rachel then reached around and undid Gretchen's bra. Her breasts, very white in the overhead light from a single bulb, bounced free. Gretchen looked at her large nipples in the mirror and was about to put her hands over them, but Rachel stopped her. That was ridiculous. Childhood religion, perhaps, and not like Gretchen. Rachel did not care that Hyman was sleeping with Gretchen, as she was with Kells. Theirs was a time long past modesty.

"Has it occurred to you that we are free? Totally free? I had a nightmare about it last night."

"A nightmare?" said Gretchen. "About freedom?"

Rachel put her hands onto Gretchen's breasts and began to slowly caress them. "I dreamt I was free in the world with a man and an apartment and a car and I was terrified. I only stopped being frightened when I ran back to the camp where the guards let me in and fucked me, before killing me. I liked that too."

Gretchen gave a murmur, Rachel thought of recognition. She did not protest.

Rachel gently kissed Gretchen's nipples one after the other. Perhaps she was only used to men. "We will put stars on these. They said we should wear the feathered costume."

Gretchen shuddered with pleasure. Rachel added two golden stars. She then took the lipstick and began to apply it to Gretchen's lips. "Purse your lips, Gretchen."

She then kissed Gretchen on the lips and Gretchen let her and kissed back hard. "Do you think that girls have more fun?" Rachel asked her.

There was a sharp cry from behind the other wooden screen which prompted the Chinese man to snore again, mumble guttural things in his own language, and cough and spit.

Then Gretchen was kissing Rachel once more. They were going to have to put the lipstick on all over again.

"Five minutes, darlings. Five minutes to stage. Hands off squelchy bits, my dears," the Mother Cat called down the stairs.

Gretchen and Rachel stepped from behind the screen, pale and quiet despite their make-up, dressed as showgirls in bodices of dark, electric-blue feathers, several of which had fallen off. Kells, despite the width of his shoulders, towered in a blue chiffon top over black tights and red high heels. Rachel thought he only looked partly like a woman, but that would delight, tease and inflame the audience. She still was not quite sure if he was really scared, or playing a game with himself, trying to find out who he was.

Tonight, Hyman was dressed in an American officer's uniform and, with his hair neatly parted, looked exactly like Clark Gable in *Gone with the Wind*.

"Are you just going to tap dance?" Rachel asked.

"Don't worry, I have my plan of campaign," he said.

XIII

"HEY, MO!"
When Rachel has gone, I go and find the bandleader, Mo, slumped in an armchair, pretzel crumbs over his light blue suit.

"Hi there, Hyman man. Got a cigarette?" he says, opening his heavy-lidded eyes.

I give him one.

"I bet you'd like to make a lot of money, Mo," I say, lighting his cigarette "Take over the girls' act? I'm going to sell them to you for nothing and give you money as well. How about that? I can make you almost rich and that might make a musician famous. In exactly a week, I may need a car. Or even a van. Early in the morning. I have papers. Do not look so surprised. This is what I want you to do, my friend. Do you know where I can make a long-distance call around here?"

Later, I stand in the wings of the little stage as the girls bring the house down. The more innocent and gauche Kells becomes, the more the audience love the three of them. The place is packed so tight there is standing room only. When they come off there is cheering and cries of "encore", but then I step onto the stage to a roll of drums and there is a deep, dark blue and awkward silence.

"You know who I am, don't you?" I say, with the American accent I have been practicing. The Mother Cat says most of her regulars speak English and I intend to repeat a few of the lines in German. I stand in the spotlight in the uniform of the United States Army Air Force. There was one backstage on the rails, to my surprise. I have the rank of major, like Clark Gable. I wonder what the real major left the Katzenmutter Club wearing. Probably something sequinned.

"You know who I am, don't you?" I say. "Frankly, my dear, I don't give a damn."

Immediately, there is laughter. I feel such relief!

"I do not know anymore, quite what I am," I say. "And if I do, I must keep quiet about it."

They laugh again. I hold out my hands and turn over the palms. "I never laugh in the morning until I've had my morning coffee and that's well after I've made love. It's a bonus when you like a lady you have fallen in love with. Someone to have coffee with in the morning. A little innocent liquid."

There is a shout from the audience. A pretty young boy in pink.

"Do you still believe in love and truth after playing Rhett Butler in *Gone With The Wind*, sir? And will you come home with me? Will you *ficken* me. *Bitte!*"

There is more laughter, they are with me now, and a man in red chiffon begins to argue with the boy in pink.

I hold up my hand and say in a quiet voice, "I try so badly to believe there is truth and love. That love is real. Then frankly in the morning . . . Honey, I couldn't give a damn . . ."

There is universal applause and laughter for this, and the Mother Cat begins to bang a large wooden spoon on the bar, the signal that the act is about to be paid a bonus collected from the audience. I salute the audience as Clark Gable.

"Always choose dishonour before death, folks, and don't make a song and dance about it."

I then turn around wiggling my bottom at the audience and as the band strike up I begin to beat time with the tap shoe on my better leg.

There are shouts of more. *"Mehr!"*

I plaster my hair across my forehead and add a too familiar tooth-brush moustache, made from Gretchen's dark hair. When I turn back to the audience for a second time my whole demeanour is changed, the dance is a one-legged goose-step, still keeping a beat. I move my right arm in a stiff and now forbidden way. Equally familiar and prohibited is a red and black swastika armband. There is silence and an audible intake of breath.

"Now, you know who I really am, don't you, *meine Lieblinge?*"

My voice is one of total command.

There is pandemonium and one man in a dress flees from the room.

"Hands up all those who wanted to sleep with me? *Bitte?* Do you want to sleep with me now? Now there is no danger of my having you shot afterwards? If you do not measure up. Shot at dawn. *Im Morgengrauen erschossen.*"

I make a suggestive movement with my hips and see a man in a blue dress to my right start to smile. There is a ripple of nervous laughter. A few boys and girls get up with a stiff-armed Nazi salute, possibly ironic, but most do not. The image is too stark, the voice too good.

I salute back. "That can get you into trouble, you know. Sent to the camps. Perhaps you would like it there. Perhaps that is what you want. All those hungry men!"

I then goose-step as best I can in a small circle and stare at them. I point at a man at the bar.

"Do you have the same loving wife as at the start of the war? If you have, you have not been trying. There's nothing quite like a world war to hide illicit sex. I bet you don't, you naughty boy. I bet you pushed the fat wife, the dumpling, *der Leberknödel*, out into the street and the shrapnel and ran quick as a rat for the shelter and found a svelte mistress. Or mister. Or perhaps your sweet little daughter? In that short pleated dress. You taught her to play with your pink mouse, *die rosa Maus*. Then you strangled her and sent her home to mother. That is the way of things. I blame the American bombs. They shuffle people like cards. I'm sure you know who I am. But I do not. That's good, isn't it? If I do not know who I am, then I cannot possibly have done anything wrong. Nothing is as true as that. We are all little innocents, *kleine Unschuldige*"

The audience roared with laughter this time. I kept my foot tapping.

"Do you remember how to march? How to beat a drum? I do not remember how to march. Not at all. I think I will go into politics. They are crying out for people like me."

A man near the stage wolf-whistles.

Mo and the band are still looking worried and start to play a soft shoe shuffle. I realise they want people to dance.

"Shall I have a go first?"

I turn and the drummer of the black band begins to play a beat and to my surprise my feet start to move even more. I really begin to move. I start a more energetic tap dance and then stop and face the audience. I begin to tap dance around my burned leg and then lift that one too. The audience clap along with the beat and I dance for a whole ten minutes until it begins to hurt in my left leg and my back and I stop and bow.

"Isn't it amazing how the beat gets you going!"

The drums begin again and the saxophone screams in. I dance some more.

"I have to go now, *meine leiblinge*. I am a wanted man. I am wanted everywhere and nowhere!"

There are howls of 'encore!' but I go backstage and stay there. I am trembling and empty. I look out again and all the audience, those boys who are in dresses and those who are not, are standing up and there is more shouting, ironically I hope, of *"Sieg Heil"*, but I fancy not. The shout thunders around the club. The white faces are featureless in the applause. I think of the white silkworm cocoons in the boiling water. So few escape. So few moths flutter out of the open window into the mulberry tree.

I go back onto the stage and they cheer for five whole minutes. They shout for me to stay. It is an ugly, angry shout. I turn to them and say, "It is truly amazing what any individual can do when they have to. It is truly amazing what a people can do . . . When you believe in who you are. I can do magic tricks. I can rule the world. I can make your best lace underwear disappear. Do you know who I am? Do you know who you are? I am the tap dancer who forgot he could dance. Will you let me be the tap dancer? Your *Stepptänzer*. Will you let me be? Let me be? *Ich leibe Sie alle*, I love you all."

These are the last words I say to the audience. Many are laughing. Others are sitting quiet and frightened. The Mother Cat looks at me strangely, a mixture of knowing and terror. The cramped basement stinks of dreams and fear.

We get home, after a lift half-way in a rubbish truck.

XIV

"TONIGHT IS WALPURGIS night . . . The night of misrule," I shout.

A week later we are still talking of the performance. That, and a decision I have reached make me feel ecstatic, and light-headed. It is a year since I ran up a hill of broken stones in Berlin on fire.

Rachel wants to speak. I see she is upset and I go over and take her hand. At first she pulls away; the man she saw on stage is different from her sensitive Dr Hyman. Then she grabs my arm and says, "You wanted to tell them who you were? In the club. Who we thought you were?"

"Yes. But I borrowed this handsome evening suit from the club after I changed out of that uniform, which I also have brought back for emergencies. In case we have to give someone the slip."

"It is not a joke, Hyman, said Rachel. "We can't go back there."

I laugh. "They know who I am. I am them . . . They knew who they wanted me to be, standing before them at the microphone. Oh yes, they knew. How they laughed. You can fake anger, but you can never fake laughter. The laughter from self-recognition. Of fear. In front of them, I am all of them. I am Germany. I am their whole world. Even the sensitive ones who the Nazis wanted to kill. I am their whole world up on stage. But not quite in the way they thought. I am not a saviour, although I can do tricks. And I can tap dance. Who taught me to fucking tap dance? Himmler? They knew who I was up there. I know because I was one of them. The worst. And I am so happy. I was glad to confess I was who they wanted me to be."

Rachel shakes her head. She is very serious. She stands up in the middle of the living room, flanked by two settees. The curtains are not drawn.

"If anyone was watching your act. From Lucy . . . Or the Americans tidying up. They may come for us. It may all be over tonight . . . I want to confess, too."

"I do not think this is a good idea," said Kells, as I sit down in an armchair.

"I mean, confess to you all. Not the authorities," she says.

"To us?" Kells puts his hand on her shoulders. He has changed back into the familiar blue dress.

"If she wants to confess, let her confess," I say, jumping up. I still feel exhilarated, drunk almost from my one stage performance.

It is infantile, I know, but fun. I have an idea. "Yes, this is *Walpurgis Nacht*, April 30, the night of misrule, when the physical can conjure the supernatural. When everything can be turned on its head. When anything can be reversed. Let my love confess. Let our love confess. Come to me, Rachel. Kneel here on the carpet. Let us do this properly."

Rachel looks surprised and her curls tremble. Then she comes and kneels before me on a Turkish carpet. Her hair shines in the moonlight that floods the room in between the passing squalls of rain, which patter on the windows and transform the waters of the small lake into molten silver.

On the settee Gretchen looks filled with dread at what Rachel is going to say.

"My sin is that I obeyed orders," says Rachel, looking up at me. "I obeyed orders to the letter, without question. I obeyed orders like a good German, even though I am Jewish. It is comic. I should be laughing. I was part of the resistance. I obeyed. But I shot . . ."

"Is that all?" I say, interrupting, making an elaborate sign of the Cross. "There are many shootings in a war. Bang, bang, bang! And there is no one to witness your often unreliable witnessing. Bang, bang. Bang. You are completely absolved and forgiven, my child. And it really doesn't matter if you are Jewish. Christ was. This absolution is all conquering. Next please."

"But . . . ?" Rachel is protesting.

She stands.

"Next please! You cannot stand in the way of forgiveness, Rachel. Lucy? You are next." I turn to Kells.

Kells comes and kneels before me.

He takes a long drag of his cigarette. The filter is smeared with the vampish lipstick he is wearing.

At first I think he is going to get angry. His eyes are murderous. Then he says:

"I am a coward. I was a coward all the way through the war. I would not let myself feel. And even when it was all over, I still wanted to find the devil who had caused it all, Hitler, when it was those like me. I . . ."

I stop him with a raised hand.

"Enough, you are forgiven, my child. Not even one *Ave Maria* is needed." I say. "He who has the bravery to rebel is always an innocent. A paratrooper who puts on a dress is a hero. Next please. Gretchen?"

Kells gets to his feet with a smile.

Gretchen kneels before me.

"All I was doing was trying to stay alive, wanting food and shelter and then sent poor children to the . . ."

"Enough," I say. "You are forgiven a million times by God and all his mad saints. Including St Lucy. In the end you rebelled too. You manage to be happy in the worst times and you can sing like a nightingale. You took great risks, for humanity, as did you all. Even if you were not working for the side you thought, or doing what you thought was intended. You were about Holy Work that God should have been doing when he was having a sleep somewhere."

Gretchen stands slowly and kisses me.

"These are not your sins," I say to them all. "They are sins of characters you were forced to create. I will not confess. Hyman Kaplan has nothing to confess. The Hyman Kaplan I have created. Hyman Kaplan is a good man."

There is a feeling of relief in the room. As if cords had snapped. Bonds.

Then I say, "We must beware that our consciousness makes us feel like gods. That the universe is as clever and as sensitive and talkative as we think we are. The beauty of the world makes us feel forever innocent and childlike. Then we get upset when our delicate plans fail in the face of the raw power and wanting that surround us. How gently we treat each other as we ascend the rickety staircase of love, from the sexual to the eternal is possibly all that matters. I can only say what is true for me. And our relationships with perfect strangers, those fleeing the past in a place like Berlin. They truly set us free."

There is a silence, only broken by the sight of a bird, a felt-winged owl, flying across the silver lake. We are all standing and embrace each other.

"How long can this magic last between us?" says Rachel, her eyes wide. I know she is sincere.

"Tonight at least," says Gretchen, with a laugh. "Come, let us all go to Kells' room. I feel wonderful. Wonderful!" I am never quite sure when Gretchen is being serious of late. She is much harder to read than the other two.

Rachel pulls Kells to his feet. Tears stream down his cheeks. A little unsteady, he puts his arms around both girls and goes out into the hall. I go after them.

I am sure they think I am going with them as they start towards the stairs and the bedroom.

But I am already opening the front door. I know what I have to do. There is a cold draught of the night air and the muddy smell of the lake.

I turn, smiling, and say.

"Happy *Walpurgis Nacht*. Go enjoy yourselves. Each other. I wish to go and think by the water. I need to quieten my racing mind. I will be with you a little later. Be kind, my silk moths. That is all we can ever be. Do not try to understand the light. Lucy is the light which brought us all together. Go into the bedroom and fly on moonbeams. *Ich liebe Sie alle*, I love you all!"

XV

RACHEL BECKONS TO me, "Come Gretchen."
Rachel and Kells already are standing on the first step. There is still an air of breathless realisation and release in the hall. Like after a storm.

The smell of flint and gunpowder in the heavy air.

I go back and kiss Hyman again on the cheek. He is smoking a cigarette in an ebony holder like an Oranienstraße pimp, holding the cigarette holder hard between his teeth. I am glad he is not joining us . . . I enjoyed his amateur dramatics of the confessions but there is increasingly an air about him I do not like and do not trust. I have let our sexual relationship go on because I am so close to the others and them to him. But perhaps I have had more experience of the type of man he really is. He looks wary of me at times. Although that may be because I have told him when he will die.

His grey-blue cigarette smoke curls up to the yellowed ceiling. I turn and follow the others. Outside, perhaps at the other shore of the lake, I hear a sound and turn back. Then an owl hoots. I shiver.

"I will join you, by and by," the man we call Hyman says again. "I want to see the moon on the lake. Fly my little moths . . ."

Then he is through the door and gone.

There is something about the way he says those words I do not like. I am still alive because I am good at spotting tricks and insincerity. Especially with men. When they are phoney. When they are going to betray. And he has been behaving oddly. Like he expects something to happen. It is not the first time I am suspicious of him. I hope he stays by the fucking lake.

I follow Rachel and Kells up the stairs and close the door of the bedroom. Rachel and Kells are already kissing by the bed. There is no jealousy anymore. Before I close the door I hear the scrape of a chair leg on the wooden floor downstairs and the sound of the front door opening and closing. Hyman had forgotten something. What is he up to now under the light of the spring moon? I half want to go to the window and look out, but Rachel comes over and kisses me, silencing the questions and pulls me to the bed as Kells turns off the creamy yellow glow of the oil lamp and the bedroom is relit in the spectral silver of the moonlight. I have a strange feeling, a premonition of great danger.

I sigh. I wait for the chasm of the past to ambush me, but a vision of my secret history does not come. The faces I see are not the Jewish children in the transports, or my dead father being led away, but those of Rachel and Kells. They are kissing me, showering me with kisses, and pulling me onto the bed, their mouths on mine, mouths that taste of the same lipstick. Then I give myself up to the physical human consolation and sacrament of sex. I give myself to the night.

XVI

I GO AND sit on one of the wicker sofas covered in everlasting flowers by the lake. I have always thought these sofas have an altar-like quality, suitable for the sacrifice of naked bathers. Perhaps I am going to be a sacrifice. Perhaps I want to be. Perhaps I must be.

Or perhaps I am being pompous.

I make myself comfortable and take a sip of my glass of excellent cognac, which I went back for in the kitchen, and another pull on my American cigarette. Even with death close, life is so good. There is a rainbow ring around the moon and those colours dance on the water as well as the yellow-white ball, which looks substantial enough to touch. This beautiful moment will never come again. The truth is, I have to heal myself. I have to let Anton Brauner, "Mr Brown", be overcome by the goodness of Hyman Kaplan. I have to let my friends go. For them to be safe. I have to find the woman who gave me the gardenia and who I have, no doubt, betrayed. In this life or the next. I am sitting here, true to that flower. It is the intention that counts.

A water bird screams to my left. It flies out into the centre of the lake, causing bright ripples. It calls again. Is someone there?

"Hush," I say to the bird. Someone may come for me tonight because of a phone call I made, because of a bargain I struck. They will honour that bargain because they still think I have all the Lucy papers. And Mo the musician will come in the morning to take the others away. Who will come for me tonight? After I called Lucerne 666? It may be the lady to whom I gave the flower. It may be death. I remember Rachel's play. "Ho, Pylades, tis death," I say.

A stick on the beach cracks like bone.

"Am I a good man?" I whisper to the night. "I am covered in blue dust and running from a holy yellow fire that is my burning flesh on a hill of stone I raise my hands to the heavens triumphant as everyone stops shooting . . . I am too alive to die . . . I am free from the past . . ." I say it, missing my friends already. It is hard, so painful, to leave them.

"Am I a good man? Can Mr Brown be a good man?"

Another bird calls loudly, but melodiously. Is that really a nightingale? The song comes again and again, but then there is silence, calm and the cold approaching dawn. The ripples cease in the centre of the lake, which reflects the Sea of Tranquillity. My hand goes to the automatic pistol in my overcoat pocket, the one with which I shot the dog. The night bird calls again. It is calling me. That is all. Then my hand is on a knife I took from the kitchen. I know I am not going to use the knife or the gun. The knife is by an envelope. An envelope that contains the white flower.

To my left the darkness moves.

XVII

"RACHEL!" I HEAR my name shouted from below as I wake.

There is a banging at the front door and more shouting. I try to disengage myself from the other two, without waking them. There is lipstick and mascara on the pillow and the warm smell of intimate flesh framing the sharper reek of lovemaking. There is both a weight of bodies and a softness, like the heft of good silk, as I pull free. Then I am scared, I shiver like a child. I can really love again. I laugh out loud. It is so simple I want to sing.

But there is more knocking. I put on a Chinese silk dressing gown from the club that belongs to Gretchen, pull on her slippers and open the bedroom door, as I hear Kells and Gretchen waking behind me.

I hear Gretchen whisper and Kells kiss her, and an excitement and nervousness bunch again in my solar plexus. I feel breathless, triumphant and, this is most important, attached to the others, as if I could lose myself in them and not care. I feel Kells' kiss on Gretchen's lips, as if it is my own, and the sudden racing of her heart. I feel Gretchen's kiss back to Kells, burying her tongue in his mouth, as he has in mine. I stop, giddy. I have been born. I feel like singing, as choirs of angels sing in me and sit glowing in the mulberry tree outside and all around the lake. I fly in skies of impossible blue. I had never expected such a night like that, and feel now empty and yet completely fulfilled, human to the power of being human, and without a shred of guilt of what has gone before, even on that last day in the camps, and in a world that has taken on the gold mosaic shimmer of a Byzantine altar.

"Rachel," my name is called again. The knocking is louder.

I steady myself on the banister at the top of the stairs, wiping the sweat from my body down to my pubic hair as the dressing gown falls open. The day is warm already and I am still half-asleep, the song of it all still inside me. I pull the dressing gown silk around me and fasten the cord belt and run down the uncarpeted stairs.

I can see the image of a man through the stained and opaque glass of the front door.

I stop. I bite my lip in a moment of panic. I used to bite my lip while playing the cello. Hyman would not bang on the door. Is this how it ends?

Has everything caught up with us? The world? For being happy?

"Hey, in there," said a deep voice I recognise.

It is Mo from the Katzenmutter Club.

I open the door.

"What is it?"

"He done dead."

"Who?"

Mo looks upset. "Hitler. Clark Gable. It's Mr Hyman. He dead."

"No!"

I fall, faint, the passageway dissolves and spins, and Mo grabs me and I try to stand and fail and then shake myself. Rachel does not faint. Rachel is strong.

"No, no. This cannot happen now," I say. Strangely, deep in me, the angel choir continues to sing. "Where is he?"

"Down by the water on one of them spiky sofas. The wicker ones with the little flowers. He cold as the stones with his cigarette burned down and a glass still in his hand. He staring out there, into the lake. Staring out there. In that big old coat of his. I says hello, and he says fuck nothing so I felt for his pulse in his wrist and his throat. Then I drinks his brandy. I say to myself, he is dead. He not going to drink the brandy. One thing I can say is that he looked happy. Too happy to be dead, if you ask me. But he is."

I start running across the road to the sofa on the small beach.

Mo comes after me, but slower. He lights a cigarette.

We both gaze at the wicker sofa and the everlasting flowers, the blue and pink and white, which are becoming brighter by the moment as the sun comes up.

There is no one there.

I turn to Mo, angry. "Where the fuck is he?"

Mo looks up and down the beach. "He was . . . I am telling you he was. Look, here is the glass. And the cigarette holder. He was dead. Dead, as I'm alive standing here."

I am shaking my head. "You must have been mistaken. He must have gone for a walk." Then I burst into tears. "We must find him."

Mo puts his hand on my shoulder. He then says quietly, "He is done dead. Dirt plastered on his face. Maybe he fell. We just had a war, babe. I seen too many dead people. On the way home. Once in a motherfucking tree, all hung there like ornaments on a Christmas tree. But old Adolf really died happy."

I stare at the musician. "You called him, Adolf?"

"Yeah. I know he done look like Clark Gable, though he didn't so much a week ago. But everyone wanted him back as Adolf. The tap-dancing Hitler. He really got them out of their seats, man. All the pansies. He knew which buttons to push. It's safe to laugh now."

"Is it?" I say, before I can stop myself.

I start to run up the beach, but Mo catches me and holds me hard by both wrists. He smells of the smoke and damp of the club.

"No babe, you got to get out. All of you. Get back to the house. Get the others. You coming with me. You all got to get out. There were some bad cars up the road a while. Three big, black old Mercedes, maybe police. Maybe worse. They not taxis. Have you got people looking for you? I'm a black man in a black band who came over for the Olympics and stayed too long, that has kept himself alive all the way through the war in snow-white Berlin by keeping well away from cats in black cars. I stick to what I know, my trumpet. Blow it and it makes a noise. But you got a spot whenever you want it at the Katzenmutter. And, guess what?" Mo's smile increased from ear to ear. "We got invited to play the muther-fuckin' Eldorado. It's another girly-boy pansy club. For a short time it was the SA headquarters until Hitler iced all of the leaders by a creepy blue lake way down south. They will love your Mr Kells in his pretty blue dress. You get only the best, rich white-boy pansies in the Eldorado on Motzstraße. And then we can get out to France, to the French Riviera."

I am still in shock when Kells and Gretchen come out and help Mo get me inside. They sit at the table in the room overlooking the lake. Gretchen has the black party dress she had on last night and looks detached and calm. Kells, as Lucy, is wrapped in the counterpane and has traces of make-up on his face and a smudge of mascara. Mo quickly repeats what he told me.

Gretchen says softly, "How did he die?"

"If he is dead, where's the body?" asks Kells. "Hyman has proved damn hard to kill in the past. In the battle for Berlin. There never were more bullets fired in a single day."

Kells looks surprised at himself. He has spoken with such confidence. A confidence I thought had deserted him.

"Perhaps if people were after him, he wanted to take the heat off you," says Mo. "He may be leading them off you. Dead. They came for him alone. Be glad."

Kells pours himself a glass of brandy from the table and then hands one to all of us.

Gretchen has gone out herself to make sure there is no one on the wicker settee. She comes back, after ten minutes, shaking her head. "There is no one there," she says with a puzzled frown.

After that we all sit, drinking the cognac.

Mo looks at his watch. Kells puts down his cognac glass. "However much we drink, it is not going to make a difference. There was one time I relied on Hyman dying and me being a hero. Now I don't know what we will do without him."

Mo drinks the rest of his brandy, and then drinks Gretchen's.

"Let's go," says Mo. "Lets go to the Katzenmutter. Let's get back to normality. We had some American Marines in and they are still there, drunk and naked and probably married to Kurt or Dieter or one of the other girly-boys by now. But I really have a feeling that we got to fucking blow."

I nod and put my arms around the silent and pensive Gretchen before I go upstairs and begin to gather together our personal things, which do not amount to much. In the room where we made love, I look in the bedside table for the small, shiny automatic pistol, but it isn't there. There is a sheaf of money, but nowhere near the amount I thought. Hyman must have put the rest somewhere safe. There is a noise behind me.

Kells has followed me and hesitates for a moment over the uniform Hyman brought back from the club and then puts on the dress and the wig he had been in the night before. He places the uniform into a shopping bag. He then takes all his clothes off again and I help him put the bra and panties back on as Gretchen comes in and hugs him.

"My father is in a mental hospital in California thinking his son is Billy the Kid," Kells says, with half a smile, and Gretchen and I laugh at this return of sanity.

"I do not believe Hyman is dead," Kells then says passionately.

"He's dead," says Gretchen. "I told him it was today he would die and he laughed. I have a gift . . ."

We look at her open-mouthed. She is in shock too.

"We have to go. We have to go now," I say.

All three of us clatter down the bare wooden stairs and out to Mo's rusting blue Opel Blitz van. There is a plaster on my left heel where my too-small high heels have been biting into my flesh. I am not wearing stockings.

Mo looks approvingly at Kells as Lucy and then laughs and shakes his head. Kells rides in the front of the van, while Gretchen gets in the back with the one small, two-tone suitcase she once told me was her mother's.

XVIII

"WE ON OUR way, Kells," Mo says to me, with a weird look in his eye.

The van does not start on Mo's first attempt. The engine then roars and congas into life and we judder forwards and are off, continuing unsteadily up the road, which bends around the small lake and we are almost opposite our house when I see a car coming towards us, an all-black Mercedes-Benz 230 saloon with the big headlights, a heavy car, like the Buick I crashed in the forest.

Mo puts his big, pink-palmed hand on my leg, probably out of habit with anything in a dress, and I, to my own surprise, pull his be-ringed fingers sharply apart, as I had once been trained to do.

"Quit that, bitch!" Mo says, wincing, in his best tough guy voice. There are times, when dressed as a woman, that I want to murder every man in sight with a cheeky grin on my face, just like Billy the Kid.

I give Mo by best, most innocent, well-dressed going-to-Mass smile.

"Okay, honey-bunch, I got your news," says Mo. "You broke my motherfuckin' hand. Why you do that? What is it with you?"

I sigh. I am watching as the approaching car, the black Mercedes saloon, followed by two identical others, draws level and stops. One of the other cars then blocks our way and Mo brakes to a halt with a jolt.

"I done with this motherfuckin' foolishness. I out of here," he shouts, and opens the door and runs back up the road.

Everything I can see is as real as if it has just been made, and I am not afraid. I hear and feel Mo's footfall on the muddy verge. I feel free. I regret my fear and how I treated Gretchen.

The car that has drawn level is full of men. I glimpse a machine pistol. The car then accelerates up the road and I jack myself over to the driver's seat. In the pedal well Mo has left a canvas laundry bag with sheet music and in the bottom a comically large pistol that may be from the First World War, or Billy the Kid, and a pair of binoculars. I look up at the car facing us and almost instantly behind us there is a burst of automatic fire and the dull explosion of an anti-tank mine. In the mirror I see a man by the leading black Mercedes pointing a machine pistol towards our van. Surf's up! Candy thunder.

Fear rolls back through my body.

"Get down!" I shout to Gretchen and Rachel and I am wondering whether to go for Mo's ancient pistol. The third Mercedes draws level. In the back sits a neat man with a homburg hat and huge, square-shaped glasses and a tall, elegant, blonde woman in a large hat and a veil. I know who they are. I think of the death camp tattoo on the arm of the woman I had known as the Empress Theodora. This time there are no Mad Hatter costumes. The woman turns to me and nods and then speaks to the driver, who speeds off around the lake towards our villa, followed by the car that was blocking our way, and then by the one behind us. All the time I expect a burst of fire to come ripping through the old, rusting metal of the van and leave us dripping blood onto the road. Why don't they fucking shoot?

I ease off my high heels and, put the van into gear again, and we move off slowly. As our van starts labouring its way along an avenue of trees, I glance to my right through the cab window across the lake and at the wicker settee with the blue and white and pink dried flowers on the lakeside and I see a figure there, standing.

A figure that is unmistakably the man I christened Hyman, waving.

My burning man.

Waving goodbye? Waving hello to the approaching cars that will kill him? Or is a white flower about to be passed from hand to hand?

A tree is now in the way and then three, and when I can see over the lake again the figure is not there. I keep the van going. I should turn back, but I have to think of Rachel and Gretchen. I want to be back on my fucking board.

It is too Lucy. Better to drown in your own nonsense than another's absurdity.

The sun peeps out with an understandable degree of suspicion and lights up the dew on the leaves and everything makes way for the splendour of the day.

I keep going. That's what we all do. I am going to keep going until I find an ocean to surf in.

There is a weird breaking sound away in the distance, beyond the lake, beyond a few wild cherry trees in blossom. It is not gunfire, or one of the mines exploding. It's more fundamental than that. I feel the tearing inside my chest as much as hear the sound. I feel the sound as emotion. The sound is like the snapping of a ship's cable. The breaking of ties. The falling of a building. Or the world turning on its head.

Then the sensation is gone.

"What's happening?" says Rachel, when we have gone a quarter of a mile.

I blurt out, "I saw Hyman. At the other side of the lake . . ."

"Are you sure?" says Gretchen.

"Yes . . ."

"Stop!" yells Rachel. "We have to go back for him."

"Yeah," I say. I hold up the old gun I have found. "We got this."

And I am turning the van around. I am turning the van around on the narrow road.

No one believes the people in the black cars will spare us a second time. Even me. There is only the noise of the engine for a few moments.

"We have to go back," says Gretchen reluctantly. "We cannot leave him to them." I can see it is against her every instinct. This is the kind of love in Dante I had once imagined possible and tried to tell Betty about. Fuck.

The van's wheel sticks in a rut in the road. The engine stalls. I try and try, but the van will not fucking start.

"We are going to have to walk," shouts Gretchen, who has undone the van doors and is walking back along the road with her mother's two-tone suitcase. Her coat is too big and she looks like a refugee. Rachel follows her and after trying to start the van one last time, I search around in the back and find a big pair of rubber boots, which I put on. The same kind of boots I used to walk through the fields of bloody dead. I take the pistol and slam the door of the van and set off after the other two, going back for Hyman, the burning man, with my carrier bag in one hand and my blonde wig in the other. I toss the wig away. I do feel. I feel fear. But there is no hiding anymore. Like jumping from a plane.

Fuck it. *Macht Nichts*.

I stop and look through the binoculars across the lake at the house. There are no cars there now. Where have they gone? Are they round the back of the house? They surely cannot have driven across the fields at the other side of the house, into the minefield.

Gretchen is determined. She sticks out her chin, her hand in Rachel's. To go back is all we can do. I am sure Lucy will kill us. It is hard to walk in these rubber boots. Yet, I feel good, I feel every blade of the roadside grass as I catch up to the other two. I feel the majesty of the new shoots in my rubber boots.

"Wait for me!"

A breeze rolls the lake mist back down the road, like the future coming to meet us, and then Gretchen starts to sing and we all join in. *"He's the boogie woogie bugle boy of Company B!"*

I am scared, truly scared, but I do not care.

There is a scent of new blossom on the warm spring wind.

XIX

WHEN WE COME around the bend in the road at the side of the lake, we are able to see the house again with the small section of beach and the wicker settees. Then I see him.

"He is alive. Hyman is alive . . ." I say, unsure of what this means.

"Yes, I am, Gretchen," he says.

He is lolling on one of the wicker settees. The old Citroën car is out of the garage and on the road. In his lapel is a white flower. A gardenia.

We all go up and hug him and kiss him. He should still be scared, but he seems amused by the whole business. He regards it as a huge joke.

"My old friends in those big black cars seem to want me around. Don't worry, they are not here now. There is another way across the minefield. They will join us later . . . Smell this beautiful flower I have been given by an old lady friend! Any past disagreements are forgiven and forgotten . . . There is a house we can go to in the city. Not far from the Katzenmutter. It will be quite safe." Rachel does not stop hugging him and Kells keeps shaking his head in a kind of wonder. But my doubts start to come back. Who exactly did he contact? Who were the people in the cars? The people with machine-guns. There is something very wrong . . .

I see my mother . . . I see my mother, her arms folded, refusing to come to Europe with my father. Warning of the broken future. I see every line on her face and the scarf with red roses I gave her. I have never seen her like this, real as day, and then she is gone and

I see my father, hanging from a gibbet and jump, startled. I hear the cheap hemp rope creak as he swings a few degrees one way and then back the other, by the barbed wire fence in a camp. Men are laughing. I shudder. Then he is gone too.

"Come on, Gretchen. We can all get into the Citroën," Kells says.

The house is a grand mansion on a street that runs at right angles to the river. The building is one of the few untouched by the war and inside there is a high, echoing hall with a chandelier and a white marble staircase leading to a salon on the first floor. There are several settees and a chaise longue, and heavy open curtains with green tassel ties frame the floor-to-ceiling windows. In one corner there is a huge stove with yellow and white tiles. An aspidistra in a pot has had its leaves recently polished.

"One would think the war and Herr Hitler never happened," says Hyman, as if performing a magic trick. He sits down on one of the leather settees and leans back, arms outstretched, and there is such a self-satisfied, arrogant smirk on his face that I begin to hate him.

Not just distrust but hate.

And the more I do, the more I find in the past, his masterful playing of the victim, his subtle taking over of Rachel, his gradual domination of all, his sexual seduction of each of us. He controls us.

Why was I so blind?

I ignore what he says and walk over to the table by the window. On it is a collection of waistcoats. I lift one up and a moth flies from the one below. A purple silk waistcoat with solid silver buttons of the type my father wore. I know it is not my father's, but that makes no difference to me.

"In a few days we will be able to get out of Berlin," Hyman is saying.

"Where will we go? says Kells.

"Wherever we like," says Hyman. "We are free and the war is over."

"I would like to go to the South of France," says Rachel, snuggling close to Hyman on the settee.

"Do you know this house?" I ask Hyman.

"We should have a drink," Hyman is saying, "There must be some around. Yes, I know this house. Apparently, it is mine."

"And these waistcoats?"

"Oh, those. I must have made a little collection of them."

"Where did you get them? They are Turkish waistcoats."

"There have always been Turks in Berlin."

I finger the weighty buttons. I can see my father on horseback wearing such a waistcoat. Different villages or different circuses or different acts wore individual waistcoats. He had buttons like these specially made. They were for our act and I see him riding around the ring, laughing. I am riding too, around the ring, cutting strings on balloons with a knife. I have my knife in my pocket. The one that can shave a pig.

"My father had a waistcoat like that."

"I am sure there are many such waistcoats. Especially among the gypsy circus people."

"That are now no more."

Kells is staring at me. He has taken his rubber boots off and put the pistol from the van on the table. "Hey quit, Gretchen . . . Lighten up. You should be glad. We should be happy. We are all together again."

I pretend to laugh. "With Hyman our ringmaster as usual?"

At this Hyman stands, and his face is no longer amused. "Perhaps you want to go back to the house by the minefield or living like a rat in the bombed buildings?" he says.

"Is that how you see me, Hyman? A rat?"

My anger is rising. I can see clearly.

"No, Gretchen, I love you. You know that. *Ich liebe Sie alle*, I love you all."

Perhaps it was that cloying phrase. His catchphrase. Perhaps it is everything about that day that does it, the black cars and Mo being killed. And how we were so upset when we thought Hyman was gone and so longed again for our master.

I say to Hyman, "I am sick of men like you telling me what to do. Men like you killed my father. Now you think you have us as your slaves. Not me. Your poor Rachel is in love with you because she has to have a master. Kells believes there is wisdom in you, but it is only the way you play on our weakness. I am not a rat. I am not one of your silkworm cocoons. Why have you brought us here? To kill us? So we tell no tales now we are no longer useful? Will you keep our clothes too?"

I turn to walk towards the door.

"Do not go, Gretchen. That would be a great mistake," Hyman says. His voice is much silkier. I stop.

"Why? Because you love me?"

"I do . . . But there is going to be a sweep of the houses around here. My friends told me. If you are caught out you may be killed . . ."

My mind goes back. I think of the terror of being caught outside the shelters. To my father being led away.

I look round and see his hand has gone towards his suit pocket. I see what is perhaps the outline of a pistol. Rachel is standing too.

"So these are your true colours?" I say, nodding towards the pocket.

"I am protecting you all. I will protect you . . ."

"When your friends come to kill us?"

"No . . . I have found an old love again . . . I will protect you . . ."

"From ourselves? I have heard that before. Because you are the master race?"

"I have never been that kind of German. I am too fond of pretty things."

He takes his hand out of his pocket.

Then he says, "Come here, my darling. It was a hard night for me. Remember? Come here and let me hug you? The war is over. Forget about Lucy's games. Come here, darling Gretchen. *Ich liebe Sie alle* . . ." he says again.

"Those words have always reminded me of the equally impossible and insane Nazi slogan *"Alles fuer Deutschland"* Everything for Germany. It's easy to see the results of that sort of thinking outside the window. I do not trust you . . ." I say.

I am frightened now. I feel a pulse in my temples and my hands tremble. I am frightened like my papa should have been when the Gestapo led him away, joking. Never again. I know Lucy wants us dead. The new or the old. They are coming for us . . . I do not trust Hyman, or the new man inside him. His hand is going back to his pocket and the gun.

"Are you going to shoot us, Hyman? Are you going to shoot me?" I step closer. One step, two, three . . .

The knife is in my hand and travelling forward.

"No!"

Rachel shouts and throws herself in front of Hyman.

My knife goes in under her ribs. So easily. Like into butter.

Her blue-green eyes staring, pleading into mine.

Rachel drops and I slash Hyman's throat. I do it exactly. Like I used to cut balloons when standing on a trotting horse in the circus ring. He looks surprised. There is a choking noise. His hands stay by his side and I bring my arm back and slash again, deeper. So deep it hurts my wrist. He falls upon Rachel, coughing and gushing bright red arterial blood onto the polished wood floor.

There is blood on the white petals of the gardenia.

Kells stands over them, shaking his head, his mouth open. Rachel and Hyman quiver and are still. "He could have been telling the truth, couldn't he . . . ?" he says.

"No. He was the devil," I say. "There has to be a reckoning." Then I scream. I scream fit to break the windows.

I throw myself down by the corpses and bathe and wash my hair in the blood. I soak it up with my hair.

This is our custom.

I wash myself in their warm blood so I do not have to ask for forgiveness of God or man or the devil. I rub the blood into my hair so that the ghosts will not follow me. It goes into my eyes and up my nose . . . Into my mouth. I glance at Kells and there is fear on his face. I kiss Rachel on the lips.

I stand back in horror.

"Look at this . . . look now at what I have done in the name of righteousness . . . I have more blood on my hands. This is Lucy . . . This is her trick . . . This is what I am. What I have become . . . Even when I refuse to obey, I obey. Even when I refuse to be part of the vileness and rebel, the killing goes on and I am the killer. We must have better."

I drop to my knees looking at the fallen bodies. "The only way out of this maze . . . Of obeying . . . Is to feel . . . Everything. That is what is being lost . . ."

Kells touches my shoulder.

"Go and find something to burn them with and the house," I say to him. "I am sure his friends are coming to kill us. And find some men's clothes."

He does not move. "How could you? We . . ." he stammers.

"Go and find something to burn them with," I say again, as Kells stands there in shock. I get up. Blood drips on the wooden floor.

He must realise what I have said is true and goes in search of kerosene or brandy and matches in the kitchens and a suit from a bedroom. I wipe my blade on a cushion and put the knife back in my pocket. This house will be demolished soon if we set it alight. They will find two burned bodies, like so many others in the city. Nothing will be done. No one will care. I am sorry for Rachel, but not for that creature Hyman, or whoever he is . . .

I can taste their blood.

I go through Hyman's pockets and take his pistol and a passport and stroke the hair of Rachel and give her another kiss and my knees nearly buckle under me. She looks like she is asleep. A child asleep. She tried so hard to be good. Her eyes are closed and her long lashes knit together. There is nothing I can say to her. If I had not acted then I would not have acted at all. Kells comes back into the room with a can of kerosene and there is a pungent smell as I throw it on the bodies and then light them with a whoosh of blue and yellow flame. He picks up the other pistol from the table.

I run to the kitchen and try to wash the blood off my hair and face. It will have to do. Kells is pulling me to the door. The hall is full of smoke.

"Where will we go?" Kells says, as we step out into the street. I can already see the flames catching on the thick curtains on the first floor. I hurry along, pulling him with me in an oversize suit he has found. I turn to him. I want to stay with him. I love him.

"We'll not go anywhere, Kells. How can we be together? After this, after everything? And you do not even know my full name. My gypsy name."

"I can't leave you. I won't."

He is in tears.

"Go tell the army you went a little mad. They are. But they understand and permit wartime madness again now there is a peace. Go to your home and your Betty. My real name was not on the papers. I'm going back to find my mother," I say.

"Please, Gretchen."

I kiss him gently on the lips.

"Don't be sad. We probably had the best love of our lives. You and I. We fell through the floor. We flew. I'm sorry for Rachel. She never really left her camp. She is free now, also."

I kiss him again, with all my passion. He tastes the blood.

"Goodbye my darling . . ."

Kells does not say a thing. He looks very small in his chalk-striped business suit with wide lapels. A child too. He sits on a large block of stone in the ruins at the other side of the street, watching me disappear into the greys and browns of the bomb sites. I stop and wave. Behind him the house is burning and he must feel the heat. I see a pillar of flames and sparks. I know he wants to come after me, but he gets up and walks slowly back to the River Spree.

I turn and pick my own way alone across the wasteland.

328

ACKNOWLEDGMENTS

I WANT TO thank my wife, the painter Alice Beckett, for her continual inspiration and for proof-reading this book, and Jonathan Pegg, Clive Cookson, Bhaskar Roy, Stephen Fry, Mary Tomlinson, Professor Gerard Woodward, and my publishers Christopher and Jen Hamilton-Emery of Salt.

This book has been typeset by
SALT PUBLISHING LIMITED
using Neacademia, a font designed by Sergei Egorov
for the Rosetta Type Foundry in the Czech Republic. It is
manufactured using Holmen Book Cream 70gsm. It was printed
and bound by Clays Limited in Bungay, Suffolk, Great Britain.

CROMER
GREAT BRITAIN
MMXXIV